Story Over

Haunted by childhood memories and ~~...~~ likely going mute, Erin embraces a quiet life in Vermont. A life away from all the mistakes she has made and the people she's hurt. A peaceful existence with her horses. A cynic by nature, she doesn't buy into what she soon learns. Apparently she's part of an unending connection between twenty-first century Broun women and medieval MacLomain men. When a Claddagh ring crosses her path, she's compelled to steal it. A bad move because the ring is meant to find true love. Something Erin feels she stopped deserving a long time ago.

Of dragon blood, Chieftain Rònan MacLeod is by birth, half MacLomain. While raised to protect the future King of Scotland, he lives life with an open mind. The idea of a ring binding him to one lass seems far-fetched. However, when a woman named Jackie calls to him from the dark edges of the Celtic Otherworld, he swears an oath to save her. That means traveling to the future to protect her before she's taken by the enemy. The only problem? She is not where she should be. Instead, he finds a beautiful, defiant lass named Erin. Now he must make a choice. Continue seeking out Jackie or protect the one he's with.

Thrust back in time to ninth-century Scandinavia, rònan and Erin find sanctuary with his Viking ancestors. With help from not only King Naðr Véurr Sigdir but his offspring, they learn more than anticipated. Something that will either damn them or set them free. Drawn to one another, heat flares. A fire neither could have imagined. Scorching. Searing. Unavoidable. One they must fight if they want to save those they care for most.

Will they be able to protect wee Robert the Bruce from evil when they end up back in Scotland? Or will their repressed feelings be their ultimate doom? After all, it's supposed to take the oath of a Scottish warrior to save a future king. Not the oath of a warrior who ended up forsaking all because he lost his heart along the way.

~Oath of a Scottish Warrior~

Oath of a Scottish Warrior
The MacLomain Series-Later Years
Book Three

By

Sky Purington

~Oath of a Scottish Warrior~

Dedication

For Mom.

Loving dragons would have never been possible without you.

You have been my rock. My best friend. You taught me how to set goals and how to be strong. More than that, you made sure I never gave up on my dream.

You've always believed in me and repeated two words over and over.
Ones I live by…ones that have made me the woman I am now.

"Keep Writing."

I will, Mom. Promise.

I love you deeply and I'm more thankful than you know. xoxo

COPYRIGHT © 2016
Oath of a Scottish Warrior
Sky Purington

Edited by *Cathy McElhaney*
Cover Art by *Tamra Westberry*

Published in the United States of America

~Oath of a Scottish Warrior~

Chapter One

North Salem, New Hampshire
2015

ERIN PULLED HER motorcycle into the driveway of the old Colonial and killed the engine. Here she was. Back again. With a heavy sigh, she swung off the bike, removed her helmet, untied her hair and shook out her wild mass of raven curls.

For days now, she had been avoiding not only this place but her closest friends, Cassie, Nicole, and Jackie. She might love them but this thing they were doing with perfect strangers wasn't for her. Honestly, she wondered at their sanity. It was one thing to support each other because they shared the Broun name and faced life-changing disabilities. It was another thing entirely to buy the load of crap the people at this residence were dishing out.

Time-travel. Magic. Witches. Wizards.

Medieval Scotland.

She eyed the Colonial and frowned. It seemed their Broun lineage was connected not only to the house but to a medieval Scottish clan. The MacLomains. Supposedly, Cassie had traveled back in time and hooked up with their thirteenth-century clan chieftain.

Bullshit.

But Erin couldn't just bail on her friends so she popped in briefly before heading home to take care of her horse. Since then, the owners of the house invited her back and wanted her to bring her horse with her. So between her friends' endless badgering for her to return and the overly generous offer, she'd finally relented. Was it bizarre that perfect strangers had invited not only her friends but Erin and her horse to stay here? Very. Yet the way she figured it, somebody needed to get to the bottom of things and it might as well be her.

Erin took out her lighter and flicked it on and off as she eyed everything. Much like her place in Vermont, the house was quaint and freshly painted, with a large, well-kept barn and plenty of woodland. The foliage was bright but already blowing off in the wind. Another week or so and the trees would be barren.

"You dinnae look anything like what I expected," came a deep voice.

Typically, she saw everything and anyone around her before she was noticed. She'd learned to do that a long time ago. Yet somehow she had missed him. But where was he? She pocketed her lighter and played it cool. After all, she knew right where her knives were. And her gun. Eyes discreetly scanning her surroundings, she said, "I could say the same thing about you."

"Even when you cannae see me?"

Like the owner of the house, Bradon, the voice had a thick Scottish accent.

Erin might have only met Bradon once, but she knew whoever just spoke wasn't him. Hand on the hilt of the blade in her pocket, she stuck close to her bike and called out, "Show yourself."

She blinked once, twice, before a man appeared, leaning against the old oak in front of the house as if he'd been there all along. But she knew damn well he hadn't been. Had he? It had been a long night and an equally long drive. Still…

You didn't miss a man like him.

For more reasons than one.

He had short black hair and vibrant green eyes. A black t-shirt hugged broad shoulders and did nothing to hide his cut torso or the tats running down his well-muscled arms. Jeans outlined his long, strong thighs and ended in a sturdy pair of boots.

Damn, he was hot.

Not one to beat around the bush, she said, "Who are you?"

Evidently not one to beat around the bush either, he said, "Rònan MacLeod." His brows perked. "And based on your appearance, I'd ask the same of you."

"My appearance?"

"Aye." He eyed her up and down. "You dinnae look at all like you did when you came to me."

Came to him? *Okay*. But she'd go with it until she knew more. "So how do I measure up now?"

Arms crossed over his chest, he eyed her up and down again. "Bonnie enough I suppose."

"You suppose?"

Something flared in his eyes that looked a lot like lust. "Like I said, bonnie enough."

Erin was about to respond when a pick-up truck pulling a horse trailer rumbled up the drive. Her horse was here. Done with *Rònan*, she waved the truck forward until it parked closer to the barn. Though not thrilled about bringing her baby here, she was grateful that Bradon and his wife, Leslie, had said it was okay. While tempted to drive her down in her own pick-up, the weather had been too nice and she figured there weren't many more days left to ride her bike.

Big-bellied, the driver hopped out and nodded at the back. "She's been quiet."

In a perfect world, only a friend would have driven her horse down but she didn't have any of those besides the ones already here. She headed for the back. "Open it up."

Eager to lay eyes on Salve, she waited impatiently as he unlatched the door. When he opened it, she frowned and tried to remain calm. "That isn't my horse." Her eyes shot to him. "Where the *hell* is my horse?"

The man looked at the horse then at his clipboard as if that would answer her question. "You were there when she was loaded." He shook his head. "I stopped off for a quick coffee. That was it."

Erin knew he was telling the truth. She had tracked him via the company he worked for.

"That horse looks just like Tosha, aye?"

It was one thing to see Rònan from afar, but another thing entirely to see him up close. When she glanced over her shoulder, he was *right* there. Shit, he was tall. The top of her head barely reached his shoulders. And his eyes might have been startling before but now they about drowned her with their intensity. Not just green but bright like fresh cut grass in sunlight.

"Back off," she muttered before turning her attention to the horse. "Seriously, where the fuck is my horse?"

"You were there when we loaded her. And you're here now."
The guy held up his hands and shook his head. "I haven't opened
this thing since."

"Hell if you didn't," she fumed and strode for her bike, calling
over her shoulder, "You saw what she looked like so you know
that's not her. You're not getting paid. That isn't my horse."

"Then it's mine," he called after her. "Because we don't ship
horses for free."

"Fine," she muttered as she put on her helmet and swung onto
the bike, so worried about Salve her stomach was in knots.

Yet the darn thing wouldn't start.

Again and again.

Damn it. She was going nowhere fast. Erin ground her jaw,
hung her head and ignored the commotion behind her. Ignored the
sound of the truck backing out. She had watched Salve walk into that
trailer in Vermont. There could be no doubt that it was her horse.
Yet she also knew what Tosha looked like. A horse that should have
already been here.

So she knew Rònan was absolutely right.

What she didn't expect to see after the truck left was the horse
trotting into the barn on its own as if it belonged there. Confused,
she frowned at Rònan when he joined her. "Why did he leave the
horse?"

"Because I told him to." Arms crossed over his chest, Rònan
walked around her bike and looked it over with interest. "Because
it's Tosha."

She frowned. "Impossible." Her eyes narrowed on the barn.
"Odd that she headed in there like that."

"The horse knows where she belongs," Rònan said. "She
doesn't need help finding her stall."

She arched a brow at him. "Assuming the stall door was
miraculously left open."

"Och, no need," he enlightened. "The door would open for
Tosha on its own."

She stared at him for a long, incredulous moment before she
shook her head. "You're outta your mind." Then she scowled.
"Don't you find it strange I showed up with Tosha when the horse
should've already been here?"

Rònan shrugged. "I've seen far stranger things."

12

Erin shook her head again, pulled off the helmet and swung off the bike. "That horse obviously isn't mine."

"It seems nothing appears as it should," he murmured as he crouched beside the bike and eyed it more closely. "Just two wheels. Interesting. Requires more balance."

Erin ignored him and pulled out her cell phone as she headed for the house. First, she needed to call her neighbor to see if her horse was still in Vermont. Though she saw Salve get in the trailer, it seemed like the logical thing to do. Thankfully her neighbor picked up. While she waited for him to swing over to her barn, she leaned against the oak and kept an eye on Rònan. He remained fascinated with the motorcycle. What was the matter with him? Hadn't he ever seen a bike before? Pretty hard not to living in these parts. Then again, he was Scottish so who knows.

Within a few minutes, her neighbor confirmed that Salve was definitely *not* at her place.

Well, at least she wasn't totally losing it.

Still, where was her poor horse?

Erin hung up and headed for the front door. She was about to knock when Rònan called out, "Nobody's here."

Somebody had to be here. Where else would her friends be?

Instead of questioning Rònan she took matters into her own hands, grateful when she found the door unlocked. Rather than straining her voice and calling out to see if anyone was around, she made a thorough sweep of the house. He was right. The place was empty.

After a quick search, she grabbed a bottle of whisky out of the kitchen cabinet and poured some into a small glass. Time to call the company she'd hired to haul Salve. Leaning against the counter, she dialed then cursed when it went to voicemail. After she left a ranting message, she downed the whisky and sighed. She should never have come back here. What a mistake.

Erin watched Rònan out of the corner of her eye as he came into the kitchen and took a swig of whisky directly from the bottle. Considering her standoffish personality, some men might avoid her, but not him. He leaned against the counter and met her eyes. "So your horse isn't here. What will you do now?"

"Take a taxi back to Vermont." She crossed her arms over her chest. "Then figure out what's going on from there."

"A taxi?"

"Yeah, that thing that'll pick you up and drive you anywhere you wanna go." She frowned at the blank look on his face. "Wow, you're a few cards short of a full deck, eh?"

"A full deck?"

Christ. Enough of this. Erin headed for the door but he caught her elbow. When their eyes locked, she almost yanked away. *Almost.* Something about him made her want to stay near yet run away at the same time.

"'Tis clear ye dinnae like being here nor do ye trust me." He leaned closer. "But I need to ken yer actions, Jackie."

Eyes narrowed, she processed two things. First, how thick his accent suddenly became. And second…Jackie? Why did he think she was her friend, Jacqueline?

Erin trusted men about as much as she trusted the world ending tomorrow. That meant he wasn't getting anything out of her. So she kept her poker face on. "Where are my friends?"

He didn't miss a beat. "Where's Leslie and Bradon?"

Heck if she knew.

"Out apparently." This time, she *did* yank her elbow away and left the house.

He followed. "Out where?"

"How would I know? I just got here. You saw me arrive," Erin reminded as she strode toward the barn.

"Aye, but that means nothing."

"Uh, it sorta does. It means I have no clue where everyone is."

Erin figured that was a good place to end the conversation as she entered the barn. With any luck, he'd get bored and head in the opposite direction.

But no.

Rònan was right there.

She stopped at the second stall and shook her head. "Tell me that's not the horse I just hauled from home."

"'Tis Tosha." He draped his arm over the edge and stroked her muzzle. "The stall was empty until you brought her back."

"No," she said, enunciating each word. "I did not."

Rònan shrugged, still stroking the horse's muzzle.

Done trying to figure out the whole horse thing, she squared off. "So who are you again?" She planted her hands on her hips. "And *why* are you here?"

"I'm here because you called for me." He leaned against the stall, his eyes again doing a slow roam down her body. "From the Celtic Otherworld. Do you not remember?"

Her brows perked. "Celtic Otherworld?"

This guy was seriously off his rocker.

"Aye," he said softly. "The Celtic Otherworld."

Erin ground her teeth and left the barn. Sure, Rònan seemed a little daft when it came to motorcycles and taxi's but there was no way everything Nicole and Jackie shared was true. Where were they anyway? When she dialed Jackie, it went straight to voicemail. So she tried Nicole. Same thing. All right, time to call a taxi. Yet before she could search out a local service, her phone went dead. Super. First the bike then her cell. Figures.

"Why do you keep flicking that fire on and off?"

She sighed at Rònan's question and leaned against the front of the barn. "What's it to you?"

"Just curious." He leaned against the barn beside her. "'Tis risky to do around so much hay."

She knew that better than most. The truth was she hadn't realized she was flicking her lighter. Just a habit at this point she supposed. So she pocketed it and grunted, "My habits are my business."

"Aye." He shrugged as if he understood. "I ken the need of habits."

"Ken?"

His brows lowered as if she was the one a few cards shy of a full deck now. "Ken." He seemed to struggle with the best way to explain before saying, "It means to understand."

"Ah." She kept eying him mostly because he was well worth looking at. "So what's your habit, Scotsman?"

He grinned and eyed her again. "Lasses."

She cocked the corner of her lip. "Oh yeah?"

His brows rose as if he thought she might be interested in that fact. "Aye."

"Then let's get one thing straight now." She gave him a pointed look. "I won't become one of your habits."

But *man* had it been a long time since she'd had sex. Far too long. So she knew being around this guy wasn't a good idea. Because he was just the type she'd be willing to ride.

Almost as if he could hear her thoughts a slow grin crawled onto his face and he winked. "Then I'll try to keep my habit under control when you're around, lass."

Erin cursed under her breath when her heart skipped a beat and heat flared beneath her skin. She didn't do relationships but she'd sure as hell go for a one night stand. Her eyes shot to the house. Or an 'afternoon' stand. Aw, hell. What was she thinking? Enough with this. Time to figure things out.

"I need answers." She leaned her shoulder against the wall and faced him. "Where is everyone? And again, who exactly are you?"

"I told you already." He remained where he was, casual as could be. "Rònan MacLeod."

"Yeah, got that." She held his gaze. "But I'd like the whole story. Why are you here and not my friends? And why does your accent thicken on occasion?"

She conveniently set aside Nicole and Jackie's chatter about medieval Highlanders. No way. No how.

"I'll tell you why I'm here, Jackie," he said. "If you tell me why you look so different."

So they were back to that.

It took everything she had not to step away when he fingered a lock of her hair. She wasn't a huge fan of having her personal space invaded. Yet, like before, she didn't pull away.

"So the missing lass finally arrives," came a soft voice.

Erin's eyes shot to the Scotsman who strolled out of the barn. This one was nearly as hot as Rònan with his pale grayish blue eyes and mahogany streaked black hair. The stark difference between the two was that he wore a blue and green plaid, tunic and tall black boots.

Hand on the hilt of the knife in her pocket, she narrowed her eyes. "Do I know you?"

"You *should* know all of us by now…" He eyed her with almost as much interest as Rònan had. "Erin."

"Erin?" Rònan's eyes narrowed on her. "When were you going to share as much?"

16

Before she could answer, the guy who had just arrived spoke to her. "Darach's the name. But I'm sure you've already heard of me, aye?"

Jackie had mentioned his name. Regardless. Him showing up here didn't make the tall tale any truer. Even in light of his strange outfit. It couldn't be all that difficult to find clothes like that or to have them made.

Erin ignored Rònan's question and shot her retaliation Darach's way. "Yeah, I've heard of you. And seeing how you seem to know who I am, maybe you could tell me where my friends are." She inflicted just enough threat into her voice. "Now."

"Och, she's not so trusting is she," Rònan said to Darach, his eyes flickering from the hand in her pocket to her face.

He knew she had a weapon. Good.

"Nay. She isnae." Darach eyed Rònan. "Bloody hell, Cousin. I never thought I'd see you in modern day clothing."

Rònan shrugged. "I thought it was best to try and fit in."

Fit in? Erin rolled her eyes. These guys were determined to play the part of Highlanders who traveled through time, weren't they? She almost said as much but something about the shit-eating grin on Rònan's face knocked the wind right out of her. He really was good looking and hell if he didn't know it.

Erin frowned at the unexpected twinkle in his eyes when he caught her staring. Screw that. She headed for the house. When Darach caught up, she hid her surprise at what sounded like genuine distress in his voice. "Are you sure Jackie's not here? Bradon and Leslie assured me she would remain here under their protection."

"Under their *protection*? C'mon." She shook her head. "I'll bet you're the one who fed her and Nicole all this 'time travel protect the future king of Scotland' crap to begin with, huh?"

"If you'd bothered to spend more time here you wouldn't need convincing." Darach followed her into the house. "But at least you're here now so we can keep you safe."

"I can keep myself safe," she said.

Erin stopped in the foyer as Darach muttered something indiscernible before he started romping through the rooms and calling out for Jackie.

"Your friends are in medieval Scotland," Rònan said, so close behind her that she jumped. The guy was admirably light on his feet considering he was so large. He'd be good at stealth.

"Yeah, sure, they're in medieval Scotland." Erin rolled her eyes, headed into the kitchen and poured another shot of whisky. "Whatever you say."

"'Tis true." He leaned against the doorjamb. "Cassie is at MacLomain Castle and I just left Nicole with Niall at the mountain. They're all safe enough for now."

"Right. Niall. The guy Nicole can't stand. I heard a little bit about him." Her eyes went to Rònan. "But not a word about you."

Rònan didn't seem all that concerned.

"Nicole and Niall have come a long way since you last saw her," he said. "'Tis safe to say she'll be his wife soon."

Erin chuckled and it felt strange. Laughing wasn't her thing. At least not for a long time.

"I can't imagine Nicole hooking up with any one guy let alone marrying him." She eyed Rònan. "So you just killed your story."

"Hooking up?" Rònan said.

"Hell, you really should have visited this century more." Darach returned and poured himself a shot. "It means coupling."

"Ah." Rònan's eyes never left her. "Then they have definitely hooked up. Often. And in enviable ways. Niall's a lucky bastard."

Erin got the impression he was fishing for a certain kind of reaction. Feeling her out. Baiting her without meaning to. Like a man who flirted with and had sex with *far* too many women because he could. Because they never said no. As if he sensed she was on to him, Rònan's brows lowered sharply before he frowned and looked away. Now he reminded her of a guy who was just caught cheating. Heck if she didn't know what one of those looked like. Because she did. *All too well.*

"So why did you think I was Jackie?" Curious, she kept her gaze on Rònan. "Who's she to you?"

Darach cut in before Rònan could answer. "Niall filled me in on your visions." He frowned at his cousin. "But Jackie cannae be meant for you."

"'Tis likely why you followed me here so swiftly, aye?" Rònan's eyes narrowed and his brogue thickened. "Worried that I might win her over upon first sight, Cousin?"

18

Darach's eyes narrowed as well. "Not in the least."

"Alrighty boys, if it's gonna be a contest to see who's got the biggest dick, take it outside." Convinced these morons didn't mean her any harm, she tossed aside her black leather jacket and sat on the counter. Rònan had the right idea when he drank directly from the bottle, so she took a swig.

Erin lowered the bottle slowly when the room grew unnaturally quiet.

Their eyes were locked on her.

Or should she say the ring on the chain around her neck.

"What?" Erin fingered the Claddagh ring. "It showed up on my finger after I visited last time. I'm not sure why." She shrugged. "No worries. I was gonna return it."

Total lie. Well, partly. Inexplicably drawn to it, she'd stolen the ring. She intended to return it. Or so she kept telling herself.

"'Tis one of the four original rings." Rònan cocked his head. "You were able to remove it from your finger?"

"Yeah, sure." But for some reason when she put it back on, it didn't feel right. Yet when she tried to tuck it away, she felt sick to her stomach. So she ended up putting it around her neck. "It's a pretty typical thing, taking off a ring."

"You know what that Claddagh ring means, right?" Darach asked.

Oh, she'd heard the far-fetched tale from Nicole. They were rings meant to bring together true love between Brouns and MacLomains. "I know what the rings are supposed to mean and just to be clear, I don't buy it for a sec."

Erin tried her damnedest to keep her breathing even when Rònan came close and fingered the ring. Her eyes fell to the light layer of stubble on his strong jaw and the cut of his firm but sensual lips. When her nipples tightened in response to his proximity, she wished she'd worn a padded bra. Yet for some reason when he inhaled deeply and his knowing eyes met hers, she knew it had nothing to do with her nipples.

No, this guy had razor sharp senses far beyond simple eyesight.

Disarmed by the flare of his pupils and the way he shifted closer, she went still. Too still. Despite efforts not to, she stopped breathing. If she wasn't mistaken, he did too.

"We need to figure out where Jackie is. Better yet, why Bradon and Leslie aren't here watching over her," Darach said, clearly interrupting the moment on purpose. "After all, didn't you swear an oath to save her?"

"Aye," Rònan murmured, noticeably disappointed in himself for becoming distracted.

"An oath? That sounds serious." Obviously, they were determined to keep up with this game of theirs so she went with it. Anything to further understand what was going on. "And what exactly were you supposed to be saving her from, Rònan?"

"As your friends already told you, Brae Stewart and her evil demi-god Laird," Darach said then downed a shot of whisky. "But there's no way they've got Jackie." Yet his expression was troubled. "Bradon would have told us."

Right, because Bradon was apparently from medieval Scotland too. Leslie, his wife, was a modern day Broun like Erin and her friends.

Erin started to talk but her voice broke off. Her vocal chords just fizzled out. Crap. This was happening more and more lately. Instead of clearing her throat and trying again, she headed outside. She'd just reached the oak out front when something changed. Shifted. At first, she thought it was the weather but no, it was still bright and sunny.

"Time to go, lass."

Erin barely processed Rònan's words before he flung her over his shoulder and ran for the barn.

What. The. Hell.

She had little time to flail before he plunked her down between stalls. The horses were agitated but the men seemed to know what they were doing as they swiftly started saddling two of them.

Erin might've dismissed everything else Nicole told her but she remembered the names of the horses. The black one that had arrived in her trailer today was obviously Tosha. That meant 'satisfaction' in Scotland. The other horse, a pale thoroughbred with a blond tail and mane was called Eara. That meant from the east. But why were they only saddling two when there were three people? She eyed the third horse. Bradon's.

"What's going on?" she said hoarsely, glad her voice was coming around. She shook her head. "Just to be clear, I'm not going anywhere and if I were, I'd be riding my own horse."

"Not this time," Darach muttered as he swung onto Tosha.

Erin tensed when Tosha's eyes met hers. Something felt *really* off about this. Though remarkably calm considering the strange weather kicking up outside, the horse seemed to be trying to say something.

To her.

"What, Sweetheart?" she murmured.

"Ride," whispered through her mind.

Louder than thunder, a roar echoed around the barn.

"Bloody hell." When Rònan tried to swing Erin up onto Eara, she shook her head and backed away.

"We need to go, lass," he growled and strode after her when she darted away.

"I ride alone," she reminded and headed toward Bradon's horse.

When Rònan grabbed her around the waist and pinned her arms, she couldn't reach her blade. So she kicked her heel hard into his shin and thrust her head back. He grunted and his grip loosened. She was about to remove herself entirely when Tosha reared up.

"Och, nay. Release Erin!" Darach yelled at Rònan and swung down from the horse. "Erin, ride Tosha."

Thunder crashed. Wind-driven snow started to whip up outside.

Rònan released her and nodded at his cousin as Darach headed for Bradon's horse and Rònan strode back toward Eara. But the men didn't get far before all hell broke loose. Spooked, Eara reared up and Bradon's horse started running in circles in the meager space it had. So Darach ended up on Eara and Rònan on the other horse.

Tosha, however, remained calm and Erin wasted no time swinging up into her saddle.

The minute she was on, Tosha bolted.

While alarmed, Erin did her best to remain calm. The horse didn't need to be any more spooked than it already was. By instinct, she knew Tosha would never respond to the usual commands. No, this one was a free spirit. A lone soul. And Erin well understood that. So she leaned down and murmured, "Easy now, girl. Remember that I'm on your side, okay?"

The weather—regrettably—was not.

What greeted her when they exited the barn was the polar opposite of what it had been when she entered. Angry, violent, black clouds rolled overhead. Autumn leaves whipped in a thick, twisting maelstrom.

Erin knew controlling Tosha would be impossible so she held tight.

Strangely enough, the horse raced toward the tree in front of the house.

Not good.

"Tosha," she warned. "You've gotta stop, Sweetheart."

Forget that. The horse had a mind of her own. Erin barely had a second to realize Rònan and Darach caught up before leaves whipped so thickly that she was unable to see a thing. Then something happened. Everything changed dramatically. Her ears popped, vision blurred and the temperature chilled.

Yet Tosha barreled forward.

Erin's vision cleared. Instead of racing toward the oak, they were racing through a forest. Then they broke free of the woods and headed straight for a gushing waterfall.

"Oh my God!" she tried to cry but nothing came out.

Massive, deadly, they were heading for a merciless wall.

Tosha never slowed.

Never stopped.

No, she brought Erin straight toward certain death.

Chapter Two

Scotland
1281

RÒNAN WATCHED ERIN with interest. She sat alone on the far side of the cave with her back to the wall and a brooding expression on her face as she eyed one of the original Highland Defiances. The massive stalagmite rose hundreds of feet to touch the ceiling in an area that was the lower part of the mountain.

They'd been here for several hours now. Though Erin clearly thought they were done for when they arrived, all had made it safely inside when Niall used magic to split the waterfall.

"She doesnae much like company, aye?" he said to Nicole.

"That's an understatement." Nicole sighed, her eyes on her friend. "But don't take offense. She's always been that way. We're grateful for the time we get with her."

"You haven't spoken much of her." He meant to look at Nicole but couldn't seem to pull his eyes from the defiant, lonely lass across the way. "You two were talking for a bit. Why is she so withdrawn in light of everything you just shared with her? I would think she would want to remain close to you in such a foreign place. Especially considering everything she's learned."

"Shit, Hon. That's a loaded question if ever there was one." Nicole chomped on a bit of meat and shrugged. She was about to say more when Niall plunked down beside them and pulled her onto his lap. The two kissed each other soundly before Nicole shook her head and nodded at Rònan. "He's sweating Erin."

"Sweating?" Niall said through kisses down her neck.

"Worried about her."

"Ah." Niall gave her one last kiss and eyed Rònan. "She seems well enough, Cousin. If not a bit…"

When he trailed off, Rònan finished his sentence. "Lost."

"Lost," Nicole echoed. "Good word for it. But," she said softly, "she's the most solid 'lost' person I know."

"I dinnae ken," Rònan said, eyes still on the raven haired beauty. Because she *was* a beauty at the very least. And the last person he expected to find when he traveled to the twenty-first century for the second time in his life.

He had fully expected to encounter Jackie, the beautiful blond he'd seen in his visions when in the Celtic Otherworld. Instead, he found Erin with her long jet black curls, petite, firm body and a face that didn't possess the angelic qualities of Jackie but something far more…tempting? Striking. Sensual. Black Irish and designed by the dark gods he'd say. Pale, immaculate, with full lips and thickly lashed, unusual colored eyes. Though they must fall in the blue spectrum, they appeared deep violet with starbursts of paler violet at their centers. Eyes that were designed to pin a man where he stood.

Eyes that understood tempered heat.

Cool heat that exploded at its heart but kept quiet.

A soundless explosion. A frigid fire.

"Erin's her own woman," Nicole continued. "She has been since we girls came together and I suspect long before that. While I might be the most vocal of us all, she's the most effective in her own way."

"Effective?" Niall asked.

"Yup." Nicole's eyes were on Erin. "We four Brouns were a support group. Cassie pulled us together so she was always sorta the leader. I say what's on my mind so I called bullshit when I saw it. That meant trying to keep everyone open about their disabilities. Jackie was the wise one. Quiet, withdrawn, but always knows the right thing to say. And Erin, well, she always made sure we kept communicating, that we never lost touch. She had a thing about that even though she's not a big talker by nature."

Nicole grinned. "And though it pains me to say because I'm becoming a kick ass fighter, Erin was always our muscle if people started crap with us."

"I find that hard to believe knowing you." Niall sniggered. "Besides, she's smaller than you."

"I know, *right*." Nicole chuckled and nodded at Erin. "But trust me, that chick could probably take you both down before you saw her coming." She grinned at Niall. "I think it was you that told me powerful things come in small packages."

"Aye." He cupped the back of her neck and pulled her in for another kiss before she could say anything else.

"Cassie went blind. You face going deaf," Rònan said. "What's Erin's disability?"

Nicole's lips didn't leave Niall's for a second but her telepathic words *did* float through his mind. *"Figure the odds of me telling you that. Go find out for yourself."*

It seemed he wasn't the only one who was curious because Darach had just plunked down beside Erin.

"Och," Rònan muttered and stood. He was heading in that direction when Grant Hamilton intercepted him.

The arch-wizard lifted a brow. "A moment of yer time, lad?"

Rònan bit back a sigh. "Aye."

He loved his uncle but he had poor timing. Regardless, he accepted a skin of whisky and sat with Grant before the fire. But he made sure to sit at an angle that allowed him to keep an eye on Erin and Darach. Out of curiosity, of course. Because even though she wasn't here, he had to remain focused on Jackie and his oath to protect her.

As if he read his mind, Grant led out with that very thought. "Have ye had another vision of Jackie?" His eyes went to the child sleeping beneath the blankets nearby. "The wee Bruce seems safe enough for now but still, where's yer mind at, lad?"

Rònan knew what Grant thought. That if Jackie made contact, he would abandon the king to fulfill his oath to the woman who had come to him in his darkest hour. Though frustrated, he understood his uncle's concern mainly because he understood his own nature. How fiercely loyal he could be, especially to someone who had come to his aid like Jackie had.

He was half dragon.

Half beast.

He was also half MacLeod and half MacLomain.

But what should probably mean the most and leave no doubt about his unwavering devotion to Robert the Bruce was Rònan's new title, Laird MacLeod. Yet some might question if he took his position as seriously as he should...as they hoped he would.

"I will protect the wee Bruce before all else," Rònan said, not obediently but firmly as he met Grant's eyes. "Jackie hasnae come to me again. But if she does, I will let ye know." He frowned. "She wasnae in New Hampshire, yet I dinnae sense harm around her. Have ye any idea where she might be?"

"Nay." Grant's eyes never left his. There was a slight hitch in his voice that he'd never heard before. "I sense nothing."

Grant was powerful so under normal circumstances that should be a good thing.

Yet he got the impression it was not.

"When and if ye do sense something, tell me what ye want me to do," Ronan said.

"Aye, lad," Grant said softly.

For all his reassurances, they both knew Ronan was merely trying to convince himself he would do one thing when he'd likely do another. He would go to Jackie if she reached out. Yes, he'd spent his life training to face the evil that might someday be thrust upon the future King of Scotland. That was his duty. His calling. Yet deep down, he would never let a lass suffer in the Celtic Otherworld. Not after she somehow saved him. Because she had. His light in eternal darkness.

So though he had been trained to protect the king, he had become a liability.

A false hope some might say.

And both he and Grant knew it.

Hell, likely all of the Next Generation knew it.

Yet Grant's next words led him to believe that though he wanted Robert the Bruce protected, he also remained concerned about the Broun/MacLomain connection. Then again, igniting the power of the ring through love worked toward such a goal.

"Both horses are here," Grant murmured. "Tosha and Eara." His eyes went to Ronan. "Why did you not ride Eara? She is connected to Jackie."

"The storm." Ronan shrugged. "Darach took Eara. I rode Bradon's horse."

"'Tis not good if ye've a true need to find yer lass," Grant murmured.

"I've a need to find her," Ronan assured. "But the horses seemed to have a mind of their own." His eyes stayed on Grant. "And we both know that evil finally found its way to the twenty-first century. To the Colonial. So great and thorough was it that only our last hope saw us…"

"Shh," Grant bit out as his eyes shot to Darach. "Say no more."

They both knew that if the old oak's magic had become a part of this, then they were closer to the end than anyone wanted to admit. And his son, Darach, like Rònan, was their last hope to fight this evil.

And the enemy would only become more vicious.

"Rònan," Erin whispered.

His eyes shot from the burning fire in the center of the cave to Erin. It sounded like she was right here but she still sat next to Darach. He frowned. As if she sensed his confusion, her eyes met his.

The fire flared and sparks shot up nearly a hundred feet.

"Och," Grant muttered. "Ye need to choose yer battles and choose them wisely, lad. For a lass like that isnae one that can be ignored."

What did he mean by that? Before he could ask, his uncle vanished. So did everyone else in the cave. The only one left was Erin. Her arms hung loosely over bent knees and she stared at the fire. Was he dreaming? Was this real?

Though he stood and called out her name, the flames only grew taller. More vicious. But fire didn't scare him. Rather it was his friend. Though it flared at him, he headed in her direction. Even as the flames crawled up his calves, he felt no pain. The interesting thing, however? He had no power over it like he usually did.

Yet he sensed no evil.

He had nearly reached Erin when her gaze again met his. Shocked, he realized that fire didn't just reflect in her eyes but actually burned *within* them.

"What's the matter with you?" she said, frowning.

Rònan blinked several times. Not only was the fire gone from her eyes but everyone had returned to the cave just as they had been before. Nobody had moved except him. Just like in his vision, he stood in front of her.

"Are you well, Cousin?" Darach asked.

Was he? He had no bloody clue. When he glanced back, he discovered Grant still sat where he'd left him. The arch wizard's eyes narrowed as though he knew precisely what had just happened.

27

While tempted to question his uncle further, Rònan decided he'd prefer to stay here and investigate. So he sat down next to Erin, his frown still in place. "Have you a love for fire, lass?"

Her brows flew together. "Come again?"

"Every Broun is a witch but 'tis not always clear where their magic lies," he explained. "I thought mayhap you might have already figured yours out."

"Listen, I'm not in the mood for this right now, okay?" She kept frowning. "I'm still trying to wrap my mind around the fact that everything Nicole and Jackie said is true." Her eyes flickered to his plaid before she sighed. "Believing in magic, witches and wizards is gonna take time. Never mind that I might possess magic."

"And dragon-shifters," Darach reminded gently, his eyes on Rònan. "You need to believe in them as well."

"Right." Erin swallowed and he swore she shifted a little closer to his cousin before her eyes met Rònan's again. "Just learned about that before you headed this way."

Rònan narrowed his eyes. Had he seen that vision of her because she'd just learned what he was? Though tempted to further explore the possibility, he wasn't overly fond of her eying him the way she was. He was used to lasses adoring him, not looking at him with a mix of wariness, distrust and mayhap a wee bit of disgust.

He much preferred the flicker of lust he caught in her eyes back in New Hampshire. Better yet, the scent of it.

"I willnae hurt you, lass," he said softly.

Erin offered no response and her eyes didn't warm any. Rònan ground his jaw, surprised to feel a flare of anger. It seemed the dragon within didn't like her contempt either.

Darach came to his defense. "Rònan would never hurt a lass." He shrugged and winked. "Outside of the evil one we face."

"So it's all true." Erin's eyes went from the wee Bruce to Darach. "You and your cousins are trying to protect the future King of Scotland from an evil bitch named Brae Stewart and her dark Laird, who's only appeared as a massive black cloud so far." Then her eyes went to Rònan. "A cloud that brought you to the Celtic Otherworld and did things to you that you don't remember. It was there that you supposedly saw Jackie."

"Aye." Rònan nodded. "'Twas because of her that I made it through the darkness."

28

Nicole and Niall joined them as well as Logan, the current MacLomain Laird.

"Move over," Nicole said, plunking down between him and Erin. When he scowled at her, she shrugged and spoke telepathically. *"Eye on the ball, buddy. Jackie's meant for you, not Erin, remember?"*

So they assumed.

Guilt flared at his traitorous thoughts. Rònan scowled more fiercely and sat down on a rock beside Niall. His cousin and closest friend eyed him with amusement. "Ye seem to be lacking yer usual humor, lad."

"Ye cannae really blame him," Logan said. "He set off to find one lass but came back with another."

Their words were tempered with magic so they would not reach Erin's ears. Even so, though Nicole and Erin were chatting, the men continued their conversation telepathically.

"It seems all these Broun lassies are bonnie, aye?" Niall prodded, knowing full well Rònan was disgruntled because he was attracted to Erin when he was set to save Jackie.

"We dinnae know with any certainty who yer meant for, Rònan," Logan said before his eyes went to Darach. *"Or you for that matter."*

"Ye and Jackie spent time together in the twenty-first century," Niall reminded Darach. *"How was it betwixt ye?"*

"You know damn well how it was. Nothing but lusty stares between them," Nicole cut in and frowned. *"Now stop talking telepathically until Erin knows how to join in. It's rude."*

"'Tis just habit, lass," Rònan said.

"What's up with you and habits?" Erin said, eyes on Rònan.

Everyone looked at her.

"Rònan started on me back in New Hampshire about habits." Erin scowled. "Now he's talking about them again."

Nicole bit the corner of her lip. "He didn't say anything…"

When she trailed off, Rònan finished her sentence. "Aloud. I didnae say anything aloud."

"I think she can hear ye speak within the mind, Rònan," Logan said. *"Say something else."*

Rònan shrugged and asked something he remained curious about as he looked at her. *"Why is turning that stick of fire on and off one of your habits?"*

Her pupil's flared and she came to her feet. "How the hell did I just hear you talk but I didn't see your lips move?"

"It's okay, Erin." Nicole stood. "Everyone can speak telepathically. Though, for some reason, you can only hear Rònan right now."

Erin's brows drew down. "Bullshit."

"I get your reservations but it's true," Nicole said. "He just asked about your obsession with lighters, right?"

Erin's expression went blank. Something she did to hide her feelings. He had noticed that early on. "I don't know what you're talking about."

"Yeah you do." Nicole gave her a knowing look and squeezed her hand. "And while I totally respect your privacy, there are a lot of things you're gonna have to get used to here. Magic being at the top of the list."

Erin pulled her hand away. Other than that, she showed no signs of distress. Her face remained emotionless. He wondered what had happened to her that she'd perfected such a look. Because something had happened. Something that made her guard herself against the world.

Something he was desperate to figure out.

Rònan clenched his jaw, frustrated with himself. He preferred open, fiery, lusty women who said what they thought and enjoyed him as much as he enjoyed them. Not lasses like Erin who wanted nothing to do with life and all it offered.

"I won't get used to magic or anything else with Rònan around," whispered through his mind.

It was Erin speaking. But when he looked at her, she was focused on Nicole. She had *no* idea he could hear her thoughts. Or at least the ones directed at him.

She stopped talking to Nicole when Grant joined them. His uncle's eyes were kind when they met Erin's. "Might I have a word alone with you, lass?"

After she nodded and went with him, Rònan spoke aloud. "Are any of you hearing Erin's thoughts?"

Everyone shook their head. Nicole looked perplexed as she joined him. "So you obviously can, eh?"

"Aye, the ones directed at me."

"And she can hear yours," Nicole murmured, giving him a sly look. "Interesting."

Now Nicole was much more his type with her open attitude and frank opinions.

"I dinnae think Erin much likes the bond we might be forming," he muttered. "And I dinnae like that I cannae make sense of it."

"Well, worry naught, Cousin," Darach said. "Erin has agreed to stick by me whilst in this century so that you might keep your oath to protect Jackie."

Nicole snorted.

Niall chuckled.

Logan smirked.

Rònan crossed his arms over his chest. "Is that right?"

"Aye." Darach shrugged. "'Tis the verra least I can do for you considering all you went through in the Celtic Otherworld."

Rònan rubbed his chin and considered Darach. His cousin had been very obvious about his initial desire for Logan's lass, Cassie and managed to develop a cozy enough friendship with Nicole before she arrived here. Then there was the rumored attraction betwixt him and Jackie. Now he was determined to stick close to Erin.

"You dinnae have any issues finding lasses here in Scotland," Rònan remarked. "Yet you cannae seem to get enough of our futuristic Brouns."

"Och, 'tis just a way for Darach to keep evading his Da and becoming the new Hamilton chieftain," Niall said.

"Take it easy, guys," Nicole interjected. "Now's not the time to sweat who matches up with who." She nudged Rònan's shoulder. "Besides, what do you care? It seems to me Darach's helping you out. I mean seriously, a few days ago you were hell bent on getting to Jackie and don't tell me it was just because you were determined to protect her."

Before he could speak, she kept going. "*Jaqueline* this. *Jaqueline* that. Such a *bonnie* lass you were set to protect and damn if you didn't fly outta here faster than hay going up in flames when you heard Darach was flirting with her."

31

"I wasnae flirting," Darach defended. "For the most part."

"Hay going up in flames," Rònan said softly, shooting Nicole a quizzical look as he recalled what he had so recently warned Erin about with her 'lighter' back at the barn. "Why would you use such a comparison?"

"I dunno." Nicole shrugged, a little confused. "It just popped into my head."

Things just seemed to be getting odder and odder.

Too many strange coincidences.

"Why does she carry that lighter?" he asked. "Why does she flick it on and off like she does?"

Nicole's eyes stayed with his as she debated on whether or not to answer.

"Please," he said. "I need to know."

"She should tell you."

"But she willnae. So you must."

Nicole sighed and started shaking her head when Niall said, "Please, lass. If my cousin thinks 'tis important then 'tis."

Nicole's eyes met Niall's for a long moment before she nodded. "Okay." Her gaze went to Rònan's and her voice softened. "She flicks the lighter on and off to remind herself how damaging fire can be. It's her way of controlling the flame...of feeling in control..."

When she trailed off, Rònan murmured, "Is that all?"

"No," Nicole whispered. "It's also her way of remembering her dad the way she last saw him." Her eyes met Rònan's. "Engulfed in flames."

Chapter Three

"I DON'T SEE what the big deal is about me wearing this ring," Erin mumbled.

"'Tis not safe hanging around your neck such as it is," Grant said. "It could too easily be lost."

"This chain is pretty strong," she tried to reassure yet again. "It's not going anywhere."

"But it will, lass. Easier than you might think." The chain suddenly fell but he caught it. "See?"

"Don't mind him," an attractive older woman said as she joined them. "My husband tends to take matters into his own hands on occasion." Her eyes fell to the chain he held. "Literally." She held out her hand to Erin. "I'm Sheila. A Broun originally from the twenty-first century."

Ah, this was one of Leslie's cousins who had traveled back in time early last year. Regrettably, time went by far quicker here and while Leslie was pushing thirty, her cousins who stayed with the Next Generation of MacLomains in the medieval period were in their fifties. Something about the past trying to catch up with the future.

Erin shook Sheila's hand. "Nice to meet you."

"You too." Sheila slid an arm around Grant's lower back and kept smiling. "Bear with him. He tends to forget how daunting it is for us Brouns to travel back in time." She nodded at the ring and then held out her hand so Erin could see. "I wear one too. Trust me, they won't bite."

She had paid attention to everything Nicole told her when she first arrived here. These were Darach's parents. Erin was amazed by the transformation in Grant's body language once Sheila arrived. He went from being tense and serious to warm and relenting.

"She's right, the rings won't bite," said another older woman as she sat on the other side of Grant. With silver wisps in her dark multi-colored hair, she was as attractive as Sheila. And her smile was just as warm when she held out her hand. "I'm Torra MacLoed, formerly Torra MacLomain."

Rònan's mother.

Erin swallowed, cursing the emotions she kept well-disguised. Why hadn't meeting Darach's mom affected her like this? Then again, there was something very different about this woman. Like Grant, she seemed to look right inside Erin's soul with her piercing blue eyes.

They possessed an unnatural wisdom.

Sheila sighed and looked at Grant and Torra. "Sorry but you two at once is a bit much for any newbie time traveler."

"No, it's okay," Erin murmured as her muscles unlocked and she relaxed beneath Torra's gaze. She shook the woman's hand. "Nice to meet you."

"Will you not reconsider Grant's request, and wear the ring?" Torra said, her voice almost hypnotic in its softness…sweetness.

But I stole it. It's not mine. So no.

Yet she pulled it off the chain and slid it on her finger. "Of course. No problem."

A soft smile came to Torra's lips. "See, that wasnae so bad, aye?"

Grant said nothing but he seemed far more pliable as he kissed Sheila's temple. Yet she didn't miss him removing the chain from her lap nor the interested yet very slight perk to his brow when Rònan joined them.

Not *again.*

It seemed wherever she went he followed.

It had been one thing to realize everything Nicole and Jackie said was true but an altogether different thing to learn that dragon-shifters existed.

That Rònan *was* one.

Which meant that his mother might be too. Yet when her eyes flew back to Torra's she felt nothing but peace. A sense of calm that usually didn't belong to her but she was hard pressed to complain about.

"So ye've met my son." Her voice remained soft and lulling. "He will watch over ye, lass."

"He doesn't need to."

"But he will." She cupped Erin's cheek. "Trust him, aye?"

"I don't trust anyone."

"But you will."

Torra pulled back when Rònan sat next to Erin, his deep voice vibrating through her when he said, "Who are you talking to, lass?"

Her eyes went to him. "Isn't it obvious?"

"Nay." He gestured with his hand. "Uncle Grant and Aunt Sheila are walking away and you're speaking to a rock."

Erin's eyes shot back to where Torra, Grant, and Sheila had been sitting. Grant and Sheila were already on the opposite side of the cave and there was no sign of Torra.

"Holy shit." She blinked several times and shot to her feet. "What the hell?"

"'Tis all right," Rònan said and stood.

When he came too close, she put a hand against his chest then pulled it back sharply. "You need to step away. Right now." She shook her head, irritated when repressed emotions pushed their way to the surface. "You're something out of my worst nightmare."

Most men knew better than to get this close but not Rònan.

He didn't budge an inch.

No, he grabbed her wrist when she tried to stride away and gently walked her back against the wall, growling under his breath, "So you *do* feel something."

When his hands met the rock on either side of her head and his body became a cage, she froze. She was former military so she knew her way out of just about any situation.

Just about.

In this case, she needed to keep in mind that he was *not* human and she'd never dealt with that before…or so she hoped.

He didn't touch her and kept his words careful. "Who were you talking to when I joined you?"

Though tempted to say it had been his mother, she had no intention of sounding insane. "Myself."

"I dinnae think so," he said. "Tell me who."

"I told you," she said. "Myself."

"I'll ask Grant and he'll know," Rònan said. "Why not tell me now?"

Erin narrowed her eyes and held his gaze. Heck if she'd back down. "Because I wasn't talking to anyone except Grant and Sheila."

His eyes narrowed a fraction. He didn't buy it.

Erin locked her jaw and remained still. He was too much man for any one woman. While she wanted no part of it, she was well aware of the muscles flexing in his strong body. The anger he kept at bay. Because it *was* anger. Deep, repressed…but there.

Her eyes dropped to his plaid and she worked at keeping her breathing even. Easier said than done. Nobody should look so good with a damn blanket wrapped around his waist. But everything about him was masculine, lethal…damning. A guy like this would be her ruin if she let him. Then again, he wasn't a 'guy' by any means but a monster. The epitome of why she'd joined the military to begin with.

"Step away, Rònan," she warned. "Or else."

If she wasn't egging him on before, she was now. And like her, Rònan wasn't the sort to back down. He leaned close, so close that his whispered words fell near her ear. "Or else what?"

Erin had already measured the distance between his broad shoulders. The length of his torso and legs. The potential power he held in check. He was if nothing else, six foot seven inches worth of well-trained muscle and easily more than twice her weight. And while some might say his weakness lay in his vulnerable groin, she knew better.

His weakness was in his mind.

Though she would be wise to take advantage of that, she was in a bad mood born of unexplainable circumstances so she figured she'd test him.

"Dinnae do it, lass," he advised, voice low.

He knew exactly what she was after.

Good.

Pulling out the dagger she'd lifted from Darach earlier without him knowing, she jabbed at Rònan's stomach. When he pulled back, she crouched and swiped his leg. He jumped. But that cost him when she pulled out a dagger she had swiped from Nicole.

She jabbed its hilt into the tender part of his heel when he fell and rolled away. With most men the hit to that nerve would make their ankle buckle when they hit the ground but not with Rònan. Even so she was ready and side-kicked the foot he had to have been over-compensating with.

Rònan grunted but it barely fazed him.

Fine.

She wasn't done.

36

When he spun to seize her, she grabbed a small rock she'd had her eye on and whipped it beneath the foot he meant to brace himself on. Like an eighteen wheeler trying to find traction on ice, he started to roll. When he did, she came to one knee, tagged him beneath the chin and grabbed his nut sack. By the time he slammed onto his back, she had slid another knife out of her boot and wedged its tip tight against his throat.

Neither moved as she straddled him.

But she found no glory as she glared down at him.

No, the smug bastard had nothing but a small, approving grin on his face.

"Nicely done," he murmured. "Though you could still use some work on your technique."

"My technique was flawless," she growled.

"Nay," he replied. "Had it been, you would have chosen the larger stone. I would've fallen forward and suffered the cut of your blade before I even hit the ground."

She narrowed her eyes.

He kept grinning.

"I was proving a point," she said. "Not trying to kill you."

Whipping the right rock *would* have made a better show. Then she might have thrust her blade, but pulled it back in the nick of time. Her point would've been better proven. Even if it was only to let him know she was not someone to toy with.

"Dinnae make such a mistake again," he whispered softly, pegging her mishap. "'Twill cost you your life."

Though Erin knew she should pull away, she couldn't.

Instead, she stared into his green eyes and hated that he might be right. Then there was the feel of him beneath her. The flex of his strong body. So much restrained power. And it *was* restrained. She felt the tension locking up his every muscle. More than that, she felt something else.

The prod of his erection against her backside.

She had fought men before. She knew how turned on they could get. But this...him, was different. Because of their height difference, she had to straddle his stomach yet she still felt him behind her. Waiting.

Heat flared beneath her skin and she fought back tremors. Just the tip pressing against her ass was more than enough to make her breathing choppy. Hell if she didn't want to lift and slide backward. Hell if she didn't want to see exactly what she'd awoken in this beast.

"Well, look at that!" Niall said. "Looks like I'm not the only MacLomain who can be taken down by a Broun."

Erin ground her teeth and swung off Rònan before unexpected and much-despised lust got the better of her.

"I've said it a million times before but damn, you seriously rock, Sweetie." Nicole came alongside as Erin stood. "That was *awesome!*"

Careful to keep emotion from her face, Erin nodded. There was no reason to say, "Thank you," or anything else. She hadn't taken Rònan in the least. No, if anything he had somehow taken her.

But Niall and Nicole were determined to have fun as they grinned at them. Niall kept making comments about how Rònan was brought down by a Broun and Nicole kept patting her on the back.

Frustrated, and done with it, Erin headed toward Darach. He seemed somewhat sane. But as she did, the ground started shaking. Already familiar with how messed up everything to do with medieval Scotland was, she backtracked fast and grabbed her blades off the ground. If evil or magic or whatever was coming, she'd have a weapon in hand.

"Erin…is that you?"

Jackie? Her eyes whipped to the fire. Nothing but flames.

"Erin? Can you hear me?"

Eyes still focused on the fire, she frowned as the shadow of a face formed.

Jackie? It couldn't be. Could it?

"'Tis nothing but evil," Rònan said as he grabbed her wrist and pulled her after him. "'Tis all an illusion, lass."

But how? While she loved her friends, she'd always had a soft spot for Jackie. The woman was too damn vulnerable in *real* life never mind this place or any Otherworld.

"No," she ground out, trying to stop him. But Rònan was fast and tossed her over his shoulder yet again. So she tried to stop him with her blades only to find them gone. Simply vanished.

What the *hell*?

"Sorry," he grunted as he started climbing. "I would let you down if I thought you'd follow."

She squirmed and tried to fight him. "So you took away my weapons?"

No response.

Like all of the oddities here, none of her moves worked against him. Nonetheless, she kept trying. But her jabs and stabs didn't slow him in the least. While she cursed over and over at him in her head, Erin remained silent as he climbed swiftly. Any normal person would be yelling, even screaming, but she fell silent. She didn't work that way.

Never had and never would.

Rather, she focused on her hatred of a man that gave her no options. A dragon creature. And she'd do well to remember that. So when he plunked her down at the top, she shoved away, stood at the top of the cliff and looked down at the cave far below.

"Come on, Erin," Nicole urged.

"Jackie's there." Erin stared down. "I can feel her."

"No, she's not. Not there. Not anywhere near here. It's all fuc..fun-like magic." Nicole grabbed her hand and met her eyes. "Are you hearing me or what?"

"Fun-like?" Erin snorted. "What're you high?"

"Nicole's trying not to swear around the wee Bruce," Niall informed as he pulled Nicole after him.

"'Tis a good habit she's trying to break," Rònan grunted as he yanked Erin after him.

Erin tried to fight him but like their tromp up the cliff, she seemed unable to utilize her training. It was like she was along for a ride she couldn't control and she hated every second of it.

She *hated* losing control.

"What about the horses?" she asked. "Where are they…"

The words died on her lips when they entered a cave that had the top of an oak tree growing inside it. She'd never seen anything like it. It was huge. If that wasn't enough, her jaw about hit the ground when a tall, golden warrior appeared out of nowhere. Phantom warriors and animals alike drifted around him. Actual *ghosts*.

"That's the Celtic god, Fionn Mac Cumhail," Rònan informed. "He will lead us to where 'tis safe."

"It seems nowhere is safe," Grant murmured as he passed them to meet with the god.

"What happened down there?" Erin said. "Is Brae Stewart here?"

"Aye and nay," Rònan said. "She and her laird are trying to infiltrate the mountain but havnae been able to yet."

"Then why are we leaving?" She shook her head. "Shouldn't we sit tight while we're still safe enough?"

"Something tells me we won't be for much longer if Fionn's here," Nicole said. "He only tends to come around right before it's time to scoot."

"Great," Erin muttered and eyed her friend, thinking about the conversation they'd had earlier. She might not like this situation but she was more concerned about Nicole. "Considering you're pregnant, shouldn't you lay low somewhere? I mean this evil is after Robert the Bruce and my ring, right?"

"Aye," Niall grumbled, answering for Nicole. "But my lass is determined to be at the heart of things."

"Not at the heart," Nicole said. "Just sorta skirting alongside is all." She shrugged when he scowled at her. "Hey, I'm not gonna bail on my friends when they need me."

"If I have a bullseye on my back, I'm fine with you bailing if it means keeping your kid safe," Erin informed. "I know how to handle myself. You shouldn't be anywhere near me. Maybe you should hang with Cassie. She probably needs a friend right now."

Erin cursed the catch in her voice when she mentioned Cassie. She was still trying to process that her friend had gone blind.

"Nobody knows how to handle themselves here, Erin. Besides, Brae and her sidekick aren't interested in Cassie or me anymore seeing how our rings glow and," Nicole trailed off when Grant interrupted them.

His eyes locked on Rònan. "You will go where your kin is strongest. Those with like blood." Then he looked at Nicole, Niall, Erin, and Darach. "You will travel with him. Torra and I will protect the wee Bruce and meet you there soon. We willnae divide and conquer this time but stand as one."

"What does that mean?" Erin asked as Grant turned away. "Where are we going?"

"If he's talking about those with blood like Rònan, I can only think of one place." Nicole bit her lip and shook her head. "And I'm not sure you're gonna like it, Hon."

Erin had no time to question before something started to change around them. Like in New Hampshire, there was an odd pressure drop and the wind kicked up. While she wasn't thrilled about Rònan pulling her close, he was an anchor in what quickly became a twisting cloud of near nothingness. Though he tried to tuck her against his chest, Erin preferred to see what was coming so she kept her eyes locked on her surroundings.

It was as if the tree wrapped around them. Varying shades of green soon became blue then white then a heavy, thick fog. Only when it started to lessen did she realize that Darach stood close behind her. Too close. Not touching but almost. Still close enough that her claustrophobia kicked in. Bad. Real bad. She didn't care where she was. They needed to move.

"Back off," she growled. "Both of you."

Darach backed away, but not Rònan. Then she realized how tightly he held her and how aroused he'd become. Her eyes shot to his and she saw the lust he struggled to control. Something about it set her skin aflame even worse than earlier. Did the air get thinner? She couldn't breathe.

What *was* this?

"Holy *crap*, is that you Tait?" Nicole cried.

The strange world she had nearly sunk into with Rònan snapped shut and another reality opened. They stood at the end of a long pier and Nicole was being swung around by yet another tall, well-muscled dark-haired man.

Except this guy was no Scotsman.

Or so she assumed based on the way he was dressed.

Erin shifted her hand to the hilt of the blade tucked into the back of her pants, grateful it had reappeared. She backed away from Rònan and took in her surroundings. Dozens of piers ran alongside theirs. Inland, a massive group of buildings stood well protected between a high wooden wall and behemoth white-tipped mountains. But that's not why she kept her hand on her weapon

No, that would be because of the towering men surrounding them.

Bearded men clad in fur and leather, with heavy boots and tons of tats.

It was a good thing Darach spoke because Rònan still seemed caught up in lust.

"'Tis nothing to fear, lass," he said. "These are our Viking ancestors."

Vikings.

Sonofabitch.

Nicole had mentioned traveling back to ninth-century Scandinavia. So she tuned into Nicole and Tait's conversation. Maybe in his mid-twenties, he seemed pretty happy to see her. Tait. Hadn't Nicole mentioned that name? And hadn't she said he was a little boy when she met him?

Erin eyed him up and down.

He wasn't a boy anymore.

As if he sensed her watching him, Tait's gaze swung her way. When their eyes connected, a low growl came from Rònan's chest. A warning. The other Vikings shifted, their muscles flexing, and Erin suddenly got the feeling she was surrounded by animals, territorial beasts…wolfs?

No…something else altogether.

Dragon-shifters.

This is what Grant had meant when he said Rònan needed to be around those with like blood. His Viking ancestors.

Tait eyed her for another second before he broke the tension.

"Uncle Rònan." He held out his arms. "Welcome."

Uncle Rònan? Damn, they couldn't be more than a few years apart.

Gotta love time travel.

While Rònan might have gone all alpha moments before, he snapped out of it and embraced Tait, laughing as he patted him on the back. "Good to see ye, Tait, my lad." Then he pulled back, eying him. "Ye've grown a wee bit since we last met."

"Yes." Tait chuckled, clearly glad to see Rònan. "Now we are the same height."

"Where's Heidrek?" Nicole asked, positively beaming. "I can't wait to see him."

"He's visiting a nearby village right now." Tait's brows arched. "I'm surprised you recognized me. It has been almost twenty winters since we last saw each other."

"You've got your dad's eyes, kid," Nicole said. "There's no mistaking them."

Tait grinned. "So I've been told." He embraced Darach with as much vigor as he had Rònan. "Good to see you again, Uncle Darach."

"What about your Uncle Naðr Véurr, the King?" Nicole asked.

"My father will be returning soon," another Viking said, his voice deep and gravelly as he eyed Erin. For that matter, all the Viking men watched her a little too closely. So she stood up straighter and narrowed her eyes.

"And you are?" Nicole asked, straightforward as ever.

"Bjorn Sigdir," the man responded, his posture tense. "First born son to Viking King, Naðr Véurr Sigdir."

Erin recognized a die-hard soldier when she saw one and he was just that. Watchful, distrustful, ready to fight at any given moment. And, like the rest of them, handsome as sin.

"Oh, no shit," Nicole exclaimed as she looked him over. "I can totally see it now. All quiet wisdom, good looks and repressed fierceness."

"And who are the guys heading back down the dock?" Nicole asked.

"My brother and cousins," Tait said.

"Your brother?"

Tait ignored her question and refocused his attention on Erin. "And you are?"

Rònan and Darach responded at the same time.

"This is Erin," from Darach.

"She's mine," from Rònan.

Bjorn's eyes narrowed. "Is that so?"

Rònan's eyes narrowed as well. "Aye."

Tait chuckled, and Niall rolled his eyes.

Losing patience, Erin set them all straight. "Like Darach said, I'm Erin." She frowned at Rònan. "Unlike Rònan said, I'm *not* his nor am I *any* man's."

Tait cocked a brow and looked from her to Rònan before he spoke. "Might I walk with your woman, Uncle Rònan?"

Seriously? Erin shook her head and started down the dock, throwing over her shoulder, "If you wanted to walk with me, you should've asked *me*. Now you're shit out of luck."

Who did these men think they were? She didn't slow down in the least but kept walking. It didn't take long for Rònan and Tait to catch up. The next thing she knew Rònan walked on her left side and Tait was on her right.

So Erin stopped short. She could feel someone else's presence close behind her. Too close. She whipped around.

Bjorn.

"All right, you bunch of deluded screwballs." Erin held up her hands and walked backward. "You all need to step off, you hear me?" She pointed at Bjorn and Tait then narrowed her eyes on Rònan. "*Especially* you."

Before they could argue, she spun around and strode down the dock. She didn't care how foreign this place or its people were. She wasn't about to deal with bullish men or show an ounce of fear. Her world might be turned upside down but she still had her shit together.

She *always* had her shit together.

One long stride. Two. Three. Four. Five. Six. She looked over her shoulder to make sure no one was following her. But when she started to take her seventh step a sudden wind whipped overhead and blew her hair forward. On instinct, she pulled her blade free and crouched.

But nothing could've prepared her for what flew overhead.

Mammoth, long, serpentine and black scaled, something far beyond her wildest imagination. Dear God. No, not God. He had nothing to do with this. But the Devil surely did. Her heart hammered and her throat closed.

When the beast landed, Erin didn't hesitate. She faced her childhood nightmare the only way she knew how. She ran and whipped her dagger at what could only be a dragon.

Chapter Four

RÒNAN SCOWLED AS he eyed Erin on the bed. When she flung a blade at Naðr, the Viking King had made sure she went right to sleep.

"She knows I'm a dragon shifter. Bloody hell, she knows they are too and it was obvious they weren't the enemy," Rònan muttered. "Yet she still threw a dagger at him. At the bloody King. What was she thinking?"

"This is sensory overload for her," Nicole said. "And for Erin, that means to fight and defend then fight some more. That's just who she is and I think it's great. She's fierce."

"Aye, fierce." He sighed. "And none too bright."

That brought her around.

Though Nicole had no idea Erin was awake, he did by the slight tension that rippled up her body.

Her small, curvy body.

He needed to get his mind off of the way she looked lying on that bed. Not sprawled out and sensual but curled into a ball. Needing protection.

Worth protecting.

But hating any that came too close.

She called to him. Hell, she called to all dragon-shifters and he had only just discovered it when he traveled through time with her in his arms. Something about the magic of the tree combined with them actually touching. Now he and every other male dragon sensed her and were drawn to her for various reasons.

Protecting her wouldn't be easy. She believed she was strong…that she could take on anyone. Maybe she could. Maybe she couldn't. Either way, she was vulnerable and tuned into dragon frequency. She didn't understand how bad that was. Dragons were lusty and territorial when they spied something they wanted. And they would all want her.

The thought made Rònan's blood boil. She was his. But she wasn't. How could one man be torn between two women? The one that saved him and the one that needed saving. He should focus on Jackie.

Erin would never accept his help.

There was a fire in her besides her headstrong, feisty attitude. A fire born of magic. A fire that she had no idea she possessed. And there was something more. Something that called to dragons above and beyond. But what? Whatever it was, it was extremely strong and unbelievably compelling to his kind.

Did Grant know? Is that what he meant back in the cave when he told Rònan to choose his battles wisely? That a lass like Erin wasn't one who could be ignored. Did he sense that she would appeal to dragons? And if he knew, why would he send her here of all places? It was one thing for Rònan, a Highlander shifter to sense her but another thing altogether for the Viking shifters. They worked on a different level, their genes not necessarily less advanced but far more…aggressive?

Then there was her astounding beauty.

That didn't help.

Because it was a wild beauty that brought out the beast.

"Erin's awake," Rònan said softly.

Nicole glanced at the bed. "Then you need to get out of here so I can talk to her."

"She wears a ring now." He ground his jaw and shook his head. "So no, I cannae."

"Nor can I," Darach said.

Rònan didn't bother glaring at his cousin yet again but kept his eyes on Nicole when she perched on the side of the bed and touched Erin's shoulder. "Hey, girl. You awake?"

"Obviously," Erin murmured, eyes still closed.

"Then get up and talk to us."

Erin cracked open one eye and it landed on Rònan. "Sure, once he leaves."

Why did the lass dislike him so much? Yes, she had an issue with fire. Yes, she had seen terrible things. But why was it landing on his shoulders?

46

"No," Nicole said firmly. "You need to sit your ass up and talk to us before we deal with the Vikings who have been nice enough to offer us protection."

Erin cracked open the other eye and frowned at Nicole. "You always were a bitch."

"Yup." Nicole shrugged. "Some things never change."

"Get off." Erin sat up, mumbling, "You know I love you but hell, woman."

"I know you do. Just like I love you." Nicole squeezed Erin's hand then returned to Niall's side.

Erin pulled a fur around her shoulders and eyed them with distrust. Though she appeared disgruntled as she gained her bearings, her features soon smoothed over to that emotionless mask she wore so well.

Her eyes narrowed on Rònan first. "Stop looking at me like that. You don't own me."

Then her eyes shot to Darach. "And you're running a little too sweet. I don't go for sweet so don't bother if you're making a play for me."

Erin's eyes met Nicole's. "And you." She shook her head. "You're too caught up in all this crap to see straight."

At last, her eyes landed on Niall. "That means you're the guy most likely to give me straight, unbiased answers." She wrapped the fur tighter. "So tell me exactly what's going on and what I can expect from these Vikings."

Rònan almost shook his head but realized Erin was doing what worked for her. Finding someone who didn't need her and didn't desire her. That meant Niall was the only one she trusted to give her the unfiltered truth.

"You are safe here, lass. At least for now," Niall said. "You've traveled back to ninth-century Scandinavia and are with our Viking ancestors. Nobody means you any harm."

"But they're like him, aren't they?" She nodded at Rònan. "Dragon shifters."

"Aye." Niall's eyes flickered from Rònan to her. "All the men born to the King and his brothers save Heidrek are dragons."

"See, that's no good." She patted her body as though looking for weapons. "Seriously not good."

"I willnae hurt you," Rònan ground out. "Nor will the Vikings."

"Uh huh," she muttered as she gave up looking for blades and grabbed a few off the wall beside her.

"I'm sorry," Nicole mouthed at Rònan and frowned before she spoke to Erin. "Seriously, Sweetie, nobody's gonna hurt you. You don't need those."

"I'll be the judge of that." Erin tucked several blades into her pants and boots as she stood. When she rocked a little both Rònan and Darach went to steady her.

Erin flipped the last blade she grabbed outward, her voice not quite threatening but firm. "I'm good. Thanks."

While Rònan wasn't pleased that she loathed him, he felt comfort knowing Darach seemed to be in the same boat.

Like too many times since he'd met Erin, Rònan wasn't quite sure how to handle her. She had no soft side, just hard edges. That's if you weren't looking at all her curves. His eyes fell down her body as she tucked more blades to the point of ridiculousness. So many tight, little curves in all the right places.

He didn't realize he growled with need until Nicole batted him upside the head. "Stop it, dumbass."

Rònan frowned but Nicole managed to snap him out of his sudden stupor. Meanwhile, Darach took advantage.

Ever debonair and too suave for the likes of a decent dragon-shifter, the bloody wizard managed to get close enough to hold her elbow as she regained her balance. Had it been Rònan, he would have done what he did back in the Defiance's cave and brought Erin against the wall. He would have caged her in and demanded answers.

He would have shown her how different their bodies were.

How much control he had over her.

Rònan blinked at his own thoughts. They were so different than the ones he usually had with lasses. Especially with one he recently learned watched her father burn alive. What was the *matter* with him? His behavior made less and less sense.

"Really, I'm good," she snapped at Darach then shook her head, softening her voice as she stepped away. "I got this."

Erin was so incredibly different than Cassie or even Nicole that he knew his cousin didn't know what to make of her. Getting close to the lass would be nearly impossible. She was too defiant, too distrusting.

Yet Rònan wanted her.

So much that it alarmed him.

What alarmed him even more was how he seemed less focused on saving Jackie. Assuming she needed saving. But she would at some point and he needed to remember that.

"So I'm surrounded by Vikings and dragon-shifters," Erin murmured.

Nicole nodded, concerned. "Yeah."

"Okay," Erin said under her breath and rested her backside against the bed. It was a subtle yet defensive stance to make her seem relaxed. But Rònan saw the way she braced her legs and the way her muscles remained tense.

She was set to lash out.

"I'll sit tight until we're ready to head out." Erin gestured at Nicole then the bed beside her. "Why don't you sit with me until I get this figured out? I can protect you as well if not better than most and you know that."

"Our Viking ancestors mean to welcome us," Niall said, tone low and even. "And we'll let them."

"Maybe you will." Erin's tone was just as even. "But not me." Her eyes went to Nicole. "And not anyone with me."

"I trust these people, Erin," Nicole said. "Just as much as I trust you."

Erin's brows didn't shoot up or draw together. Instead, her face remained emotionless. "You've met them what, once? And now the one Viking kid you met is a full grown man. One who hasn't seen you in nearly twenty years." She shook her head. "Why do you trust him or any of them for that matter?"

"I told you what the Viking King and his brother did for me the last time I was here," Nicole said. "How could I not trust them?" She frowned. "Besides, they'd do anything to protect the MacLomains and anyone related to them. They're blood and that means something. Simple as that."

Erin eyed Nicole for several long moments. "You *really* trust them?"

"I do," Nicole replied. "With all my heart."

"Even considering I tried to kill that..." She cleared her throat, obviously having trouble saying it. "That dragon."

"His name is Naðr Véurr and I consider him a friend," Nicole said. "One I know would never hurt you even in light of your actions." She shrugged. "My guess? He already knows exactly why you did what you did."

Something Rònan would love to know as well. Sure, dragons might be frightening at first but for Erin, they were downright terrifying. Not only was it obvious in her actions but in her random thoughts flickering through his mind. Thoughts he tried to block so she could have her privacy, but was unable to shut out.

"I'm sorry that I came up behind you when we traveled here, Erin," Darach said. "I only meant to protect you, not upset you."

Leave it to Darach to take advantage of Erin's slight softening.

Erin nodded but frowned. "Don't do it again. I'm not into tight spaces."

"Aye, of course," Darach said.

Though her eyes skirted around Rònan, he knew she wanted an apology from him too. And while a part of him was tempted, a bigger part, the dragon within, refused. He meant to keep her safe and he did. If he got aroused in the meantime, there wasn't much he could do about it. She was a beautiful, tempting female and he was feral.

Rònan scowled.

Feral?

Where had that thought come from? Rònan had a lot of reasons for pursuing lasses but that word had never popped into his mind.

"The Viking King and younger male dragons have stayed here to help protect us," Nicole said. "His brothers, their wives, and daughters are at the dragon lair. Female dragons are even rarer than males and they want them kept away from any potential harm."

"These Viking shifters will protect us with their lives," Nicole continued. "As it is with the Scots, family and honor mean everything to them. I for one think that's awesome so we're gonna get our butts out there and not only thank them but hang a little."

Tongue in cheek, Erin merely nodded. "As usual, it's your way or the highway." Before Nicole could bite back, she continued, voice a little softer. "And I'm all about keeping that kid in your belly safe which means keeping his mom from stressing out too much over her friends."

"Damn straight." Nicole put her hand on her stomach and used her unborn child for all she or he was worth. "Best to keep Mom happy."

Though he sensed it was the last thing she wanted to ask, Erin said, "You want me to lose some of these weapons, Mom?"

"Heck, no. You're hanging with Vikings now." Nicole snorted. "And they respect a woman who can fight."

"As if we Scots dinnae," Niall mumbled as he pulled Nicole back against him, put a hand over her stomach and kissed the top of her head.

"Oh, I know you like a fighter," Nicole murmured, nestling her backside against Niall in invitation.

"For Christ sake you two," Erin muttered and got busy making sure she knew where all her weapons were. Rònan bit back an impulsive growl when he smelled a flicker of arousal that wasn't Nicole's. No, it was hot and sweet and belonged to...

"Alright, alright," Nicole said and reluctantly pulled away from Niall. "Let's go."

They had plunked down in Scandinavia during winter so before Erin made it out the door Rònan managed to swing a fur cloak around her shoulders. She might not have said it aloud but he heard her mild 'thanks' whisper through his mind. Interestingly enough, it cheered him up considerably.

Rònan was surprised by how much Erin's contempt had affected him. He didn't like it. *At all.* In general, he was happier than most so it made no sense.

Not really.

In truth, what lad liked being rejected by a lass? Especially when he was used to women adoring him.

"I cannae quite imagine how she's meant for either of us," Darach said softly as Erin, Nicole and Niall walked ahead. "She doesnae seem fond of men in general."

"Nay," Rònan agreed. "She doesnae."

He and Darach were close but not as close as he was with Logan or especially Niall. He always sort of figured it was because Darach's element was air. And air, after all, fueled fire. Some might say that was a good thing but in their case, it had always seemed more like a battle of wills. Both were to become lairds of their clan. Rònan had stepped up and done what was expected of him but his cousin avoided it. And, despite their connection, he didn't respect Darach's avoidance.

Whether or not you liked it, you did what was expected of you. For your kin. Your clan.

He had.

And Darach should.

Yet Rònan thought there might sometimes be more than that between them. Though a wizard, his Ma was the all-powerful dragon-shifter of the MacLomains and MacLoeod's and Darach's Da, the most powerful wizard. Grant and Torra were remarkable and the ultimate leaders of the MacLomain clan. Were Rònan and Darach wary of each other because of that? Because they somehow felt they should measure up to their parents and in doing so become the strongest? And if so, could they be equally strong like their parents or would there forever be a nugget of competition between them? A need to be on top.

While Rònan was dominant by nature, he knew Darach repressed just as much dominance. The problem? Like his element, air, it shifted and remained unseen. A power that he masked and only used on rare occasion. But it was there. That Darach kept it hidden made Rònan wary. He preferred a lad's strength to be out in the open and easy to evaluate.

"We should stay close to Erin tonight," Darach continued. "It seems these Vikings find her," his eyes shot to Rònan, "just as alluring as we do."

"You mean the Vikings who are dragons." Rònan tried not to bristle at the careful yet prodding tone of Darach's voice.

"Aye," Darach said bluntly. "The dragons."

"As you said, she doesnae seem fond of men in general," Rònan said. "More than that, dragons. So though I agree we should stay close…enough, I wouldnae worry overmuch."

He made sure he kept his voice casual when he said 'enough.' Let his cousin think that perhaps Rònan remained open to another lass's advances. That's what Darach expected of him. And, all things considered, he *should* remain open to another lass's advances…shouldn't he? A frown settled on his face as they plodded through the snow to the great building at the heart of the Viking ring fortress. His thoughts baffled him. Earlier today, he was determined to find and keep Jackie safe.

Now all he could focus on was Erin.

When they entered the main building, it was to find the room half full. Multiple fires crackled along the center of its long length and flames burned in bowls hanging from the ceiling. Drums and flutes played. People ate and chatted at random tables. It was a healthy, happy community that flourished.

A community willing to welcome those sought by true evil.

A community willing to protect them.

When King Naðr Véurr waved them over, they headed that way. Though past his sixtieth winter, he had very little silver in his hair and remained as strong as ever. Having been king of this Viking clan for over forty winters, Rònan wasn't surprised in the least by his continued virility. Not only was he a powerful and honorable man but a strong and noble dragon.

The only one of them who stopped short when the King encouraged them forward was Erin. Though the others continued, Rònan remained by her side, careful not to touch her. "Come, lass," he murmured. "He willnae hurt you."

"That's him, isn't it?" she whispered. "The dragon I tried to kill."

How could she possibly know that? "Aye, 'tis the Viking King." He kept his voice firm because he knew she would respond to that tone best. "He ensured you slept afterward and holds no ill will toward you."

"Why?"

"Because he's wise and must know 'twas nothing personal."

"Oh, it was personal," she assured. "All the more reason for him to make sure I'm dead."

When Nicole glanced back, wondering if she was needed, Rònan shook his head. Thankfully, she listened and continued toward the head table.

"He kens your need to protect," Rònan said. Because why else would she have thrown the blade at the king when he was in dragon form?

"Kens," she murmured as her eyes shot to his. "So he *understands* that I tried to kill him and still welcomes me? Seriously?"

"Aye, lass," he murmured, surprised when Queen Megan headed their way. Though older, she was as lovely as ever. While

Rònan sensed Erin was tempted to take a step back, something about the way Megan approached worked. Maybe it was the fact she kept her eyes locked with Erin's or maybe it was because she had just as many weapons strapped to her body. A woman that armed would likely appeal to his lass.

His lass?

Bloody hell, Erin was as far from being his as any lass could be.

Yet he wasn't immune to the interest radiating off of Tait and Bjorn, who sat alongside the Viking King. That—to his dragon way of thinking—made him a smidge more territorial than usual.

With a wide, warm smile, Megan took Erin's hands and squeezed. "Welcome. It's so good to have you here."

Instead of saying hello or thank you, Erin's eyes narrowed. "You sound like a New Englander."

"Do I really? Still?" Megan's smile broadened. "Awesome. Because though I've been here over twenty-five years, I originally traveled back from Maine in 2014."

Erin started to talk but snapped her mouth shut, a dumbfounded look on her face.

"So Nicole didn't tell you that part, eh?" Megan chuckled, wrapped elbows with Erin and led her forward.

After that, Rònan didn't hear much and he knew it was because the Viking King didn't want him to. Rònan's powers might be strong but here, in Naðr Véurr's realm and era, nothing could touch the King's strength.

So he sat beside Nicole and Niall at the head table, truly surprised that the King and Megan plunked Erin down between them. Why would they do that? Maybe to show the Vikings that she was no enemy in spite of her earlier actions? Still, it was too much. A grand showing by anyone's standards. In all honesty, if they were to get technical, shouldn't *he* be there? A dragon shifter? A blood relative?

Instead, Tait sat down beside him.

He'd known the lad since he was in his mother's belly and had seen him several times over the years. Even so, Rònan found it suspicious that they had arrived during a time frame that put Tait so close to Erin's age. He didn't like it one bit. But hell if he would show it.

"Uncle Rònan." Tait held up a horn and nodded at Rònan's mug. "Might we toast to once more being reunited? And so close in age at that."

Careful to show none of his wariness, Rònan tapped his mug against Tait's horn and grinned. "Aye lad, and strapping ye've become."

Then they drank, eying one another.

Rònan felt Tait's sidelong look like a punch to the gut. No harm would come to Erin here. No, she would be *well* protected.

And well desired.

Viking men were direct. When they saw something they wanted they went for it. While he'd like to say the same held true for Scotsmen, he knew there was a marked difference. Most of his countrymen did a mental dance of wooing and catering to the lasses. Vikings skipped all the in betweens and staked their claim. Though some might call them Neanderthals and barbaric, Rònan knew their methods worked. Hence, the three twenty-first century women who had arrived here over twenty-five winters prior and became such an intricate part of their lives.

A *respected* part of their lives.

That was another thing about Vikings, especially those who were dragons. They might seem brutal but they were smooth in a way that melted women's hearts. He eyed the happy crowd, the tight community.

They were also fiercely family oriented.

Once they chose a woman to be theirs, she was as loved by the community as she was by the man she ended up with. Though it was the same with his Scottish clan, he could admit that somehow Vikings went about it faster and easier.

And right now Erin was with Vikings, not Scotsmen.

Not Highlanders in their element.

He took another long drag from his mug and wished she could see that his kinsmen, *his* MacLeod's, would welcome her just as warmly. Yet the minute he thought about it, he cringed. Hadn't a few of his clansmen disrespected Nicole when they'd had too much to drink? Implied that he could lay with her easily *because* she was drunk? Yes. And had he defended her? Had he punished them for their comments? No. Because he was too drunk to see how insensitive and demeaning they were.

Instead, Niall had defended her.

Not Rònan, the chieftain, but Niall.

Waking up the next morning hadn't been good at all. Not only was he hungover, but his sister Seònaid had been there *not* to flick him on the forehead as he expected and deserved but to damn him much more effectively. She kept a cool, calm voice and told him what an arse he was. How he should never have treated a lass with such disrespect and how he was a pitiful excuse for a chieftain. He knew it wasn't right, but he already had a reputation for getting too drunk. What he had *not* been known for was allowing a lass to be disrespected, under his reign or otherwise.

He got lucky, though. Nicole never judged him because she was busy fighting her own demons. Rònan, however, had not been so easy on himself. Though he wore his trusty smile and continued to make jokes, he inwardly loathed his behavior.

Maybe that was another reason he itched to fight Darach.

At least his cousin was smart enough to run from responsibility rather than become what Rònan had.

"Might you dance with me, warrior?"

Torn from his ever darkening thoughts, Rònan hoped for a split second it might be Erin. But no. It was a buxom blond leaning over the table in front of him with a come-hither look on her face.

"Go, Uncle," Tait said. "Enjoy your time here."

Enjoy his time? There was only one way to do that. He cursed his line of thinking when his eyes went to Erin. She was deep in conversation with the King and Megan.

"Please. I insist." Tait nudged his arm and winked. "You do not want to offend your hosts, do you?"

The blond curled her fingers and licked her lips. For the first time ever, he had absolutely no desire for a bonnie lass. And she was, indeed, bonnie. But she wasn't nearly…Erin. *Hell and damnation.* He needed to stop thinking like this.

"Again, I insist," Tait said.

"Aye," Rònan murmured and joined the lass for a dance. It was for the best. And to do otherwise could have caused trouble. Yet as he brought her close, his arms felt empty. He held her, she was there, she was more than desirable, but it felt like he touched nothing. Growling, frustrated with his inability to enjoy her, he pulled her even closer and tried harder.

56

But he didn't feel a thing.

Not until he saw Tait dancing with Erin.

Not until he saw the way her eyes closed in pleasure when he pulled her close.

Then Rònan felt something to be sure.

Pure rage.

Chapter Five

ERIN WAS STILL trying to decide if she should pull a knife on these Vikings when Tait asked her to dance.

"No." Her eyes skirted between the Viking King and his wife. "I'm busy talking."

"Please." Tait held out his hand. "I insist."

"Insist elsewhere." He might be hot but she was in the midst of strangers. And no matter what Nicole said, that meant she was in the midst of enemies.

"You won't offend us if you go dance," Megan said. "It might not be such a bad idea considering all you're dealing with."

"All I'm *dealing* with?" Her gaze landed on Megan. "No offense, you've been kind considering I tried to kill your man but your story's not mine. In fact, I have no story." She tried to yank her Claddagh ring off but it wouldn't budge. "Especially none of the crap that's supposed to be attached to this thing."

Tait leaned against the table and eyed the ring. "I can find a way to burn that off if you like."

The disgruntled look the king shot him made Tait shrug but not run.

"Keep it on," Megan said, not demanding but firm as her eyes met Erin's. "Otherwise, you'll have to deal with more crap than you're ready for."

Erin didn't smile but she did arch her brows. "Yeah?"

"Yeah," Megan assured.

It was still hard to believe she was talking to a woman from her era that had lived here so long but Megan made it easy. She was different. Soft yet strong. She told Erin exactly how things were. And it all matched up with what Nicole said. A modern day woman hooked up with an ancient Viking. That sort of thing happened. It existed.

Love existed.

That's what brought them together.

"Please. Dance with Tait." Megan touched her shoulder and oddly enough Erin wasn't tempted to flinch. She always felt the urge to flinch when people touched her. "He's the easiest of these Viking men to get along with. He inherited his good disposition from his parents."

Her eyes again went to Tait. He did seem pretty upbeat and easy going. So though Erin sighed she complied, unwilling to upset her hosts. But for whatever reason when she was in Tait's arms, her traitorous eyes sought out Rònan. Naturally he was still with the blond. What was with men and big breasted blonds? Seriously, there was something to be said for a small breasted brunette.

And how Rònan's hands might feel touching her breasts.

The minute she thought it an odd sensation washed over her. As Tait pull her closer, she couldn't help but close her eyes and relish a pleasure she didn't understand. Not because of Tait but because of...

"Ye bloody bastard!"

Erin staggered back as Rònan ripped Tait away.

All hell broke loose as everyone roared in support of the men rolling on the floor. Punching, kicking, they were fighting for all they were worth.

"No more!" the Viking King roared.

Yet the men kept punching and if she wasn't mistaken, steam rolled off their bodies.

Though the King's next words were softer, they were also far more effective. "Do not make me say it again."

Tait froze. Rònan did as well.

The Viking King never left his perch behind the head table as the men shook in anger and eyed one another.

The King's gaze went to Erin. "Dance with Rònan."

Dance with Rònan? She shook her head. "No."

His eyes narrowed. "Now, woman."

Erin bristled but knew better than to test him too much. "Fine."

There was no way around it. Dancing with Rònan was a bad idea.

Evidently he didn't think so because she barely had time to blink before he pulled her against him. While his arm might have come around her back and she might've let him pull her close, she was still fuming mad.

60

"What *was* that?" she growled as her eyes met his. "Who do you think you are?"

A muscle ticked in his jaw. "I dinnae know what that was."

"You don't know?" She kept frowning. "You just attacked a man for no good reason."

She was startled by the flicker of emotion that crossed his face. Better yet, how confused he seemed by his own actions. "I dinnae act like that," he murmured.

"I would hope not," she said. "It's damn unattractive."

"Aye, 'tis," he admitted. "And I apologize."

Her brows lifted in surprise. She hadn't expected that. *Not at all.* She figured he would get cocky because he got what he wanted.

"*Why* did you do it?" she asked again, growing less frustrated and more curious. "There has to be a reason for your actions."

He shook his head. "I dinnae know." A frown settled on his face and she had to appreciate how honest he was. "I saw the pleasure you took in Tait's arms and I couldnae fight a feeling of rage."

"You mean jealousy."

"Aye, mayhap. Rage fueled by jealousy." His eyes held hers. "And that doesnae happen to me. Ever."

Erin ignored the jolt of awareness that shot through her. She had always been picky about men and especially disliked the insecure ones. Yet Rònan seemed as far from insecure as a guy could get. "I don't understand." Then she said something she wished she hadn't. Something that made her sound a little too aware of his actions...of him in general. "You seemed happy enough with the Viking woman."

"Aye, happy enough I suppose," he admitted but she didn't miss the flare of renewed interest in his eyes. "And though it shouldnae, it pleases me that you noticed."

While she meant to make a comment about him not getting hopeful, instead she said, "Why shouldn't it please you that I noticed?"

"Because I assume Jackie is the lass meant for me."

"Ah." She shrugged and worked to keep her voice level as she became more and more aware of him. He made her nerve endings spark in a whole new way. It was alarming and she didn't like it. "Well, I'm all for you being meant for Jackie. She's a good woman."

"Aye," he agreed. "So it seems."

They might be talking about him being with another woman, but she was well aware of his arousal.

"Until I find Jackie, I mean to keep you safe," he grunted.

He said nothing more as his hand splayed and his fingers flexed across her back. Erin meant to speak—meant to tell him she could take care of herself—when his hand clamped down and pulled her closer.

"Rònan," she warned because she wasn't sure what was happening.

"Erin," he whispered.

Raging fire flared beneath her skin when her eyes met his. There was nothing but lust there. And it drove her crazy with need. So much need. The kind that made her blind with desire. Aroused beyond belief.

Ready.

Not only for intimacy but something more…something dangerous and different.

Erin was attracted to him before but now it was a hundred times more intense. Why? What had changed?

She knew holding his gaze wasn't good. That a great deal of what flared between them had to do with those verdant eyes of his. There was a compelling fire in them that spoke to her. Yet he was everything she despised. Well, parts of him. Not all. Because right now, in his arms, pressed against him, *what* he was didn't bother her in the least. No, it was the furthest thing from her mind. Why was it again that she so avidly disliked dragon-shifters? For the life of her, she couldn't remember.

She didn't want to.

She wanted him.

Right here.

Right now.

Erin had no idea he'd been slowly walking her backward until her back met one of the building's support beams. And she had no clue his hand was on her ass until he slowly lifted her so that their lips were much closer. Centimeters apart. Their breathing became harsher as she wrapped her legs around his waist.

God, he was rock solid and throbbing against her.

A raging ache blossomed between her legs, spread down her thighs and up her stomach. He inhaled deeply and she swore actual flames burned in his eyes. When he ground against her, she bit her lower lip and arched. One more thrust and she knew her body would let go. She was *that* close.

"Um, guys."

Nicole sounded far, far away.

"Ye need to get yerself under control, Cousin," Niall warned. Like Nicole, it sounded like he spoke from a great distance.

Someone tapped her shoulder. "You two might wanna knock it off," Nicole said. "Like *right now.*"

Something about Nicole touching her snapped Erin back from wherever she had gone. Discombobulated, she blinked several times as the room slowly came into focus. Now she knew why they were so concerned. Several Viking men, including Tait and Bjorn, stood nearby. All had their eyes locked on her with what she'd call ferocious lust. And fire flickered in each and every steady gaze.

"Put me down, Rònan," she said through clenched teeth, pulling out several blades. Rònan did as asked and repositioned himself to defend her as he pulled his blade free as well.

"I had hoped this might go smoother but it seems you are too much of a draw for the young dragons," the Viking King said softly as he joined them. "Though they will protect you, it is best that you avoid them for now."

"I've never seen this sort of behavior from them," Rònan said to the King. "I dinnae ken."

"No, it's quite obvious you do not." He gestured for them to follow. "Come. All of you. I will explain."

Erin felt a strange flutter in her stomach as Megan joined them and they headed outside. Why did she have the feeling they were about to tell her something that was going to change everything? When Rònan put a comforting hand against her back, she almost pulled away. But unlike everyone else's touch, his didn't put her off. Instead, it felt like it belonged there.

That last thought *did* make her pull away.

Erin only appreciated Rònan's touch because she was long overdue for some sexual release and he fit the bill. She conveniently ignored the fact that Tait, Bjorn or any number of the sexy Vikings didn't do a thing for her. And they damn well should have.

"Please." The King gestured to several seats around a small fire in what she guessed was his and Megan's lodge. When they sat down, the servants handed them mugs of ale.

Naðr sat across from them and contemplated Erin for several moments before he spoke. "You will not like what I have to tell you but it needs to be told."

Erin clenched her hand around the mug but kept a smooth expression. Nicole remained close for support. While Erin appreciated it, she was good. Whatever the King had to say, she was ready to hear it. "Tell me," she demanded.

The King glanced at Megan before he nodded and met Erin's eyes. "The reason male dragon-shifters are so drawn to you is because you possess dragon blood. Though it's clear that you have never shifted, you *are* a female dragon. And they are very rare. In fact, these men have never come across one that is of no relation to them."

Her blood froze in her veins. In the crazy reality in which she'd been thrust, Erin expected Naor to say just about anything…but not that. Never that.

"What did you just say?" Erin asked, shocked and confused. There's no way she heard him correctly.

"You are a dragon," the King repeated.

"Bloody hell," Rònan whispered.

Nicole squeezed Erin's hand, understanding that she was rendered speechless.

"Okay, way to drop a bomb." Nicole's eyes narrowed on the King. "You need to keep talking *now*."

"We don't have all the details and we may never," Megan said. "All we know for certain is that she has dragon blood." Her eyes locked on Erin. "And that she's not only a Broun but a DeLaunde. That, as it turns out, was my maiden name."

If she wasn't frozen before, she was downright frigid now. "DeLaunde?"

"Holy shit," Nicole whispered.

"You know the name then?" Megan murmured.

Erin tried to respond but couldn't.

"I would hope so," Nicole filled in. "Her name is Erin DeLaunde."

Megan smiled. "Of course it is."

Erin meant to shoot to her feet, to defy what she was hearing, but remained frozen in place. Stunned. In shock as too many bad memories assaulted her.

Megan strode around the fire, crouched in front of her and seized her hands, eyes warm but voice intensely firm. "You descend from me and King Naðr, Erin. You *are* our distant offspring."

"No," she mouthed and shook her head.

Flashes of her father burning flickered in her mind.

She could not be half dragon. She just couldn't be.

"So what does that mean?" Nicole asked. "That she's related to Rònan as well?"

"No. No more than you are to Niall through the Brouns. The bloodline has thinned out over the centuries." Megan kept her eyes on Erin. "Honestly, we don't know how this is possible just that it is." She squeezed her hands. "You are one of us and are always welcome here."

Here? Where was *here*? Ancient Scandinavia? Medieval Scotland? Erin yanked her hands away, stood and pulled the blades she'd pocketed when they left the main lodge. Though she had no intention of using them, they were her safety net. And boy, did she need that right now.

"You're all deranged." She backed away. "I'm outta here."

She had just walked out the door when she bumped into a hard chest.

"You go nowhere without being escorted. It's not safe."

Bjorn.

She had only backed into the lodge a few steps when she met another hard wall. When she spun, Rònan grabbed her wrists before she could use her blades. Which she wouldn't have...would she? Nothing made sense. She no longer had an identity. What was she? Who was she? One thing was for sure, she didn't want to be part of a *dragon* family.

"You need to calm down, lass," he said softly. "We'll figure this out."

"*We* won't figure out anything." When she tried to push him away, he held tight. She knew exactly what to do to get free yet instead she stilled, calmed almost. How was it that he inflamed her one second and she found absolute peace beneath his touch the next?

His eyes locked on hers. "We *will* figure this out."

65

"It's okay," Nicole said, putting a comforting hand on her shoulder. "Rònan's right. We got this."

When Erin frowned, Nicole shrugged and cocked the corner of her lips. "So you're a horse-loving witchy biker chick one sec and a dragon-shifter the next. It's all workable."

Right, she was supposedly a witch as well.

It was impossible to stop the tug at the corner of her lips. While she typically found Nicole's sense of humor overbearing, she didn't right now. What was going on with her? Lusting after Rònan for all to see then finding humor in Nicole's wiseass comments.

Nothing made sense anymore.

Okay, maybe lusting after Rònan wasn't so far-fetched. She was human. Or so she hoped. But what they'd done was completely out of character for her. She wasn't a fan of public displays of affection. Hell, any affection for that matter. At least not in a very long time.

"Let me go, Rònan," she said softly, but with just enough threat.

"Nay." He clasped her tighter. "'Twould be unwise."

Though she was tempted to spit, "Get off!" something told her not to. They were connected somehow. She might feel emotionally charged but she was no fool. Whatever was happening between them kept her contained in a way she didn't understand. And while she might want to fight them all tooth and nail, she knew that was unwise. If nothing else, she was sorely outnumbered.

Her eyes shot to the Viking King. "Two things. I want proof and some time alone to think things over. Is there someplace I can rest?"

"The proof is in your blood," the King murmured. "And something you alone must discover and accept." His eyes met Megan's. "I think perhaps you would be the best person to escort her to her lodgings."

Megan nodded and looked at Rònan. "Release her."

When he did, Megan took her hand and urged her to follow.

"Hey, I'm coming too," Nicole started but Megan shook her head. "No, only Rònan."

"I said I wanted to be alone," Erin reminded as she followed the woman outside.

"Regrettably, that's not an option," Megan said. "Based on what we saw in the main lodge, it's unwise to leave you alone. Rònan will stay with you. Bjorn will keep watch outside."

The last thing she needed was to be alone in a building with Rònan. "It's snowing and freezing out here. Bjorn's gonna stand out in this all night?"

"Bjorn is a Viking and used to the weather," Megan reminded. "No one will come near you with my first-born guarding you."

When she glanced over her shoulder at the tall man, his eyes were locked on her. "So who's going to protect me from Bjorn?" Her brows furrowed. "*Rònan?*"

"You say that as if you dinnae think I could," Rònan grumbled.

Erin shrugged and glanced at Bjorn again. He and Rònan were well-matched in height and build but Bjorn was a damn Viking. For some reason, that translated into a smidge more fierceness.

"Okay then." Her eyes met Megan's. "Who's gonna protect me from Rònan because he seems just as drawn to me as the rest of 'em."

"That, regrettably, is for you to deal with," Megan said as she led Erin into an impressively large lodge. "All I know is that not only Grant but Rònan's mother, Torra, wants him by your side at all times. He's a MacLomain dragon and best suited to guard that ring of yours."

Erin narrowed her eyes. "And why would that be?"

She knew the stone at the center of the ring was supposed to become a gem to match the MacLomain wizard's eyes she was meant for. And it was not Rònan. Besides, she had stolen the ring so technically it shouldn't be on her finger to begin with.

"Torra and Grant gave no reason and we're not in the habit of questioning them," Megan said as she nodded at a circular table in the corner of the room. "We've had food and drink provided for you." Then she gestured at a trunk. "Both of you will find a change of clothes in there."

Erin was about to respond when Megan embraced her. Freezing at the human contact, unable to hug her back, she remained aloof. Finally, Megan pulled away and eyed her warmly. "It'll be all right. I promise. Take the night to think things over. You're safe here." She glanced at Rònan. "Believe it or not, you have a friend in him."

Before Erin could say a word, Megan strode out.

A frown in place, she eyed the room. Like the others, it had a high thatch-covered ceiling. Various weapons hung on the walls and a fire crackled. Her eyes shot to the big bed and her frown deepened.

One bed.

That's it.

Considering how easily she had fallen into Rònan's arms earlier that was a really bad thing.

"Dinnae worry, lass," he murmured and headed for the table. "I'll sleep on the floor."

Erin eyed the plush throw on the floor in front of the fire. It looked comfortable enough. At any rate, he wouldn't be on the hardwood. "Yeah you will."

Because the two of them absolutely could not sleep in the same bed.

She didn't trust him.

More than that, she didn't trust herself.

Rònan filled two mugs then handed her one. It was hard to read the look on his face. He had to be working through the King's revelation just like she was.

"Thanks," she murmured and slid down against the wall. Feet on the floor, knees bent, she took a deep swig then focused on the fire. As if he sensed she needed space, Rònan slid down against the opposite wall, stretched out his legs and said nothing.

Accustomed to having her own place and complete privacy, she felt his presence like a heavy weight. He made it impossible for her to think clearly. Maybe she could get him to leave. "If you want to take a stroll or something, maybe find that blond again, I won't tell."

"I didnae want to dance with the blond to begin with," he said softly.

"Well, you should have," Erin grunted. "She wasn't half bad looking."

No, she was gorgeous.

Rònan didn't drink nor did he say a word. Instead, he eyed her with that same unreadable expression.

"Enough." Erin sighed. "Spit out what's on your mind and stop looking at me like that."

"Like what?"

"Honestly?" She shrugged. "Like I've got three heads and a tail."

She scowled at her own words. Dragons had tails.

Rònan contemplated her for another moment before he relented. "'Tis just that the only other female dragon-shifter I've met is my

Ma." He shook his head. "Besides the Viking lasses, I didnae know any others existed. And one from the future no less."

"Listen, I may not have pitched a fit back there but I don't buy what the King's selling," she informed. "So what if Megan and I share the same last name. That doesn't prove a thing. Technically I should share a last name with the King for this to make any sense."

Rònan shrugged, evidently no more concerned with that detail than the others. "Anything's possible. Mayhap his family took Queen Megan's surname to keep those like you safe."

"Either way," she said. "I still don't believe it."

"What about how the dragon-shifters are responding to you?" His eyes never left hers. "And explain what happened betwixt you and I back there?"

"As to the dragon-shifters, they're probably just drawn to the new girl in town." She shrugged. "As to you and me?" Erin was careful with her words and remained nonchalant. "Heat of the moment. It happens."

But it didn't.

Not ever.

Heck if she would admit it, though.

Rònan, however, wasn't nearly as casual about their encounter. "That has never happened to me before." His eyes remained firmly locked on hers. "I've never been consumed by another and I've *never* lost control."

"Consumed?" She snorted and shook her head. "It was just lust, Rònan. Something I know you're more than familiar with."

"Aye, lust indeed." He leaned forward, his arms now braced on bent knees. "But more than that. Something deeper. Something that took me right out of this world and sent me somewhere else." He cocked his head. "Tell me you didnae feel it too."

"I didn't," she lied. "All I felt was plain ole' fashioned arousal." She kept her eyes on his because she backed down from no man. "It happens to the best of us."

"It doesnae happen like that." His eyes narrowed. "It doesnae happen like it did betwixt us."

"It does," she shot back. "So stop trying to see something that wasn't there."

"Mayhap you're right. Mayhap 'twas just good old fashioned arousal." Rònan sat back, continued to eye her and said the last thing she expected. "If 'tis just that then why not slake your lust, lass?" His brogue thickened. "'Twas clear enough ye desire me and 'tis clear yer in need of release." He curled a finger in a come-hither motion. "Yer a full grown lass with yer own mind. Come take what ye need and be done with it."

In another place and time, she would be inclined to agree.

But they both knew damned well it was more than that.

And she wasn't willing to find out how much more.

"I'm fine right here," she said. "I'm fine not repeating what happened earlier."

"Aye," he murmured. "As am I."

Erin *knew* she should leave it alone but for some reason, she kept at him. Forget the blond. There was a more defined target. "Besides, Jackie is likely meant for you."

"Aye, mayhap," he whispered then shook his head. "But mayhap not." He set aside his drink as though he worried it would muddle his thoughts even further. "There's something unusual betwixt you and me." Again he gave her honesty she appreciated. "Though I bloody well like the feel of you in my arms, I dinnae like the loss of control I felt. 'Tis not the way of the dragon to lose a sense of itself. To act as I did with Tait before we danced. 'Twas not admirable."

"No," she agreed. "It wasn't."

But she still wondered about it. Why had he acted that way? Why had they acted like they did afterward? What *was* that? Because she refused to believe it had anything to do with mutual dragon blood. More than that, she refused to admit how all of this connected to her past.

"Why do you do that?" Rònan asked.

"What?"

"Flick your *lighter* on and off?"

Startled, Erin glanced at the lighter she must have pulled out of her pocket and started flicking. For the life of her, she didn't remember doing it. Shit. She tucked it away. "None of your business."

Rònan eyed her as though he already knew the answer and wished she would enlighten him further. "Why is it so bloody hard for you to share just one thing about yourself?"

If he only knew.

Erin stood, took another swig of ale then set aside the mug. Though catching a buzz sounded great, it was a bad idea. She was in a land and time she didn't understand. More so, she was surrounded by people she didn't trust. Including Rònan. "I'm going to bed. I expect you to be anywhere I'm not."

Always one to sleep fully clothed in case she needed to bolt, she crawled into bed. Before she pulled the blankets over her, she set aside her weapons. All save one. That blade she held up for him to see. "Keep your distance, Rònan, because I'm not afraid to use this."

"Aye, lass." He nodded. "You have my word that I willnae move from this spot."

Not completely without compassion, she nodded toward the fire. "Lie there. It looks comfortable enough."

"I'm fine right here." His eyes met hers. "Go to sleep, Erin. You're safe."

She wiggled her blade. "Damn straight I am."

While she had always slept in clothing, she hated blankets. She hated being hot. Or she got hot too easily. It was hard to know. But tonight she had no choice. Anything extra covering her felt necessary. Protective.

Hand on the hilt of her blade, she kept an eye on Rònan. He never moved, never drank, only stared at the fire. Bit by bit, and after a long while, she started to relax. She allowed the howling wind outside to soothe her and the unwavering, unmoving, presence of Rònan to finally enable her to drift off.

"Why cannae I hear you?" came a soft voice.

Erin blinked and sat up. "Who said that?"

Rònan gave no response but continued to look at the fire.

"I know yer there," came the voice again. A child's voice. A boy by the sounds of it. "But I cannae hear ye!"

She jumped out of bed and tried to speak to Rònan, but nothing came out of her mouth. Her vocal chords were on the fritz again. So she waved her hand in front of his face. Nothing. It was as if he didn't see her.

"Rònan?" she said, grateful her voice seemed to be working again.

Why was he ignoring her?

"What's the matter with you?" she growled and tried to shake him. Her hands passed right through his body.

What the *hell*? "That's impossible!"

"Dinnae yell at me," the child whimpered. "I am lost and 'tis dark."

So the boy could hear her now?

"I didn't mean to yell." She pulled away from Rònan. "I'm sorry."

"Where are ye?" the boy said. "I cannae hear ye anymore."

Huh? She spun and kept speaking yet the child couldn't hear her. This was insane. The only thing that had been different before was that she'd been trying to touch Rònan. Desperate to reconnect with the voice, she figured it couldn't hurt to give it another shot. So though it made no sense, she tried to touch Rònan again and said, "Where are you?"

"I dinnae know," the child whimpered.

He could hear her! Erin frowned and crouched beside Rònan. Drawing on military training, she kept a calm head and a level, reassuring voice though she was completely baffled. "My name is Erin. I'm your friend. Can you tell me what your surroundings look like?"

"Dark. Gray," he whispered. "Like the forest died."

Chills ran up her spine.

"Okay, that's a good explanation," she said. "Can you tell me your name?"

"Aye, 'tis Robert the Bruce."

Oh no. How was that possible? Wasn't he supposed to be with Grant Hamilton?

"We never got a chance to say hello earlier so nice to meet you, Robert," she said, still hovering beside Rònan. "I'm friends with Cassie and Nicole. You know them, right?"

"Aye, they are my friends," he acknowledged. "Someone else is here too."

Erin didn't like the sound of that.

Robert started to whimper. "I think they are going to hurt her."

She *really* didn't like the sound of that.

"Who's going to hurt who?" she responded.

"The darkness is going to hurt her," Robert whispered. "The darkness is going to hurt Jaqueline."

Chapter Six

RÒNAN JOLTED AWAKE at the same moment as Erin and recalled every detail of his dream. How paralyzed he had been. How he was unable to look at her when she crouched beside him and equally unable to feel her touch. More than that, he had heard every word said betwixt her and the wee Bruce.

"Wha…" Erin started as she swung her legs over the side of the bed and looked around in confusion. Her eyes locked on him and she whispered, "What the hell just happened? I was beside you and…" She blinked several times. "We've got problems."

"Aye, lass." He stood and though tempted to go to her, he instead refreshed his ale and relayed the dream he'd had.

Her eyes grew wider as he spoke.

"How is that even possible?" she whispered.

"While you likely dinnae want to hear it or even believe it, I suspect our shared dragon blood is the reason for our connection not only in the dream but back at the mountain." He handed her his ale. "Drink. 'Twill calm your nerves."

Erin took a hearty swig, eyes never leaving his as she stood. Having clearly tossed and turned, her raven curls were a wild mess around her shoulders. And whether it was because she had just awoken or because she was upset, the starburst of pale violet at the center of her eyes seemed to have expanded. Gods help him, she was beyond alluring. Striking. Utterly beautiful.

Determined to keep the roar of his arousal under control, he stepped away. He could reignite the fire on the hearth with magic but decided against it. He needed something to occupy him and his thoughts. Anything to keep from tossing her onto the bed and picking up where they left off earlier.

When he glanced at Erin again, she was pulling on her boots. "What are you doing?"

73

"Going to find the Viking King. I'd think you'd be doing the same." She frowned at him. "Not only Robert the Bruce but Jackie's in trouble. We need to get out of here and find them."

"Nay," he said. "We go nowhere until we hear from Grant."

"Are you out of your mind?" Erin tied her boots and stood. "Not only is a helpless kid out there somewhere but my friend is too. And by the sounds of it, she seriously needs our help."

"And where precisely do you think they are, lass?" Rònan crossed his arms over his chest. "Because I dinnae know in the slightest, nor does the Viking King or I guarantee he would already be in here sharing his newfound knowledge. What I do know is that they are nowhere near us. They arenae in this century."

"Well then we need to figure out a way to get to wherever they are," she said. "Because I refuse to sit around waiting when someone needs my help."

When she tried to stride by him, he grabbed her arm, using his height to full advantage as he narrowed his eyes. "You arenae going anywhere."

More inside her mind than he should be, he anticipated her next move. Before she could threaten him with her dagger, he flicked it from her hand with magic. Though more than tempted to physically battle her, he knew how it would end. In lust. With her legs spread and him deep inside her. And as bloody tempting as that sounded, it was the last place either of them needed to be right now.

He wondered at his line of thinking. It wasn't like him. Typically, he would have seized the opportunity to have her despite his draw to Jackie. He truly wanted her that bad. Yet now that he knew what she was, things had changed. Now that he knew she was half dragon. A creature like him. Though he was known for enjoying and respecting lasses, he could admit that he inherently respected a female dragon more. It was just in his blood to do so. And he wasn't quite sure how he felt about that.

"Let me go, Rònan," Erin warned.

He should have known better than to think disarming her would stop her. So when her knee came up, he evaded. Whatever was happening between them was progressing swiftly because though she was an excellent fighter, he easily anticipated every move ahead of time.

She punched. He avoided. She swiped her leg. He stepped aside. On and on it went as he did his best to make as little contact with her as possible. Nonetheless, his blood stirred and he was being drawn back to that place she could take him. That otherworldly place made only of desire and inescapable lust. So he did something she would hate him for later.

He murmured a chant and put her to sleep.

Rònan scooped her up before she hit the floor and laid her down on the bed. After he covered her, he sat by her side and sighed. He had never been so conflicted. So confused. Never so unsure of what direction he was supposed to go in.

"Cousin, can I join you?"

Rònan was surprised by the sound of Niall outside the door. He hadn't sensed him coming.

"Aye," he called.

"Sorry to check on you so late." Niall brushed the snow from his hair as he entered. "But your thoughts were troublesome."

"No doubt." Rònan poured Niall some ale and eyed him. "I'm surprised Nicole's not with you."

"Oh, she tried. She's been at me all night to check on you two so I had to put an end to it."

"And how did you manage that?"

Niall grinned and winked. "In the best way possible."

"Och, I dinnae need to hear about it." Rònan plunked down in a chair beside Niall and took a long swig of ale. "'Tis no easy thing keeping my lust at bay right now."

"I know the King said you should stay here but I can watch over Erin if you need to slake your lust elsewhere," Niall said. "Just be sure to go out the back way. Not only Bjorn but Tait guard the front."

"Nay, 'twould be dishonorable." Rònan frowned at his friend. "To both the King and Erin."

"Mayhap 'twould be." Niall looked at him oddly. "But I'm sure Naðr wouldnae overly judge you if you did. Just stay close."

"And what of Erin?"

"I thought you…" Niall's brows drew together in confusion. "Though you two got lusty in the main hall I thought 'twas a dragon thing." His eyes narrowed. "Are you not determined to save Jackie? Is she not the lass you desire?"

Rònan rubbed a hand over his face and sighed. Niall made a valid point. "I am set to save Jackie and will."

Niall remained silent for several long moments before he murmured, "And what of the desire for Jackie you so recently felt?"

"I've yet to meet the lass so what do I base my desire on?" he bit back and cursed the words as he said them. "I dinnae know her in the least."

"You sound conflicted. Will you save her then? Because you dinnae need to know a lass to fulfill your oath to her." Niall frowned. "Was she not there for you in your darkest hour?"

"I intend to fulfill my oath," he growled. "I just dinnae know..."

When he trailed off and scowled at the fire, Niall filled in the blanks. "You just dinnae know if she's the lass meant for you and you're feeling guilty because of it."

"Aye," Rònan whispered, thankful his friend was here and understood him so well. "I dinnae ken half of what I'm feeling right now and I dinnae like it a wee bit."

"As you likely know, some of your thoughts have brushed my mind since we got here." Niall's eyes flickered to the bed then back to him. "You cannae fault yourself for desiring Erin, Cousin. Any more than I could stop my feelings for Nicole when she first traveled back in time. I give you credit that you havenae had her yet. 'Tis unlike you not to slake your lust with a lass when you want her so badly." He cocked the corner of his lips. "So I tend to think you're rallying your strength well by recognizing that your feelings for her need to be questioned as you dinnae ken the way of it with a female dragon."

"A female dragon," Rònan murmured and perked a brow at Niall. "'Tis hard to believe, aye?"

"Aye, considering we all thought your Ma was the last of them." Niall swigged his ale and gave Rònan a pointed look. "'Tis no small thing what we learned. I respect you trying to keep your distance from her till you better ken the connection, but..."

When he trailed off, Rònan said, "But what?"

"Well." Niall continued to eye him. "I feel for you is all. 'Twas hard enough to find my way to Nicole and we didnae have half the battle you might fight if mayhap Erin is the lass meant for you." His cousin grew more serious. "You deserve the love I found with Nicole. So my advice." Niall paused for a moment. "Keep your lust at bay and try to get to know her better. Try to ken the lass she was before all of this."

"Even if I'm meant for Jackie?"

"Aye." Niall nodded. "Erin needs a friend right now. You can see her through all this. Support her. It willnae be easy to get her to accept she's got dragon blood. But you can help by understanding who she was before all this."

 Rònan knew he was right. He also knew deep down it was the reason he hadn't slaked his lust with her all ready. There was too much gray area. Too much that he didn't understand.

"You've grown wiser as of late, my friend," Rònan murmured.

"Aye, 'tis amazing how much clearer I see things now that I'm with Nicole."

"Och, 'twas a battle to be sure when you two came together." Rònan managed a small grin. "'Twas well worth the fight, though. You're both better people for it."

"Aye," Niall agreed.

A comfortable silence born of a long friendship settled between them as Rònan pondered Niall's advice. Because while Nicole was certainly a handful when they met, Erin was clearly going to be more of a challenge.

"'Twill all work out as it should," Niall said softly. "The rings willnae have it otherwise."

"Och, the bloody rings," Rònan muttered. "Whilst I'm set to find Jackie and lust after Erin, I dinnae think I'm fond of a ring locking me onto one lass for life."

"Nor was I," Niall said. "But I couldnae love Nicole more and remain grateful she was brought to me."

"'Tis Nicole, though," Rònan reminded. "If not for you, Cousin, I would have kept her as my own."

"You like to think as much," Niall said. "But did you not take a lass to your bed the verra first night Nicole arrived at your castle?"

"Well, there *was* that," Rònan conceded. "But drunk is drunk. We all slip up, aye?"

"Nay." Niall shook his head. "When you meet the lass meant for you, desiring another becomes impossible no matter how drunk." His cousin shrugged and grinned. "The cock wants what the cock wants."

A grin tugged at Rònan's lips. "And here I thought 'twould be all about my heart."

"You'd be amazed at how well your heart controls your cock in the end." Niall eyed him. "Might I give you just a wee bit more advice, friend?"

Rònan nodded. "You can."

"All right." Niall stood and wrapped a fur cloak over his shoulders. "Like me, on rare occasion you tend to turn into yourself because you dinnae like what others are telling you." His eyes held Rònan's. "Work toward not doing that. Work toward paying attention to those who love you and ken that they might see something you cannae because you're too close to the situation, aye?"

Rònan imagined he might be referring to recent developments between Niall and his Da. They had come a long way in a short time. "Aye, Cousin. 'Tis good advice."

"'Tis." Niall eyed him for a long moment before he pulled him into an embrace and clapped him on the back.

Before Niall left Rònan said, "Bjorn and I are more than enough to protect Erin. Tait doesnae need to be out there."

"I said as much before I entered but he's determined to stay." Niall paused at the door. "They can be trusted to stay where they are."

Though they both knew Rònan's dragon was rearing up against Tait, Niall was right. After he left, Rònan sat back down and eyed the fire.

But sure enough, his gaze drifted to Erin.

Her thick hair haloed her face and she looked like an angel. An angel! Erin? Closed-off, defiant Erin. But she did. What he wouldn't do to wrap his hands into her curls and pull those soft, full lips against his just once.

Yet he knew once would not be enough.

If it was like earlier, she would melt against him then work her magic and he would be gone. Lost somewhere he wasn't sure he would be able to break free from again. So though he wanted to crawl into bed and pull her close, protect her, he knew better.

Back against the bed, he sat on the floor and kept a dagger in hand. He would sit here through the night and try to figure out the dream they'd shared. What it all meant. Though tempted, he hadn't

78

told Niall about it. Not only because he sensed his friend was eager to get back to Nicole, but because Rònan felt it prudent to share with the Viking King first.

So he set aside his ale and sat through what felt like the longest eve of his life. Erin slept soundly, her breathing soft. Not once did he look over his shoulder and risk being drawn to her. Instead, he kept a close eye on both doorways. Even so, her sweet, feminine scent drifted over him and managed to keep him aroused all damn night. And nothing put him in a fouler mood than unfulfilled lust. Or so it seemed. Truth told this was the first time his lust had ever been denied.

Eventually, dim daylight arrived along with an even heavier snowfall. Servants brought in food and drink then left quietly. As he knew she would, Nicole arrived.

"Hey, you two awake?" she said softly from outside the door. "Better yet, are you decent?"

"Aye, come in," he called.

Nicole peeked around the corner before she entered and shook the snow off her hood. "Man, is it snowing out there."

"'Tis." Rònan handed her a mug of mead. "Good morn, lass."

"G'morning." Nicole's gaze went to the bed. "Erin's still crashed, eh?" She eyed Rònan. "So what happened last night? Is she okay?" Her eyes narrowed on him. "Did you two...ya know...finish what you started in the main lodge?"

"None of your damn business," Erin murmured from the bed. She cracked open one eye then the other and yawned as she sat up. "How the heck did I get here?" she started before her eyes narrowed on Rònan. "What the hell'd you do to me?"

"I didnae do a bloody thing...for the most part," Rònan grumbled. He plunked down at the table and bit into some warm bread.

"The last thing I remember I was heading out of here." Erin scowled as she crawled out of bed. "So I'll ask one more time, what did you do?"

Nicole's eyes flickered between them. "Maybe I should go."

"Nay," Rònan said. "Stay. Break your fast with us."

His need for Erin only seemed to be growing by the moment so the more people around them, the better. Anything to help keep him under control. How was he ever going to keep the wee Bruce safe and find Jackie while protecting Erin? He could barely think beyond his cock. Mayhap, no matter what Grant said, the best solution was to put her under someone else's care.

"Yeah, stay and hang," Erin said. "That way somebody'll be here to keep me from killing this guy." Her eyes remained narrowed on Rònan. "Because I know you did something to me last night against my will."

"Come again?" Nicole said.

"Och." Rònan shook his head, exasperated with the whole situation and getting more overheated by the moment. He dared not remove his tunic, though. The less flesh revealed, the better. "You were set to leave and I couldnae allow that."

"Damn straight I was set to leave," Erin spat. "Just like you should've been." She put her hands on her hips. "Answer my damn question, Rònan."

He was getting hotter and hotter.

"I made sure you rested," he murmured.

"Rested?" Her brows slammed together. "Did you use some sorta dragon magic on me?"

"Aye." His eyes locked on hers. "To protect you."

"Protect me? You took away my free will you jackass!"

He stood in confrontation when she strode his way.

Nicole shook her head, stood in front of him and put a hand against his chest, warning, "Don't you *dare* move."

His skin heated more as his emotions increased.

Nicole's eyes swung to Erin. "Hon, you seriously need to chill out, okay?"

But as he suspected she would be, Erin was furious.

"Step away, Nicole," Erin growled.

What happened next literally rocked Rònan's world and he took immediate action. *"Niall, ye better get yer arse in here right now and be well armed,"* he spoke within the mind to his cousin.

"Holy crap," Nicole whispered, gaze widening on Erin. "Your eyes."

The pale violet had expanded and brightened. But that wasn't what made him growl with need and made Bjorn and Tait come flying inside not to protect her but to take her.

No, it was that her eyes were cat-like and dangerous.

Dragon eyes.

"Oh *hell*," Nicole cried as she pulled out two daggers and turned her back to Erin to protect her from the men…including Rònan. Her gaze narrowed on all three of them and she shook her head. "You all need to put those creepy lookin' dragon eyes away *right now*."

Like his, Tait and Bjorn's dragons were surfacing.

Never once had he been unable to control his other half but apparently when a female of his kind embraced her dragon, his responded. And hell was it responding. Like his kin's, Rònan's flesh was so overheated that steam rose off of it.

"I'm not afraid of them," Erin growled and stepped around Nicole. Evidently, the lass had no sense of self-preservation. Or she just didn't understand how dire her circumstances.

Thankfully, his cousin heard his summons and likely the Viking King sensed what was happening because they arrived within moments. Naðr faced Tait and Bjorn, a thunderous look on his face. Niall, doing exactly what he should, held the tip of a sword to Rònan's neck.

"I dinnae ken your current state, Cousin," Niall warned. "But you best get it under control when around my lass and wee bairn, aye?"

Rònan was well aware that Niall was using magic to spray the men with cool mist. It was a smart move. Anything to get their temperatures down.

"Get out of here *now*," the Viking King roared at his kin.

They hesitated briefly, their hungry gazes lingering on Erin before they trudged out. Meanwhile, Megan strode in, batting Bjorn upside the head as she passed, voice disappointed. "Head to your lodge and nowhere else. I'll be talking to you and your cousin after I'm done here."

Her concerned eyes went to Erin. "Are you okay?"

Before Erin could reply which was likely going to be a scathing response based on the look on her face, Megan gestured at Naðr. "Please take the men elsewhere so I can speak to her alone."

"Nay, I willnae leave her unprotected," Rònan began, ever more thankful for Niall's mist as his body slowly cooled.

"Out. Now. You're no more fit to protect her right now than my son." Megan's eyes narrowed to slits. "And if you don't listen to me, I'll do everything in my considerable power to make sure you never step foot near Erin again."

Chapter Seven

ERIN WAS STILL seeing red after the men left. Regrettably, that wasn't just a saying in her case but the honest truth. Everything was reddish and far crisper than before. Though she knew somewhere in the back of her mind that she should be frightened, she was still too damn mad. It was one thing for the Viking King to put her to sleep, another for Rònan to have done it.

Once the men were gone, Megan became far sterner and pointed at a chair. "Sit down. Right now."

"Hey, give her a break," Nicole started but Megan shook her head sharply.

"Either keep your mouth shut or get out of here."

Nicole's eyes widened but like Erin, she sensed Megan wasn't messing around because they both sat.

Megan crouched in front of Erin. "Now you need to listen to me carefully and do exactly what I say."

Erin frowned. "That's gonna depend on what you say."

"Don't test me, girl." Megan's eyes narrowed. "I've raised several dragon-shifters so I know what I'm doing. And right now that's teaching you how to control what's going on inside you."

"There's nothing going on inside me," she lied.

"Oh yeah?" Megan pulled a small mirror out of her pocket and held it up in front of Erin. "Try telling me that again."

It took several long discombobulated moments for Erin to realize what she was looking at. Her...but not her. "What the..." she whispered as fear spiked. Her eyes looked all wrong. The color. The shape. Everything. They looked inhuman. "Oh, God."

Megan set aside the mirror and grabbed Erin's wrists before she could scramble to her feet. "Now look at me and nowhere else."

Erin was so stupefied with shock she was unable to do much else.

Instead of dishing out words of wisdom, Megan spoke about random things for a few minutes. The buildings in the village being rethatched. The most recent births. Nothing at all related to the current situation. Though Erin barely followed her, the sound of the woman's voice was soothing and slowly but surely calmed her.

"Okay, that's much better," Megan said softly. "Your eyes are returning to normal because you're releasing your anger. If a shifter lets his or her anger rule them, they will have no choice but to shift because their inner dragon feels threatened. It's much like a human releasing adrenaline when something intense happens."

Erin started to tremble, fear overtaking her even as the red faded.

"Look." Megan's voice remained soft as she held up the mirror again. "Look at your eyes now, Erin."

She shook her head and tried to push the mirror away but Megan was having none of it.

"Yes." Megan grabbed her chin and kept the mirror in front of her. Erin almost squeezed her eyes shut but not once had she avoided things that frightened her. She always looked fear in the face. And right now, that was *her* face. If she didn't do this, she would never forgive herself.

So though terrified, she looked.

Her eyes had returned to normal.

"See," Megan murmured. "No more dragon eyes."

Erin breathed a sigh of relief as she narrowed then widened her eyes at the mirror. When she tried to talk, nothing came out. Her vocal chords were being difficult. When she tried to speak again, Megan put a finger to her lips and shook her head. "No, don't try to talk just yet because it won't work." She handed Erin a mug. "Instead, drink. Calm your nerves."

Calm nerves sounded like a good plan so she took a few hearty swigs.

"Now take several deep breaths," Megan said.

So she did, her eyes flickering to Nicole, who amazingly enough had remained silent the whole time. Her friend offered a comforting smile and remained blissfully quiet.

"Finish your mead," Megan urged. "Then you and I are going somewhere."

Erin complied, somewhat amazed that she listened to this woman without question. It was a first. But there was something about Megan that spoke to her. An unexplainable level of comfort and respect that she didn't feel with anyone, not even her closest friends. She tried not to contemplate how that *may* have to do with the fact she *might* be distantly related to her.

Megan pulled clothes out of the trunk and handed them to Erin. "Change and then we'll go." Her eyes went to Nicole. "Thanks for being here for your friend but go be with Niall now. He's in piss-poor shape worrying about you with all these dragon-shifters around."

Nicole nodded and looked at Erin. "Are you gonna be okay, Hon?"

Erin wasn't sure if her vocal chords would work but gave it a shot. Fortunately, they did.

"Not much choice," Erin muttered but appreciated Nicole's concern. "Like you, I'm a survivor so yeah, I'll be fine. Thanks."

Nicole held out her arms and cocked her head. "Bring it in then."

Erin twisted her lips in reservation. Her friend knew she wasn't a fan of physical contact.

"For real," Nicole said. "I need some love."

"Okay," Erin relented and embraced her.

Nicole squeezed tight and whispered in her ear, "You want me to come with you? Because I'll totally stick by your side."

"No, I'll be all right," she whispered back. "But thanks."

Nicole sighed and pulled away, eyes narrowed on Erin. "I've got your back if you need me."

"I know."

Nicole eyed her for another long moment before she put her cloak on and left. Erin changed into the odd clothing as Megan waited. She couldn't say she was totally opposed to the outfit. The pants were made of soft leather and the tunic a lightweight material that felt like cotton.

Megan held out a leather string. "For your hair?"

"Thanks," Erin said as she tried to tie the unruly mess back.

"Let me help." Megan untied Erin's hair and pulled some sort of wide-toothed comb from her pocket. Erin stilled as Megan carefully and amazingly enough, started to work the comb through her hair without causing any pain. "Your hair's just like mine. Some might think these curls are killer but I've always thought mine were a pain in the ass."

"I couldn't agree more," Erin said. "And the weather here isn't bound to help."

Megan chuckled. "Nope, it doesn't."

Yet the woman seemed to know what she was doing because the flyaways that were in Erin's peripheral vision vanished and her hair was soon securely tied back. Megan held up the mirror again. "Take a look." Then she winked. "No worries, as long as you're not seeing red, your eyes are back to normal."

Though still wary, she took a peek and bit her bottom lip against a smile. Nobody, including herself, had ever managed to tame her hair so well. Though full, it was soft and attractive while still out of her face. "How did you do that?"

"Do you really want to know?" Megan grinned as she eyed Erin. "Because though I'd like to take credit, it has nothing to do with me having the same hair type."

"Yeah, I really wanna know," she said.

Megan handed her the comb. "Because of this. My husband had it made for me with dragon magic."

"Seriously?"

"Yes." Megan smiled as she wrapped a fur around her shoulders and another around Erin's. "But you'll find as time goes by that you won't have to worry about your hair so much."

"Why's that?" she asked as Megan took her hand and pulled her along.

"Because dragon-shifters have beautiful hair and it only seems to grow more glorious as they come into their own."

That sounded intense. Before she could overthink and start panicking again, Megan kept talking, distracting her as they walked out into the heavy snow. "I thought maybe you'd like to spend some time with Tosha."

Any thoughts of freaking out vanished when she saw the horse. This time, there was no biting back a smile, it came full force.

"Hey there, Beautiful. When did you get here?" she whispered, stroking Tosha's muzzle. "You shouldn't be out in this weather."

"She can handle the elements for a few minutes," Megan murmured, patting her. "She wanted to be here for you. Let's walk her back to the stables."

"She did, did she?" Erin said, speaking not to Megan but Tosha. "Well, I'm glad."

"Aye, 'tis good that, lass," whispered through her mind.

Erin stopped short.

"Did she speak to you through the mind then?" Megan asked.

"I…uh…"

"Of course, she did." When Megan kept walking so did the horse.

Confused, Erin followed. "You can't be serious."

"According to Tosha, it's not the first time she's spoken to you in such a way."

Erin's brows perked when she remembered the words whispered through her mind back in the barn in New Hampshire.

"It's a rare gift you know," Megan continued. "For a dragon-shifter to bond with horses."

"How so?"

"Horses inherently fear dragons," Megan said. "Naðr's brother Kol was the first of his kind to take to them. Since then only one of my children has and it's a rocky connection at that."

"But I seem to recall Nicole mentioning something about Viking magic merging MacLomains with horses. Hence Cassie's horse Athdara and Nicole's, Vika?" Erin looked at Tosha as they walked. "And isn't this horse supposed to be one of those?"

"So you *do* believe some of this then," Megan said as they entered the stables. "Good because yes. But ancient Viking magic that benefits MacLomain wizards has very little to do with dragon-shifters in general. It has more to do with a Viking who bonded with his horse on the battlefield. A connection unlike any other."

"No kidding." Erin walked Tosha into her stall, not ready in the least to try talking to her. But maybe Megan could shed light on something else. "When I showed up at Leslie and Bradon's in New Hampshire…in the future, my horse was supposed to be with me but she wasn't. Instead, Tosha was in the trailer. Any thoughts on that?"

"Hmm. Knowing all I do about magic in general now, I'd be inclined to look deeper into your horse's past." Megan handed Erin a horse brush. "When and where did you get her or him?"

"Her. Salve." Erin started brushing down Tosha. "I got her earlier in the year. She'd been ill-treated and was skin and bones. I nourished her back to health."

"Why the name Salve?" came a deep, soft voice.

Erin tensed when her eyes met Rònan's. Why was he here? Thankfully, so was the Viking King.

"Look at me, Erin," Megan said.

Fire flared beneath her skin but she did.

"Though I'm not sure I agree with the idea right now, Grant and Torra want Rònan to stay close to you so he will." Megan gestured at Tosha. "Keep brushing the horse."

When Erin glanced at Rònan, Megan shook her head sharply. "Don't look at him."

With a heavy sigh, she concentrated on grooming Tosha while Megan continued talking.

"As I mentioned before, the first thing you need to do as a shifter is learn to repress your anger," Megan said. "Dragons respond first and foremost to it. So if your human half doesn't deal with it fast, the dragon will seize control." She gestured at Rònan. "That's likely why he's usually such a happy go lucky guy. It's his defense mechanism against the dragon taking over."

"Rònan's happy go lucky?" Erin couldn't help but snort. "Hard to believe."

But she remembered how he was in New Hampshire and it was pretty close to that initially. Rònan offered no comeback but remained silent as he leaned against the stall door.

"I'm not concerned about what you believe about Rònan," Megan said. "I'm concerned about you learning to get your anger under control."

Erin shrugged. "To the best of my knowledge I've always been good at that."

She had made sure she was at a young age.

"Maybe so. But now that your dragon is awakening you'll have to learn to control it a whole lot better," Megan said. "When anger flares, you need to figure out what brings you away from it and focus on that." She nodded at Tosha. "Horses calm you so maybe focusing on them when you get upset would be a good idea."

She didn't like the idea of depending on a singular thought process to keep her from turning into a monster. "I wasn't thinking about horses earlier and still came out of it."

"Because I was there. Because I talked you through it," Megan reminded. "Next time there's a good chance I won't be. Next time it might just be you and Rònan and like you, he's trying to learn to control new emotions."

When thoughts of him putting her to sleep the night before arose, Erin ground her jaw. Despite her reservations, she did what Megan suggested and focused on the horse. She kept brushing and soaked up the soothing feeling it leant her. Not only did it assuage her anger but helped her cope with the mind-blowing reality she was being forced to accept. That she was half dragon. Half beast. So she set to giving the horse a good brush down and found a small sense of peace.

"Other odd stuff might happen to you as your dragon awakens," Megan continued. "I suspect you already had some unusual experiences before you arrived here. Time lapses or sometimes seeing things that weren't there even though you swore they were."

Erin frowned as she recalled the oddities back in the cave. "Could you clarify?"

"Does it really need clarifying?" Megan gave her a knowing look. "Did you not see Rònan's mother in Scotland even though she wasn't there?"

Rònan sounded surprised when he spoke softly. "'Twas my Ma you were talking to when I thought you spoke to a rock, aye?"

Erin nodded and sighed. "Well, I guess it's good to know I'm not completely nuts."

"No, you're not." Megan's lip curled up. "A fellow shifter reached out to you. One that clearly likes you."

"How could she like me when she only just met me," Erin murmured.

"Torra MacLeod is not only a powerful wizard and shifter but a better judge of character than most," the Viking King provided. "Some say she understands a person's soul even before she's laid eyes on them."

Erin wasn't sure what to make of that considering Torra was Rònan's mother but supposed it wasn't something to dwell on. So she remained focused on grooming Tosha and the continued peace it gave her. Yet for some reason, as she crouched and worked at the horse's legs, memories started to flicker through her mind of her father. How he casually leaned against the stall and grinned. How she grinned back.

They had been best friends.

She told him to stop flicking his lighter because he was too close to the hay. An odd habit he'd picked up after he quit smoking. She figured he just needed to keep busy with something.

He shrugged and nodded at the horse she was caring for. "All's well, Angel. Just take care of your girl."

Erin smiled as she kept brushing. "Sure thing, Dad."

Yet she worried about her father. About what would happen next. Would they make ends meet? Would they keep their house? Would everything be okay?

Or would she somehow manage to destroy everything?

"I think mayhap Tosha's tail is well brushed."

Erin blinked several times and snapped out of wherever she had gone. Rònan stood across from her as she held Tosha's tail. There was no sign of Megan or Naðr.

"Back away," she said, on guard.

Rònan took a few steps back and nodded. "I'm backing away."

"Good." She put a hand on the horse to ground herself, to keep safe. "Now get out of here."

"Nay," he murmured and sat on a stool in the corner.

"Why are they leaving us alone after what happened?" Though Erin continued to run the brush over Tosha, she eyed Rònan. "Seems like a bad move."

"Aye," he agreed. "But here I sit."

And he was sitting. Not pressuring or intimidating her with his height like he tried to do earlier. She supposed that was a good start. Though she said nothing while grooming Tosha, she figured it might not be a bad idea to try communicating with him. Especially if everyone was determined he stay with her.

"So what happened to you back there because it wasn't good," she said.

"Nay, it wasnae. I lost control." Though he spoke to her, he focused on the horse. "I apologize."

"You should," she said but realized she wasn't all that mad at him anymore. After seeing the Viking shifters' reaction to her in the main lodge, a part of her understood that he had been protecting her the night before. "And while it's not the easiest thing to say, thank you for making sure I rested." Her eyes narrowed on him. "Just don't do it again."

Rònan's eyes stayed on the horse. "As long as you dinnae give me a reason to, you have my word I willnae."

"And what exactly do you consider a reason to?"

He looked anywhere but at her. "As long as you dinnae foolishly try to put yourself in harm's way."

"If you haven't noticed, I know how to fight," she shot back.

"And if you havenae noticed, dragon-shifters can anticipate your every move," he said softly. "Or at least, I can."

She *had* noticed as much. "And why is that again?"

"I dinnae know precisely but 'tis partly because the telepathy betwixt us seems to be growing." He again focused on the horse. "'Tis odd considering we haven't lain together. I can only assume 'tis because of the dragon connection."

"What's us sleeping together got to do with telepathy?" She shook her head, still trying to swallow the fact they might be communicating through their minds. But then it seemed to be happening with Tosha so it was certainly possible. "And why aren't you looking at me when you speak to me?"

"Och, lass," Rònan muttered. "'Tis not for lack of wanting." He sighed. "Like you, I'm trying to tame my inner dragon. Outside of my Ma, I haven't been around another such as you and trust me when I say, I'm suffering a strong reaction. One I need to get under control soon if I'm to protect you, the wee Bruce *and* find Jackie."

Eyes firmly glued on Tosha, he continued. "As to the strong mental connection we seem to be forming, it typically only happens after a MacLomain wizard lies with the Broun lass who is his true love." He frowned. "Did Nicole not mention such to you?"

"Right, because you've got MacLomain blood too," she murmured. "No, Nicole never mentioned the sex thing."

"Well, if you've any questions, dinnae hesitate to ask," he said softly. "I'll help any way I can."

It sounded like he meant it.

"So you're set to protect me but can't even look at me," she said, setting aside the brush.

"I think 'tis best for now until I learn to control," he cleared his throat, "my emotions." His jaw clenched. "According to Naðr, there will be a period of difficulty as your dragon surfaces."

"Such as?"

"Scents and your reactions to them…my reaction to them," he said, brogue thickening as he struggled with his explanation. "All male shifters will likely feel the…changes in your body."

Oh, hell. "Why does this sound like some sort of supernatural puberty?"

Rònan chuckled and she got the sense he was grateful to find some humor in this crazy situation. "'Twill likely be such for us both but rest assured, I mean to keep my hands off you."

"Good goal," she murmured, leaning against the stall. Yet there was a dash of untruthfulness to her response. A wave of heat flared deep within as she eyed the way the black fur cloak hugged his broad shoulders. Then the length of his long, muscular body. Visuals of what that body might look like arose and she licked her lips.

Rònan inhaled sharply, ground his jaw and strode out of the stall without glancing at her. "Please come outside so that we might continue talking with more people around."

When she hesitated, he called out, "Please, Erin. I mean to be your friend and 'tis hard to focus when we're alone."

"What about the other dragon shifters?" she replied. "Where are they?"

"I'd imagine getting a good tongue-lashing from Megan still," he replied. "As to the ones who didnae come into our lodge, Naðr spoke with them last night."

"So I've got the whole place on high-alert, eh?" she said as she shouldered into her fur cloak and followed.

"Aye," he said, but there was a smile in his voice as they exited.

While it wasn't the best day for a stroll considering the inclement weather, plenty of people were about. History always told that Vikings were tough sons of bitches and it seemed to hold true as far as she could tell. Erin put on her hood and eyed Rònan as they walked. "Aren't you gonna put on your hood?"

"Nay." He shook his head, eyes dead ahead. "The snow feels good. 'Tis best to keep my skin cool right now."

"And why is that?" she said. "Better yet, why'd you scoot out of the stables so fast?"

"Dragons can sense many things that humans cannae," Rònan explained. "Including arousal. We can smell such from a lass." His voice thickened. "Apparently the scent of a female dragon is much stronger."

So he *smelled* that she was getting turned on back there? Well, that was one to grow on.

"Does it work the other way around?" she asked. "Will I be able to tell when you or another shifter is aroused?"

Rònan shrugged. "I dinnae know. As I'm sure you ken, 'twas not something I ever felt the need to ask my Ma."

"Understandable." She repressed a chuckle. "It's pretty easy to tell when you guys get turned on anyways. I don't think I need to smell it. But you gotta wonder what a guy smells like when he's revved up."

As if desperate to redirect the conversation, he said, "So I take it Nicole didnae tell you how she learned she was pregnant?"

"I'm afraid not." Her eyes widened a little as the truth dawned. "From you?"

"Aye." A genuine smile lit his face and she yanked her eyes away. He was already too damn fine without smiling. All those straight white teeth against his tan skin.

"I not only smelled the wee bairn but heard its heartbeat," he continued. "'Twas a truly touching moment."

"Sounds it." Despite herself, Erin was warmed by the affection in his voice. By how much he seemed to care. "You and Nicole get along well, huh?"

"Verra. Not to mention she saved me." Rònan shrugged. "I would have taken her as my own if there wasnae so much love betwixt her and Niall."

Again, she had to appreciate his honesty. "I heard a little bit about what happened to you in that Celtic Otherworld place." Though she typically wasn't compassionate beyond what she felt for horses, she was sort of warming to him. "Sorry about all that, by the way. How are you doing?"

"Honestly, I haven't had much time to ponder it since traveling to the future," he said. She sensed he wanted to glance at her but didn't. "And for that I'm grateful. While 'tis safe to say us meeting was mildly difficult, I am truly grateful for the distraction."

"Mildly difficult," she murmured, suppressing a grin. "Yeah, I guess you could call it that."

"Aye," he said softly. "But mayhap things will get better betwixt us now?"

"We'll see," she said just as softly. It occurred to her she wasn't nearly as wary of him as she had been. Rather, she felt a level of comfort as they walked through the village toward the ocean. The snow had lessened enough that she could make out the rows upon rows of piers. Bjorn was heading their way, but when he saw her, he swiftly turned and headed in the opposite direction.

Rònan chuckled. "I think the Viking dragons will be giving you a wide berth until they've learned to control themselves."

"Probably a good thing." Her eyes flickered to Rònan as she started to realize how difficult this must be for him. "You know I can hang with Megan and the Viking King to give you a break while you learn how to deal with...me. That might be the best way for you and me to get where we need to be."

Not to mention, she was way too aware of him despite all the heavy clothing. His height. How small she felt beside him. The way puffs of moisture escaped those sexy lips of his. Just looking at him invoked an unfamiliar level of desire.

"Nay, I must do what Grant asked of me." Rònan inhaled deeply and she swore he shuddered. His brogue thickened yet again. "And though I'm flattered, lass, ye might want to do what Megan suggested about fighting back anger when ye feel aroused. Mayhap focus on yer horse." His voice grew more guttural. "Because yer scent calls to me something fierce and 'tis hard."

Her eyes fell to the way he held his cloak tightly around him. If she wasn't mistaken, he was walking a little bow legged. "I take it you've got an erection then?"

"Aye," he growled. "One that isnae easy to control even with magic."

That had to suck. So she tried to make light of it. "Refer again to supernatural puberty… better yet dragon puberty."

Rònan snorted but she managed to wrangle a chuckle from him. "Aye, lass."

She realized that once she wasn't on the defense with him, Rònan wasn't all that difficult to get along with. Maybe he did have a happy go lucky nature lurking under there somewhere. Or maybe her perception of him from the get-go was simply based on her not trusting men to begin with.

"We should stop here," he said at the gates of the fortress. "'Twill be too cold on the shore and 'tis just a lull in the storm right now."

She closed her eyes and inhaled deeply, surprised to sense a change of some kind.

"The wind will soon shift from east to southeast," she whispered and ran her tongue over her teeth. "It'll bring a sharp temperature drop and far more moisture."

"Aye," he said.

Her eyes shot open and though she looked at him, he gazed at the sea. "How did I know that?"

"Dragons are creatures who rely on instincts above all else," he said. "'Tis in our nature to be more aware of weather and seasonal patterns."

Though for a few minutes she had been easing into the possibility of accepting what she'd become, a flash of fear rose up and she whispered, "I can't be a monster. I can't be my worst nightmare."

"You are no monster, lass." Rònan's voice was so soft it was nearly lost on the wind. "You are magnificent."

A chill raced through her that had nothing to do with the cold temperature. What she couldn't figure out was whether it was his spoken words that touched her or the ones he whispered through her mind.

And though you fear you've become your worst nightmare, you have not. What you are is the furthest thing from it."

Erin tried to respond but the words died on her lips. Not because her voice didn't work but because she simply had no idea what to say. Despite her close friends, kindness was not something she trusted. People always had an angle. And though she would be tempted to say Rònan's was to get her into bed, he seemed determined to do the opposite.

"Come, lass, we should get back to where 'tis warm," he said and started back the way they came.

"I don't mind the cold," she said. "It feels pretty good right now. Most of the time, actually."

"'Tis because you're half dragon." He turned back when she stopped, eyes still averted. "We get overheated quickly. Whilst you might think you can withstand the current temperatures, your human skin cannot. However, when in the form of a dragon we can withstand sub-zero temperatures for a verra long time."

Erin swallowed and shook her head in denial. "I know you're trying to educate me but…"

"But," he said when she trailed off. "I know 'tis not easy, lass, but 'twould be in your best interest to learn all you can from me. And though I haven't known you long, you strike me the sort that prefers knowledge to a general sense of denial."

No words were truer.

Still, it wasn't easy digesting all of this.

"Please." He gestured back toward the village. "We should seek shelter."

Erin sighed, nodded and joined him. "It's weird that you can't look at me."

"'Tis for the best," he assured. "Until I manage to control myself."

She *almost* argued the point. Mainly because she wanted those emerald eyes on her. Just once. To see if he could do it. To see what his response would be. To see what hers would be. But she respected what he was trying to do. A lot.

"Hey, there you guys are," Nicole said, heading in their direction with a scowling Niall hot on her heels. Her eyes met Erin's. "How are you doing? Better?"

"Yeah." She nodded. "You shouldn't be out here."

"Just like you shouldn't be." Nicole linked arms with her. "We're all heading in anyway, right?"

"Sounds good to me," Erin said.

They had only taken a few more steps when the sky started to darken and chills rippled over her. When Rònan cried out in pain, she spun. Head hung, he had dropped to one knee and held his midriff. Concerned, she tried to go to him but her legs grew sluggish and her vision blurred.

"Erin, can you hear me?" whispered through her mind. *"Can you hear us?"*

Jackie?

"I can hear you," she called. "Where are you and who are you with?"

"Oh, thank God," Jackie responded within her mind. *"I'm somewhere dark and gray. Barren. I'm with little Robert the Bruce."*

Rònan buckled over in more pain and the wind whipped up.

Erin tried to move closer to him but her limbs only grew heavier.

"I'll find a way to get to you, Jackie," Erin said. "How did you get where you are?"

Jackie responded but the words were so far away she couldn't hear them.

"Jackie," she called. "Can you hear me?"

"I can hear you, lass," came a deep voice. "Shh."

Erin blinked as the darkness and sluggishness faded. Confused, she struggled.

"'Tis okay, Erin. 'Tis me, Darach Hamilton."

Darach? What the hell? As her vision cleared, the Viking village snapped into focus.

Then more.

Grant stood in front of her with a little boy.

Robert the Bruce.

But that's not what drew her attention most.

No, it was Rònan.

Unmoving, he lay on the ground as Niall held his head and Nicole cried over him.

Chapter Eight

RÒNAN'S EYES SHOT open and he froze in fear. He was back in the dank recesses of the Celtic Otherworld. Pain shot through his body as the remnants of what they had done to him kept throbbing through his limbs. Yet somewhere far off he heard a beautiful melody. A sound that seemed to push away the darkness. He struggled to keep the sweet voice close even as it faded away.

"Shh." The woman with white-blond hair he had met here before put a cool hand on his forehead. "Relax."

His head rested on her lap. Though it seemed an impossible concept, his muscles liquefied beneath her touch and he calmed.

"Jackie?" he murmured.

"Just relax," she whispered. "All will be well."

He stared up into her beautiful eyes and nodded, believed her. How could he not?

"I swore an oath to save you," he whispered. "Just tell me how to do that."

"Love," she murmured and stroked his cheek. "Just love."

"Love you?" he whispered.

"Kiss me," she murmured before everything darkened and he could no longer see her.

But he could still feel her.

When her lips touched his, everything fell away. The darkness. The pain. All he could feel was her. Everything she was. Not soothing balm but heated fire. Lust. Desire.

His.

Their mouths opened and tongues twirled. It was a kiss unlike any other. Unique in a way he didn't understand. Unique in a way that had his blood boiling and his cock beyond eager. Needy.

Then she pulled away.

Desperate to pull her back, his eyes shot open but she was gone. Still, a voice called to him from far away. Where did she go?

"Jackie?" he said, growing more anxious. "What's the matter, lass? I cannae hear you."

"Settle down, Rònan, it's okay," came a soft voice and her cool hand again touched his forehead. Relieved, he settled back and closed his eyes.

"Thank you," he whispered.

"No need to thank me."

Though the voice was still soft, it was different. Not Jackie's in the least. Though his eyelids felt heavy, he pried them open. His surroundings blurred at first then cleared. Instead of a beautiful blond looking down at him, there was a beautiful brunette.

Erin.

"I dinnae ken," he croaked.

Their eyes held for a brief moment before she pulled away. "Nicole, Niall, he's back. He's really back this time."

"Wait," he said hoarsely but she was gone and Nicole was there.

"Hey, you," she murmured, pressing something cold against his head as Niall appeared at the foot of the bed. "You had us worried."

Before he could try to speak again, she held a mug against his lips. "Drink first."

So he did, leaning up just enough to down the mug of water in three long gulps. Before he could say more, she handed him another. He downed that one in two long gulps then fell back.

"You've been lost to us for three days, Cousin," Niall said, a mixture of frustration and happiness in his voice. "How do you feel?"

"Lost," he said weakly. "In that bloody Otherworld."

Nicole and Niall shot each other concerned looks before Niall spoke. "Nay, Brother, you've been here with us the whole time."

How could that be? Had he been dreaming? Nay, it seemed too real.

"That's impossible," he whispered but could barely keep his eyes open.

"Rest," Nicole murmured. "We'll catch up in a bit."

Rònan meant to deny her and get to the root of what was happening but he was too exhausted. He drifted off and when he opened his eyes again, cold wind blew in through the windows and he felt far more alert. He sat up and scanned his surroundings.

Sunlight dappled the floor and Erin was sound asleep in a chair next to him. Nobody else was in the room.

"What the bloody hell happened to me?" he whispered.

As if she slept on the edge of awareness, Erin's eyes shot open. "You're awake. Let me go get Niall and Nicole."

When she leapt from the chair, he grabbed her wrist and shook his head. "No, wait. What happened?"

"You've been down and out for a bit, Rònan." She kept her eyes averted. "Let me go get your cousins."

"No. You." He pulled her down until she sat on the bed beside him. "Tell me what happened, lass."

Erin inhaled deeply and looked at the fire rather than at him. "According to Grant, you had an episode that flashed you back to your time in the Celtic Otherworld. What you need to know is that Robert the Bruce is okay. He's here."

"What of Jackie?"

He swore he heard a hitch in her breath. "We don't know. But nobody knows where Leslie and Bradon are either so everyone's hoping they're together somewhere safe."

"Nay." He shook his head. "I was with Jackie. She comforted me."

"Maybe," Erin murmured. "But I can tell you for sure that you never left here. I had a strange experience outside over a week ago where I thought I saw the Otherworld. But I'm thinking now that it was just a weird slip for me because little Robert's here and not there. You passed out when I had my episode."

"Over a week ago?" Frustrated, he frowned at her. "Look at me, Erin."

"Yes, you've been down for a little over a week." She shook her head. "As to looking at you, bad idea. Remember why?"

"I remember why I shouldnae look at you," he said. "But last I knew, you had no issues looking at me."

"Yeah, well that's changed a smidge." She yanked her hand away, leaned over then handed him a cup. "Drink and I'll catch you up."

Thirsty as hell, he nodded and took the cup.

Erin walked over to the window and crossed her arms over her chest as she looked out. Rònan eyed her as he gulped down water.

She looked good. Better than good. At ease with herself in a way she hadn't been the last time he saw her.

"Grant and your mother are here. They have been since you passed out," she said. "There's no real plan in regards to our next move because no one was entirely sure you'd wake up. The first time or the second."

Rònan frowned. "'Twas that bad then?"

"Yeah, it was that bad," she said softly.

"So Grant and my Ma dinnae know what happened to me? Why I flashed back to the Otherworld?"

"No." She shook her head. "Neither do Naðr or Kjar."

"So you've met the Norse demi-god?"

"Yup." She sighed. "It's been a helluva week."

He swung his legs over the side of the bed, surprised to see he was nude. Curious, his eyes went back to her. "And why is it again you cannae look at me?"

"Every once in a while I wonder how bright you really are." She shrugged as if it were no big deal. "Uncontrollable dragon arousal. Pretty sure you know something about that."

"Aye, but I'd like to know how you know so much now," he said, testing out his limbs and how functional they really were after a week of bed rest. Thanks to his dragon blood, everything seemed about the same. "Have you lusted after me whilst I've been lying here?" Then a worse thought occurred to him and fire flooded beneath his skin. "Or did you feel it with another?"

"Yeah, Rònan, I wanted you so damn much I rode you while you were zonked out," she quipped sarcastically. "How could you not remember that?"

A grin came to his face. "You know that my cock would service you even if I were—"

"I don't ride flaccid dicks," she drawled. "And let me assure you, yours was just that...most of the time."

Rònan snorted with laughter. "At least it sounds like you've become familiar with the beastie."

He was about to continue when Nicole strolled in with Niall and Darach. Nicole's eyes widened when they locked on Rònan. "Damn glad to see you awake, Sweetie." She shook her head. "But for the second time since we've met, I've gotta ask you to put away your junk."

"The *second* time?" Niall said but grinned at Rònan. "'Tis bloody good to see you awake!"

Rònan wrapped the blanket around his waist and smiled, happy to see his cousins. More than that, happy to realize he truly wasn't in the Otherworld. Darach tossed him leather trousers. "Lasses, turn away so that my cousin might dress and we can embrace him properly."

"Don't need to tell me twice." Nicole winked at Niall as she spun away.

"Many thanks," Rònan said as he got dressed. "Have we no plaids about then?"

"Och, if only," Niall muttered. "These Vikings are determined that we dress like them. Bloody uncomfortable."

Rònan shrugged as he tied the strings, feeling like himself for a change. "'Tis not so bad as long as you dinnae get too happy." He pulled at the groin area of the pants and grinned. "Not much room for a cock in here, eh? Makes me wonder about our Viking ancestors' ability to please a lass."

"Hey, there are ladies in the room," Nicole scoffed.

All three men said, "There are?"

Nicole shook her head and chuckled. "Dimwits."

"Dimwits?" Erin said. "What kind of word is that?"

"One that's not a swear." Nicole nudged her. "Remember, I'm trying not to curse with the kid around."

"But he's not here right now," Erin reminded.

"Still," Nicole defended. "Practice makes perfect."

"All aside," Erin said over her shoulder. "Not sure how I managed to fall into the category of *not* being a lady." She winked at Nicole. "No offense."

"None taken."

"Well, Erin, I've never seen a lady take down a Viking like you—"

When Niall nudged him, Darach stopped talking.

It was then that Rònan realized a comradery had formed between Darach and Erin. He saw the way she winked at his cousin over her shoulder and how he grinned back. No need for the freedom of a plaid. Any potential erection he could've hoped for died down right then and there and a heavy frown settled on his face.

Niall seemed to catch on because he detoured the conversation and gestured at the table full of food. "Come, Cousin. You need to eat."

"Aye," Rònan grunted. He skipped embracing his cousins and plunked down. There was no reason for him to be upset about things developing between Erin and Darach, especially considering his connection with Jackie. Still, he tore into the food with angry relish.

Nicole sat down next to him and dug in with as much gusto. When he raised an eyebrow at her, she shrugged. "Hey, I'm eating for two."

Niall joined them but not Erin. She remained where she was and stared out the window as she munched on a piece of bread Darach brought her.

"I can stay with you," he said softly but she shook her head.

By the time Darach joined him, Rònan's mood was teetering toward sour when it shouldn't be. Darach and Erin were clearly meant for one another. Still, it irked him. How well would his Wizard of Air cousin be at coupling with a dragon-shifter whose element could only be fire? By his estimations, they would both go up in flames.

His scowl only deepened.

Maybe they were a perfect fit. *Maybe* they would go up in flames in a sexual sense.

"Wow, Rònan," Nicole said around munches. "I don't think I've ever seen you look so pissed off."

"Och, he's just trying to focus on his need for Jackie is all," Darach murmured.

Rònan's eyes met Darach's and his cousin offered a slight shrug. "Am I wrong?"

Their eyes narrowed at the same time.

"Hey, Darach, you promised me a horseback ride," Erin interrupted. "How about now?"

Darach grinned at Rònan but replied to Erin. "'Twould be my pleasure, lass."

Rònan's eyes stayed narrowed on his ill-forsaken brethren as Darach wrapped a cloak around Erin's shoulders and grinned at Rònan as they left.

"Phew," Nicole declared, still munching away as she made a slicing motion with her hand. "Could've cut the tension in here with a knife."

"Darach's a bloody arse if ever there was one," Rònan muttered.

"No, he's actually a good friend," Nicole said.

"Aye," Niall agreed. "Though he will make you crazy when it comes to lasses. He has an unnatural way with them."

His eyes met Niall's. "And has he had his way with Erin, then?"

Rònan didn't miss the look tossed between Niall and Nicole before his cousin responded. "We dinnae know...but does it really matter?"

"Nay, it doesnae bloody matter," Rònan growled and kept at his food. He knew his body was trying to regenerate. "'Tis probably for the best if he did...if they did."

Nicole sighed and sat back. "Listen, grouch, Darach's really been there for Erin so you need to get over it."

"Aye, 'tis clear enough he's been there for her," Rònan groused, trying to push past his discontent. It made no sense considering how much he was drawn to Jackie. "I wish them nothing but happiness."

"Good," Nicole declared. "Because Erin's done nothing but listen to you call out for Jackie for the better part of a week." She resumed eating. "So she deserves whatever affection Darach's dishing out. Anything to help her get through everything she's been dealing with."

"I've been calling out for Jackie?" he said.

"Aye," Niall said. "And Erin's been in here every day chilling her hands to keep you cool as you suffered through your fever."

"What do you mean chilling her hands?"

"'Tis a thing with her." Niall shook his head. "Though all the dragon shifters including the Viking King said that she need only put ice against your skin she decided that skin to skin touch would be better. So she'd keep her hands in buckets of snow until they were blue then defrost them against your face and body. 'Twas the damnedest thing but she did it day after day, determined to bring you back."

Rònan had no idea what to make of that. "And she didnae suffer frostbite?"

"Nay." Niall shook his head. "Your skin was bloody hot and revived her tissue as readily as she touched you."

"Aye?" he said.

"Aye," Niall replied as Nicole said, "Yes."

"'Tis bloody odd, right?" Rònan said.

"Aye," Nicole said as Niall said, "Yes."

He frowned at them in confusion.

"Niall and I are a team now." Nicole grinned. "We speak half modern day American and half medieval Scottish."

"Gods help your poor wee bairn." Rònan shook his head and looked skyward before he stood. "What else has happened over the past week?"

"Little," Niall said. "Except Erin learning about what she is."

"And I think she's making good headway," Nicole commented. "Though it probably helps that Darach's been around. He makes her feel halfway human."

When Niall scowled at her, she shrugged. "What? He does."

Rònan pulled on a tunic then yanked on boots.

"Where are you going?" Niall asked.

He tucked a few daggers in his pants, wrapped a cloak around his shoulders and said, "To find Grant."

"He's in the main lodge," Nicole yelled out as Rònan left.

The snow was considerably higher than it had been the last he remembered but it didn't slow him down any. He needed answers. He needed to know what was going on. By the looks of the sky, he would say it was late afternoon and the scant amount of people in the main lodge confirmed it. Naðr, Megan, and Grant sat alone at the head table.

When he entered, Grant stood. "Och, 'tis bloody good to see ye up and about lad."

"Aye, thanks," he muttered as he strode their way. The blond who had danced with him the first night appeared but he shook his head. The last thing he wanted was a lass. At least not *that* one.

Grant embraced him before they sat. Eyes concerned, his uncle said, "So how fare ye? We have all been worried."

"I've fared better," he said honestly, eying Grant. "Might ye share what happened to me?"

Naðr clasped Grant on the shoulder. "Megan and I will give you some time alone with your kin."

"Nay." Rònan's eyes shot to the King. "I would prefer that ye both stay so that I better ken exactly what happened."

"Nobody knows what happened, lad," Grant said. "Least of all the good King and his wife. Ye passed out when I arrived with the wee Bruce and have stayed such since."

"What of where I went?" Rònan said. "Can ye not sense it then?"

Grant shook his head, squeezing his shoulder. "Outside of knowing it was of the Otherworld, I couldnae sense a thing."

Rònan trusted Grant. He believed his uncle would never lead him astray. But right now, caught in all the conflicting emotions swamping him, he found himself questioning for the simple fact that he needed answers. Ones that might help convince him he wasn't going mad.

"We have a plan, lad." Grant kept a firm hand on Rònan's shoulder. "Ye dinnae need to fret right now."

"Tell me of this plan," he said. "Give me a sense of direction because I cannae seem to focus."

"You will hold your ground here with my brethren to help defend you," Naðr said. "We will keep you and Robert the Bruce safe."

Rònan heard what the king said but didn't miss the octave of Grant's tone when he said there was no need to fret. As if his uncle might not be totally convinced. So he directed his words at Grant. "Yet you worry over the outcome. Why?"

"Because, like with everything, the outcome is always unpredictable," Megan interjected. "And now it doesn't just involve you but one of our distant offspring who just happens to be a dragon shifter. The rules have changed and we sense the enemy is taking advantage of it."

Gone was jealousy over Erin and Darach.

Now it was just fear.

"Is Erin in danger?"

"You're all in danger," the King said. "You and Erin more so."

"Why?"

"Because you're Brouns and MacLomains and of dragon blood," Grant said. "This dark laird we fight has already taken ye once and has tried a second time. What's worse is he now knows that someone can pull ye free of him without igniting the power of the Claddagh ring first."

"Jackie," he whispered.

"No, only another dragon could pull you free." Megan's eyes met his. "Erin."

Rònan shook his head. Flashes of Jackie's face arose as she soothed him through that dark place. "Nay, 'twas Jackie."

"Mayhap Jackie whilst ye were there," Grant said. "But I dinnae need to guess whose face ye saw first when ye returned to us."

"Erin's," he whispered and shook his head. "How?"

"We don't know," Naðr said. "All we know is that Grant's instinct is right. You must stay close to the woman. You must protect her because as it turns out, she can best protect you as well."

"Och, 'tis clear she's fine without my protection." He nodded his thanks when a woman handed him a mug. He took a swig of ale, grateful to drink something that might soften the blow of all he had learned. "Darach is her new protector."

"My son is but a wizard," Grant said. "Erin needs to be protected by her own kind."

"Then how has she managed so well over the past week," he mumbled.

A small, infuriating grin came to Grant's lips. "'Tis true enough that my bairn has a way with the lasses."

Rònan narrowed his eyes.

"I cannae help it." Grant's grin only broadened. "But mayhap ye can, aye?"

What was Grant up to?

"So have ye promoted what's developed betwixt them then?" Rònan said. "Or have ye pushed her toward me?"

Grant arched a brow. "Why would I push her toward ye when ye've a need for Jackie?"

"The lass who needs to be saved," Rònan reminded.

"At least one of them," Grant murmured.

Rònan frowned. "What do ye mean by that?"

Megan shrugged. "The obvious choice isn't always the best choice." Her brows perked. "Love the one you're with?"

His brows lowered in confusion.

"Never mind." Megan shook her head. "What you need to focus on now is that you've got back-up here and a female dragon spreading her wings for the first time. She could use some guidance from someone besides my son."

"Bjorn?"

"Aye," Grant relented. "She's been spending nearly as much time with him as Darach."

Fire flared beneath his skin. Another dragon? "Has she been able to look him in the eyes?"

"Odin above, yes." Naðr shook his head. "Those two spend so much time gazing at each other I'm growing wary of it." His frown deepened and he shrugged. "Because she's meant for Darach, of course."

"Who said she's meant for Darach?" Rònan said, voice low.

"Better Darach than Bjorn," Megan said. "If she and my son go where they're heading, there'll be no stopping it."

"Even worse if it ends up happening with Tait," Naðr mentioned.

"Tait?" Rònan said, trying to keep a growl from his voice.

"Aye." Grant shook his head. "It took him longer to learn to control himself around her than Bjorn but now that he has, he and Erin seem to get along quite well."

"Too well, too fast," Megan agreed.

So Darach, Bjorn, *and* Tait were spending all their time with Erin? Bloody hell.

"I heard ye were up and about, my wee dragon," came a soft voice.

"Och, Ma, 'tis good to see ye." He embraced his mother as she joined them. "Though I'm not so wee anymore, aye?"

"Ye might be twice my size but ye'll always be my wee bairn," Torra murmured, holding him tight. "I've missed ye so much, lad."

He knew his mother. She would never admit how worried she had been because doing such meant admitting she feared she had lost him.

"I'm all right, Ma," he whispered when she wouldn't let go. "All is well."

She pulled back and eyed him over. "Ye seem to be intact but what of yer mental state?"

"More concerned with the lasses than anything else right now," Grant informed.

"Ah." Torra's regard grew wistful as they sat down. "My guess is the lovely Erin weighs on yer mind, aye?"

"Nay," Rònan denied as Grant said, "Aye."

Rònan swigged more ale as his mother continued to eye him.

"What?" he finally grumbled.

"I've never seen ye act like this." A small smile hovered on her lips. "But then ye've never come across another female dragon besides me." Her eyes went to Naðr's. "'Tis good I think that yer daughter and nieces are at yer dragon lair, aye?"

"Yes," Naðr agreed. "Now I know I was thinking clearly when I made sure he never met them."

"I would never desire them like that," he exclaimed, his eyes round. "They are like kin."

"Aye, with nearly five centuries of thinned blood betwixt ye," Torra reminded. "'Tis a lot."

Rònan sighed, suddenly wishing he was amongst his cousins instead of the elders. Well, Niall at least. And Nicole. Erin was better off wherever she was. He kept that thought firmly in mind as he remained where he was for several hours and for the most part brooded silently. He even kept that thought in mind as he ended up dancing with several lasses when the great hall filled up.

But even the strongest of men could keep a level head for only so long.

Especially when Erin arrived in Darach's arms…

With Tait and Bjorn walking on either side.

Chapter Nine

"I'M FINE, DARACH," Erin assured. "Seriously. Put me down."

"But your ankle," he complained. "You took a good fall from Tosha."

"You did," Bjorn agreed.

"You should rest it some," Tait added.

"Down," Erin repeated and frowned at Darach. "Please."

"Aye, lass." He carefully set her down but held her arm as she put pressure on her foot. As she suspected, it wasn't twisted and already far easier to stand on. "See, I'm good, guys."

Erin still couldn't believe she fell off Tosha. She had *never* fallen from a horse. But for some reason, Tosha got spooked and threw her. It made no sense. Nothing had been around her and Darach as they rode. It was almost as if Tosha decided she'd had enough riding for no apparent reason. But now that she was here, she could admit to being happy enough about it.

The main lodge was busy and as always, the Vikings were enjoying themselves with music, food and dancing. Though the crowd was thick, it wasn't difficult locating Rònan. Taller than most, he was easy to spot as he danced with a gorgeous redhead.

Putting that man in leather pants was a big mistake. At least based on the women flocking around him. But then she imagined they'd be there if he were in jeans or a kilt. But *leather*? Might as well drape him over a motorcycle with a sign saying, "Which would you rather ride, the bike or the man?" Because she knew damn well which option she'd choose.

"Here. Drink." Darach handed her a horn of ale. "To ease any ache that remains."

"Thanks," she murmured, downing half of it as fire flared beneath her skin and she tore her eyes from Rònan.

It had been a long week acclimating to what she had become. Or what she always was. A dragon-shifter witch. The witch part didn't throw her too much. The dragon part was a whole lot harder to swallow on several levels. Not only because it seemed preposterous but because of her past. Either way, she was slowly but surely accepting it.

Mainly because of Bjorn.

He was the first one who managed to be around her and their personalities were similar. Neither were overly chatty. Not once did he try to hit on her. Instead, he helped her understand what she was. How it wasn't as bad as she initially thought. And while she could admit they were drawn to each other, it was far different than what she felt around R̀onan.

R̀onan.

What *was* it with him? *About him?* Because whatever it was, she was fast becoming addicted. And the guy had been out like a light for a week. Still, they had shared moments he knew nothing about. Moments that still rendered her speechless. Like the feel of his muscular body beneath her fingertips as she tried to cool him down.

Like the feel of his lips when she kissed him.

"He's just doing that because you came in with so many guys," Nicole declared.

Erin snapped back to the present only to realize her friend stood next to her. As usual, so did Darach and what she now referred to as her 'Viking posse' Bjorn and Tait. It was their duty to protect her from their dragon cousins and she wasn't entirely opposed.

"What?" Erin frowned at Nicole. "Who?"

"Who, my arse." Darach chuckled. "You've got Rònan in a state you do. I've never seen him like this."

Erin's eyes flickered to the way the redhead ran her hand over Rònan's chest and how thoroughly he seemed to be enjoying it. "He's in a state all right." She frowned. "One that I've clearly got nothing to do with."

"All those long hours caring for him," Bjorn murmured. "Leads me to believe you do, woman."

"Someone had to take care of him," she grumbled and finished off her ale.

Tait handed her another. "Might it not have been his mother?" He glanced at Niall and Darach. "Or his cousins?"

"We tried." Darach winked at her. "But she wouldnae have it. 'Twas her responsibility seeing how they had that episode in the Otherworld at the same time."

Surprisingly enough, she and Darach had become good friends. She still wasn't sure why since he was overly affectionate and she tended to be standoffish. Nonetheless, the more she got to know him the better she liked him. Yet despite how handsome he was, she felt no spark beyond friendship and knew he felt the same. Which made her truly doubt this whole MacLomain, Broun connection.

Because Rònan was clearly set on Jackie and vice versa.

And Erin definitely should not be with Rònan.

So if there were only the four of them left in all of this then maybe the infamous connection between the clans had finally fizzled out. So how were any of them going to ignite the Claddagh rings? Because apparently that's what repelled this awful evil determined to take little Robert. Still, how do you force love? You didn't. Couldn't

"Let's go dance, Darach." She handed her horn back to Tait.

"I dinnae think—"

"I don't wanna sit here drinking." Her eyes met his and she held out her hand. "Please."

Darach joined her and shook his head. "Are you trying to make Rònan jealous?"

Was she? Erin bit the corner of her lip. Maybe on some level. "No more than you were earlier when he woke up."

"He had it coming," Darach muttered.

"Why?" she said as he pulled her close. "What'd he ever do to you?"

"As I've told you before, 'tis nothing direct just who he is in general." Darach shrugged. "I might love him but Rònan's always made a habit of taking what he wants with no care for others. If given the chance to retaliate a wee bit, I'll take it."

"Shame on you then." She frowned. "You've been hedging for days about this. Spit it out already. What'd he do to piss you off so much?"

Darach shook his head. "It doesnae matter."

"It obviously matters a great deal and it sounds like it's time to share."

When Darach remained silent, she kept eying him. Then she got it. How simple his discontent was. "He stole a girl from you, didn't he?"

"Lasses have an unnatural draw to dragon men," Darach grumbled.

"Pardon?" Her brows shot up. "You're not lacking either, Honey. Women have been all *over* you since we arrived."

Fire again flared beneath her skin as her gaze trailed to Rònan. She watched as he and the redhead left. Good, he needed to get laid. So did she for that matter. Since her eyes turned that first time, her dragon senses had been increasing. Scent. Sight. Hearing. Everything. Something was definitely going on in her body. Something that had her eying men as sexual prey when she had long avoided them. Her eyes flickered to her Viking posse. Bjorn was as much her friend as Darach but Tait…well, he spoke to her on a different level. Yet was it one she wanted to tap into?

"But it doesnae matter all that much right now, does it, lass?" Darach said softly.

Ripped from thought, her eyes returned to his. "I'm sorry." She shook her head and cleared her throat. "Bear with me. This dragon shit has me all turned around."

"Aye, 'tis okay," he said.

"No, it's not. I asked you a question then I zoned out." She frowned and searched his eyes. "What'd Rònan do to you? What happened?"

He was about to speak when a beautiful woman came up and tapped him on the shoulder. "A dance then, Highlander?"

When Darach started to shake his head, Erin nodded and backed away. "Go ahead, enjoy yourself."

"Aye?" he said, a concerned look in his eyes.

"Definitely." She squeezed his hand. "As long as you promise we'll resume this conversation later."

Darach nodded.

She held his gaze. "Yeah?"

"Aye," he assured.

"Good." She shot him one last smile then headed for the door.

All she wanted to do was lie down. Though it might have been a long week dealing with what she had become, the truth was the difficulty laid in caring for Rònan. Not knowing if he would live or die. She hardly slept or ate. Which baffled her. She barely knew him. Even so, when he passed out the day she *might have* flickered into the Celtic Otherworld, Erin felt…responsible? Guilty somehow that he fell into that unnatural slumber instead of her.

Bjorn stopped her before she left, frowning. "Where are you going, woman? It's early yet."

"Yes," Tait agreed, his eyes darkening as he looked at her. "I was hoping we might dance."

Unlike Bjorn, Tait still hadn't managed to rein in the desire he felt for her. Megan said it was likely because he was Kol's son so he came by his lusty ways naturally. Either way, she was far too vulnerable and knew it was best to keep her distance, especially when it came to dancing.

"I'm pretty wiped, Tait," she said. "Another time, okay?"

Tait nodded. "Then allow me to escort you to your lodge?"

Bjorn would be a better idea but she didn't want to be rude. "Sure, thanks."

They were just about to leave when little Robert the Bruce entered with Kjar.

"Hey there." She smiled and crouched in front of him. "I haven't seen you all day. What have you been up to?"

"Spending time with Kjar." Robert grinned. "He has been teaching me battle moves."

Her brows perked and her gaze went from Kjar back to Robert. "Is that so? And are you a mighty warrior now?"

"Aye." Robert puffed up some. "Mighty indeed."

Erin got a kick out of how good the massive Viking demi-god was with children. "Well, you're learning from the best."

She had even learned a few new moves from Kjar.

Robert frowned. "You're not leaving are you?"

Erin nodded. "I'm really tired. But I'll look for you first thing in the morning, all right? Maybe we'll get in some riding?"

"I would really like that." Robert gave her a big hug. "Sleep well, my friend."

"You too, Sweetheart."

Never having spent much time around children, she was surprised by how well she took to the future King. He was a good kid. As it turned out, Robert had no clue who she was when he first arrived so that ghostly episode was some sort of farce. As Grant said, likely trickery born of their enemy. Damn daunting thought. Hopefully it was all just a fluke that had to do with her dragon blood surfacing.

As always, it was snowing when she and Tait trudged to the lodge she'd been sharing with Rònan. Thankfully, another bed had been added. In light of Rònan's unnatural slumber, Tait or Bjorn had remained outside for their protection every night. However, she got the impression they would've done the same even if Rònan was awake.

"While I'm thankful for all you've done, you don't have to stand outside tonight, Tait," she said. "Rònan's up and about now so I should be fine."

"I do not think you'll be seeing much of the Highland dragon this eve," he said. "So I will remain."

"No." She shook her head. "It's way too early. Go enjoy yourself. If you're set on coming back later, that's cool, but you really don't need to."

"Might I come in and join you for some mead before you rest," he said softly.

Their eyes met and held. He was a handsome devil but she knew inviting him in would lead to nothing but trouble. While she liked to think she could simply slake her lust like Rònan was so clearly able to, would it be so simple? Now wasn't the time for complications. Not between her and Rònan, of course, but anything that could hinder her from watching out for Robert. And while she had no-strings-attached-relationships in the past, she sensed having sex with a dragon shifter would be another story altogether.

"I don't think that's such a great idea, Tait." She sighed. "And we both know why."

A twinkle met his eyes. "I *can* keep my hands to myself, woman."

But could she? While she didn't have nearly the same fiery reaction to him that she did with Rònan, she was way overdue for sexual release. She pressed her lips together and shook her head. "Not tonight, Handsome."

"As you wish," he said, disappointment in his voice as he leaned against the wall beside the front door. "If you change your mind, I will be right here."

"Tait," she groaned. "Go back to the main lodge and enjoy yourself. Seriously. For me."

He shook his head, stubborn. "I remain here for you."

"All right." Erin frowned. "I'm not gonna argue with you."

Before she changed her mind altogether, she stood on her tiptoes, kissed his cheek and headed inside. As she suspected, all was quiet and Rònan was nowhere to be found. Ignoring a twinge of jealousy when she imagined what he was up to, she shrugged out of her cloak and warmed her hands in front of the fire.

Food, mugs and a pitcher of ale had been left on the table. So she filled a cup to the brim and settled in to enjoy the fire and some peace of mind that Rònan was alive and well.

Alone time.

Something she rarely got since traveling back in time.

After a few hearty swigs, she studied her blunt fingernails. They would grow…change. Bjorn had tried to explain what it would feel like. How they would lengthen and become talons when she shifted. Erin swallowed back fear. Something she had been doing more and more of lately. She might keep it well hidden but she was frightened by what she would become.

"It willnae be as bad as you think, lass."

Erin jolted at the sound of Rònan's words floating within her mind. They felt different than before. Far more erotic.

So she pushed him away. *"Get out of my head."*

"Aye," he murmured. *"If only I could."*

"You can," she assured, essentially talking to herself because that's what it felt like save the fact she was instantly aroused. *"Get out."*

"I mean to protect you, lass," he said. *"And will."*

"Get out."

"Aye, then."

Everything went silent. Hopefully Rònan was busy getting busy. Erin scowled even as she thought it. Did he really just screw the redhead he was dancing with earlier? What's worse, was he speaking within her mind while he was at it? Frustrated, she downed her mug and went for a refill. But something caught her attention as she poured. A shift of shadow in the torchlight outside the back door.

So she grabbed a few daggers off the wall and snuck in that direction. Edging closer slowly, she narrowed her eyes. Someone was sitting on the ground, leaning against the building. Instead of letting them know she was there, she came around fast, crouched and held a blade to their neck.

She blinked several times. Rònan?

"Och, lass, you've an admirable way with a blade," he murmured as his eyes met hers.

It was the first time she had looked into his eyes since that first night and it hit her like a ton of bricks. Or a punch to the gut. Either way, the wind was knocked right out of her.

"Rònan," she whispered, struggling to catch her breath. "What are you doing out here?"

Erin pulled on every ounce of training Bjorn had given her. How to push past the feelings looking into a male dragon's eyes could invoke. And she had mastered it with him, Tait and the others. But as she feared might be the case, it was ten times harder with Rònan.

"I didnae want to tempt you," he murmured, clearly struggling as much as she was.

Only when a tremble rippled down his body did she realize he wore nothing but pants and boots. Worry over him managed to pull her out of her stupor.

"Why the hell don't you have on more clothes?" Erin frowned as she stood and held out her hand. "C'mon, we need to get you warmed up."

"Nay." Rònan shook his head. "I've been running too bloody hot. I'll be fine right here."

"Now," she stated, voice firm, eyes even firmer. "Let's go."

"Nay," he reiterated. "Get some rest, lass. I know Tait's around the front. I'll protect you from here."

"Stubborn," she said under her breath. But Rònan mentioning the Viking gave her an idea.

"Suit yourself." She headed inside. "I think I'll invite Tait in after all."

"Bloody hell if you will," he muttered.

She kept a smile hidden as he followed.

"In front of the fire," she ordered and poured him some ale. Focusing on protecting him helped distract her from the sheer lust she was feeling. "Strip down if you need to. It's nothing I haven't seen before."

"Nay," he mumbled as he crossed his arms over his chest and stood in front of the fire. "I've already dried my pants with magic."

Erin almost overfilled the mug as she watched him out of the corner of her eye. Damn, he was hot as hell. Heat flared between her thighs as she eyed his snug leather pants, and broad, muscled, tattooed chest and arms. She swallowed. Maybe leaving him outside *would* have been the smarter move.

Rònan inhaled sharply then released a long, slow breath as he closed his eyes, shook his head, and whispered, "Gods give me strength, you smell good."

Doing her best to keep her eyes averted, she held out a mug. "Here, drink. It'll help warm you."

"Many thanks," he murmured and took the mug. "Will you not look at me then? You did so outside and we managed through."

"Likely because I had a blade to your neck," she reminded.

"If I've the strength to look at you then you've the same strength, lass," he said softly. "Please."

"Not gonna lie. I'm too damned aroused." She shook her head and turned away. "Drink your ale and warm yourself, Rònan."

He growled in frustration. "We need to push past this if we're to protect the Bruce as we should."

"We don't need to look at each other to protect Robert."

"Aye, but we do." He downed the ale in a few gulps. "Especially if we're to battle alongside one another. Eye contact is important."

She hated to admit it but he was right. "I'll get there. Promise. It just doesn't look like it'll be happening right now." Though it was about the last thing she wanted to say for more reasons than one, she said, "Why aren't you still with the redhead? After you warm up, it might be best if you rejoin her."

"Nay." He refilled his mug and handed her one as well. "Whilst she was pleasant enough I couldnae seem to muster desire for her."

Erin almost cursed when a rush of satisfaction blew through her. "You two seemed to be doing just fine dancing."

"Only because I meant to make you jealous," he whispered. "Because I felt the same when I saw you with Darach and the Vikings."

Though she should have been surprised by his bluntness, she wasn't. Like her, he accepted what simmered between them for what it was. Simple lust based on dragon blood.

"Well, you've got nothing to be jealous of because Darach and I are just friends and me and my Viking posse have an understanding." She took several sips as she navigated around him to the fire without meeting his eyes. "All that aside, we both need to remember that not only is what we're feeling nothing more than a dragon thing but that Jackie's out there somewhere waiting for you."

"Viking posse?" he said. "Is that what you're calling Tait and Bjorn?"

"Yup."

"Why did you not take Tait tonight?" Rònan's question was a deep rumble close to her ear as he moved behind her. "I know he offered and I know you were tempted to accept."

Right. Because their thoughts mingled.

"You know the answer to that," she said softly because she didn't trust her vocal chords.

"Aye," he said. "You think it would have complicated things had you taken Tait to your bed but I dinnae ken that. Perhaps it would have eased the ache you suffer now? Would easing that ache not make it easier to focus on what lies ahead?"

She was tempted to turn and confront him but stayed put. "Not if I ended up having stronger feelings for him because of it. Who knows, there's a good chance I wouldn't want to leave here if I did."

"I saw how you were with the wee Bruce earlier," he said. "So I dinnae doubt you would do whatever was needed to protect him."

"How did you see?" she started then shook her head. "You never really left with the redhead did you?"

"I dinnae want the redhead," he murmured, words still close to her ear, his body a warm wall at her back. "I want you, lass."

Erin closed her eyes and focused on breathing evenly. "No, you want Jackie."

"Aye, part of me," he admitted. "But it feels more like desiring a figment of my imagination. 'Tis nothing like what I feel now. Here." His hand fell on her shoulder. "With you."

Hell, this was pure torture.

Blood rushed through her veins so rapidly she grew lightheaded.

120

"I can't." She shook her head but couldn't manage to step away, could not get her feet to work. "What if you and Jackie are meant for one another? I love that woman to death and would hate myself if…"

Save for the crackling fire and howling wind, the room grew quiet as her unsaid words hung in the air. As if his feet were as glued to the floor as hers, Rònan didn't move for several long moments. Yet he eventually stepped away, his voice soft. "You're right, lass. 'Twould not be right."

"I wish I knew more of this connection betwixt Jackie and me." Keeping his distance, he stood beside her and ran a hand over his face as he stared at the fire. "While some of my memories of her involve slight desire, most have more to do with her soothing voice and pale brown eyes. 'Twas a dark place and they lent comfort."

"Understandable. Jackie's a pretty peaceful person for the most part." Erin frowned as she mulled over his words. "But you mean dark brown eyes, right?"

"Nay, definitely light brown," Rònan said. "Almost golden at times."

"That's weird because Jackie definitely has super dark brown eyes," Erin said. "Guys love them combined with her platinum hair. They can't get enough of her."

"Then she must not be standing next to you," he said, voice a little guttural. "Because there's no comparison to ebony hair and violet eyes."

"Dragon eyes likely meant to lure dragon males," she reminded. "But thanks."

"'Tis true I've never met another with your eye color," he conceded. "But dinnae think for a moment you're not every bit as beautiful as Jackie…if not more so."

"Be sweet all you want. We're not doing this." No matter how much she wanted to. "Back to Jackie's eye color. Do you think the discrepancy has something to do with the Celtic Otherworld?"

"I dinnae know." He gulped down more ale. "All I know was that they werenae dark brown in the least."

Erin knew she should leave it alone but was curious. "What about her hair? Was it straight? Long?"

Though she sensed he wanted to look at her, his eyes remained as trained on the fire as hers. "Aye, 'twas long. But nay, 'twas only slightly curled. Not nearly as curly as yours. So maybe wavy is a better word."

"Strange, because Jackie's hair is straight and thick. She's got the sort of hair models would die for." Her eyes finally went to him, she was so curious. "Another possible side effect of the Otherworld?"

"I dinnae know." Evidently as curious, his eyes met hers. "Tell me more about what she looks like."

Genuinely worried that he might have been misled by the evil Brae Stewart and his life was more at risk than ever, she was able to set aside lust and *look* at him. And damn, was he worth looking at. "She's tall. Around five foot nine." Erin gave it some thought. "Full lips. Men seem to love those too. High cheekbones, thick dirty blond lashes. Oh!" She touched just to the right of her eye. "She has a little crown shaped birthmark right here."

"Crown shaped?" He cocked his head and took her hand, his eyes falling to her ring. "Odd considering there's a crown on these rings, aye?"

"That is a little odd," she agreed, shocked it hadn't occurred to her sooner.

"I couldnae tell her height as I only recall lying down when I saw her. Her lips were full enough but her lashes were as pale as her hair," he continued. "And she had no birthmark. I would have remembered that."

"This is bizarre." She took his mug so she could refill both cups. "What about her breasts? Were they big, small, medium?"

Rònan snorted. "Believe it or not, I only focused on her face."

"Well, Jackie's as lucky in that department as she is in every other," she said as she poured. "God love her, she's fully stacked."

"Stacked?" His brows perked. "I take it that means her breasts are large."

She chuckled. "More than twice the size of mine."

"It sounds like she's considerably taller than you," he pointed out, voice getting husky and brogue thickening. "I think yer breasts are quite…"

When he trailed off, she said, "Small? Yeah, pretty much."

"They well suit yer size, lass," he murmured. "And look large enough on your frame."

Her size had always worked against her in the military. But she'd trained hard and knew how to use it to her advantage. Bulk meant nothing. Skill and timing *did*. And then there was attitude. That's what always put her on top in the end.

"Honestly, outside of the whole dragon thing, I'm surprised you're into me." She handed him the mug. "From what I've seen, you seem to favor the robust type." Her eyes narrowed as she considered him. "Your mom's a tiny thing, though." Then her eyes widened. "*Please* tell me you don't have a mommy complex."

Rònan choked on his ale but managed to swallow it down. He obviously needed no translation as to what she meant. "Hell, if you're determined to keep me from you, that's the way to do it, lass." He shook his head, a mad scowl on his face. "Though you're small like her, you look *nothing* like my Ma. 'Twould be bloody alarming if you did."

"It sure would." Erin grinned at him, thrilled that they were able to look at one another without lust getting in the way. She was genuinely happy that they could just *talk*. "And luckily, you look nothing like my father."

The minute she said it blood seemed to drain out of her and pool at her feet.

Had she just referred to her *Dad*?

"Erin?" Rònan's brows shot together as he took her elbow to steady her. "Are you all right?"

"I need to sit," she tried to say but nothing came out.

Before she knew it, he scooped her up into his arms.

"No." She closed her eyes, way too aware of his body despite her conflicting emotions. "In a chair, Rònan. *Please*."

"Aye," he whispered and sat her in a chair. Crouching, he stayed close without touching. But his eyes never left her face and his voice was soft. "Speak when you can, lass."

"I can speak," she managed to croak, a whole new fear flashing to the front when she realized he heard her thoughts. When she realized he likely knew that she was losing her voice.

"Aye," he murmured. When she tried to turn her face away, he cupped her cheek and turned it back, those bright green eyes of his locking with hers. "I know, lass."

But *did* he know? Had Nicole told him? Not one to sit on 'what if's' she did her best to ignore his touch and put it out there. "So you know I'm losing my voice."

The flicker of unease in his eyes told her everything. Rònan had no idea. He must have been referring to her distress over her father.

She supposed it was better that he knew of her upcoming affliction if they were going to work together as a team to protect Robert. How he responded now would make or break him.

"I didnae know of your voice but as I see it 'tis not half as bad as losing your mind to an Otherworld you have no control over."

So his plight was worse than hers? But as their eyes held and she saw the compassion in his gaze, she knew that wasn't how he intended it at all.

He was trying to relate.

Trying to make it seem like it was no big deal.

That they were both facing something they had no control over.

"No," she whispered, glad her voice worked. "It's likely not as bad as losing your mind to the Otherworld."

Rònan cupped her other cheek, his eyes locked with hers. "We will face what we must together, lass."

Erin tried to respond but nothing came out. This time, she knew it was her voice issues kicking in. She wondered at the timing. But hell if she would shy away from it so she pointed to her throat and shook her head.

"So you cannae speak right now." His gaze never left hers. "'Tis all right." Instead of questioning her further, he sat down in the chair beside her and held her hand, eyes not on her but on the fire. "Then I'll talk." His glanced at her. "Aye or nay because I'm just as content sitting with you in silence."

Was he really? Why? But she appreciated the offer so nodded.

"Remember, you can always speak to me telepathically," he whispered into her mind.

"I know," she thought. *"But it's a little too arousing right now."*

"I ken." Rònan nodded, eyes on the fire as he spoke aloud. "We willnae do anything that makes you feel like you've betrayed your friend."

He meant it and she appreciated it. So she figured a few more internal words couldn't hurt. *"I know it's probably hard but can you tell me more about what happened to you in the Otherworld?"*

Rònan nodded. "Though I cannae recall much of my last visit, I do remember bits and pieces." He shook his head. "'Tis a place devoid of color and warmth that drains the life from you. Last time I was beaten but I'm not so sure I was this time. Then again, I'm not entirely certain I was taken by the dark demi-god this go round."

He sipped from his mug then continued. "I remember flashes of Jackie. And I recall someone singing." Though reluctant, his eyes met hers. "And because I would rather be honest with you...I remember a kiss."

Chapter Ten

RÒNAN DIDN'T MISS Erin's heavy swallow as their gazes held. This time when she tried to speak, her voice worked. "You kissed Jackie?"

Rònan made no comment about her voice because he knew she wouldn't appreciate it. "Mayhap," he murmured, eyes still on her. "But I didnae get the sense it was Jackie."

He watched closely as her thoughts flickered like shadows through his mind.

"But wasn't she the only one there?"

He could tell by her tone that she was hedging.

"Aye, I thought so," he said. "Yet she wasnae the one singing."

"Strange," she said softly. "Maybe you imagined it."

Oh, he had not imagined it.

Erin kept her features smooth but her mind still brushed his as it had all night. He tried to ignore the way she felt but it was nearly impossible. More than that, he was trying not to invade her privacy. He would much rather she open up to him. "Might you share something of yourself? I'm curious about the lass who will be fighting alongside me. Where you came by such battle skills."

Rònan saw the relief she tried to hide. She was avoiding something. Even so, he listened with avid fascination as she talked about serving in the military and about her horse in Vermont. He liked the way her features softened then hardened based on what she spoke of.

As he suspected, she possessed a level of intelligence he appreciated which was something that he rarely paid attention to with lasses. It wasn't that he thought women weren't smart, he had just always preferred their company in bed versus anywhere else. Outside of his sister and female cousins, he spent little time with lasses beyond the lusting.

"'Tis good that you've got the connection with horses," he said. "Have you started communicating with Tosha yet?"

"Actually, I have." She smiled. "A few days ago."

Without a doubt, Tosha was like the other three horses they'd found in New Hampshire and was part MacLomain wizard. "I dinnae suppose she's mentioned which MacLomain bonded with her?"

Erin shook her head. "I'm afraid not. Like me, she's pretty low key."

"Low key," he murmured, still eying her. Somehow she had been there with him in the Otherworld while she cared for him. So he went with his gut to see what he could pull out of her. "So do you sing to her as you did to me?"

When Erin stilled, he felt a surge of satisfaction. It *had* been her singing. He would have never guessed based on her tough exterior.

"Not sure what you mean," she murmured.

"Aye, but you do," he said softly. "You've the voice of an angel."

Erin barely breathed and pain flickered across her face. "Sorry but it wasn't me you heard."

Then he realized the stark truth. *This* was the sole reason she feared losing her voice. She would lose the ability to do something she loved.

But she didn't have to. Not entirely anyway.

Rònan couldn't stop himself if he wanted to. He turned her chair until she faced him and dragged her closer, locking his hands on the armrests.

"What are you doing?" she exclaimed and shook her head. "This is a real bad idea." Her eyes shot to his forearms on either side of her. "Way too close."

"Sing for me." He cupped the side of her head. "Sing within your mind."

"Are you crazy?" She frowned. "That's impossible."

"Why?"

"Because it is."

"I dinnae think so," he whispered, overly aware of how silky her hair felt, of how the pale purple in her eyes seemed to be magnifying and pulling him closer. "Mayhap not now but I think you should try at some point. I think you might be surprised."

"You need to move away," she whispered, closing her eyes as her cheek leaned into his touch. "For Jackie."

Her thoughts didn't just flicker through his mind but started to flood. Desire. Need. She fought an overwhelming draw to him that she was barely able to control. Feeling the pull just as intensely, he was impressed that she managed to fight it. She was already growing as a dragon. One that would be an admirable ally. Yet the lust, the connection they shared at this moment, still filtered down to one thing…one certainty.

"'Twas you who kissed me in the Otherworld," he whispered.

"No," she whispered, eyes still closed. "I kissed you here."

He cupped her cheeks, reveling in the softness of her skin, the flawlessness of it. "Why?"

Her eyes slowly opened.

They were no longer human but dragon.

Rònan had a split second to register that before he seemed to be sucked into a memory of the Otherworld. There was no sign of Jackie. Just endless gray and death. Mournful wails on the wind. A shiver raked him as he tried to move but his body was unresponsive. His eyes slid shut. He was dying and the wails were drawing closer. Coming for him. Closer and closer.

Then the singing came.

Singing that drowned out the wails and pushed them away.

Erin?

Soft lips met his but he couldn't open his eyes. A tear—*her* tear—rolled down his cheek. It had never been Jackie who kissed him but Erin.

Despite how far away from his body he felt, passion roared up and gave his limbs strength. Eyes still closed, he cupped her cheeks and returned the kiss. Soft at first as he tilted her head. Then he kissed her more deeply. She tasted so sweet, hot, delicious, so different than all the others. He swore his blood started boiling when her mouth opened and their tongues touched. Tasting, sampling, both groaned before the kiss started to grow wild.

"Hey guys, great news!" Nicole declared before she murmured, "Oh, damn."

Ripped from oblivion, Rònan's eyes shot open at the same time as Erin's. She was straddling him on the chair and he was moments away from taking her. He'd pulled down his pants enough and it seemed he downright ripped hers.

"Here, cover yourselves quick." Nicole whipped a fur at them. "And put away those dragon eyes."

Rònan had no idea what to make of any of this. Why had Erin embraced her dragon without being angry? Better yet, when had she ended up on his lap? The memory had been so brief. The kiss not nearly long enough. He had a few seconds to mull it over before Niall and Tait strode in.

"Och," Rònan muttered as he wrapped the fur around them enough to cover what shouldn't be seen. "Might ye give us a moment?"

Erin blinked several times and her eyes returned to normal as they flew to Tait and she blushed. With no means to control it, Rònan's inner dragon shot the Viking a triumphant look.

"Erin?" a lass said as she walked in a few seconds later.

Erin's eyes went wide. "Oh my God, Jackie!"

Jackie? His eyes shot to the tall blond. *Bloody hell.*

Nicole being Nicole took charge and started shooing everyone out. "Okay, let's give them a minute to," she cleared her throat, "to readjust themselves."

"Sonofabitch," Erin groaned and swung off of him. "How did I end up on your lap?" Before he could respond, she shook her head. "Forget it. It must've been a dragon thing. One we obviously still have no control over."

Rònan eyed his erection with despair. "I cannae seem to will away the beastie's need with magic."

"What?" Her eyes fell to his cock then widened. When she licked her lips, he pulled the blanket over it and scowled. "That doesnae help any lass."

"Sorry. I just…it…" Her frown was as deep as his when she grabbed another pair of pants out of a trunk. "That shouldn't have happened." Then she yanked off her shredded pants. "I can't believe Jackie's here."

He tried but for the life of him, he couldn't pull his gaze from her slender legs and tempting wee arse. So much smooth, firm, mouth-watering skin.

"Stop that," she growled as she pulled on fresh pants. "Did you *not* catch that Jackie's here?"

"And do you not recall our talk of dragon puberty?" he growled back, galled that he couldn't get a simple erection under control.

"Then take care of yourself." Erin yanked on one boot. "Stroke one out." She yanked on the other. "But get that under control soon then meet me in the main lodge."

"We need to talk," he started but Erin shook her head, wrapped a fur around her shoulders and strode out. He sighed, more upset than he could ever remember being. For more reasons than one. Instead of pleasuring himself as she so eloquently phrased it—oh, he got the gist of her modern day description—he focused on breathing. Damn lass. It must be nice to walk away from what had happened so easily.

Thankfully, with her gone, he was able to get himself under control.

He needed to talk to her now.

Because Jackie was *not* the lass he saw in the Celtic Otherworld. She was *not* the lass he swore an oath to.

He could only suppose that lass had been the enemy all along and hell if she hadn't played the part well. Too well. Which made him wonder.

After he pulled on a tunic, he headed for the main lodge. Though it was crowded, it didn't take him long to locate Erin. She might be with her friends but Tait and Bjorn were hovering nearby as usual. Blasted Vikings. Tait's eyes met his and despite the compromising position he had found them in, it was clear the man had no intention of giving up his pursuit of her. While he and Tait typically had more lighthearted personalities, their mutual desire was creating unneeded friction.

And clearly affecting their moods.

Though Erin didn't look his way, Nicole did. "There you are." She grabbed his hand and pulled him over, making introductions. "Jackie, this is Rònan." Then she gestured between them. "Rònan, Jackie."

Jackie offered a soft, tempered smile. One he imagined wrapped most men around her little finger. But he wasn't most men.

"Nice to meet you, Rònan," she said, studying him curiously.

"You as well, Jackie."

When his eyes flickered to Erin, she looked away. *Hell.*

131

Nicole nudged Rònan and kept smiling at Jackie. "Mind if I steal him for second?"

"By all means." Jackie's eyes flickered over the room. "Is Darach here?"

"You just missed him," Nicole said as she yanked Rònan after her.

They were about halfway through the crowd when Nicole thanked a servant for a horn of ale and handed it to Rònan. Exasperated, she scowled at him. "For Christ sake, you left with one woman then I find you ready to screw Erin. I thought you two were steering clear of each other?"

"We were. At first," he groused and downed half his horn. "But I didnae want her to be alone."

Nicole rubbed her forehead and kept eying him. "Did you sleep with the redhead first?"

"Nay," he scoffed. "I never really left but you'd not know that because you were off with Niall."

"Right." She shrugged. "I can't keep my hands off of him." Her eyes stayed with his. "Well, Jackie's here now so you and Erin better get a grip."

"Jackie's not the lass I swore an oath to," he said softly. "She isnae the one who came to me in the Otherworld."

Nicole's jaw dropped. "Are you serious?" Her eyes narrowed. "Or are you just saying that because you wanna sleep with Erin?"

Rònan's frown deepened. "You think that ill of me then?"

"It's not a matter of thinking bad of you, Sweetie. I just know nothing about dragon-shifter males and females being around each other." Nicole's eyes searched his and she shook her head. "The Otherworld's been screwing with you in a real bad way and now you and Erin have this attraction neither of you knows how to control."

"Och, 'tis bloody frustrating." He downed the rest of his ale. "'Twould be best if I go to sleep and start fresh on the morrow."

"Nay, my lad," his mother said softly as she came alongside. "Ye'll be joining me in the Viking King's lodge so that we might better ken what's happening."

While tempted to argue, the look in her eyes broached no room for argument. Even if she were not his ma, he wouldn't argue with Torra MacLeod. Nobody of MacLomain blood would save possibly Grant and he had yet to see that happen.

So by the time he plunked down once more at Naðr's fire with a fresh horn of ale, only the few Torra wanted were there. Grant, the Viking King, Megan, Erin, Jackie and Rònan. Though their personalities struck him as vastly different, it was clear that Erin and Jackie were close as they sat together.

Naturally, Grant led the conversation, his eyes on Rònan. "Leslie and Bradon fled New Hampshire with Jackie when they learned you were taken by Brae Stewart to the Celtic Otherworld. Wishing to take no chances by remaining vulnerable in the future, they fled to Scotland. When and where they ended up shall remain a mystery because you are too entrenched and part of what Brae and her dark Laird are doing."

Before Rònan could respond, Grant shook his head. "And now you are lust-ridden over Erin because she is a dragon."

"Mayhap 'tis not just because she is half dragon." His eyes wandered to Erin. Back to flicking her lighter, she stared at the fire with a frown. Jackie, however, met his eyes, clearly interested in what he had to say.

Grant's brows perked, his brogue thickening despite their company. "So ye've love for Erin then despite yer oath to Jackie?"

"I never said a bloody thing about love." He cringed at the intensity of his words. Erin never reacted but kept at the damn lighter. "Either way, Jackie isnae the lass I made an oath to."

The room fell silent and though she didn't look at him, Erin's fingers stilled on the lighter.

Jackie finally broke the silence. "I'm not?"

Rònan shook his head and met her eyes. "You look nothing like the lass who called to me. Who helped me through."

"That's okay." Her eyes were remarkably kind as the corner of her lip tilted up. "Because by the sounds of it, I'd rather not be trapped there."

"Nay, you wouldnae," his mother said, her eyes meeting his. "Are you sure, Son?"

"Aye." He nodded. "Definitely. She even sounds different."

"Then we can only assume that the enemy is masking himself as a lass to lure you in, Rònan," Grant said.

"Mayhap but somehow I dinnae think so." He shook his head, unconvinced. "She was too kind. As to her calling to me from the

Otherworld, the verra reason I went to the future, it seemed too real. Too intense."

"Evil can seem that way when it tries to lure," his mother reminded.

"Nay." He shook his head, still trying to catch Erin's eye. "Whoever helped me in the Otherworld the first time, even the second time, wasnae evil in the least."

"Nay," Grant murmured. "It wasnae, was it?"

Caught by the octave of his uncle's voice, his eyes shot to Grant. "You believe me then? You believe that the lass who called to me wasnae evil?"

"I believe that you believe it, Nephew." His eyes flickered to Torra then back. "How different were her features from Jackie's?"

"Yeah, I'd like to know that too." Erin's voice was whisper soft as her eyes swung to his. "Because my take on it is that you're just thinking with your dick."

Though tempted to retaliate with anger, he saw the flicker of hurt in her eyes. More than that, he felt it in her thoughts. She had no idea what to make of this. How she should feel. If not Jackie, who was this unknown woman he had felt so strongly about? Honestly, if their positions were reversed, he'd feel the same way.

"When it comes to you, aye, mayhap I have thought with my cock too much." His eyes never left hers and he dealt only in honesty. "But there's more betwixt us than that and now that I know 'twas not your friend I swore an oath to, I'm coming for you, lass. I need to better ken what this is."

Erin's brows dropped. "You're not coming for anything, buddy."

"Enough," the Viking King cut in. His eyes went to Jackie. "I know that Bradon and Leslie kept you safe. Have you had any dreams of this Otherworld? Of Rònan? Any strange episodes that make no sense?"

"None." She shook her head. "Before today, I've never seen Rònan."

Grant's eyes met his. "That doesnae mean she wasnae there, Nephew."

"Grant's right," Torra added. "There's too much unknown to be certain of anything."

Rònan saw where this was heading and wanted no part of it.

"I tire of this. I'm a laird now and lead my own clan." Rònan swigged down his ale and stood, his eyes flickering between Torra and Grant. "What did you call us in here for then? To tell me I couldnae have Erin despite me telling you Jackie's not the lass for me? That I must wait and see how this all works itself out?" He ground his jaw. "I grow tired of doing what everyone else wants. I grow tired of being a pawn in a game I dinnae ken."

He saw no point in trying to work through the mysterious dynamics of an Otherworld he remembered so little about. For the most part, his memories of being there had been ripped away. What hadn't been torn from him was what he had here. What he understood.

And that was Erin.

Though Erin's eyes had returned to the fire, Rònan tossed aside his horn and looked at her. "Lass, you know where I stand. Come to me or dinnae."

Nobody said a word as he left and he was glad for it.

He knew his own mind.

He knew what he wanted.

And being told that he might be without his wits in the damn Otherworld didn't work for him. So he trudged through the snow, his fury only growing with his confusion. The wind whistled but he didn't pay attention.

Not at first.

Until the flakes died away and he recognized the sound.

Then he had only a split second to realize he no longer walked on snow.

No, he walked on barren rock.

His knees gave out.

Then his body.

And yet again he laid unmoving in the Celtic Otherworld.

Chapter Eleven

"HE'S ALWAYS BEEN a stubborn lad," Torra murmured. "Some things dinnae change."

"But they need to," Grant said. "He runs from things when he should face them."

"Did he not face them again and again?" Torra's hard eyes met Grant's. "Take care how much ye expect from my bairn when he's the only one repeatedly brought into a world we dinnae ken, aye?"

"Ye know what I speak of—" Grant started but Torra cut him off, her eyes narrowed.

"I know that 'tis not yer bairn but mine. 'Tis more than enough for me to have the final word right now." Her eyes narrowed further. "Is it not?"

"Aye, mayhap—"

"Och, nay mayhap!" Torra bit back. "Ye've no concept of what I'm going through."

Erin was done with this. Completely over it. So she squeezed Jackie's hand and met her eyes while Grant and Torra argued. "I've got to go make sure Rònan's okay. Wanna come?"

"No." Jackie's voice was soft and understanding. "I see what's happening between you two. Go find him."

"There's nothing happening between us," Erin said. But she knew there was. Something that had just become far more readily available when he denied it had been Jackie he swore an oath to.

The corner of Jackie's lip hitched up. "It's okay if there is." Her eyes searched Erin's and the strange, peaceful bond they'd always shared calmed her frayed nerves. "Rest assured, I never met him before today."

Erin considered Jackie for a moment. Her friend was telling the truth. So she leaned over and kissed her cheek, whispering, "If you need me, you know where I am."

Jackie's eyes met hers. "Go."

Erin nodded before she strode out, throwing over her shoulder, "I'm going to check on Rònan."

Grant and Torra were still busy arguing and the Viking King and Megan simply watched her silently as she left. The only ones who seemed opposed to her destination were her Viking posse. Bjorn and Tait fell in beside her as she trudged through the snow.

"I do not think this is wise, woman," Bjorn said.

"I agree," Tait answered.

"Why?" She stopped and eyed them. "Do you know something I don't?"

"Nay." Bjorn shook his head, disgruntled. "Just that something feels off about all this."

"Of course, it does. This whole situation is a genuine clusterfuck." Her eyes flew to Tait's. "And you're just jealous."

"Yes," he agreed then shook his head. "But there is more to it, Erin. Something…" He seemed to struggle with his words as he looked at Bjorn then her. "There is something very wrong."

"Yeah." She looked between them. "There's a ton wrong with all of this."

"And Rònan's at the heart of it," Bjorn warned.

"Part of it," Tait said.

"Enough." Erin flung her hands in the air and shook her head as she kept walking. "Rònan's been screwed hard through all of this. While I don't know where I stand with the guy, I'm not gonna leave him alone."

Before she could enter her lodge, Bjorn grabbed her arm. "No, it is more than that. I sense trouble."

Tait clustered her from the other side, distressed. "Unnatural trouble." His hand fell on her shoulder. "You go no further, Erin."

When she saw Grant and Torra exit Naðr's building and head in her direction, she shook her head. "No, enough with this." She shoved away and glared at her Viking posse. "If you're determined to be my bodyguards then stop them not me."

Before they could respond, she darted inside.

The fire was down to embers and Rònan was in bed.

"Rònan?" she said softly, not sure if she wanted to wake him or not.

He lay on his back unmoving. She sat beside him and kept her voice just above a whisper. "Rònan?"

Nothing. No response. As far as she could tell he was sleeping soundly. Deep down she knew that made no sense. He had only come in here a few minutes before her and was angry to boot.

Yet he slept soundly.

Just like he had for the past week.

Worry spiked and she touched his cheek as she had done so many times before. He felt cool to the touch. Far too cool.

"Rònan?" Her worry turned to outright fear. "Can you hear me? Wake up."

Though his eyes remained closed, he murmured, "What are you doing here, lass?" He shook his head. "You shouldnae be here."

"But I am." Erin leaned closer. "Can you open your eyes?"

"They are open," he whispered.

But they weren't. Erin was about to tell him as much when he cupped her cheeks and brought her lips down to his. Though startled, it took half a second to melt against him. Just like that, they were back where they left off earlier.

Except this time Jackie wasn't a factor.

But the truth was both had too easily forgotten there was a factor at all when they kissed earlier.

Somewhere in the back of her mind, she knew she was losing herself to his touch. But as it had been before, it was impossible to pull away as their tongues tangled and the kiss deepened. *Unlike* before, she was aware of their every move as he pulled her until she straddled him. How his strong hands felt when they dug into her hair as the kiss grew more and more intense. As everything happening grew far more vivid.

An ache didn't just grow but exploded between her thighs. Painful in its intensity, she would swear that she whimpered into his mouth. But then they were both groaning so it was hard to know. It felt like actual fire flickered over every inch of her skin when he grabbed her ass and ground his erection against her.

She had never been so aroused that her vision blurred.

She had never been so aroused that the flesh between her thighs felt this swollen.

Throbbing.

Drenched.

Clutching at his tunic, she ground against him, desperate to fill the hollow ache between her legs. This time, when he ripped her pants, she knew it was happening. This time, when he pulled his pants down just enough, she felt every long, hard inch of the aroused man pressed against her. Not stopping, desperate to take what she needed, she rolled her hips up until she had him where she wanted him then slowly sank.

Rònan inhaled sharply and his eyes flew open.

Dragon eyes.

When red shadowed her vision she knew her dragon was responding.

For a moment, he seemed confused by his surroundings but soon became as ensnared as she was by what was happening between them. Head dropped back, she groaned and bit her lower lip as she worked her way onto him. Due to their size differences, she was vaguely surprised she managed to take all of him.

But she did.

Every last inch.

Raw lust emanated from him as his lips fell open and he squeezed her backside, lifted her just enough then thrust upward. She cried out when her womb contracted in a mix of pain and pleasure. Their eyes held as they breathed harshly.

There would be nothing remotely romantic about this. Nothing that spoke of love.

No, this was *all* harsh need.

Overdue lust.

Pure unadulterated sex.

They might be fully clothed and wearing boots, but it didn't slow them down any. Her skin was so overheated it felt like she was literally going up in flames as he bent his knees slightly and placed his feet on the bed. His large hands nearly wrapped around her entire waist as he lifted her again and started thrusting.

Not slow, easy thrusts but sharp, hard, determined ones.

Hands braced back on his steely thighs, she watched him from beneath half-mast lids as the feeling of fire and sweet pleasure wound its way through her. An indescribable feeling that crawled up her torso and down her legs. Around her neck, over her shoulders, and down her spine.

A spicy, heated scent rose between them.

A scent that called to her on a whole new level.

It was their combined scent made of both human and dragon arousal.

And it turned them into animals.

Rònan inhaled sharply again, growled then flipped her beneath him so quickly what little breath she had whooshed out of her. Then it was just a mad frenzy as he squeezed her wrists beside her head and thrust like a deranged madman. She wasn't much better as she braced her feet and met him with equal vigor.

There was violence to the way they moved.

The way their eyes locked and he held her down.

Their dragons warred against one another as they struggled to get closer, as the beast inside him tried to dominate. But she knew when she wrapped her legs around him and exerted more control, that he only had so much power over her...over himself. Whatever mutual understanding they found as their thrusts increased grew more desperate, culminated as their eyes held.

Now they both growled.

Challenged.

Competed.

And she liked it.

Loved it.

So much so that her body started to shake and tremble not only from the excitement of the moment but from the searing pleasure that wrapped around her. While it started as fiery tremors, it soon became a mini-bomb of climaxes that had her crying out before the mega explosion came and she outright roared.

Rònan's growls grew more guttural moments before he locked her wrists over her head with one hand. Then a deep, ragged groan broke from his chest as he braced himself up with the other hand, thrust sharply and locked up against her.

Chest arched, her eyes rolled back in her head as his throbs heightened her ongoing orgasm and her body kept fluttering and jerking. Even her jaw trembled and teeth chattered as her muscles seemed to ricochet off her bones. She'd never felt anything like it...anything so all consuming.

It seemed like a long time before she drifted down. When she did, he was braced on his elbows with his head bent beside hers and his breathing still just as ragged. Then it took a while before the red cleared from her vision. When it did, it was replaced by leaden gray.

Confused, she blinked several times.

"What the hell?" she whispered as her eyes flickered over his shoulder to the barren landscape around them. "Where are we?"

Just as confused, at least for a moment, Rònan's eyes met hers before he pulled away and frowned. "Bloody hell." He shook his head, more and more upset as he helped her sit up. "You're really here, aren't you, lass?"

"That depends on where 'here' is." She took in their surroundings, overly aware she had no weapons on her. "Doesn't look too promising."

Jagged mountains rose all around them, cut through by a dry riverbed. Trees were barren and spindly. Long grass was dead as it blew in an eerie sounding wind.

"Nay, 'tis not promising in the least." Rònan adjusted his pants, yanked off his tunic and ripped it in half. Then he tied either side of it around her waist, creating a skirt over her pants to hide the damage he'd done. He was so much larger than her the material nearly wrapped twice.

Chills went through her as she began to understand what she was looking at. "This is the Celtic Otherworld, isn't it?"

"Aye. A place I cannae seem to break free of." His upset eyes met hers. "I didnae," he started then broke off as his frown deepened. "Och, lass." He squeezed her shoulders, brogue thickening. "I shouldnae have taken ye like that. I knew something was wrong, that I'd somehow been brought here but then when ye came to me I was back in the lodge." He shook his head. "Then I lost control."

"Hey, sleeping together was a mutual decision so don't beat yourself up over it." She frowned at their surroundings. "I think we better worry less about us and more about how to get out of here."

"You dinnae seem all that frightened," he said softly.

"I am but I learned a long time ago how to control my fear." Her eyes met his and she wondered how much she was ready to share about the week he'd been passed out. She supposed it might as well be everything. "The truth is while I haven't actually been here before, I've seen this place."

Rònan's eyes searched hers and he seemed to understand. "Come." He pulled her after him. "Though there isnae anywhere safe here, I'd feel better over there."

Erin understood what he meant when he led her to a wide rock next to the base of a nearby mountain. Though it didn't offer them much protection, it was better than being out in the open. Before she sat down, she gestured to him. "Help me pick some of this long grass."

"Why?"

She started yanking up grass. "Let's just call it a backup plan."

Though he shot her a quizzical look, he nodded. "Aye, then."

After they gathered up a few armloads, she tore a piece of material off the tunic tied around her waist and wrapped a few bundles. Then she headed for a nearby tree and picked up as many arrow sized limbs as she could find. Her eyes met his. "I'd suggest you gather up rocks."

"Rocks?"

"Yeah, small to fist-sized if possible," she said. "The sharper the better."

His eyes narrowed then he nodded when he figured out what she was up to. Fortunately, he was smart enough not voice it in case something or someone sinister was listening. By the time they sat on the ground with their backs to the rock and eyes on their surroundings, she had several piles of rocks, sticks, and bundled grass.

"Now tell me," he said. "What do you know of this place, lass?"

Erin picked out two especially sharp rocks and gave him one. Then she took a stick and handed it over. "Whittle while we chat. It's a good way to keep our minds off how creepy this place really is."

The corner of his lip hooked up as he eyed her skimming the rock along the end of the stick. Naturally, the goal was to make it into a sharp point.

Though she wasn't quite sure how she felt about speaking telepathically, she figured it was the best move possible considering where they were.

"I know about this place because I was somehow in and out of it with you," she said into his mind. *"And in answer to your earlier*

question, yes, I like to sing. I thought it might lend you some comfort."

"And 'twas you who kissed me, aye?" he responded.

Erin knew his eyes were on her face even as he kept at his stick. She was impressed by how smoothly he worked the stone and how quickly he set aside a well-pointed stick to start on another.

"Yes, I kissed you," she said. *"Let's just call it a heat of the moment move."*

"'Tis hard to imagine you craving such a moment when I was unable to kiss you back."

Erin arched a brow at him and couldn't stop a small grin. *"Have you looked at yourself lately?"*

Their eyes held for a moment before she dragged her gaze away, set aside one stick and started on another.

"Thank you then," he whispered into her mind. *"Between your bonnie voice and that kiss, it helped. In truth, I think what you did tore me free from this place."*

"In theory, maybe." She sighed. *"But it looks like I can bring you back just as easily."*

"'Tis not nearly as bad with you here," he said.

"That's only because I've put you to work." She snorted and eyed the endless gray rock. *"A damn good idea in these parts I'd say."*

"Aye," he agreed. *"But usually, I run a lot weaker when here. 'Tis strange I dinnae feel that way this time."* She knew he was watching her out of the corner of his eye. *"Mayhap you bolstered my energy in a way even Brae Stewart and her demi-god chieftain couldnae have anticipated."*

"I would've thought I drained your energy." Erin chuckled. *"You definitely got in some exercise."*

"Aye," he agreed, a smile in his voice as he finished with his stick, set it aside and picked up another. *"'Twas unstoppable."* He bent his knees and braced his booted feet on the ground. *"'Twas verra good."*

She set aside a stick and started on another, keeping a grin well-hidden as she discreetly eyed the bulge forming between his legs. *"You're getting turned on again, eh?"*

"Turned on?"

"Aroused."

"Och, aye. You seem to have a way with my beastie." He scowled. *"And 'tis a bloody uncomfortable thing when wearing trousers."*

"Your beastie." She chuckled again, surprised he kept pulling humor out of her when she could rarely muster it in the real world never mind this Celtic hell. *"You like to call it that, don't you?"* Erin couldn't help but wink at him. *"Not to say it doesn't have some ferocious qualities to it."*

While she sensed he wanted to joke, his expression grew serious as he started working on another stick. *"All aside, 'tis important that you know how thankful I am that you took the time to nurse me back to health. 'Twas admirable, lass."*

"No problem. I say you deserved it." She set aside her stick and started on another. *"You were determined to save Jackie and look out for me and Robert the Bruce at the same time. That's pretty admirable."*

Erin conveniently left out how poor it was that she lusted after him despite Jackie.

More than ready to change the subject, she said, *"I noticed you didn't fix my ripped pants with a flick of your wrist. Does that mean you can't use magic here?"*

She heard the surprise in his voice. *"Aye, perceptive of you."*

They started on more sticks at the same time.

"I try to pay attention." Her eyes met his. *"My bigger concern, however...since she's not technically part of this Otherworld, can Brae Stewart use magic here?"*

"I dinnae know." He shook his head. *"I havenae seen her use it here thus far so mayhap not."*

She was about to say more when his hand fell on her thigh and he shook his head. Alarmed, her eyes went to where he was looking. Someone was coming and based on the blackness surrounding them, it was nothing good. Erin pocketed some rocks, grabbed her lighter and focused on keeping fear repressed. It would do her no good right now.

Rònan pulled her up and squeezed her hand as they waited.

They didn't have to wait long.

The dark smear on the horizon shifted closer in a heartbeat and a beautiful yet sinister woman with black hair stopped in front of them. Erin didn't need to guess who she was.

Brae Stewart.

Brae looked at Rònan. "Ye just cannae get enough of this place, aye, dragon?"

Then her eyes met Erin's and narrowed.

A sense of recognition flared between them.

Had she somehow met Brae before? Because though she'd been here in brief flashes when trying to bring Rònan back, she didn't recall meeting anyone else. But she looked *so* familiar.

Brae's eyes stayed on Erin as she held out her hand. "If ye've a need to save yer dragon and avoid meeting something so sinister ye'll never be the same again, then give me the ring without strife, lass."

"Will you let us go free if I do?" Erin asked.

Brae nodded, clearly surprised by her response. "Aye, we will."

Erin knew there was only one way to handle this woman so she pretended to contemplate before she sighed and glanced at Rònan. "Sorry, but I'm not up for much more of this place."

Rònan frowned as she yanked off the ring—thankful she was able to this time—and held out a closed fist to Brae. "It's all yours."

If Erin wasn't mistaken, relief flickered in the woman's eyes as she went to take it.

Bad move on her part.

Erin tossed the ring up and lit her lighter, burning Brae's palm. When she yelped in pain, Erin took advantage of the moment and snagged the ring while side-kicking the Scotswoman in the stomach.

"Gimme the—" she started but Rònan was already on it.

He winked and tossed her a bundle of grass. Lighting it, she swung back around and went at Brae. She staggered back and leapt as Erin swiped low. Though she knew damn well Brae had caused nothing but harm, something was keeping her from turning lethal.

But Erin knew how to hurt someone.

So she whipped a small rock hard at Brae's forehead. It hit dead on and brought her to her knees. Erin thrashed the burning grass close, swamping the woman in smoke before she tagged her in the face.

"Bloody hell," Rònan said before he yanked Erin back and nodded to their right. "We've got to go, lass."

When she glanced in that direction, she understood why he sounded so urgent. Something huge and blacker than sin was heading their way. At the heart of it a man. Dark, glorious and evil but a man nonetheless.

One she recognized.

One she was more than willing to confront again.

"Fuck, no," she spat. Never one to flee, Erin slid the ring back on her finger, shook her head and yanked away. Before Rònan could catch her, she scooped up several sticks and another bushel of grass and strode toward the darkness.

"Bloody hell," Rònan said again.

"I've missed ye," the dark stranger whispered, his words reaching her long before they should have. "Are ye here to stay this time?"

Erin's steps slowed the closer she got to him.

Was she?

Was it time?

"Ye fight well," he murmured, his features becoming clearer and clearer. "I always knew ye would."

Erin stopped, vaguely aware of her loosening grip on the makeshift weapons as she whispered, "I know you."

"Aye." Though he was a ways out, he still managed to reel her in closer.

From far, far away she heard Rònan calling to her but couldn't remember why she should heed his cry. Why she should do anything but focus on remembering the dark man drawing closer.

"Erin," whispered sharply in her ear.

"I'm fine, Jackie," she assured, eyes glued to the man approaching.

It never once occurred to her that Jackie wasn't supposed to be there.

"No, you're not fine, Erin," Jackie said. "Look at me."

"I will," she assured. "In just a sec."

"No, now!"

Erin had a split second to recognize the urgency in her friend's voice before two horses barreled past.

Tosha and Eara.

Eara flew by but not Tosha. When the horse reared up, her attention refocused on trying to calm her.

"Get on me!" the horse cried.

When her eyes met Tosha's, she snapped out of whatever spell she'd been under and swung up. Confused but suddenly desperate to escape, she caught the sticks Rònan tossed to her before he swung onto Eara. When Brae stumbled to her feet, Erin whipped two sticks. One lodged in her shoulder and the other in her thigh, bringing her to her knees again.

Erin had no idea what they were racing toward except it looked like a cliff.

And all that was beyond was an ocean.

"Shit," Erin muttered under her breath. When she looked over her shoulder not only was the dark stranger racing after them but three dark mini clouds. Those had to be the *Genii Cucullati,* the nasty spirits born of the Celtic Otherworld Nicole had yapped about back when Erin first arrived in Scotland.

It turns out Nicole's yapping held a whole lot of truth.

"Tosha, not the best direction to go in!" she said, her eyes on the cliff again.

"'Tis the only direction, lass," Tosha said. *"Hold on tight."*

Erin might not trust the world in general but when it came to horses, they made more sense to her so she listened. She leaned down, held onto Tosha's mane and glanced at Rònan and Eara as they sailed over the cliff.

"Damn, are you kidding me?" she said to Tosha.

As she expected, the horse gave no response but leapt over the cliff as well. She didn't scream. Instead, she leaned down, pressed her face against Tosha's mane and figured if she was going out there was no better way to do it than on a horse.

This horse.

For a split second she wished it was Salve but felt a certain sense of peace that it wasn't. Her horse didn't deserve an ending like this. Not that Tosha did either.

Wind rushed by her face as they plummeted. A frigid wind that strangely enough, suddenly turned warm. She had no time to contemplate what that meant as they free-fell toward the ocean. Focused on remaining calm, on the certain inevitability that this was her end, Erin relaxed.

After all, this was an end that she had long deserved.

Or should have.

Because instead of splashing down the wind stopped and it felt like Tosha leapt a fence. Jolting up, she tried to make sense of her surroundings. An ocean no longer rushed at her but warriors raced in from either side.

Erin might be caught off guard and totally baffled but she recognized danger. When a warrior rushed up from the left, she whipped a rock at him. When another came from the right, she stabbed a stick into his side. She tried to make sense of her surroundings as Tosha flew onward. It was by no means a Celtic wasteland but just as rugged a landscape. Just as threatening in its own way.

Her eyes widened on the massive castle sitting on a cliff overlooking the ocean. She punched a guy in the face who got too close as she took in its staggered towers and numerous wall walks. She whipped more rocks at another as she took in its mighty dimensions and fierce nature.

Like her, the castle seemed to fight against its surroundings.

Fight against anything that meant to take it down.

Anything that thought it couldn't withstand all that was thrown its way.

"Come, lass," Rònan roared, falling in alongside her as too many warriors rushed in around them. They had just broken onto the rocky stretch in front of the castle when wind rushed over her. Eyes to the sky, Erin forgot to fight as she gaped. Monstrous serpentine bodies flew overhead and roared fire down.

Dragons.

One was prisms of blue. The other was black. Both were mighty. With gigantic wings and endless scales, they fought against those coming in from either side.

After that, it was all some sort of fairytale mixed with remnants of a nightmare from her youth. Except this time, it wasn't set to destroy her but…save her? Seeing your worst nightmare come to life and have it be your ally, not your enemy was incomprehensible. Some might say impossible.

Yet she was living it.

Her eyes flew to Rònan in confusion.

Big mistake.

Her vision blurred and he vanished off of Eara. For a moment she thought he might have been yanked off by the enemy. Then she processed what rose up overhead. A great, emerald body with massive wings and lethal talons.

She couldn't be seeing straight but knew she was.

It was Rònan.

Oddly enough, as Tosha raced toward the castle, any fear or disgust she might have felt toward dragons vanished. Instead, a warm glow started to snake through her veins. Almost like the feeling after a few shots of whisky but far better. Then an overwhelming feeling of power rushed through her. When a red haze fell over her vision, Erin realized she was responding to the dragons. This time, it wasn't sexual but a driving need to protect them. Somehow they belonged to her as much as she did them.

"Ye must not embrace yer current feelings right now or ye'll shift, lass," Tosha said. *"And 'tis not good to do that just yet. Not in current company."*

It hadn't occurred to her that she might be heading in that direction until she saw the glistening sheen of her skin. It almost seemed to glow. She had no time to fear it as her eyes were snagged by the shadow creature demi-god fluctuating in the air in the direction of the dragons.

Most specifically Rònan.

"This time, I will destroy the MacLeod," the dark man warned within her mind. *"Then ye will come be with me, lass. As it always should have been."*

"Not gonna happen," she muttered aloud. Though it was nearly impossible not to give into whatever her body was doing, she trusted Tosha's advice. They were almost to the first portcullis when the dark shadow rushed after Rònan.

Her heart leapt into her throat.

Hell no.

Going with her gut—a voice deep down inside—she mustered all the energy she could and whipped the remaining stick she'd whittled in the Otherworld straight into the center of the foggy mass. For a split second, she thought she saw the stick glimmer. Or was it her ring? Either way, though it only sailed through the darkness, the demi-god had a surprisingly strong reaction to it. The ground shook as the monster released a mighty roar of anguish then vanished. In response, the *Genii Cucullati* poofed away.

Confused by what appeared to be the defeat of their leader, the remaining warriors started to flee only to be swiftly incinerated by the dragons. At least most of them. It looked like a few were being taken prisoner.

Hoots and hollers of victory exploded around her as Tosha trotted into the courtyard. It took Erin several moments to realize the crowd was cheering for her. Uncomfortable, she stayed on the horse and tried to smile but found it impossible. Way too much sensory overload. The red haze in her vision faded away as a tall, well-muscled blond came alongside the horse.

"Greetings, lass. Welcome to MacLeod Castle. I'm Rònan's Da, Colin MacLeod." He offered a compassionate smile. "Stay put, I'll get you and Tosha to where 'tis quieter, aye?"

"Thanks, that'd be great," she murmured but couldn't say much more as her voice caught. No shocker considering her surroundings and who spoke to her. What a way to meet Rònan's father. Frozen by emotions on a horse.

Erin was never more grateful than when they entered the quiet stables and she realized her friends were here waiting for her.

Nicole, Jackie, *and* Cassie.

"Take some time alone with your friends, Erin," Colin said. "I'm sure Rònan and your Vikings will be waiting outside for you when you're ready." Before she could respond, he squeezed her hand, his eyes lighting with warmth. "Thank you for saving my son."

Erin nodded and finally managed a few soft words. "What about little Robert? Is he here? Is he okay?"

"Aye." Colin nodded. "Ye'll see him soon enough."

After he left, she slid off her horse and though she wasn't a fan of too much contact, she had no problem embracing her friends.

"I'm so glad you're here and okay," Cassie mumbled.

"Me too," Jackie murmured.

"You had us worried," Nicole added.

They held each other for a long minute before Erin finally pulled away but continued to hold Cassie's hand as she peered at her. It was hard to believe she was blind. But like Nicole with her impending deafness, her friend didn't want to be coddled. So Erin kept it light.

"I heard you lost your sight, Cassie," Erin said. "How are you doing with it? Hanging in there?"

"Not counting the Otherworld crap we're all dealing with, I'm good." A small, content smile came to Cassie's lips. "Surprisingly good."

"Glad to hear it. I knew you'd handle it like a champ." She squeezed her hand. "Never doubted it for a second."

"Speaking of handling things," Nicole said. "Though I've had a chance to thank you individually, now that I've got you all together I want to thank you all so much for the hearing aid you bought me." She grinned and cocked her head as though listening to something. "It's amazing how much I can hear now."

"Our pleasure," Cassie said, still smiling.

"I'm so glad you like it," Jackie said.

"And I'm glad to see you're actually wearing it." Erin winked. "Seeing how stubborn you can be."

Nicole shrugged and grinned. "I just needed to work through some things is all."

"Well, I'm glad you did," Cassie said. "You and Niall both." She was uncannily accurate with her aim when she put her hand on Nicole's belly. "Now you both can work as a team to teach your little one not to be so stubborn and mule-headed like his parents once were."

Nicole snorted and cocked the corner of her lip. "And what makes you think we've changed any?"

"Right." Jackie chuckled. "But as far as I can tell, Niall's had a positive influence on you."

Nicole's brows lowered. "You say that as though I needed it."

"Enough, ladies," Erin intercepted, not in the mood for one of the minor tiffs the two could get into. "I need someone to catch me up on what's going on before I head back outside. I need my head on straight before I deal with that crowd."

When a stable boy tried to lead the horse away, she shook her head. "Just show me to Tosha's stall and I'll take care of her."

"Everyone knew something was going down in Scandinavia but your Viking posse seemed to sense it first," Nicole said as her friends followed her and Tosha into a stall. "They said they tried to stop you from going into your lodge that night but you were having none of it."

"I was worried about Rònan." Erin unstrapped the saddle. "He was having a rough time."

"Yeah, everyone understood that," Nicole said. "Unfortunately, nobody figured you might be sucked into the Otherworld along with him."

"So what made everyone figure it out beforehand?" Erin said as she pulled off the saddle and hung it. "What exactly did they sense?"

"Darkness and evil," Nicole said. "All around you for a long time."

"I don't get it." Confused, Erin frowned. "For a long time? I'd only been in there a few minutes before Rònan and I ended up in the Otherworld."

"Nope. Incorrect." Nicole shook her head. "Your Viking posse was right behind you when you entered the lodge. Yet when they stepped inside, there was no sign of Rònan and you were sound asleep on the bed."

"No." Erin shook her head. "I can assure you that Rònan and I were right there." She cleared her throat. "And we definitely weren't sleeping."

"And I can assure you, it was only you, Erin," Jackie said softly. "I know because I spent the better half of a month caring for you."

Chapter Twelve

ARMS CROSSED OVER his chest, Rònan leaned against the outside of the stables and eyed Tait. "Ye dinnae need to wait out here. Erin will be just fine." He nodded at the boisterous crowd. "Go celebrate and enjoy my clan. I insist."

"While thankful for your hospitality, we prefer to lay eyes on Erin before we go anywhere," Bjorn said.

Both Vikings ignored the numerous lasses trying to get their attention every bit as much as Rònan did the ones sidling up to him. And that was a first. Not a day had gone by when he didn't have a lass or two or even three tucked against his side. But they no longer held any appeal. At least not the ones in his immediate vicinity. No, if anything he was becoming uncomfortably aware that he had lain with most of them.

Tait, clearly sensing his thoughts, shot him a small grin. "It will be interesting to see Erin's reaction to your endless fans."

Rònan narrowed his eyes. "As if ye didnae have enough of yer own back in Scandinavia."

"Aye," Tait relented. He smirked at several lasses who again sidled up next to Rònan. "Something tells me it will be different with you." His eyes went to the women. "Surrounded by so many all the time."

"Enough." Bjorn frowned at Tait. "You are a Viking dragon enjoying your kin's hospitality. Remember that and behave better."

Tait scowled but said nothing more as Rònan again ushered the women away, trying his best to be kind about it. Yet he grew frustrated. Not with the lasses but with himself. Mainly because he realized how focused he had been on the next set of thighs he'd settle between rather than working toward being an admirable chieftain.

"'Tis bloody good to see ye well, Cousin," Niall said. Just in time, his friend leaned against the stables beside him, fending off women before they drifted too close to Rònan. "Ye need to stop vanishing for such long bouts."

Rònan had been filled in on what happened after he left and how long he'd been gone. This time around, Niall held out more faith that he would return alive. Not to say a hearty embrace wasn't involved when he reappeared.

"Aye, 'tis good to see ye well indeed," Logan said, leaning against the stables on his other side, a secondary stopper to any lasses attempting to approach. "I've had word sent to MacLomain Castle about recent developments. Though Connell is overseeing everything well enough, Machara's parents have joined him there."

He had seen little of Colin and McKayla MacLomain since this all began. Rònan nodded. "How fare our aunt and uncle? It has been too long since I last saw them."

"Good." Logan chuckled and nodded at the Vikings. "Aunt McKayla got it in her head to write about them. Apparently, she's started having visions about them and lasses from the future."

Rònan frowned. "Our lasses?"

"God, nay." Logan shook his head. "They arenae Brouns."

Not relieved in the least, a response died on his lips when Erin and her friends finally came out of the stables. Thanks to Rònan's father, the clan knew not to crowd her or even cheer for her until the celebrations later tonight. That should have been something Rònan saw to but it hadn't even occurred to him until his mother filled him in. He knew Erin didn't like to be touched, never mind being made the center of so much attention no matter how well-intentioned it was.

Rònan only held back long enough for Erin to lead Cassie to Logan before he took Erin's hand and tried to pull her after him.

"Hey, slow down, Rònan." She pulled her hand free before turning back. Her eyes went to Tait and Bjorn. "That was you guys back there in dragon form protecting me, wasn't it?"

Both nodded.

"Thank you." She hugged Bjorn first and Rònan did his best to keep a frown off his face.

"Thank you both so much," she reiterated as she embraced Tait.

Rònan didn't realize he was stepping forward until Niall grabbed his upper arm, shook his head and murmured into his mind, *"Wait your turn then go about it correctly, Cousin. Take advantage of the fact you're Laird here and act accordingly. Impress her. Woo the bloody lass, aye?"*

Though Rònan scowled at his friend, he knew he was right.

But how to woo a lass? They had always just fallen into his arms. And was he truly ready to make such efforts for a lass's affections? To focus on just one when there were so many? As he thought of all Erin had done for him, how she had felt in his arms earlier, he knew without hesitation that he was willing to make the effort. No, he *needed* to if he stood any chance at…what? Forever? Love? The gods only knew. One thing was certain, he didn't like her in another man's arms.

Tait, of course, took full advantage of Erin's hug and held her longer than necessary. Like Rònan, the Vikings were taller than most so had the advantage of lifting her up to hug her. Something that conveniently involved a wee bit too much body contact.

At least, when it came to her Viking posse.

So when Tait finally released her, Rònan didn't take her hand and pull her after him again but instead held out the crook of his elbow and offered the most charming smile he could muster. "Welcome to my castle. Might I escort you to your chamber?"

When she hesitated, he was shocked to feel his heart slam into his throat. What if he had no chance with her? What if the sex was nothing more than sex and she was truly interested in pursuing one of the Vikings? He couldn't stop her if that was her wish. If he'd learned nothing else about Erin, it was that she had her own mind and no man could force her to go in a direction she didn't want to go.

"That'd be great," she finally said. "Thanks."

When she took his arm, he breathed a sigh of relief. He still stood a fighting chance. Though tempted beyond reason to scoop her up to show every man here that he wanted her, his gut told him to keep with what he was doing. What Niall suggested. *Wooing* her.

Again, he was thankful to his Da that the crowd wasn't boisterous but parted as he walked her up the stairs. Instead, all smiled broadly, thanking her softly as she passed. After all, it was no average day that they welcomed a lass who had just saved their laird and most likely their clan.

He still wondered exactly what had happened both here and in the Otherworld. The last he saw she was speaking to the demi-god shadow as though she knew it...or *him*. The next thing he knew, she snapped out of whatever spell she was under. Then, thanks not only to his Ma and Uncle Grant but the Vikings, they were pulled back here to MacLeod Castle.

According to Grant, this was where Jackie had said they would end up. Because, as it turned out, Jackie was the only one who made contact with Erin in the Otherworld.

Rònan still wasn't entirely sure why Grant and his mother so readily trusted a lass they had only just met, but could only be grateful they had listened to her. Yet still, how had Erin defeated the evil demi-god? Better yet, had she or was it but another ruse by the enemy? These were concerns he and his immediate kin shared though they said nothing to his clan.

More magic and warriors than usual would be defending the castle tonight lest the enemy somehow returned. His clan would think nothing of it as his Da, the former laird, had always exercised an abundance of caution after battles in the past.

"This place is damn impressive," Erin said softly as they entered the castle and she took in everything. He had never paid much attention to the great hall until seeing it through her eyes...literally. Their thoughts were bonded enough that he saw how majestic the high ceiling and tall stained-glass windows were. The way she felt as her eyes swept over multiple fires burning on monstrous hearths. How awed she was by the massive tapestries depicting sweeping, angry oceans with dragons flying overhead. Though glorious in its own right, she especially liked the stalwart angles and dangerous edges of the castle.

"Many thanks, lass," he said.

His mother greeted them by embracing Erin and holding her tight. "Again, I find myself so thankful to you, lass." She pulled back and held Erin at arm's length. "You saved my boy. For that, I will forever owe you."

"Thanks, but you don't owe me a thing." Erin shook her head. "The way I figure it we're all working together as a team, right? If I'm going to bat for someone, it's not because I want them to feel like they owe me but because I respected them enough to go to bat for them to begin with."

When Torra's brows shot up, Erin shrugged. "That's how it was in the military and if nothing else, I'm a proud American."

"Aye," Torra said with approval. "You take pride in the people you call yours and would defend them until your dying breath, aye?"

"Absolutely."

Torra's eyes went from Rònan to Erin, her regard a bit too curious for his taste. He wished she didn't ask what she did in light of so many people standing quietly nearby, eager for gossip.

"So my son has earned your respect? If so, why?"

"He has," Erin said without hesitation. "Not only because I know he worked toward making Nicole happy when she needed it most but because of his devotion to protecting Robert the Bruce, Jackie and myself."

Rònan puffed up with pride. She truly thought that of him? She was that impressed? Then her next words took him back down to scale. Words that let him know she was more than aware of the endless women eying him with a, I've-had-you-before-and-will-have-you-again look.

"Even despite his frivolous ways with women," Erin said. "His heart's in the right place."

Though his mother showed no outward sign, he didn't miss the flicker of amusement in her eyes. "Aye, dragon lass." Torra's eyes searched Erin's. "I believe at long last his heart truly *is* in the right place."

Rònan felt Erin tense at being addressed as a dragon but he also felt the rightness she experienced at being called such. She was truly accepting what she was.

They had only taken a few more steps toward the stairs before his sister and another cousin blocked their way. Grant's daughter, Lair came forward first and took Erin's hand, eyes soft as she introduced herself then said, "Welcome, Erin. Thank ye for what ye've done for my kin."

"Nice to meet you too, Lair." Erin nodded. "And my pleasure as far as your kin goes."

Next came his sister, Seònaid. He didn't miss the slight widening of Erin's eyes as she looked up and said, "Wow, you're Rònan's twin aren't you?"

"Aye," Seònaid said as she embraced Erin. Though his sister spoke so softly nobody could hear, Rònan didn't miss it with his

159

superior hearing. "'Tis obvious my brother didnae mention me. Dinnae grow upset with him, aye?" He heard both the smile and purpose in her voice. "'Twas only because his mind was so thoroughly occupied elsewhere."

"It's all good," Erin said before Seònaid pulled away. "You're the sort I'd much rather meet in person instead of hearing about you first anyway."

"Aye?" Seònaid eyed her. "Why is that?"

"Because I prefer looking you in the eyes rather than forming an opinion of you based on what your brother said," she provided. "No offense, but it might've been biased."

Rònan was caught off guard when Seònaid asked, "And your opinion is what having only just met me?"

His sister cared nothing for what others thought of her any more than he usually did.

"Based on how you defend those you care for, I'd say you're my kind of girl," Erin said. "And I look forward to getting to know you better."

"So yer a bit o' a diplomat." A wise look entered his sister's eyes. "'Tis good that."

If nothing else, Rònan always paid attention to Seònaid's take on people. She had liked Nicole. That was no surprise. Nicole might be blunt and stubborn, but there was no one you'd rather have at your back. Yet he had never heard Seònaid say what she just had to Erin. Something so political. When his sister stepped back and her eyes met his, he was surprised to see it for what it was. His sister thought Erin would be a good addition to this clan. What they needed.

She also thought Erin was the perfect match for him.

He barely had a moment to process that before a voice he knew all too well muttered, "Och, step aside, ye bloody bastard," and yet another cousin dropped to a knee in front of Erin and lowered her head before offering her sword and meeting Erin's eyes. "Cousin to Rònan, my name is Machara MacLomain. My devotion and sword are yers. I thank ye for fighting so fiercely to protect my kin."

Dealing with Machara was always an ordeal so Rònan was curious how Erin would handle it. Though tempted to intercept, the sharp look his sister shot him kept him quiet.

"Trust that Erin can handle this," Seònaid whispered into his mind.

And handle it she did in the most unexpected way.

Erin cocked her head and narrowed her eyes on the sword Machara continued to hold out. "That's a good looking blade." She ran her finger along the blunt edge then touched the other side, clearly not interested in being political or winning anyone over in the least. "Sharp as hell." Her eyes met Machara's. "I'll bet you sharpen it yourself."

"Aye. Nobody else is allowed near this blade." Machara kept holding it out. "Would you like to hold it?"

"Would I ever." Erin grinned when Machara handed it over, murmuring, "It's heavier than I expected. Damn near perfect." Her eyes flickered to his cousin before returning to the sword. "But that makes sense. It's made to suit your size."

Rònan thought for a moment he was wrong and that Erin was playing to the clan after all. But when she swooped it a few times with pure admiration in her eyes the suspicion fizzled away.

Machara watched the way Erin handled the blade with admiration. "Keep it if ye like."

"Though tempted, I've got to say no." Erin reluctantly handed it back, her eyes meeting Machara's. "I couldn't do this blade justice. It's not suited to my size. Thank you though."

"I can have it welded down to suit ye," Machara offered.

"Again, thanks but..." Erin moved closer and whispered in Machara's ear something that made both him and his cousin smile.

"Well then, lass," Machara said as she pulled back and spoke loud enough that all might hear. "I shall meet ye in the MacLeod armory later and we'll have a blade welded to suit yer needs, aye?"

Erin nodded. "I'd like that."

"As would I." Machara stepped aside, met Rònan's eyes and gestured up the stairs. "Might ye see the lass to her chamber then, Cousin?"

"Gladly." When Erin slid her arm through his, he led her up the stairs. The hall fell unnaturally silent as they walked.

"Why is everyone so quiet again?" Erin said into his mind.

"Because they show you honor."

"Did you ask them to do that?"

161

Though tempted to take credit, he knew better. Erin deserved the truth. *"Regrettably, nay. 'Twas my Da who ensured you would not be overwhelmed any further. That my clan would show their thankfulness in a more respectful and reserved nature."* He sighed. *"My apologies that I didnae think to make sure of it before him, that I was so narrow of mind."*

Erin's eyes met his and held for a moment before they went to the wall. To all the weapons glittering in and out of the endless torchlight. *"Again, I'm impressed. This place is amazing. I can only imagine the history it shares with the MacLomains."*

"This castle has a long history," he said aloud but softly when he knew they were beyond earshot of everyone. "Ages of which it was held by the MacLomain's main rival, enemies all."

"And who was that?" She skimmed her fingers along the weapons hanging between the torches as they climbed.

"Us, the MacLeod's." When her eyes shot to him in confusion, he wondered if this was any sort of conversation he wanted to have right now. "Did you not know that the MacLeod's and MacLomain's were longtime rivals before my parents came together?"

"I didn't," she said as they reached the top of the stairs. "When did they get together?"

"About twenty-seven winters ago." He put his hand to her lower back and led her alongside the balustrade overseeing the great hall. "Before that, the MacLomains and my clan were arch enemies. For centuries, in fact."

"No shit." She continued to admire the castle. "Why's that?"

"As I heard it told the MacLeods and MacLomains saw things differently. Several Broun and MacLomain couples dealt more directly with MacLeod strife including Adlin MacLomain and his love," Rònan said. "'Twas as simple as that until my parents came together and formed a truce betwixt the clans."

"So your clan were the bad guys." She offered a rare grin as he led her up another set of stairs. "That definitely lends a bit of intrigue to the story."

"Intrigue?"

"Sure." Her words trailed off at the top as she eyed his chamber. "Wow," she whispered taking in its large size, the multiple arrow slit windows staggered by three wider windows. The multiple wall-bracketed torches. The huge hearth that took up a quarter of the room with a crackling fire. More so, her eyes shot to the bed.

His bed.

Though it had long been his masterpiece with its intricate dragon headboard, it suddenly looked sinister. A place that he had brought far too many lasses.

All the wrong lasses.

"Nay." He shook his head, grabbed Erin's hand and pulled her after him. "This room isnae for you."

"Why?" she argued. "It looks comfortable and I'm tired."

"Ye might find yer old room more to yer liking brother," Seònaid said into his mind.

"Nay." He shook his head. *"It hasnae been used in ages and 'tis far too small."*

"Ye might be surprised," Seònaid said. *"We had an unexpected visit from Adlin MacLomain whilst ye were away. He thought mayhap ye'd want some changes made before ye returned."*

Though Adlin MacLomain had long since passed away, his ghost was known to pop in on very rare occasions. He had already helped Niall and Rònan with the weapons they created for Nicole. Now it seemed he was up to more mischief.

"Where are we going?" Erin frowned as he led her back down the stairs then along another long, narrow arched corridor. "I would've been just fine crashing for a bit in that other room."

"Nay," he said. "There is somewhere more comfortable."

The room he led her to overlooked the ocean on the highest level at the backside of the castle. Unlike most chambers, it had its own private wall walk. When he opened the door, he was dumbfounded by what he found. Gone was the room from his youth. In its place, a chamber even larger and more sweeping than his current one.

"Oh *damn*," Erin murmured as she walked in.

"Bloody hell," Rònan whispered.

With help from what could have only been magic, walls had been removed, combining several rooms into one. Even the length of the wall walk had been expanded with animal skins pulled back on either side so the roar of the ocean filled the room. The hearth was a masterpiece but not as large as the one in the other chamber. He actually preferred its size because the other gave off too much heat.

A table with food and drinks sat in the corner and a tub steamed with water. Torches burned and some of his favorite nautical dragon tapestries now hung on the walls.

Yet nothing was as astounding as the behemoth four poster bed framed on either side by torches. However, it was the headboard that drew their attention.

"Incredible," Erin whispered as she walked over to it. "Look at this workmanship. Unreal."

Rònan's eyes narrowed. Not only did it put the one in his chamber to shame but it depicted not one but two dragons. Entwined, there was both a sensual and fierce sense about them. As though they fought for dominance yet were willing to share, to be as one. When Erin traced her finger through the grooves and over the masterful curves of the larger dragon, fire flared beneath his skin. Flashes of her riding him flickered through his mind and he almost groaned. Determined to set aside his intense lust, he focused on pouring two mugs of whisky and handed her one.

"Thanks." She took a hearty gulp and kept eying the dragons, as affected by them as he was. "Interesting artwork, Rònan." Her eyes met his. "Is this room yours then? Better yet, the bed?"

"Nay." Overheated, he invited her to join him on the wall walk. "The first chamber I brought you to was mine."

"I see." She leaned against the railing and eyed him. "So why didn't you want me to crash there for a bit? Afraid all the other girls might get jealous?"

Rònan shook his head and debated how much to tell her. In the end, he went with the truth. She deserved it at the very least. "Nay, I didnae want you lying where others had."

He almost said 'so many others' but decided that level of honesty was unneeded.

Erin crossed her arms over her chest. "Are you serious?"

"Aye, never more so."

Their eyes held before she dragged her gaze to the sea. "While I appreciate it more than you know, you need to understand that I'm not looking for anything substantial. I don't do relationships."

Rònan almost said he agreed but the words caught in his throat so he took another swig of whisky.

"So what's the deal with this chamber? Better yet, that headboard," she said. "Why are there two dragons on it? My guess is a male and female. Is this your parent's room?"

"Nay." He shook his head. "Besides, only my Ma is half dragon. Not Da."

"Then what's up with it then?" She frowned. "Is this Seònaid's room? Is she a shifter with a husband I haven't met yet?"

"Nay, my sister isnae half dragon." Rònan scowled, feeling more and more uncomfortable. "'Tis just an extra room that will be yours as long as you're here."

Erin's eyes narrowed. "Why are you lying to me?"

Why *was* he lying? But he knew. He wasn't sure what her reaction would be. But he supposed he might as well be partially truthful because she would find out eventually. "This was my chamber when I was a bairn. Some updates have been made since including a new headboard."

"Ah." She grinned. "So this was your room when you were a kid?"

"Aye," he said. "'Twas much smaller then."

"Well, I imagine you were too." She shrugged and kept a smile on her face. "Then again, I'll bet you were big even then."

Before he could respond, she gestured at the wall walk. "Was this here?"

He nodded. "'Twas not as large, though."

Her brows perked as she peered down at the long drop to the ocean. "I'm surprised your mother was okay with you having access to this."

"Och, I was flying when I was a wee one," he scoffed. "And I ran hotter than most so 'twas a good choice for me."

"Right, flying," she murmured and took another sip of whisky, the purple in her eyes flaring to life in the dying sun. "So why did you end up in a chamber with fewer windows and a bigger fire?"

Rònan knew he looked guilty when he offered a sheepish grin. "Nothing gets a lass out of her dress faster than a hot chamber."

Erin snorted before she outright laughed. "You're serious aren't you?"

Rònan shrugged, cocked the corner of his lip and nodded.

Erin contemplated him with that same smile lingering on her lips. "So why do I get the impression that you're looking for a little more between us?" She shook her head. "When it's clear you like to play."

When he hesitated, she said, "Just say what's on your mind, Rònan. You already know where I stand and that's not gonna change." Erin gave him a pointed look. "Nothing you say is going to sway me so you might as well keep things on the level."

"On the level?"

"Just keep being honest because I'm right here, right now, but not forever." Her eyes stayed with his. "And I'd think better of you if you did. I kinda like the idea of us being friends."

Friends?

Nothing about this conversation was going in the direction he wanted.

Or was it?

He had no idea. Everything about Erin was a first.

"Aye, being friends is good," he agreed. "But you should know that..." He cleared his throat and worked at wording things correctly. "I find myself embarrassed by the lasses here..." Rònan shook his head. "Nay, not by the lasses but by my behavior up until now. How frivolous I've been."

"Really? You're having regrets?" Erin cocked her head and he tried not to get distracted by the way the wind tried to loosen her wild curls. "Why?"

"For a lot of reasons." Rònan set aside his mug and braced his elbows on the railing as he stared at the horizon. "Lasses aside, I haven't behaved as a new Laird should. Though my parents and even my sister have always supported me, I've not missed their occasional looks of disappointment." He shrugged. "Until now, it hasnae bothered me but then I suppose I figured I had plenty of time to prove my worth. And as I saw it, a lad should take advantage of his youth whilst he has it."

"But now?" she prompted. "What's changed? That I'm here?"

"In some ways, aye. You've had a profound effect on me to be sure. But 'tis not just that." He shook his head. "Something about being taken again and again to the Celtic Otherworld is making me reevaluate things." He frowned at the sunset. "Much like that sun, I feel like I'm sinking into the horizon, drifting further and further away from this reality. The more that happens, the more I appreciate everything I took for granted."

"But not all the women?"

"Nay." He sighed. "Though bonnie, kind lasses all, they seem to be the last thing I'm missing."

"It sounds to me like you're growing up, Rònan." Erin took another sip of whisky, her eyes lingering on the ocean as well. "Happens to us all at one point or another."

A comfortable silence settled between them before she continued. "On the off chance the enemy's still out there, that bastard in the Otherworld isn't gonna get you in the end." Her determined eyes met his. "None of us is going to let that happen."

He saw by the conviction in her eyes that she meant it.

"Thank you, lass."

What neither said was that they might not have a choice.

"While I know it's probably the last thing you want to talk about," Erin said. "What do you make of our experience in the Otherworld? The fact that you were there the whole time while I was apparently snoozing away in Scandinavia." She leaned back against the railing and kept her eyes on his. "If what everyone's saying is true then there's no way you and I had sex. More than that, even though I miraculously appeared here, was I really with you in the Otherworld to begin with?"

Rònan couldn't help but take her hand, never more serious. "Aye, you were there with me, one way or another. As to the sex?" He grinned. "Even if 'twas not real 'twas an unforgettable experience."

He *almost* said it was one well worth experiencing again but he figured that was *not* what Niall meant when he urged Rònan to woo her.

"Those are a whole lot of repressed thoughts there." Erin's lips curled up slightly. "And I'm sure as hell not opposed to repeating that unforgettable experience as long as you know it goes no further."

That was about the last thing he thought she would say and tried like hell not to show too much of a reaction. "'Tis a tempting offer, lass."

When his blood stirred, he leaned against the railing facing the ocean once more.

Erin shook her head, her eyes falling to a groin he kept out of sight. "Aroused again I take it?"

"Aye." He resumed drinking and growled into his cup, "You well know I cannae control it around you."

"Flattered," she murmured and kept sipping from her cup. "Look at the bright side. At least we can look at one another and chat now without wanting to rip each other's clothes off."

"Matter of opinion," he muttered. Determined to get his erection under control, he changed the subject. "So why did it seem as if you knew the dark demi-god in the Otherworld?"

Clearly startled by the topic switch, she inhaled deeply and shook her head. "I have no idea."

When he frowned, she continued reluctantly. "All right, let's just say he looked like someone from my childhood."

"He?" Rònan frowned. Fear for her made his chest tighten. "Lass, the demi-god has never appeared as anything but a black mass. Do you mean to say you saw the form of a man? One you once knew?"

When Rònan sensed Erin closing up, he shook his head and gently seized her upper arm. "This is important. If the dark laird is not yet defeated, whatever you know could verra well save not only our kin but the wee King."

Though he knew she wanted to fight him, there was a sharp intelligence in her eyes that told him that she understood how dire the situation was. "I," she started then trailed off, obviously trying to gather her courage. "There was a…something bad happened to me when I was a kid. When it happened, he was there…that man."

"What does he look like? Does he have a name?"

Both fear and defiance flashed in her eyes.

"He's dark. His looks, everything." She pulled away. "No name."

Though tempted to demand more details, he also knew that pushing her would not be good.

"I need to rest," she said and headed back inside, clearly finished with the conversation.

"Of course." Rònan followed her in and with the flick of his wrist, her bath water was warm again. He gestured at the trunk at the end of the bed. "My guess is you'll find a change of clothes in that."

"Yeah, okay." She sat on the edge of the bed, discontent. "Thanks."

When he hesitated, her eyes met his. "I need you to go, Rònan."

"Aye, lass," he murmured. "Please eat if you've the chance."

Though all he wanted to do was stay and comfort her, he well understood that her pain was something she was long used to tackling alone. So he left. Not surprisingly, Tait and Bjorn stood guard outside the door, weapons in hand.

"Bloody hell," he muttered, eying them. "Ye dinnae need to be here."

"We watch over our kin," Bjorn said.

Rònan narrowed his eyes. "Not too closely I hope."

When Tait made to speak, Bjorn shook his head sharply and spoke for them both. "We protect our kin, Highlander. Never would we disrespect her."

Rònan was about to say that his own warriors could watch over her just as readily but his Ma appeared before he could.

"Bathe and dress in full MacLeod regalia," she said, eyes stern. "After all, this is an eve that will either make or break yer future, Son."

Chapter Thirteen

ERIN HAD NO idea what time it was when she awoke, only that she would much rather stay in the bed. Nothing had ever felt more welcoming and comfortable. Nonetheless, she heard bagpipes trilling from somewhere in the castle so figured the celebrations were underway. Oddly enough, the bathwater was still warm so she enjoyed it thoroughly before exploring the contents of the trunk.

Nothing but dresses.

Though reluctant, she put one on, thrilled to find that it fit her like a glove. After she pulled on boots, she dried her hair the best she could in front of the fire. Like Megan said, it was changing. Instead of frizzing out of control, it was full and smooth, silky almost.

Taking her time to enjoy some food and whisky, she mulled over her conversation with Rònan. Should she have told him so much? Thankfully, he hadn't demanded more answers when she shut him down. Good thing because she still had no solid explanation and she did not like dealing with people when she didn't have all her facts straight.

Even so, she had the overwhelming feeling that Rònan wouldn't judge her either way. That despite tackling his own issues, he would have wanted to help her through her troubles. The problem? Her troubles ran deep and long.

But she couldn't focus on her past right now. She needed to make a show of it tonight, so she finally headed out. Erin smiled when she found her Viking posse outside the door. "Hell, guys, if I knew you were waiting around I would've sped up the 'get ready' process."

While Bjorn seemed unfazed by her appearance, Tait sort of snapped to like a soldier who had almost drifted off when he was on duty. Bjorn held out his elbow to escort her but she didn't miss the way his eyes flickered over her with admiration.

"How fare you, woman?" he asked when she wrapped elbows and they started walking.

"Tired," she answered honestly, repressing a chuckle when Tait walked alongside, nearly tripping over himself as he eyed her.

"You look beautiful," Tait stuttered. "Very much so."

"Thanks." She yanked at the top of the dress. "Because I'm seriously not into this look."

"It is always good to see the shape of your legs in trousers," Tait complied obediently, eyes glued to her overabundance of cleavage. "But Scottish attire agrees with you too."

"Tait," Bjorn warned as little Robert the Bruce came flying down the hallway.

"Erin!"

Thrilled to see him, she crouched and gave him a big hug when he flew into her arms. It felt good to be around him again. Out of all this bullshit, he seemed to be the only one who made sense.

"I didnae think I would see ye again," Robert said into her neck. "I thought ye were dead."

"No way." She stroked his hair. "I like to stick around."

"Stick around?"

"Stay close to you."

"Aye, 'tis good," he murmured.

It was clear he had no intention of letting go, so she lifted him and carried him on her hip. "Where's your mother? Is she here?"

"Nay," he said. "Laird Grant is my protector until I see her again."

"Then you're well protected," she assured. "Because he's the best."

"Aye," Robert agreed. "He says ye are too."

"Really?" She smiled. "Smart man."

"Do you know where you are going, woman?" Bjorn said from behind.

"Yes," she said over her shoulder. "I pay attention."

Erin weaved through several halls and down stairs before she eventually arrived at the top of the stairs leading to the boisterous great hall below.

"Ye may set me down M'lady," Robert said.

When she shook her head, he did the same. "Please, 'tis only proper that I escort ye down, such as ye are."

Erin's eyes met Robert's. "Such as I am?"

"Aye." Robert nodded solemnly. "A great lady who saved a clan, who saved a laird."

Appreciating the serious look in his eyes, she set him down and crouched. "Are you sure you're all right?" She narrowed her eyes. "Because we can always avoid the crowd and go horseback riding or something."

"Och, nay." He shook his head. "'Twould be ill of us both not to join the MacLeod's right now."

A part of her was sad that a little boy felt so much responsibility but another part understood. In a weird way, she had been in the same position at his age.

"Okay, then." She stood and held out her hand. "Lead the way."

"Aye," Robert agreed and took her hand. Unlike the peace Rònan's father bought for her going up the stairs earlier, it was an entirely different story going down.

While she might've thought the concept absurd weeks ago, Erin was overly aware of all that had come to pass. Now she was going down the stairs with the future King of Scotland and two Viking dragon bodyguards trailing them as the crowd roared.

For her.

She should have drank more whisky.

The more the crowd cheered, the more her world closed in. She didn't deserve this. Never had, never would. The only thing that kept her going was the little hand in hers and...the man waiting at the bottom of the stairs.

Rònan.

Erin had never seen him dressed quite like this. He wore a long sleeved tunic. With tall black boots, his black and yellow plaid was wrapped to perfection with a shiny brooch at his shoulder.

He looked downright respectable.

Truly handsome.

Noble.

Not that he wasn't damn hot in general because he was but right now, hands locked behind his back, stance tall, he appeared...not just a gentleman but proud of what he wore. Proud of his uniform. And something about that, something about seeing him taking responsibility, made walking down the stairs easier.

If he could be strong, so could she.

With a renewed sense of purpose, she made it down the stairs. Little Robert stopped at the bottom, turned and bowed to her before he lifted her hand to Rònan and said to him, "Care well for my friend, Laird MacLeod."

Rònan bowed in kind to Robert. "Aye, my future King." Then he took her hand and lowered his head. "Erin."

Her heart leapt when their eyes connected. Why did that always happen? She didn't bother trying to talk because she didn't trust her vocal chords. Instead, she wrapped her elbow with his and let him walk her through the cheering crowd.

"They only mean to thank you, lass. 'Twill be for a short time," he said into her mind. *"I can lead you away from them if you like."*

Erin was tempted to say yes and bolt until her eyes found her friends. They fell in at her side and Jackie took her free hand. That's all it took.

Though she might have always thought she didn't need them, something about this moment reminded her that she did. That good friends were everything. She squeezed Jackie's hand and offered them a smile of acknowledgment before they fell away and she ended up standing in front of the largest fire in the hall. When they stopped, the crowd quieted and a servant handed her a mug.

Rònan's hand slipped into hers as he addressed the crowd. "Thank ye all for showing Erin such respect!"

The crowd roared to life again.

"Would you like to speak," Rònan said into her mind. *"Because 'tis your right."*

Speak? To this many people? Was he out of his mind? *"Hell, no."*

"Aye, then, lass."

With a hand to her back, he raised a mug in the air.

The room grew silent.

"Might we all toast to a lass we never saw coming. One that I couldnae be more grateful to." They cheered and nodded their agreement as they held their mugs in the air before drinking.

When they calmed, he set aside his mug and made a point of meeting their eyes before his gaze turned to her, his voice just loud enough. "Thank ye for saving me, lass. More than that, thank ye for saving my clan. Ye put my welfare and my clans before yers. 'Twas truly heroic and willnae be forgotten."

Another loud round of cheers filled the great hall and her cheeks warmed. Not sure what else to do, she nodded and did her best to smile.

"Now I urge everyone to celebrate and enjoy themselves," Rònan declared. "Yet as always in these times, remain ever vigilant."

"Aye!" many roared as the pipes resumed and the crowd's attention finally focused not on her but on partying.

Rònan's eyes turned her way. "Have you eaten? Are you hungry?"

"I'm good. I ate upstairs," she said. "Thanks."

He nodded and murmured, "You look verra beautiful, lass."

His eyes flickered over her not lewdly but with admiration.

"Hmm." She cocked a small grin at him. "Look at you acting so respectable."

"'Tis good, aye?"

"It is," she acknowledged and winked. "Though I wouldn't put away the bad boy entirely."

"I don't think that'd be possible," Nicole said as she and Niall joined them. She shook her head and grinned at Rònan. "Gotta say though, I'm super impressed by the change in you." Nicole tugged at his plaid. "And way to clean up, Sweetie."

Niall snorted but grinned with affection at Nicole. "As I recall, the last time you were here your behavior well suited Rònan's."

Erin eyed her. "Oh yeah? What'd you do?"

Nicole waved away Erin's question. "Nothing worth dredging up."

"Then I'll just get it out of Rònan later," Erin said.

"Nay." Rònan chuckled and shook his head. "'Tis not mine for the telling."

"What am I missing?" Jackie asked as she joined them. "What'd Nicole do now?"

Nicole groaned. "Nothing. Enough about me." She eyed Erin up and down. "I say we get busy complimenting Erin on how *awesome* she looks in a medieval dress."

"Yeah, sure," Erin muttered, scowling as she yanked at the low front again before eying Jackie. "Sorry, but I don't pull this stuff off nearly as good as you do."

There was no point complimenting Nicole as well because she was always in pants. *Exactly* what Erin would like to be wearing right now.

"I'm just more accustomed to wearing dresses," Jackie said. "Or skirts at least."

Honestly, Erin was amazed every man in this joint including Rònan wasn't falling over themselves to get closer to Jackie. Between her tall, voluptuous body, and stunning face, never mind hair, it was a wonder she wasn't surrounded. Not to say quite a few weren't hovering.

She was more than surprised to see several of them eying her instead of Jackie. Even despite the fact Rònan kept a possessive hand against her back. A hand she just couldn't seem to bring herself to ask him to move.

"Hey, I haven't seen Darach," Erin mentioned. "Everything okay with him?"

"Apparently he's at Hamilton Castle making sure it's as fortified as possible," Rònan said. "Hopefully, he'll arrive soon. 'Tis important that he remain close to the wee Bruce."

"I think he's just trying to avoid Jackie," Nicole said. "He didn't hang long with the Vikings either once she showed up."

Jackie frowned and Erin swore her friend's cheeks reddened a little. "Why would he be avoiding me?"

Nicole shrugged. "Beats me."

But Erin saw the brief look tossed between Niall and Nicole. They knew something. Clearly not wanting to stick around for the remainder of the conversation, Nicole grabbed Niall's hand and led him away. "C'mon Brute, let's go dance."

When Jackie's eyes met hers, Erin shrugged. "Don't sweat Darach. From what I hear, he's not good at sitting still for too long."

Jackie stood up a little straighter, frown deepening. "I'm not sweating anything." She sighed, her eyes flickering to Erin's Viking posse. "I think I'll go visit with Tait and Bjorn. They've been good to have around the past month." There was a certain softness to her voice when she murmured, "Who knows, maybe Heidrek will show up." Her eyes went to Erin. "But I'll stay with you if you need me."

"Naw, I'm good." She nodded at the Vikings. "Go have fun. They need it as much as you do."

The minute Jackie was out of range, Erin turned to Rònan. "I'm worried about her. I never got a chance to meet the Viking King's nephew Heidrek but Jackie obviously did. Is something going on between them?" She scowled. "And what the hell's up with Darach and don't tell me you don't know. You and your cousins are thick as thieves. I'm sure they've got you all caught up on what happened while we were gone."

"Thick as thieves?"

"Just tell me what's going on, Rònan."

"Aye, lass." He steered her beyond the crowd until they were in a somewhat private corner. Erin was impressed by how well he politely turned away several women who approached him in the short distance they walked. But then a few men were hovering close clearly wondering if Erin might soon be available.

"It looks like a few around here aren't convinced you'll keep me by your side for all that much longer," she mentioned.

"They couldnae be more wrong," he said softly.

"Sure. However you wanna play it while I'm here. Just remember I'm not staying." Her eyes met his. "Okay, so what's going on with Jackie and Heidrek? And Darach?"

Rònan kept a hand against the wall to the upper-right of her head, his body angled inward so that any approaching would steer clear. "I dinnae know much about Jackie and Heidrek except that he returned to the Viking fortress whilst we were in the Otherworld. Well, whilst I was there anyway. From what Niall tells, they bonded well and Heidrek intends to pursue your friend."

"Pursue her how?" Her eyes narrowed. "Isn't this the kid that hit on Nicole when he was a teenager?"

"Aye." Rònan chuckled. "But he isnae by any means a teenager anymore and still remains heir to the throne based on the Viking King's wishes."

"I don't get it." She frowned. "Why doesn't he want his firstborn, Bjorn to take it?"

Rònan shrugged. "He has always felt Heidrek is best suited."

"Is Heidrek half dragon?"

"Nay." Rònan's brows arched. "I think it says a lot about the lad for Naðr to want as much considering. But until you and your friends traveled back, I've spent little time with my Viking ancestors so I dinnae ken the dynamics."

"Good enough." Her eyes narrowed. "Now tell me what's going on with Darach. I haven't known him long but avoiding defending Robert doesn't strike me as part of his M.O."

"M.O.?"

"Method of Operating."

"Ah." Rònan shook his head. "Nay, 'tis not how Darach usually...operates." He took a swig of whisky and shrugged one shoulder. "Like I said, he's not good at staying in one spot overly long."

"Oh no, you don't." She leaned closer. "No evading the question."

"'Tis not in the best taste to speak of my cousin's private affairs, aye?"

"Rònan," she warned. "Either tell me or I'll go badger the hell out of Nicole and Niall." She arched a brow. "I'd like to think things won't get that far. That you and I really are friends."

"What does us being friends have to do with me sharing my cousin's secrets?"

"Everything I'd say." She widened her eyes. "Especially considering your cousin might very well be meant for my friend and I wanna know if she's getting ready to be hurt." Then to add emphasis and make sure they were on the same page. "And nothing says Darach and I aren't still meant to be together so I need to know what I'm dealing with."

"You and Darach?" He frowned and shook his head. "Och, nay."

"Why not?"

He shifted closer, his eyes deadly serious, brogue thickening, voice deeper than usual. "Because despite the bloody Vikings determined to watch over ye, if yer here for anyone 'tis me and only me."

"Settle down with the alpha shit." But she wasn't moving away as he shifted even closer, his sheer size a solid wall that shut out their surroundings. "Tell me what's going on."

His eyes held hers as he trailed a lone finger down her arm then pulled it back as though he didn't realize what he was doing. It occurred to her then how well behaved he was trying to be. Yet she didn't miss the billowing of his plaid. Erin cursed under her breath when desire shot through her.

Arousal.

"Don't inhale, Rònan." Her brows flew together and she shook her head. "Just tell me what I need to know." She softened her voice and eyes. "Please."

"You cannae tell Jackie." His expression turned serious. "Promise me, lass."

"Jeez, I feel like I'm in high school all over again. And I'll say it like I would've back then." She shrugged. "What you tell me is gonna depend on what I tell her. And it's all going to depend on how much it'll hurt her. Sorry, but I don't mess around when it comes to my friends any more than I imagine you do when it comes to your cousins."

"Aye," he whispered. His eyes searched hers for a long moment before he relented. "It happened the night you danced with Darach at the Viking fortress. The night you thought I took the redhead to bed. Do you not recall leaving my cousin with another lass? Do you not recall telling him he should enjoy himself?"

"I do. I did." She nodded. "What of it?"

"Well…he did," Rònan murmured. "Enjoy himself that is."

It took Erin less than five seconds to figure out what all the hype was about and why Rònan was so evasive. "So Darach got laid and now he feels guilty because what…he's got a thing for Jackie?"

"Laid?"

"Had sex."

"We dinnae know with any certainty he got *laid* but aye, 'tis assumed he did based on his avoidance of your friend," Rònan said.

"Well, damn, you should've just told me because hey, I'm the one that pushed him in that direction," she reminded.

"Aye." He frowned. "Why did you do that?"

"I dunno, because he seemed so lonely and I wanted to do the guy a solid. I knew it wasn't going to happen with him and me so figured I was doing him a favor." She shrugged. "Besides, Jackie's dating a few guys and though she might present herself as a gentle flower, my girl's doing just fine in the sex department."

"So she wouldnae mind if he laid with another knowing he might be meant for her?" Rònan said. "Truly?"

"I didn't exactly say that but…" She squeezed his hand. "I'll talk to Jackie. I'll make sure she understands what I do about Darach."

An undefined emotion flickered in his eyes. "And what precisely is that?"

"That he has a kind heart like she does," she said bluntly. "And she better practice the forgiveness she believes in so much now."

When he started to speak, she shook her head and looked anywhere but into his eyes. "Don't ask me to elaborate because I won't."

"Aye," Rònan murmured. "I willnae push you, lass."

Erin's eyes went back to him. He had every right to demand answers like she just had. But he wouldn't. She wasn't sure which emotion prevailed. A flicker of guilt because she'd insisted that he give her answers about one of his closest friends. Or feeling grateful that he was compassionate enough not to do the same.

"You dinnae need to feel so much right now, Erin," he murmured. "This eve is for you. For all you've done for me and mine."

As always, he sensed her turbulent thoughts.

Their eyes held for a long moment before he stepped back and held out his hand. "Might we dance, lass?"

She flinched. "Dancing's not really my thing."

"You did just fine at the Viking fortress. Besides, you dinnae need to do much but let me hold you." A soft smile came to his lips. "Please. 'Twould make my clan happy."

Her eyes fell to his groin. "And what about the *beastie*?"

The corner of his lip curled up. "I'll risk it."

"I bet you will." Yet she allowed him to lead her into the crowd which not surprisingly gave them plenty of space.

When he pulled her into his arms, the moment felt almost surreal. The lavish dress swooshing around her ankles. How incredible he looked as he brought her close but didn't grope. It was all on the up and up. Respectable. Erin was well aware of his parents and sister standing off to the side. How they watched them with curiosity and if she wasn't mistaken, approval.

"Your family is staring at us," she mumbled.

"Aye, expect that for a while," he said. "They're trying to ken me...us."

"Uh huh." She rested her cheek against his chest, far too aware of his strength and heat. "It's weirding me out, though."

He rested his hands against her back. "I'm sorry. There isnae any help for it."

"Because they're not used to you acting like this," she guessed.

"Aye." He chuckled. "'Tis an understatement, that."

"Why are you really doing this?" She pulled back and met his eyes. "I've told you I'm not sticking around. Not only that, there's still a distinct possibility Jackie *is* the Broun meant for you."

"I dinnae feel a thing when I look at Jackie." His eyes held hers. "But I do when I look at you. Even if you dinnae stay, 'tis this thing I feel when you're near that has changed me into…something better."

"Jackie's gorgeous, kind and amazing," Erin pushed past her lips. "You just need to give it time and get to know her."

"Nay." He shook his head, convinced of his words. "There is something about her that doesnae speak to my heart. She isnae who she seems to be." When Erin tensed at his words, he continued. "'Tis no offense to your friend but even if I wasnae caught by you, I would turn from her. The lass doesnae know her own heart but offers those around her only what they expect of her. What they wish to see."

Erin hated how well he had pegged her friend.

But she knew why Jackie was the way she was.

"Sounds like you've given this too much thought," she remarked with an edge of irritation. Because whether or not she thought he was right, he was talking about her friend.

When she tried to pull away, he held her tight and tilted up her chin until their eyes met. "I might have been frivolous and not someone I'm proud of for far too long, but I ken people. And I'm not wrong about Jackie." His eyes were so damn genuine she couldn't look away. "I dinnae find fault in your friend for the battles she fights. 'Tis none of my concern. What is my concern?" His thumb brushed gently over her chin. "*You*. You're the only lass I worry about and no other."

"You need to stop it then." She shook her head and pulled away. "I'm tired and going to bed."

Rònan caught her hand before she went too far. "I have to stay down here whilst my clan celebrates." He shook his head. "I cannae abandon them to run off with a lass as I have far too often in the past. 'Tis time for change."

181

While Erin understood where he was coming from, her mind only heard one thing.

"There are too many lasses willing and able where you suddenly seem not to be."

"Do what you need to, Rònan," she threw over her shoulder. "See you tomorrow."

Erin was halfway up the stairs when her Viking posse fell in behind her.

She was three-quarters up the stairs when the crowd below erupted in another round of cheers. More uncomfortable than ever, she offered a quick wave then booted it. As soon as she made it into the hallway and clear of prying eyes, she spun on Tait and Bjorn. "Guys, I appreciate your devotion but I seriously need some space."

"Maybe the last thing you need is—" Tait started.

"We understand," Bjorn intercepted. "We will escort you to your chamber then give you privacy, woman."

"Why won't you just give it a rest and go have some fun?" She shook her head. "I'm totally fine. The enemies are defeated."

"There are always enemies about," Bjorn said softly. "Go rest, Erin. You will not stop us from protecting you. I vow, it will not happen."

There really was no dissuading them. Erin flung her hands in the air and strode down the hall. "Have it your way. I'm beat."

Eager to crawl into bed and escape this day, Erin froze at the threshold of her chamber. Grant sat in front of the fire with Robert on his lap. When she approached, she realized the kid was crying against his chest.

"Oh no," she murmured and crouched in front of them, trying to meet Robert's eyes. "What's the matter, Honey?"

He turned his head away, voice catching. "Nothing is wrong, M'lady."

Erin sidled around until she could meet his bloodshot eyes. "That would be Erin to you." She cupped his cheek. "Now tell me what's going on."

"'Tis not admirable," he whispered around tears.

"I beg to differ," she said softly. "I think anything you have to share is admirable."

"Och, nay," he murmured and sniffled. "This isnae."

"All right. That sounds serious." She took his hand. "Any chance I can take Laird Grant's place so we can talk?"

Robert eyed her for a long moment. "I wouldnae want to offend Laird Grant."

"Me neither." Her eyes met Grant's. "Would it offend you if I sat with Robert?"

Grant smiled softly and stood. "Not at all if that is what he wishes."

Erin sat and took Robert, who curled up on her lap but not before his eyes went to Grant's. "Ye willnae go far, aye, Uncle?"

"Nay, lad." Grant stroked the side of his head. "I'll be waiting just outside the door whilst ye speak with yer friend."

"Thank ye," Robert whispered and rested his head against Erin's chest.

Erin nodded to Grant then held Robert as he sobbed quietly. She said nothing at first just let him cry. When his sniffles became less frequent, she murmured comforting words. "You're going to be okay. Nobody's getting close to you with my friends and me around."

"Aye, Erin," he whispered after several long moments. "But that doesnae make missing my Ma and Da any less so."

"No." She stroked his hair. "I can't imagine it does."

"I know that makes me weak and not fit to rule my country someday," he said.

"That's where you're wrong," she said. "I think a great ruler should value his parents, what makes them so special. I think if more leaders valued their upbringing and took pride in family this world might be a better place."

"Why?" he whispered.

Erin bit back tears. Her life and mistakes had no place here.

Comforting someone who could make a difference *did*.

"Because our family makes us who we are," she said. "They teach us compassion and forgiveness. They give us a sense of belonging that we can pass on to others."

"And that can help me lead Scotland?"

"Maybe. Yes," she said. "Remembering that you understand unity. That people can truly care and watch out for each other."

After several long minutes and a few more sniffles, Robert sat up and met her eyes. "Do ye mind if I ask ye something?"

"Not at all."

"It might seem untoward."

"Nothing you could say would seem untoward."

Little did she know what was coming.

"Yer friend Cassie went blind and yer friend Nicole is going deaf." His quizzical, innocent eyes stayed with hers. "What ails ye, Erin?"

She might not be a fan of saying it to anyone else but for whatever reason, she had no such issue with Robert. "I'm losing my voice."

"So ye willnae be able to talk?"

Erin shook her head. "No."

"I am sorry," he said, heart in his eyes before he rested his head against her chest again. "Might I ask ye something else?"

"Yes."

Again, little did she know what was coming.

"Were ye close with yer Ma and Da?"

Her response caught in her throat as she stroked his hair.

"Erin?" he murmured when she didn't respond. Heck if he wasn't already the diplomat he would someday have to be. "'Tis not an answer ye need to give."

But he had put it out there. That meant she needed to answer it to strengthen their bond so that he would trust her without question.

"My mother passed away when I was very young," she finally said. "My father raised me and was my best friend."

"I'm sorry," he whispered, nuzzling closer. "So ye found this sense of unity and family with just your Da?"

"I did." She bit back emotion. "He was incredible."

"'Twas just him, though," Robert said. "What made him so special?"

"He watched out for me," she said. "He believed in me and my dreams."

"What were your dreams?"

Erin almost said it didn't matter but something stopped her...something born of the past. More importantly, she didn't want to lie to Robert.

"I wanted to be a singer."

"Like a minstrel?"

Erin almost smiled at the terminology but felt too sad. "Yeah, like a minstrel."

Robert wrapped his arms around her waist and kept his cheek against her chest. "Will ye sing for me, Erin? I would verra much like to hear it."

Erin stared at the fire and swallowed hard.

The last time she'd sung was to lend Rònan comfort when he fell into that unnatural slumber. To do it again seemed like tempting fate. Would this be the final time? Would the last note die along with her voice?

"*Please*, Erin," Robert whispered.

Though momentarily frozen, the sound of desperation in his voice touched her.

"Okay," she said hoarsely and cleared her throat. "Okay."

So though terrified...she sang.

For Robert, to Robert, she sang.

~Oath of a Scottish Warrior~

Chapter Fourteen

NO MATTER WHO you are when you hear it for the first time, listening to an angel sing will change how you see things. How you *feel* about things. The sound gets inside your soul and does not let go.

Because of the wind tunnel created by the wall walk in her chamber, Erin's sweet voice carried down to the hall below. A sound he swore would continue to echo off the walls of his castle for centuries to come. A haunting, peaceful sound that would feed the soul of this great beast until it was nothing but dust.

Rònan stayed with his clan as he told Erin he would. But he had stopped drinking and remained as merry as possible without her there. It was no easy task. He would have preferred to fight arousal all night as long as she was in his arms. Though she seemed convinced he wanted to stay so that he could be with another lass, it was the furthest thing from his mind.

"Erin has a bloody beautiful voice," his Da said as he joined Rònan in front of the fire. "Your Ma and I are verra impressed."

Despite the joyous occasion, it had been Erin's singing that put everyone in a gentler mood. One that had women and men embracing. One that had everyone searching out their wee bairns and traveling off to celebrate with their immediate kin. A voice that made everyone grateful they were still alive and their families were close and well-protected.

"'Tis good that," Rònan murmured. It was clear his parents liked Erin.

"We're equally impressed with yer behavior tonight, son," his father said. "But we remain curious."

"About what?" he said, eyes still on the fire. He hadn't always pleased his parents over the years, but he never doubted their love for him. So what was happening now almost seemed too natural.

Was he playing right into their hands? Into what they ultimately wanted for him? And if he was, would that be such a bad thing? No. Did it lend him contentment? No. All it did was make him realize that he was late becoming the man he should have already been.

"Will ye let her get away so easily?" his Da said.

Would he let Erin get away so easily when she was obviously different than the rest? For too long he had lived the way he wanted to, determined to be judged by no one. Living by his own free will. Things went as he saw fit, especially once he became laird. To be devoted to one lass seemed almost unthinkable...until Erin.

"Erin has her own mind. She will do what she wants." Rònan looked at his father. He knew there was more to this. "Might ye ask the question truly on yer mind?"

"Aye, lad." Interest lit Colin's eyes. "Do ye love her?"

"Love?" By instinct, Rònan shook his head. "I know nothing of it. Do I *like* Erin? Aye. Verra much so."

His father contemplated him for so long, Rònan almost repeated himself.

"'Tis a good start," Colin said at last and stood. "Might ye not join her then?" He arched his brows. "To keep her safe that is."

"I thought I might sit here a while longer," Rònan said.

"Yer Ma and I want the great hall to ourselves," Colin informed. "'Tis a rare day that a lass's singing clears it so. She gave this clan an added level of peace that even yer Ma and I were unable to give over these long years of unrest. "

"Aye, Da. 'Tis true enough." All night he had wanted to run as fast as he could to Erin's chamber but had waited it out...had done what was right. But Rònan knew as he stood and embraced his father that he'd been given the clear to at last leave.

Still in Colin's embrace, his da whispered in his ear, "Ye've made us proud in ways ye dinnae even ken yet."

Rònan nodded and pulled away. "Sleep well, Da."

He didn't wait for a response but took the stairs two at a time.

Anything to get back to Erin.

Anything to lay eyes on her again.

Dragon-shifter—young and in the best shape of his life—Rònan was still winded when he slowed outside her door. And it wasn't from exertion.

Nay.

It was from pure nerves.

As always, Tait and Bjorn stood silently outside her door.

"All is well," he said softly. "I'm here now."

Bjorn nodded his acknowledgment but didn't move. Not that he intended such, Rònan knew that even if he managed to cut both down by sword these men's spirits would still watch over her.

"Then ye have my thanks." He embraced them. All contrary emotions aside, as laird his top priority should not only be the safety of his clan but gratefulness to men who cared so much for their own. Especially those who were his ancestors. Odd thought that he likely descended from one of them.

He was about to enter when Bjorn shook his head and stopped him. Though Rònan frowned, he soon understood why. Erin was asleep in front of the fire and Grant was lifting the slumbering wee king from her lap.

When his uncle exited with Robert in his arms, Rònan didn't miss the edge of warning in Grant's soft voice. "Ye care for her like no other lad, or ye've me to face."

Rònan nodded before he entered. Though tempted to leave her resting peacefully, he couldn't keep his hands off her. So he scooped her up, brought her to the bed, laid her down and removed her boots.

Then he debated.

The person he had always been would have crawled in next to her, nuzzled her awake and enjoyed a good night of romping. But he could not do that now. It would seem wrong. And that was…disgruntling? Upsetting? No, not in the least. What he felt right now was something different. Bad yet really good.

Confusing.

Something he knew he should be proud of but still left him unsatisfied in a way he couldn't figure out. When had he gone from a man who had women fawning over him and readily available to…this?

What *was* this?

Yet he wasn't growling in frustration. And he might've not that long ago had there been a bonnie lass asleep in his bed who didn't awake immediately upon his arrival. Because they *always* knew he had arrived whether or not he touched them. He had liked to think it was because they liked his looks or skills in bed or even eventually that he was laird. And mayhap sometimes it was one of those reasons. But deep down he knew it was usually another altogether.

They were drawn to, yet wary of, the dragon.

But not Erin.

She remained asleep and not phased in the least by his presence. Even while she dozed he sensed it was because she was comfortable with him on a level her wakeful mind didn't yet realize. So he took the opportunity to gaze at her for far too long before he plunked down in a chair in front of the fire.

"Hell," he whispered, eyes lost. Whatever had come over him made the blood in his veins speed up. It had his muscles tense and his breathing irregular. There was nothing normal about it.

Long hours passed as he mulled over the changes in his body.

The changes in his mind.

In everything he ever thought he knew about himself.

The sun had barely crested the horizon and the sky was a deep purplish black when Erin shot up in bed. Within seconds, she flew outside. In the state of half-slumber, half-awareness that dragons were so good at, he bolted after her. Luckily, he caught her seconds before she dove over the wall walk's railing.

"He's right there!" she cried. "I can stop him!"

Though he said nothing to Erin about it, he had spoken to Grant, his father, and all close kin telepathically about how she apparently saw a 'man' in the dark demi-god shadow. Nobody could give him a solid answer about what that might mean except that it was dire…and clearly connected to Erin.

"There's nothing here, lad. It must have been a nightmare. She's safe for now." Grant's assurances flickered through his mind as Rònan pulled Erin into his arms. *"Keep her close."*

"Erin," Rònan said as soothingly as he could manage, trembling when he realized how close she had come to plummeting to certain death. Not that the dragon in him would have let that happen. Still. There were too many unknowns in everything going on lately.

"No!" she cried, beating against his chest when he whipped her around. "Don't take him from me!"

"Nay, lass." Rònan walked her back against the wall and held tight, still trying to soothe her the best he could. He stroked her hair, body, anything he could manage while keeping her in place.

190

And it seemed to work because she eventually calmed and murmured, "Rònan?" against his chest.

"Aye, lass, all is well," he whispered, still stroking her hair.

She pulled back and her gaze rose to his as thunder rumbled across the sky.

"How are you here?" she whispered, her eyes not quite focused.

Rònan cupped her cheeks, sickened with worry, brogue thickening with emotion. "Lass, yer at my castle. MacLeod Castle. Do ye not remember?" He brushed his thumbs over her cheekbones, trying to ground her, trying not to show how desperate he was. "Tell me you remember."

She blinked several times, eyes wide before her vision seemed to clear and her eyes locked with his. "Rònan?"

"Aye, Erin," he said. "I'm right here."

"Rònan?" Her eyes studied his before she exhaled sharply and nodded. "Thank God, it's really you," Erin murmured before she shook her head, wrapped her arms around his waist and pressed her cheek against his chest.

"Where were you, lass?" he said softly. "What happened?"

When Erin whispered, "I'm not sure," he knew she wasn't entirely truthful.

"I think it was just a bad dream," she said.

Rònan knew it wasn't the right time to question her further so he simply held her and debated what he should do next. Urge her to sit and drink whisky to soothe her nerves? Or mayhap encourage her to get more rest. In truth, he wasn't opposed to holding and comforting her for as long as possible. Anything to stop her heart from racing and to help her through this.

Then she moved.

And not in a way he anticipated.

Subliminal, as if she didn't realize she was doing it, her hands slid up beneath the back of his tunic. Her fingers were soft, barely touching as they explored the muscles of his lower back. It was almost as if she was touching him for the first time.

Then again, they had never done all that much touching just lusting.

His eyes slid shut at the intimate contact. He couldn't remember a lass's touch feeling so good...so powerful. When her gentle fingers rode up his back, one lone finger feeling each vertebra, heat followed in its wake. A heat that also shot in the other direction, stiffening his cock within a breath. When she turned her cheek and inhaled deeply, a low groan vibrated deep within her chest. He knew why. For the first time in his life, a lass caught the scent of *his* arousal.

"You smell so good," she moaned softly.

While it was about the last thing he wanted to do, he managed to whisper, "Nay, lass. You dinnae need this right now. Let me get you back to bed."

"No," Erin growled against his chest. "No bed." She pulled back enough that their eyes connected. "I'm not tired."

Rònan shook his head when she started yanking at his tunic, determined to remove it.

"Lass, we should talk," he argued as she shoved and pushed to the point that he bent over and let her have her way.

"Lass," he repeated as her hands rode up his torso and over his shoulders, her eyes alight with admiration. "You might have just had an episode that involved the Otherworld. Why dinnae you lie down and rest some. Relax. I'll get you something to eat."

His words grew softer and softer as her fingers trailed over his dragon markings. Women had touched them before but they had never responded like this. When Erin's fingers glided over them, pleasure shot through him. A feeling so profound, his muscles tightened along with his ballocks. Whatever it was obviously had something to do with her being half dragon. The feeling was so impossibly intense he almost yanked up her dress and took her right there.

"These aren't just average tattoos are they?" she whispered as her breathing increased. Erin flexed her fingers over them. "They glow and…" Her eyelids grew heavier as purple flared brighter in her eyes. "Warmth and pleasure is spreading up my arms." Her eyelids shut entirely and her lips fell open as another soft groan erupted. "God, the feeling is spreading everywhere now."

Her eyes shot open moments before he smelled her arousal.

"What are they, Rònan?"

He debated how much he should tell her…how much she could handle. But then they had never glowed beyond the Celtic Otherworld so he knew there was so much more to this.

192

"Do what I expect of you," she murmured. "Tell me the truth. I can handle it."

"Aye, lass." Rònan put his hand over hers. "The markings became visible when I reached my full size but they were there long before that. I felt the sting of them the first time I shifted when I was still a wee one."

Her eyes studied his. "I get the sense the sting was pretty bad."

When he hesitated, she gave him a pointed look. "I can take it, Rònan."

"I know you can." She deserved to know. "While a dragon shifter feels the transition from human to dragon acutely the first time, there is a particular sting in the shoulder and arm region when we first develop our wings. 'Tis those spots that somehow formed the design of my markings."

"Interesting," she murmured and swallowed. "Will I develop similar tats, I mean markings, after I shift for the first time?"

"I dinnae know. My Ma didnae but the Viking male dragons all have them," he said. "I dinnae know if the Viking female dragons do."

"I already have a little bit of ink so more tats wouldn't bother me," she said. "Neither would the pain of shifting for that matter."

He searched her eyes. "Nay?"

"No." Erin shook her head. "I had a moment during the battle when my skin started to change…when I was starting to shift. Tosha told me to fight it because I wasn't ready." Her eyes narrowed slightly as she contemplated. "Potential pain doesn't worry me." Erin's eyes stayed with his. "Becoming something else does. Something I thought I hated."

"But you dinnae anymore?" he said softly.

"I don't think so," she murmured. "Between getting to know you and the Vikings then feeling that connection when you all shifted to protect me, I'm starting to wonder if my dislike wasn't misplaced."

Rònan tilted up her chin so her eyes stayed aligned with his and kept his voice gentle. "Though you dinnae need to share such now, I hope you'll someday tell me why you had such dislike to begin with."

He was pleased when she didn't shove away but held his gaze. "Maybe. If and when I'm ready."

"Aye," he whispered. "'Tis good that."

It took everything he had to pull his hand away and fight the need to take her, but he did. He might be more confused than ever about his emotions in regards to her but he knew one thing...he wanted her beyond simple lust.

He needed to truly know her. To keep her friendship.

Not only that but he wanted her mind and heart.

It was hard to know when exactly that had happened but it had.

Erin, it seemed, had another plan entirely as thunder rumbled and she started to untie her dress, eyes never leaving his.

"We dinnae need to," he started but she shook her head and said, "But we're going to."

"Erin, I dinnae want you to think," he began. The rest of his statement died on his lips as her dress fell. There was nothing more beautiful than Erin back dropped by an angry sea and black clouds flickering with lightning. Her hair was wild and her eyes brilliant.

Then there was her body.

Fire flared so hotly beneath his skin he wasn't surprised when steam rose off of him.

"You don't want me to think what, Rònan?" she murmured, her eyes unusually sultry as she held his gaze.

He couldn't remember for the life of him what he didn't want her to think as he tore off his plaid, closed the distance and lifted her onto the edge of the wall walk. Unable to voice another damn word, he spread her legs, dug his hand into her hair, tilted back her head and closed his lips over hers.

Everything he had experienced when she kissed him in the Otherworld felt a thousand times more intense now. The heat and silkiness of her tongue against his. The softness of her skin as he wrapped an arm around her lower back and pressed close without taking her.

Her arms wrapped around his waist as the kiss took on a life of its own. There was no way to know how much time passed as their tongues explored. In its own way, it was the most sensual thing he had ever experienced. How they held each other and simply kissed...not to say the kissing was simple. No, it was deep and profound and thorough.

When icy rain started falling, he didn't feel it any more than she did. Nothing touched them as their skin sizzled and they lost themselves in the feel of each other. Only when she grabbed his arse and groaned into his mouth, " Rònan," did he realize how desperate she was for more.

So was he for that matter.

"Not here," he managed against her lips. "Not like this."

She pulled back a fraction, met his eyes and wrapped one leg around his waist. "*Exactly* like this, dragon."

Something about the way she said it, the way she dared as her skin grew dewy and her eyes started to turn, made him lose control. While somewhere in the back of his mind he was determined to make this a romantic experience, it suddenly became impossible. Growling, he grabbed her arse, pulled back enough then thrust hard.

"Oh hell," she cried out and wrapped her arms over his shoulders as she bit her lower lip.

Ròjan released a ragged breath when he realized what he had done. "I'm sorry," he tried to say but nothing came out as he lost himself in the feel of her tight heat.

"It's okay," whispered through his mind as her nails dug into his shoulder blades. *"You're just,"* she started before a quiver rippled through her. *"You're larger than what I'm used to...even if it's possibly our second time."*

"I'm sorry," he managed aloud this time, voice ragged. "I wasnae thinking clearly."

But he didn't need to fret because it wasn't long before she responded.

"Ròjan," she whispered close to his ear as she wrapped her other leg around him. "I don't want you to think right now." She nipped his earlobe. "Just *move* already."

When she pressed even closer and shifted her hips, he no longer had a choice.

He moved.

When he did, it was fast and full of so much need he soon lost himself yet again. *Nobody* felt like her and moved against him like she did though he seemingly had all the control. Thunder roared and lightning flashed, but he was only aware of Erin. How her head fell back and bliss overtook her features as his pace increased.

There was something about that.

The way she took such pleasure from the way they felt together.

Rain fell harder. They were drenched. But they were so overheated that an arctic blast could have blown through and not only their lust but their dragons would have kept them warm. This was their element. Chill and nature. Rawness. A unique sense of vulnerability.

Yet he knew better than her that they were half human.

More than that, he knew in this form the only thing they could truly survive was fire.

So when he carried her inside, he ignored her denial and brought her onto the bed. Rònan didn't entirely realize what he was doing until he flipped her onto her knees on multiple pillows to suit the difference in their torsos, made her grab the headboard then slid back into her. Only then as she groaned and slammed a hand over the male dragon carving did he understand.

He wanted her to see what the artwork really was.

Them.

Together.

A new beginning.

He gripped her hip and put a hand over the female dragon as he moved first harshly then slowly, pacing the passion that would seize them far too quickly if they let it. If they didn't learn to control the dragon they might never get out of bed again. Lust might become their world.

And he wanted *more*.

Rònan wanted her to stay in this castle with him, to be his voice of reason, the voice of wisdom that would complement and aid his clan so well.

He wanted her to be Lady of MacLeod Castle.

"Oh, hell, Rònan," she panted. "Too much information."

Damn. Erin could hear his every thought. Yet somehow it only increased her arousal despite her negative response. She wanted to run from this but at the same time stay.

His movements grew more intense, more driving, as a strange need overtook. One he had never felt before. A need to claim her as his own, not just as a wife but as a *mate*. This was not of the man's making but the dragon within. Though it was something he would never do without speaking to her first, he could fantasize.

So he spread her legs further and drove into her with more eagerness than he knew he was capable of. Sweat slicked their skin

196

as passion exploded. She braced her hands more firmly and took him, crying out with pleasure.

When her climax began, her limbs weakened. Wrapping one arm around her waist and the other across her chest, he pulled her back against him. One more thrust was all it took to send them both over the edge and he roared as their bodies jerked against one another's.

There was no sweeter release to be had than this. Holding her close as they both let go. Cheek pressed against her hair, he closed his eyes and yet again lost himself in the feel of her. This place they could go that was untouchable and so very much theirs.

Eventually, Rònan leaned back on his calves but didn't let go of her. No, he relished every moment of his body floating down from where she had taken him. More than that, he enjoyed the long-lasting remnants of her release. A letting go that only ended when her breathing slowed and she slumbered.

Careful to handle her gently, he laid her down. Though tempted to leave her nude, he had heard her thoughts back at the Viking fortress. He knew she slept in clothing to protect herself. So until she truly felt safe, he would not take that from her. Though he wasn't entirely sure how she would take it, he grabbed his tunic and put it on her. It was something that Nicole did with Niall's tunics and he found it...nice.

He wanted that same sense of 'nice' with Erin.

He wanted another way to wrap himself around her...to get closer.

As an afterthought, he grabbed her lighter from her boot—aye, he knew she hid it there—and slipped it into her pocket. He understood that it was another form of safety.

Rònan sighed as he gazed at her. Gone were the days of trying to get a lass out of her clothes. Now it seemed it was best to clothe a lass he truly wanted to keep in his bed...or this bed...maybe someday *their* bed? Well aware that Erin might not want him nude either, he wrapped his plaid before he lay down and pulled her close, her back to his front. No need for a blanket despite the cold. They ran too damn hot.

How bloody nice it was to be with a lass who preferred a good nip to the air.

Though he only meant to wrap his arm around her waist, his hand slid up beneath the tunic and rested on her stomach. Small and smooth, her abdominal muscles were well defined. She clearly took good care of herself. But having learned of Erin's training in her *military* and how well she fought, that was no surprise. What *was* a surprise was the other feeling touching her stomach invoked.

Wee bairns and what it might feel like if his was growing inside of her.

Rònan almost frowned at the thought but didn't. Mostly because he could think of no one better suited to carry his child than Erin. His heart slammed into his throat. Was he thinking this because of Niall and Nicole's pregnancy? Nay, somehow he knew he wasn't. While right now might not be the best time, he had no doubt that the lass in his arms would be...what? The best choice to house his bairn? Nay, that seemed cold and indifferent.

He inhaled the scent of her hair and pulled her even closer.

If anything, he would be privileged to share a wee bairn with Erin.

Honored.

Not yet of course. Not until things had been worked through and the wee King was safe. He knew she wasn't taking anything that would inhibit his seed from taking root. It wouldn't matter anyway as he was half dragon and could control conception. Still he wondered...why had Erin not mentioned their 'unprotected sex' as Nicole had called it with Niall. Was she not worried about becoming pregnant? Either way, Rònan intended to speak with her about it soon. Not his recent revelation but her thoughts on bairns in general.

Wee bairns...his own...

His heart quickened at the thought. The rightness of it...them. How there might not be one but two, twins like him and his sister. Maybe two boys...or two girls. The last thought he had before drifting off was of two girls running around his castle with their raven curls, big purple eyes, and defiant attitudes. Wee dragon shifters that knew how to keep their Da on his toes.

"Dad, is that you?"

At first, Rònan couldn't understand why his wee one was using twenty-first-century terminology to address him and shook his head as he chased his daughter around a corner.

"Oh my God, Dad?" Erin cried.

Ripped from his dream, Rònan shot up in bed. Somehow Erin had already made it to the wall walk without him knowing. Though it was clearly late morning, the day was gray and leaden. While tempted to cry out her name and run to her, he sensed something indefinably powerful fluctuating around her. So he got out of bed slowly and moved her way. He prayed to every god listening that whatever was around her didn't sense him.

"Dad?" She leapt onto the wall walk. "Don't go!"

True terror set in when she flung out her arms and shook her head. "I'm right here!"

Maybe stealth wasn't the best answer.

"So am I Erin," he cried as he raced toward her. "'Tis Rònan, lass."

This time, he was too late.

She went over.

Darkness swooped toward her so fast even his dragon eyes barely caught it.

But they did catch something.

Light fighting the darkness.

Rònan leapt onto the wall walk and shifted to a dragon, determined to save her as she fell. The only problem? He raced toward nothing but ocean. She was nowhere to be seen.

Roaring in rage, he searched and searched. No sign of her. Erin was truly gone. No pain was greater as he flew over the ocean and used his heightened vision to see beneath the dark water. He had failed to protect her even as he held her close. Erin was gone, taken by evil. The sea sizzled beneath him as rage and sadness seized him. It took several moments before he realized his dragon tears had caused the watery disruption.

"Highland dragon," Bjorn roared into his mind. *"Come back now."*

It had been ages since he heard the secret frequency on which Bjorn spoke to him. One that the Viking King taught all those with his blood. A frequency no one could hear but his own kind.

Hope spiked as he flew back. Rònan had a split second to shift and land before Tait yanked him into Erin's chamber. Meanwhile, Bjorn murmured a chant and sealed off the wall walk with magic.

Then he had another short second to see his Ma and Grant enter before Bjorn whipped him around, slammed him against a wall and slapped a scrap of plaid against his chest. "*This* was left on your bed, Highlander. *What* does it mean?"

About to roar back in rage, his eyes were ensnared by the plaid, and he instead murmured in disbelief, "It means we need to get to Castle Stewart fast."

His eyes rose to Grant's across the room and his uncle spoke what he was thinking.

"Not in this era. We need to travel through time again."

Chapter Fifteen

Scotland
Near Stewart Castle
1228

"DAD?" ERIN SAID over and over, confused and so sad she could barely see straight. "Where'd you go?"

Everything was black. She couldn't see a damn thing.

"Shh, it's okay," came a feminine voice as a soft hand slipped into hers. "Your vision will clear in a few seconds, okay? Trust me. Divine intervention does this every time."

Divine intervention? Wonderful. Add that to the list of screwed up happenings in her life lately. Though tempted to lash out, she didn't. Instead, she felt contentment when she slipped her hand into a pocket and found her lighter. Yet it was sliding her hand into a pocket not quite where it should be. What was she wearing?

"Are you all right?" A cool hand met her cheek. "Can you see me now?"

After several blinks, a woman slowly came into focus. Blond and beautiful, her lips curled into a small smile. "My name is Treasa and you're safe." She looked over her shoulder. "She can see now."

Erin's eyes swept over her surroundings. A forest. But it had changed from what she saw earlier. The trees were no longer barren but green and vibrant. It was a different time of year.

When a man crouched beside Treasa, Erin's heart jolted. She *knew* his face. "No," she cried, tears coming to her eyes as she shook her head and tried to back away. "Not you again."

Before she could slide her hand into her pocket again, he seized it and shook his head. His voice was remarkably gentle. "I know you have a lighter in there." His blue eyes comforted. "I also know you dinnae mean to use it. You dinnae need to fear me, lass. I mean you no harm."

"The hell you don't," Erin whispered. She still remembered his face flickering through the flames of her worst childhood memory.

"But mine wasnae the only face, aye?" the man murmured, his eyes unwavering as he evidently read her mind. Whatever he was doing with his steady gaze was definitely relaxing her.

"There was another face in the flames," he said softly. "One you saw again recently."

She was about to respond when the man stood and spun moments before Rònan, her Viking posse, the horses and surprisingly enough, Darach arrived. Erin had never been so relieved to see them. Equal relief was in Rònan's eyes when they locked on her.

"Watch out. This guy's big trouble, Rònan," she whispered into his mind.

"Nay, lass," he replied. *"Have no fear."*

Her eyes widened when Rònan strode her way then pulled her into his arms.

"Och, lass, you gave me a good scare," Rònan murmured.

He held her so tightly she finally had to say, "Getting short on breath, Hon."

"I'm sorry." Rònan loosened his grip and eyed her. "How do you feel? Can you stand on your own?"

"Kinda hard to know with you holding me up but I'd say yeah."

Rònan stepped back but held her arms until he was sure. Then, like Darach, he embraced the man who evidently brought her here. "Bloody hell, I wasnae sure I'd ever see ye again, Cullen Stewart."

Erin frowned. How did Rònan know this guy? A man who had haunted her worst nightmare?

"Somebody needs to tell me what the hell's going on," she said, not overly concerned about breaking up their reunion. Only when she caught Tait eying her outfit did she realize her clothing wasn't exactly what it should be. No wonder the pocket was so low. Her eyes shot to Rònan. "Care to share why I'm wearing your shirt?"

He merely shrugged. Though he worked at a sheepish expression, it came off more smug and territorial than anything else when he glanced at Tait then her. "I know you prefer to sleep in clothing and 'twas the closest thing available after you drifted off."

"I never told you I like to sleep in clothes."

He tapped his temple. "Nay, you thought it."

"Right," she muttered, not particularly in the mood to thank him as she rolled up the way-too-long sleeves. "Well, it fits like a damn potato sack."

"We'll get you a change of clothes when we get to my castle," Cullen assured.

Rònan grabbed a satchel off of Tosha. "No need. I brought clothing for her."

Erin nodded absently, eyes narrowed on Cullen. "I'm not going anywhere with you until I get some answers." Though tempted to run as far from him as possible, she was no coward. "I wanna know exactly who you are and *why* you were there on the worst night of my life." Then her eyes went to Treasa. "And I haven't forgotten that comment about divine intervention. You better get explaining that as well."

Treasa nodded. "You got it."

Erin wondered at the strange bite to her accent. Sort of half medieval, half modern day Scottish.

"Go change in the cave, Erin, then the rest of us will join you so that you might get the answers you seek," Cullen said. "Though we're on my land, trouble is always afoot."

Rònan nodded, took her hand and led her into a small cavern she wouldn't have guessed was there based on the thick shrubbery in front of it. She was never more relieved when he pulled out pants, a tunic more suited to her size and boots.

"I'm really glad you didn't bring a dress," Erin commented as she grabbed her lighter and pulled off his tunic. She was startled to feel a little reluctant before she tossed it to him. She'd never worn a man's shirt before. Though it was ridiculously large, it smelled like him and that totally worked for her.

Not only did her thoughts turn him on but his eyes were back to doing that slow walk down her body they were so good at. There was no stopping her own arousal as she recalled what they'd done earlier. How unbelievably good the sex was…the passion. The sweet sting left between her thighs soon became a raging almost painful burn of desire.

Their eyes locked and she almost growled at the blatant want in his eyes. Yet she was fast learning that when he brought out the growl in her, it meant their dragons were taking hold. Right now there was no time for that. So she was quick about yanking on the pants and shirt, well aware that he had shifted closer.

"Those are some naughty thoughts you're having," Erin murmured as she sat and pulled on a boot. She was about to put on the other when he crouched in front of her and took it.

"Allow me," he said.

She narrowed her eyes as he took his time loosening the strings with one hand while caressing her foot with the other. "What're you doing, Rònan?"

His eyes were a smidge too innocent when they met hers. "Helping you with your boot."

"I've been putting on my own shoes for a long time," she said. "Pretty sure I can handle it now."

But this had nothing to do with her shoes and they both knew it.

"I thought I lost you back there," he said softly and squeezed her foot gently. "'Twas an indescribable feeling, lass."

Her heartbeat kicked up a few notches at the look in his eyes, at the tone of his voice. Flashes of his thoughts arose. How serious he seemed to be getting about her.

"I told you this can't be a forever thing." She shook her head, not entirely sure if she was shaking it at him or at her own words. "I made that *real* clear."

Rònan held her gaze for a long moment and though she knew he had a lot to say about it, he instead slid on her boot and laced it up. "'Tis best for now that you get the answers you seek from Cullen."

Erin clenched her jaw when her skin heated with emotion. Though desire was always there, this had to do with something else entirely. Had she *wanted* him to be more persuasive here and now? Did she somewhere *way* in the back of her mind want to stay with him?

He cupped her cheek, evidently understanding her feelings better than she did at the moment. "We'll speak more of this later, Erin."

"Nothing to talk about," she muttered under her breath as he headed for the entrance to call in the others.

Her Viking posse stood guard at the entrance as everybody else sat on various rocks and Rònan joined her. While she typically preferred to face things alone, she was grateful for the supportive hand he slipped into hers.

Cullen sat across from her with Treasa by his side. They were the sort of striking couple she imagined Darach and Jackie would make if they hooked up. Cullen with his rich dark hair and Treasa with her pale blond locks.

"As you heard outside, my name is Cullen Stewart," he began, his eyes firmly on Erin. "My sister is Brae Stewart."

No shit. "*That's* why she looked so familiar." Her eyes widened as the truth slapped her in the face. "She's your twin!"

"Aye." Cullen nodded. "I dinnae know how much you've been told but she murdered me in battle many years ago. When she did, I became an angel but ended up embracing evil so that I might better defeat her. Unfortunately, it didnae go as well as I'd hoped and I was banned to the twenty-first century by the Celtic god, Fionn Mac Cumhail."

An angel? That explained the whole divine intervention thing. But what was an angel doing in her worst nightmare? While beyond uncomfortable sharing that frightful day with anyone, it looked like she didn't have much choice.

"So why are you back here and not in the twenty-first century then?" Erin frowned. "And again, why were you there...that night? Because you *definitely* didn't seem angelic."

"'Twas a truly difficult night," Cullen said softly. "And anything divine would have only seemed sinister in your state."

Erin's throat started to thicken. "It was...you were..."

Cullen's eyes stayed on hers and she swore a faint glow came from them. "You didnae kill your father, lass," he said softly. "'Twas never you that ignited the hay nor was it the lighter he always flicked on and off. 'Twas the evil demi-god now seeking you."

"I don't understand," she whispered, only faintly aware of Rònan shifting closer and squeezing her hand. "How can you be sure? I saw the...it...through the flames...flames that started when I arrived..."

"I can be sure because I was there, Erin. There to save you from him," Cullen said. "The man you saw in the Celtic Otherworld. He who means to keep you every bit as much as he tried with your friends and will likely try with Jackie."

She didn't have to glance at Darach to know he tensed.

"It was this dark laird who lit the hay on fire. He made sure your father was trapped inside," Cullen said. "It was also him that made sure you saw a dragon that night. Something that became a part of your worst nightmare."

Erin's throat was so clogged with emotion that speaking was impossible. Long repressed memories screamed through her mind. Her dad roaring at her to take her horse and get out of the barn. But the fire was everywhere. Its flames alive with faces. The man from the Otherworld and Cullen. For the past thirteen years, she'd been convinced they were part of an illusion she created to cope with what she had done.

Because fire always followed her. It was something she could ignite with a mere thought.

Something she kept secret from the world.

Rònan's arm snaked around her lower back, a solid wall of support when his pained eyes met hers. He knew now. All of it. Somehow she had been strong enough to block it but no more.

"That's why you flick the lighter," he whispered into her mind. *"To make sense of things. To keep everything normal. Something you could do with the flick of your finger rather than with your mind. 'Twas also a connection with your Da after he died. A way to let him know you didnae blame him if he had mistakenly lit the fire."* She felt his sadness for her. *"And 'tis why you dinnae like tight spaces. Because of your Da being trapped and the suffocating feeling you sensed from him."*

Erin nodded once but offered no response as she tried to pull herself together. She survived but the barn had burned to the ground and took her dad with it.

She was unaware a tear slid down her cheek until Rònan brushed it away and shook his head. *"It was never your fault any more than it was his, lass. Now you know the truth."*

Determined to get a grip, she cleared her throat and returned her attention to Cullen. "Why did the bad guy want me to see a dragon? And *how* were you there?"

"After I reconnected with Treasa in the twenty-first century, God gave me back my wings," he said. "And with them came extra knowledge. Information I assume given to me because of the great love Grant Hamilton and his former patriarch Adlin have for Him. I dinnae think God was entirely pleased that one of the Celtic gods had grown so dark. Not only that, I know my Father has a great deal of love for this country."

"Exactly what information were you given?" Erin said.

"That you deserved a fighting chance," Cullen said. "After all, the bad guy meant to take you that night. Had he, none of this would have happened. The MacLomains would've already been defeated, the wee Bruce taken and Scotland's future entirely different. A future that would have ended in a demise far worse than what this country already faces. 'Tis always best in any possible scenario that Robert the Bruce become king and leads Scotland in the direction it must go."

"So when you went to the future it wasn't 2015 but 2001?" Erin said. "Because I was only fourteen when this happened."

"Nay, I was in the year 2015 originally," Cullen said. "But once I got my wings time-travel became possible again. Soon after, Treasa and I were able to come home."

"Your parents must be glad to see you," Darach said.

"Not yet," Treasa said softly as her hand wrapped with Cullen's. "We only just arrived. And we've been away for far too long."

"What happened back at my castle?" Rònan asked Cullen. "Why did you take Erin back in time?" He frowned. "Why did you not speak with me first?"

"My apologies, Laird MacLeod...Rònan," Cullen said, respect in his voice. "I didnae mean to frighten you like that. Whoever this evil is, he knows I'm tracking him. Though 'twas years ago for Erin, the battle we waged at her barn only happened for us recently. He knows she is half dragon and is using that to get to her."

So she had not defeated the monster after all. She saw the flicker of distress that passed between Rònan and Darach.

"If the dark Laird was able to go to the future and affect Erin's fate, why did he not do the same with her friends?" Darach asked, his voice growing cautious. "The Broun lasses?"

There was an odd flicker in Cullen's eyes when they met Darach's. "I cannae speak toward the lives of her friends as I was only given leave to watch over Erin. Since they all lived normal lives and now wear a ring, I'm inclined to think 'twas the dragon blood that somehow allowed him to track Erin and not the others."

"Which means he's tracking our Viking blood," Rònan murmured.

"Aye," Cullen said. "'Twould seem so. Though your enemy is Celtic, he has a connection of some sort with the Norse as well."

Erin shook her head, baffled by all of this. Yet right now she needed to focus on that awful night from her childhood. So she cut into the conversation.

"There's something about that night that makes no sense." She was able to set aside her sadness as her anger grew. "Because of him, I hated and feared dragons. How is that something to use against me?"

"Would it not be in his favor if you disliked dragons, even yourself when you discovered you were one?" Cullen said. "I think he hoped you would dislike them so much that you would flee to him. That you would see him as human and normal despite how verra inhuman he is." He cocked a brow. "When you were in the Otherworld, did you not for a moment fall beneath his allurement? His dark beauty?"

"Yes," she said, angrier by the moment that she was nearly duped. "But I'm still unclear about something. Why is it that he, the evil one, drew me when you, the good one, infuriated me?"

Cullen eyed her for several moments. "Do you really want to know?"

Something about the way he was looking at her simultaneously put her on edge and at peace. "I do."

He contemplated her for far too long before he nodded. Though again tempted to run in the opposite direction, she held her ground as Cullen approached. His eyes went to Rònan. "Might I take her hand, Laird MacLeod?"

Irritated, she answered for Rònan. "Sorry, but shouldn't you be asking *me* that?"

"He means no disrespect, lass," Rònan said into her mind. *"He intends to show you something truly difficult."*

"That doesn't change the fact he should be asking me," she replied.

"'Tis just his way of respecting us."

"There is no 'us' but 'me'." Erin was sorry the minute she said it but she was used to standing on her own two feet. And he needed to understand that lust and love were two separate things. Lust didn't equal 'us' and love...well, that wasn't part of her vocabulary.

Despite her words, he squeezed her waist and nodded at Cullen. "Please dinnae speak to me but my lass."

"Your lass?" she said but not nearly as sharply as she could have. *"You're pushing it."*

Rònan gave no response as Cullen's attention focused on her and he held out his hand. "Will you take my hand, Erin?"

Would she? Should she? What was he going to show her? Erin eyed him, debating. He scared her far more than the dark laird. But again, what good would running do? She needed to face this…whatever it was.

So she took his hand.

Instant warmth filled her that had nothing to do with dragon blood. No, it had to do with something far different. Her eyes widened as huge white wings spread out from Cullen's shoulder blades and not only his eyes but his skin started glowing.

"I will show you something that I made sure you forgot," he murmured.

"Holy crap," she whispered as her surroundings started to turn white.

Then fiery red.

Only vaguely aware of Rònan's arm keeping a firm hold, she was suddenly in her teenage body living out the final moments of that horrific night again. The barn was inflamed but the faces and the dragon were gone. She stood outside, shaking and terrified. Erin had tried to go back in but the fire had ravaged the place. There was no way her dad had lived. Only she and her horse had made it.

"Oh, God," she cried and fell to her knees. She tore her eyes from the flames and looked upward, trying to search out the divinity she had always believed in. *"Why* have you done this?" Erin squeezed her eyes shut and realized she was blaming the wrong person. Somehow she'd been responsible for this. Whether she had lit the fire with an errant thought or was never convincing enough when she tried to get her dad to quit flicking that damn lighter.

Either way, *she* was responsible.

Nobody else.

Tears blurred her vision so much it took several blinks before she realized someone was walking out of the barn. No, not one person but two.

It couldn't be.

She blinked a few more times and stumbled to her feet. "Dad?"

"I have to go now, Angel," he said softly.

"Why?" She tried to run to him but couldn't seem to move her feet. "You're alive! You don't need to go anywhere."

Her words sounded odd even to herself. As though unconsciously she knew he did.

He offered no response as he looked at her with love. Her eyes shot to the man by his side. Tall, dark and handsome, he had been one of the faces in the fire. Fury rose and she shook her head. "Don't you take him from me!"

"You make sure you sing, Erin," her dad said. "Live your dream."

"No." She shook her head. "No, Dad, don't go!"

But it was too late. The dark haired man spread his white wings and wrapped them around her father moments before a white light shot toward the sky and they both vanished.

"No!" she screamed and leapt toward him only to find herself no longer in her memories but in Rònan's arms. The barn had vanished. It was quiet and she was in a medieval Scottish cave. Cullen no longer had wings but knelt on one knee with his head bent.

"It was *you*." Her eyebrows slammed together and she tried to lunge at him but Rònan made it impossible. Erin shook her head, eyes narrowed on Cullen, voice lethal. "You took my dad from me."

Cullen remained silent with his head lowered.

Why was he doing that? Submission? Regret? What?

"He honors you." Rònan held her tighter when she tried to move. "And he honors your father's passing. 'Twas he who made sure your Da made it safely to Heaven. And 'twas he that kept you safe from the dark demi-god until now."

She shook her head, overwhelmed. "Heaven," she whispered. "I don't believe in any kind of Heaven."

"Mayhap not now," Rònan said softly. "But you once did, lass."

Had she? Did she? Maybe once upon a time but after that fire no more. Yet as she replayed the events of that night in her head, other memories from earlier in her life resurfaced. Her father and her praying for her mom's soul...that she might be in peace wherever she was. While they weren't overly religious, they always murmured a prayer before dinner and Dad wore a cross until the day he...died.

Died.

But not gone entirely.

No.

Erin put a hand over her mouth, eyed Cullen and allowed the truth to sink in. He had made sure her father found peace and that he was far beyond suffering. No matter what unexplainable things happened that night, one thing was for sure.

Dad was at peace.

"Thank you…for everything," she mouthed but nothing came out.

Though he wasn't looking at her and she hadn't spoken aloud, Cullen whispered, "'Twas my honor. I only wish I could have saved him but 'twas his time." Then, not making a big deal out of it in the least, he returned to Treasa's side.

The next thing she knew her arms were around Rònan and her face was pressed against his chest. After that, things were a blur for a while. Though outside of herself, she knew she cried and that she released long repressed emotions. So much heartache she had no idea she still carried. But somehow when Cullen showed her what she'd forgotten, she was able to see how much it had affected her life.

Who she had become.

Not a bad person just someone very closed off. Someone who kept people at arm's length.

"Hell," she muttered at last and pulled away from Rònan. Only then did she realize that Cullen and Treasa were gone. Her Viking posse remained at the entrance with their heads bent and Darach sat on her other side. She wiped away the last of her tears and frowned at him rather than look at Rònan. "So you stuck around for the sob show, eh?"

"Aye," he murmured. "'Tis what friends do, lass."

"Thanks," she whispered. "I'm lucky to have you both around."

"Aye," Rònan agreed gruffly.

When her eyes at last turned his way, it was to see him wiping a hand over his face before he stood and turned away to scoop the satchel off the floor. But she didn't miss the glistening on his cheeks beforehand.

Tears.

For her.

"Ronan," she whispered but it was too late. He had gone outside.

"All my life I've known my cousin but have yet to see him mourn like this. Ronan doesnae deal in tears," Darach said softly. "He cares for you deeply, lass."

It was on the tip of her tongue to say he shouldn't but she suddenly realized that her long held self-loathing was no longer valid. Nonetheless, over a decade of feeling and reacting a certain way didn't vanish in a single moment. So she said what felt natural. "He'll get over it. They always do."

Darach frowned. "I dinnae think so."

She stood, determined to get back to what made sense. "Hey, you got a blade on you? I don't like being without a weapon."

"Aye." He handed her a small dagger.

She eyed the noticeable bulges in his clothing and curled her fingers. "I'll take one more."

He sighed. "You dinnae need them here."

"Hand one over or I'll take it when you're not looking."

When he hesitated, she offered a lopsided grin. "I've done it before and I'll do it again so let's make this easy."

"Och, so that's where my missing blade went," he muttered as he handed her one.

"Guess I should've kept my mouth shut." She winked and tucked her blades away. "It's always more fun to scoop 'em off you when you're not looking."

His brows arched. "More than one?"

She nodded. "You need to keep better track of your weapons, friend."

"I'm a seasoned warrior and yet you still managed it," he mumbled. "You've a way with thievery."

Erin shrugged. "Call it what you will. If I'm not provided with weapons, I find a way to get them." She headed for the exit. "C'mon warrior. I imagine they're waiting for us."

By the time they made it outside, everyone was ready to travel. Ronan gestured to Tosha. "She's yours to ride, lass."

She nodded and said, "Damn straight," as she swung onto the horse. Other horses were here which she assumed Cullen had arranged. Ronan rode one taller than Tosha and well-suited to his size.

212

"Are you well, Erin?" he said, coming alongside as they made their way through the thick forest.

Never more thankful that he was back to normal, she nodded. "I am, thanks." Concerned despite herself, she said, "And you?"

Their eyes locked and as quickly as his lust could feed hers, the silent strength in his gaze filled her just as readily. "Aye, lass, I'm well."

"Good."

They fell into a comfortable silence as they traveled. It didn't take her long to figure out he was giving them both some space. She needed as much and appreciated it.

She kept playing over the events in the cave. Everything she thought she understood had changed within minutes. She had *not* killed her father. More than that, he hadn't caused that fire himself. No, some ancient Scottish enemy *had*. Though circumstances were dire, for the first time in far too long, she felt remarkably free.

Free of a prison she had put herself in.

Free of a prison she had put her father in.

More than that, she was free to finally let go and realize that her father was in a better place. So was she because of it.

Eventually, the woods thinned and gave way to a sweeping field overlooked by what she soon learned was Stewart Castle. Stately and almost majestic, it was back-dropped by a mountainous cliff.

The whole effect made one think twice about approaching. Even so, Erin couldn't help but compare it to MacLeod Castle. Where Rònan's castle sat on a cliff daring the wind and ocean to weatherize it more, this castle seemed far too protected and safe. Some might call it beautiful with its staggered wall walks and towers but she much preferred the hard edges of a castle that had withstood the ages of time via the sea.

There was more beauty in that.

In survival. In how it fortified you if you didn't let it eat you alive.

If you still remained standing when life had seemingly beaten you down.

Erin inhaled deeply. In the end, what did she know of being beaten down? Nicole had been by her circumstances but as it turned out, maybe not Erin. Instead of having to go into foster care, she ended up with an uncle and cousins until she was eighteen. He wasn't around much so she pretty much fended for herself. Still, it wasn't as rough as it could have been.

"You lost your father in a terrible way and formed your life around it," Rònan's words whispered through her mind. *"You're allowed to feel beaten down."*

Though grateful for his support, she didn't look his way but kept her eyes on the castle as they approached. Only when she saw people running across the field in their direction did she realize how self-absorbed she'd become.

"Cullen?" a woman cried as she staggered over the last drawbridge. "Is that ye, Son?"

A tall, handsome man followed her who based on his similar looks had to be Cullen's father. Pain mixed with joy as he wrapped his arms around not only Cullen but the woman and they all embraced.

"They are his parents, Alan and Caitriona Stewart," Rònan said softly, steering their horses past them. "A family coming together once more. Something we didnae think would happen."

Erin knew nothing about the proper way to greet them so she did what Cullen so recently did for her. She lowered her head and kept quiet. Everything she felt now wasn't based on his divinity but what he had so clearly given up when he left his home.

He had been a son and well loved.

Just like she had been a daughter and well loved.

They'd just entered the courtyard when a young woman strode up alongside her. At first, Erin thought nothing of it and meant to keep her head down.

"Will ye not look at me then?"

Recognizing the voice, her eyes shot to the woman.

"Good, ye see me." The woman squeezed her hand, leaned closer and whispered harshly, "Might ye save me then?"

Erin shook her head, confused.

Though the woman was younger than the last time she saw her, one thing was for certain.

She was Cullen's sister, Brae Stewart.

Chapter Sixteen

"*HOW* MUCH YOUNGER did Brae look before she vanished from your sight?" Alan Stewart asked for the fifth time as he paced in front of the fire. He made a gesture with his hands. "Did she wear her hair piled on her head like this?" He kind of groped at his hair before he skimmed his hands alongside his neck. "Or was it in braids? Sweet as it always was?"

They had arrived here almost two days ago and though Alan was very happy to have his son back, he remained disgruntled about his daughter.

"It was sort of half up, half down," Erin said as she had a few times already.

 Rònan knew that Erin had come to terms with her past and was doing her best to help out Cullen's father. More than that, she wanted to repay Cullen in any way she could for taking care of her father and keeping her safe.

Catriona spent the early part of the evening hosting and had recently joined them in a large antechamber off of the great hall. She didn't allow Alan to continue his ranting much longer before she said, "Enough, good husband. The poor lass has told you all she knows. By the sounds of it, Brae wasn't all that much younger." Her eyes met Erin. "The hair style you're describing sounds like the way she wore it for a time three winters or so ago."

Erin nodded. "I don't mind Laird Stewart questioning me. My father would've done the same had I been in Brae's position." Her eyes flickered between them. "I can't imagine how hard this has been on you both."

Catriona squeezed Cullen's hand when he sat beside her. "It has been difficult but at least our son has been returned to us." A warm smile curled her lips when she looked at Treasa. "And his betrothed. 'Tis truly good to see ye again, lass."

"Aye, 'twas more wonderful than ye know to visit my village and be amongst my own again," Treasa said. "And to once more be at Stewart Castle with Cullen and all of ye."

It had been eventful since the Stewart clan reunited with Cullen and Treasa. Rònan had given Erin a thorough tour of the extensive castle with her Viking posse right behind. Now that it was confirmed the enemy was not defeated, they were more vigilant than ever. Though he felt moments of irritation when he wanted privacy with her, he could only be grateful they cared so much.

Like Darach, who had been filled in on the events at MacLeod Castle, he was deeply upset that the dark demi-god had survived. Though Rònan knew his defeat had almost seemed too easy, he'd remained hopeful. When Erin bathed earlier, Rònan took the opportunity to speak with Darach in the armory.

"So not only you and I but the Vikings are to protect Erin whilst our cousins and kin watch over the wee king for now." Rònan frowned at Darach. "I'm surprised Niall wasnae sent considering he has the sword I'm meant to fight this evil with."

Rònan's father had given the sword to Niall when he was younger. Since then it had been re-forged with magic by not only the great wizards, Iosbail and Adlin MacLomain, but also by Alan Stewart. A weapon that had once defeated a great evil and apparently was meant to do so again.

"I dinnae question my Da when he orders me to go somewhere," Darach replied. "Though I know ye'd prefer Niall."

While grateful Darach had been so supportive of Erin, he was more on edge with his cousin than usual. "'Twas ill of ye not to be at my castle though it seems ye clearly arrived at the last minute. Jackie was looking for ye and the lass could use the protection now more than ever. Mayhap even the friendship."

"Jackie had her friends and all of ye to protect her." Darach studied a particularly long dagger and tested its weight. "Someone needed to check on my castle to make sure the people were well tended."

"Last I knew 'twas not yer castle but yer Da's, aye?" Rònan leaned against the wall, crossed his arms over his chest, and frowned. "'Twas ill timing that ye were set to oversee what ye should've been seeing to long before this. Especially considering the

Broun lasses and the wee king need ye more than ever. 'Twas what ye bloody well trained yer whole life for, Cousin."

While Darach might be evasive when it came to certain things, he wasn't one to turn from an upcoming battle. Arms crossed over his chest as well, he faced Rònan. "Dinnae try to lay blame my way. 'Twas me who spent plenty of time in the twenty-first century making sure the Broun lasses knew and trusted at least one of us before being thrust back in time. 'Twas also me who worked with a few of them before they came so that they might defend themselves better."

Rònan narrowed his eyes. "Mayhap, but I think ye were there more for the lusting than anything else."

"Ye can think what ye bloody well want," Darach bit back. "It doesnae change the fact that the lasses had somebody there. Me. And what about ye? Ye dare to judge me? Ye couldnae be bothered to go to the twenty-first century until ye had no other choice. And why? Because ye were too busy doing yer lusting back here and neglecting yer duties to yer clan."

The conversation would have grown far more heated had Cullen not joined them. And though both were tempted to argue despite his presence, they knew their brethren was going through enough. So now, hours later, they listened to Alan Stewart mull over his daughter's odd ghostly appearance and made a point of not looking at one another. Because if they did, the argument would likely flare up again. Only this time telepathically.

"I think if we should take nothing else from this experience, husband," Catriona said. "'Tis that our daughter isnae as evil as we were led to believe...likely not evil at all."

"'Tis my greatest hope." Alan frowned at Cullen, his words thickening with emotion. "But all aside, she murdered her own brother in battle. 'Tis lucky that God gave ye another chance at life after ye gave up yer wings."

Cullen remained vague about exactly how that had happened but it was clear to all based on the way they looked at each other, that Treasa was at the heart of it.

"Aye." His eyes remained on Treasa. "I've never been so lucky."

"Nor I," she murmured.

"So ye know nothing of why Erin would have seen Brae such as she did?" Alan asked Cullen.

"Nay, Da." Cullen shook his head. "I can only hope that 'twill lead to good things and help all of us find resolution one way or another."

Rònan knew that Cullen didn't trust the situation any more than the rest of them. Who knows how the dark Laird might be trying to get to Erin. He also sensed that Cullen repressed a great deal of fury when it came to his sister. A fury that he suspected Alan and Catriona were well aware of. But there could be no blame laid for that. Cullen had every right.

Yet at this moment, Cullen's focus was on anything but his sister.

No, he only had eyes for Treasa.

"I think mayhap 'tis time for us to step away from heartache and focus on joy for a little while," Catriona said softly as she watched Cullen and Treasa eye one another. "Do we not have a wedding to attend then?"

Eager to wait until they returned home so that they could be with their families, the two had waited to marry. Yet Caitriona recognized that her son wouldn't wait much longer. Unlike the clandestine wedding they had tried years ago, she decided nothing would better suit the joyous occasion than the added bonus of marriage.

Rònan stayed close to Erin when everyone started to filter outside and up the path to the wide area beside the mountain behind the castle. He kept a hand against her back as they walked and murmured close to her ear, "You look more beautiful than ever, lass."

And she did.

There was a new glow to her that he knew had to do with her accepting that she couldn't change the past. More than that, it no longer controlled her.

His heart still broke over what she'd suffered. Rònan had never felt so much compassion or sympathy for anyone. He was impressed by how strong she'd become because of it. Yet it had taken its toll and for some reason made her remain distant to a man's affections. Something he was determined to push past when the time was right.

When she was ready.

Because of the wedding, she was once again in a dress that highlighted her petite figure to perfection. It was deep purple, drawing out her eyes so well that when men weren't gawking at her body and face, they were ensnared by her gaze. And it was getting to be too much. Mostly because though he made it clear he wanted her, Erin didn't reciprocate. She did not flirt with others, but she certainly didn't act as if she were his. Then again, she wasn't. Not yet.

But she would be.

"You don't look half bad yourself," Erin murmured in response to his earlier compliment.

His blood stirred when she eyed him over. Laird Stewart made sure he had a fresh MacLeod plaid and his clan's brooch. So he was once more in full regalia except this time his tunic was sleeveless. It seemed that difference worked because her gaze kept returning to his bare arms. She liked not only the markings but the muscles.

"Treasa looks fantastic." Erin grinned. "Though her dress rocks, I'm almost surprised she isn't wearing pants."

She referred to how much Treasa had apparently embraced the twenty-first century. Like Erin, Treasa and Cullen apparently had motorcycles and enjoyed riding.

"I think I'd like to visit your century once all of this is over and ride a bike," he said. "After hearing all of you talk about it, I grow more intrigued."

The corner of Erin's lip shot up and her arousal spiked. "You'd look damn good on one." She cast him a curious sidelong glance as they made their way onto the lower half of the mountain. "It's hard to know if it'd give you much of a thrill though seeing how you can fly. I tend to think that might feel a lot like the freedom of the open road but far better."

"Aye, mayhap," he agreed. "But you misunderstand. I think I'd like to try it with you because it's something *you* love to do."

"Ah." Erin didn't look at him but she did allow him to take her hand as they made their way through the crowd. "This place is amazing." Her eyes went to the massive bonfire before she gazed up at the sheer rock face behind it. "I bet it's even more gorgeous up there."

"'Tis." He glanced up as he bought two skins of whisky from a peddler. "'Twas where Bradon and Leslie first coupled."

"Really?" She chuckled. "And how do you know that?"

He handed her a skin and grinned. "Secrets dinnae keep well in our clans."

"Good to know." She kept eying her surroundings. "I'm sorta shocked they ended up living in the twenty-first century after having been here and back in your time. I've yet to see MacLomain Castle but I've heard good things."

"Leslie was determined to go home and her Highlander wouldnae be without her." Rònan gestured at the rock face. "Would you like to go up and watch the wedding from there?"

"Actually, I would." She grinned. "It's not every day a girl gets to watch her guardian angel get married and that looks like a great vantage point."

"Aye," he agreed.

Grateful for the opportunity to get her away from the crowd and mayhap talk a bit, he led her up a fairly steep path. He knew better than to tell her to be careful. Erin could more than handle herself and would likely not appreciate the advice. As he suspected, she made it up quickly without being winded in the least.

They sat on a rock that gave them a perfect view of the couple marrying below. Small white clouds raced past a nearly full moon, casting shadows over the castle and forest.

"So I imagine Leslie and Bradon sat right here, huh?" she said after a swig of whisky.

He shrugged. "I dinnae know."

Rònan knew she was working toward a question but wasn't sure how she should phrase it. He wouldn't either. What he did know, sadly enough, was that there was only one answer.

So he kept his voice soft. "I cannae help but know what you're curious about, Erin." He tried to meet her eyes but they were locked on the fire below. Yet he had to continue. This needed to be said despite how hard it was. "I am not Bradon, lass. He was brother to Laird MacLomain at the time and didnae have the same responsibilities as I do." He sighed. "So though tempted, I couldnae live in the twenty-first century even if I wanted to. I willnae abandon my clan."

Erin remained silent for a time as she continued to stare at the fire. She wore that emotionless mask and her face was unreadable. It was the longest damn moment of his life. Would she hate him? Did this mean there was no hope for them? Either way, he would do what he had to even if it meant losing her. He'd made an oath to his clan and it was long past time that he see it through.

Eventually, her eyes met his. When she spoke her words weren't emotional in the least but strong and even. "You know, you're really starting to impress the hell out of me, Laird MacLeod. I'm proud of you."

He hadn't realized how shallow his breathing had become until she responded. How much he worried about whether she would understand. Then again, he imagined there was another reason for his response. Erin had actually *wanted* him there. Though it was hard to know if she desired a relationship, this felt like a step in the right direction...somewhat. Because there was another thing to be learned from her unsaid question.

She still intended to go home.

And not to his home.

Erin nodded down at the couple taking their vows in front of the fire. "So I don't suppose Cullen will be able to show off those gorgeous wings when he kisses Treasa, will he?"

"This clan's laird is a wizard and the Lady of the Castle a mystic so 'twould not surprise me." Rònan realized she was trying to detour the conversation. "The clan knows he is an angel so anything is possible."

"That's really cool," she murmured. "I think it's amazing how accepting all your clans are of all the various mystical beings."

"'Tis easy enough when everyone's raised around such," he said. "'Tis less mystical, and simply normal for them."

"True enough." She leaned forward when Cullen cupped Treasa's cheeks and kissed her. "Looks like they're..." Her eyes widened when a faint glow emitted from the Stewart and his wings appeared. Then her eyes moistened when Cullen closed his wings around Treasa. "Damn, that's so sweet...beautiful."

All he could think of was how much he wanted to close his wings around Erin. Though he had never met the Viking female dragons, he knew they were smaller than their male counterparts. And though his mother might be fierce, she was little more than half his size in dragon form. That meant Erin was likely close in size. So if they were ever dragons together, his wings would easily be able to wrap around her.

Well aware of his thoughts, Erin's eyes met his. She said nothing at first, just stared at him. When she spoke, he was surprised by her words. "Now that we know the bad guy's still out there, I should practice shifting. Because one way or another, I know damn well that I can better protect Robert in dragon form."

It was true. She could.

"Aye, she can and she should." Tosha's words whispered through not only his mind but Erin's. *"'Twould only be to the enemy's advantage if she shifts for the first time when he once more appears. 'Twould verra well mean not only her demise but that of those she seeks to protect."*

"See," Erin said. "I'm right."

"Aye," Rònan agreed, proud of Erin for being so brave. Because something like this took more courage than most people could imagine. "As soon as we get back to my castle and Grant and my Ma are with you, then you will try shifting."

"So it's dangerous?"

"Nay," Tosha said at the same time Rònan said, "Aye."

"Okay," Erin said slowly, eyes narrowed on him. "No offense, but I tend to think the horse who is half MacLomain mystical wizard probably has a little extra wisdom. Why do you think it'd be dangerous, Rònan?"

"I'm half wizard too," he muttered. But the truth was he worried about her. What if something happened and she hurt herself? "'Tis hard to know what to expect the first time you shift."

"All right. You were super young when you shifted for the first time." She frowned. "Outside of the pain that eventually created your tats, did something bad happen? Did you keep something from me so I wouldn't be frightened?"

"Nay. All went well enough." He shook his head. "But I was verra young and had a mother dragon to teach me."

"I see." Erin eyed him. "So are you telling me you think yourself incapable of taking care of and teaching a dragon what to do the first time it shifts?" She tilted her head. "If so, that pretty much tells me that having kids is off your radar because isn't there a good chance if you had a child they'd be half dragon? Or were you planning on letting your mom do that part of raising your children for you?"

Rònan's brows flew together and he frowned at her unexpected questions and borderline accusation. His mind reeled over her talking about children. Though he knew she spoke of bairns he might someday have with another lass, all he could think about were his thoughts a few short days ago. A desire to have children with *her.*

A desire that only grew stronger.

Before he could respond, she said, "How safe do you think we are here from the enemy?"

"Verra safe," Tosha answered for him. *"This that happens now is divine intervention. Soon enough you will have to go back and protect the wee king. Until then, 'tis verra likely nothing can touch you here."*

"Anywhere here?" Erin asked.

"Aye," Tosha said. *"But time is limited. Cullen was only given a small window of opportunity to keep you here. Something he wasnae even given permission to do for the wee King."*

Erin nodded and clenched her jaw before she stood, faced Rònan and planted her hands on her hips. "Alrighty then, Sweetheart. Let's go do this then."

He frowned. "Do what?"

"You're gonna take me somewhere private away from all these people and I'm gonna shift."

Rònan snorted. "You're out of your bloody mind, lass."

Erin's frown met his. "No, I'm thinking real clear right now. You heard what Tosha said."

"Och," Rònan scoffed. A flash of fear made his temperature spike. "'Tis not the right time or place for such a thing."

"You're right, it's not a good place," she agreed and started walking. "That's why you're gonna bring me to the right one."

"I willnae," he said, unmoving.

"Fine," she threw over her shoulder. "Then I'll get my Viking posse to help me."

His eyes narrowed. She better be bluffing.

"You willnae," he called after her, not budging, convinced she would come back to argue.

He should have known better.

Erin didn't bother responding but vanished down the path.

"Erin, get back here," he called. "You dinnae know what you're doing."

Was she truly seeking out Bjorn and Tait?

"Erin," he called again.

Still no response.

Bloody *hell*.

"Fine then," he muttered and went after her. He had just made it around the bend before he stopped short.

Erin was waiting and cocked a grin at him. "Good boy." She made a flourish with her hand that pointed in several directions at once. "The next move's yours. Lead the way."

Though more than tempted to throw her over his shoulder and bring her back to the castle, he knew that wouldn't go well. And Cullen and Treasa did not deserve that on their wedding day.

"Good boy, my arse. Fine then," he growled and headed back up the path. "Come."

"Sure thing." He didn't miss the smile of triumph in her voice. Troublesome little dragon.

He had spent ample enough time at this castle in his youth so he knew the land well. Only one spot struck him as far enough away. That meant walking the shore and putting another mountain between them and Stewart Castle. Sure, the noble thing to do would be to bring her back so she could change into pants first but he was far too frustrated.

Determined as she was, Erin made no complaints as she followed him down the less steep but far longer path that led down the backside of the mountain to the loch. And though he muttered no less than half a dozen times, "This is a bloody bad idea," as they followed the shore, she never said a word. No, she held up her skirts, kept her head held high and moved right along.

What he was most impressed with, however, was how well she managed her fear.

A fear that was very much there.

But Erin pushed it aside and kept focused on what she felt she needed to do. That meant embracing what she was so she could save Robert the Bruce. Despite himself, Rònan admired her more and more as she walked along the dark beach toward something that had been her greatest fear for so long. Though he knew she had more courage than most, a tremendous amount of pride filled him. This lass would do anything to protect those she cared about. Anything at all. Fear did not rule her in the least.

Yet it continued to fill him.

Would he be able to walk her through this shift? What if something went wrong? Was she right, did he depend too heavily on his Ma and Grant? Had he been for too long in one form or another?

The moon had started rolling back down the sky when they reached the area of shore he knew would be best. The openness of the loch beyond the second mountain would give her room to fly without clan Stewart or any nearby villages seeing her. More than that, there was a tight alcove of trees nearby that would give her a place to shelter when she shifted back. Because if he knew one thing, she would be in an odd state of shock when she did and being out of the wind would be best.

"They're giving me more distance than usual," Erin finally said. "But I know they're there."

Rònan didn't have to glance over his shoulder to know Bjorn and Tait trailed at a distance. They knew exactly what was happening. Though as a general rule he wanted Tait nowhere near Erin, this time he felt relief. Maybe there was comfort in numbers...or was it his way of escaping taking this on alone?

"No Viking posse." Erin's eyes met his. "I want only you here for now, Rònan." She inhaled deeply then whispered, "Just you."

When another flash of fear raced through him, he repressed it. She deserved better. "Aye, lass." Though it was the last thing he wanted to say with Tait and Bjorn nearby, he said, "Though you can remain clothed, 'twill likely inhibit how you embrace your dragon."

"Uh huh, that makes sense I guess," she murmured and pressed her lips together as she eyed her dress. Erin being Erin didn't overly contemplate things but cupped her hands over her mouth and yelled into the darkness. "Gimme a little privacy already, guys. Turn around."

He knew that both complied but Tait wasn't above peeking. Damn Viking.

Rònan kept his breathing even and eyes somewhat averted as Erin stripped down. But as always, escaping arousal was impossible.

She shook her head. "Get control of that erection, because I seriously need to focus."

Yet another reason he should not be here for her first shift. All he wanted to do was throw her on the ground and have his way with her. Clearing his throat, he dragged his mind from romping and focused on everything she was facing right now. More than that, the reason she was doing what she was.

To help save Robert the Bruce.

What made him get control of himself in the end was how much she deserved to be treated with respect. Erin was a hero. That firmly in mind, he didn't focus on her body but her eyes when she was ready.

"You can do this one of two ways because it seems two emotions bring out your dragon. The one way you will have to do on your own. The other, I can assist you via my dragon," Rònan said, not entirely sure why he gave her both options when he had no idea if he could control himself. "So either you give into anger or lust."

"For real?" Erin snorted. "That sounds like a no-brainer."

"It does?" he asked, truly unsure where her mind was until it became blatantly clear.

"Come here then."

"Dinnae you want to know more of what to expect, more of—"

That's all he managed to get out before she strode over, pulled his lips down to hers and kissed him hard. For a brief moment, he felt guilty mostly because he had no idea in the least if his dragon magic could help her shift. It seemed like a sound theory and something inside told him he could do it. But now with her soft lips against his, he wasn't so sure.

"Erin," he murmured between kisses, trying like hell not to pull her into his arms and touch every inch of her. Though his eyes were closed, the red haze of the dragon quickly filled his mind's eye. Her hands abandoned his cheeks to slide up beneath his tunic before she wrapped her arms around him and pressed close.

It was then that he felt it.

Her dragon.

Cupping her cheeks, he wrapped his tongue with hers. One swoop, two, three, then he pulled back enough that their eyes locked. When her brilliant purple dragon eyes met his, he stopped breathing.

He knew what he had to do.

How, he would never know, but he did.

So he turned her and brought his mouth close to her ear while simultaneously pressing close. "You think you can be a dragon but still you fear so much." He nibbled her earlobe, then dared. "You can do nothing to save the wee King. You are not fit."

Rònan felt the beast in her bubbling to the surface. The pure rage she had repressed in life for so long. He gripped her hips and spoke through clenched teeth. "You arenae one of us though you try."

Her dragon responded to both his touch—the lust—and his taunting—the anger.

But she needed more.

His magic.

So he let it free. A type of magic he had no idea he possessed until he felt her dragon and human mind bite at his...plead with his. Unable to push anymore cruel, untrue words past his lips, he gave into the burning pain that ran along his dragon markings.

The original pain he had felt when he shifted for the first time.

All of it fed into her body.

His pain became hers.

When she cried out and arched, he held tight, frightened for her while at the same time realizing he had to let her go.

"I'm scared, Rònan," she whispered moments before she screamed at the top of her lungs.

Though everything in him wanted to keep her close and safe, he let go and stepped back. When she fell to her knees, the Vikings came closer. But they didn't interfere any more than Rònan did. Instead, he sensed they were a wall of support not only for Erin but for him.

Rònan took a few staggered steps back as she started to whimper.

"Rònan, stop this," she cried from far, far away into his mind.

"Nay, lad," Tosha whispered. *"Dinnae. 'Tis time ye set her free, aye?"*

He kept shaking his head as her pain and confusion became his. Terrified for her, he realized he had likely made some sort of awful mistake. After that, everything blurred. Her thoughts, emotions, their connection.

"Erin," he roared. Though determined to save her, he was unable to move when Tait and Bjorn grabbed his arms.

Immobile, he watched in both torture and amazement as the air twisted around Erin. Black at first and then every shade of purple...her dragon colors. Slowly but surely, he felt her pain lessen as her vision changed along with her body. His struggles lessened along with hers and pure awe took over.

He had seen a lot of beautiful things in life but nothing so stunning as what was left behind when the air stopped spinning around her. While small, she was magnificent. Almost iridescent, deep purple scales glittered along her serpentine body.

But that wasn't the best part.

No, that would be her eyes.

When they turned his way, even the Vikings took a ragged breath.

The palest of purple with starbursts of darker purple at their centers, they were…ferocious.

"She needs someone to show her how to fly," Bjorn managed, his heart beating as rapidly as Rònan and Tait's.

"I will," Tait said though his words came out as a weak, wanting whisper.

Erin tested her feet and swung her head back and forth.

"No, it should be me," Bjorn said softly.

Though he wanted to deny both men, Rònan still couldn't manage to speak as he watched her. Fortunately, she took matters into her own hands—or talons—when her head swung down and one brilliant eye looked directly at him. "No. You."

Hearing her in his head for the first time as a dragon felt like he had transcended to a different plane. One made of eternal bliss and unparalleled pleasure.

Erin's Viking posse didn't stand a chance.

Rònan roared and shifted within a blink.

As it was when they were in human form, she was barely half his size.

And just like in human form, she wasn't intimidated in the least.

Instead, she peered up at him and dared, her words sharp and direct. *"Show me how to fly, dragon or I'll figure it out on my own."*

There was no hesitation in his response. No thinking things through. He wasn't human now. He was a dragon. She listened or she didn't.

"Aye, then." He walked around her and sniffed the air. *"Like I taught you back at the Viking fortress, we dragons sense the weather. We can feel everything. Always test the wind first. If there's no sheer, take flight. If there is a sheer, work with it. Always take off*

not against it but with it, especially if battle is ahead. Working against a heavy wind can weaken you greatly."

"But how do I fly to begin with?"

Rònan cocked his head at her and knew she heard the humor in his voice. *"Flap your wings and fly, lass. At your age, you might be surprised by how easy that is."*

"My age?"

"Aye." He chuckled and realized training Erin would be quite simple. Challenge her. *"You're verra old to be taking your first flight. 'Twill be interesting to see if you can even manage it."*

Rònan didn't banter with her any further but flapped his wings and took off, hopeful she would be aggravated enough to follow. He counted the long seconds as he lifted up over the loch and refused to look back.

Please let her follow me. Please let her be able to do it.

Because of his superior hearing, Tait and Bjorn's words met his ears from the shore.

"It was unwise of him to taunt her like that," Tait said. "Foolish Highlander."

"I agree," Bjorn said. "I do not envy his position."

For Bjorn to say as much spoke to Rònan. Gods above, he had done this all wrong. Erin was unable to take flight and remained flapping around on shore hating him. He should have been more patient. He should have remembered that she had no idea what she was doing and had trusted *him* to teach her.

Mortified, Rònan banked a left to turn back only to have his wing clipped hard as Erin sailed by him, fury in her searing purple eyes. Confused and surprised, he watched as she dipped down, body wobbly before she leveled out and shifted her wing so that she flew back in the opposite direction.

Bloody hell. Her Viking posse wasn't worried about her but *him*!

Erin flew back to the shore and though her landing wasn't particularly graceful, she did it. Then she tucked her wings by her side in what was clearly a posture of unhappy defiance. Bjorn and Tait lowered their heads to honor her before they made quick work of leaving her be.

Obviously in a state, Erin proceeded to tromp into the forest, her newfound wings scraping the limbs and bending the trees before the air shimmered and her dragon vanished. Rònan shifted when he landed and ran after her. As he knew would likely happen, she had made it to the small glen he always loved as a bairn. By the time he got there she'd fallen to her knees and her head was bent.

"Erin?" He raced to her. "Are you well, lass?"

Her eyes met his, the last of her dragon fading away. She shook her head and managed a few whispered words before she passed out.

"Why did I ever think you might be the guy for me?"

Chapter Seventeen

THERE WAS NO sweeter bliss than feeling her new body for the first time except the way she felt when she looked into *his* eyes. Emerald eyes that stayed with her the whole time. A green dragon that towered over her and kept her safe...until he shunned her.

Though Erin jolted awake, it took more effort than she expected to sit up. She felt like she had boulders attached to her limbs. Confused, she tried not to panic as her vision blurred.

"'Tis all right, lass," Rònan said softly. "Your vision is but readjusting to being human again."

"Enough with the vision issues," she croaked and wiped her hands over her eyes. "They're getting old."

"Aye," he murmured.

Erin blinked a few times and acclimated to her surroundings. They sat in a small clearing surrounded by trees. Salt drifted on the wind so she knew she was still near the loch. As she became more and more aware, she recalled standing on the shore with Rònan. Of him pulling her close. Such lust.

Then her vision went red.

After that, things were fuzzy but sharp at the same time. There was pain...at first. Then a sense of freedom she had never felt. Something new...different...better. *Wings.* Erin looked from arm to arm. Not wings but definitely arms. She had little time to process that before flashes of another dragon again arose. A green one far larger than her, arrogant and defiant in its strength.

His strength.

When her eyes met Rònan's, everything flooded back. How his dragon taunted her and said she was too old to get the hang of flying. How demeaning he was. How demeaning he *had* to be to get her where she needed to be.

"Did you really?" she whispered.

She felt all the insecurities flickering through his mind. The same ones he'd had as they walked the shore to get here. How worried he was that he wouldn't be able to teach her. Then she heard all his deepest thoughts. How he felt like an ass. And how he wished he could turn back time and handle it differently. But there was another emotion. One she appreciated more than all the others.

One, thank God, he showed her when he spoke.

An emotion that made no apologies for his behavior.

Eyes firm, voice just soft enough, he took her hand and nodded. "Aye, lass, I did everything you remember when in dragon form." He clenched his jaw, banking all the apologies he wanted to offer and looked at her with the sort of hard admiration shared amongst fellow soldiers. The sort of look she worked hard to win from men in the military. "And never have I been prouder than I was of you today. You are not only a strong warrior but a fierce dragon."

She almost said, "Damn straight," but realized only two words suited the moment. "Thank you."

Flashes continued to flicker through her mind of flying, of the defiance she felt toward him that made her spread her wings for the first time and flap. After that, it was pure, unbelievable euphoria. Sure, she shot after him, whacked at his wing, then everything went downhill but still…she flew!

She *did* it.

She faced her worst fear, more so her worst nightmare. Not many could say that. Flopping back on the grass, she stared at the moon barely visible through the thick foliage and felt like she had climbed the tallest mountain. Between learning the truth about her past and embracing her dragon, she felt free in a whole new way.

Rònan lay down beside her and stared at the moon as well. Like her, he was releasing a whole lot of tension. Though her dragon might have been furious at him, her human half was touched by how hard he had tried. How much he cared. She'd never met another man like him.

As if he read her mind because he likely had, he said, "Have there been that many then?"

"That many what?"

"Men in your life that you can compare me to."

Erin rolled her eyes. "Likely not close to the number of women you've had."

232

"Och. I suppose I deserve that," he said. "Why not so many men for you then? 'Tis surprising with your beauty."

"Not that I think I'm all that, but people can be considered attractive and not be inclined to sleep around," she enlightened.

"Mayhap," he agreed, a grin in his voice. "'Tis hard to imagine, though."

She liked that he didn't look at her and make this a mushy moment. That alone made her answer readily. "I worried that I might hurt them like I did my dad."

A short silence stretched before Rònan murmured, "You worried about killing them with fire."

Erin bit back emotion. "Yeah."

"'Tis why you dinnae like being touched," he said. "'Tis also why you didnae pursue anything beyond sex."

She really did love this guy...and how blatant he could be.

"I never knew for sure if I killed my dad so yeah, I kept things brief enough to get the job done but even then there was always a level of stress involved. That's why I sleep with clothes on to this day. Just a habit formed of wanting to try to cuddle a little afterward but realizing I might need to get out of there fast. I realized that even that amount of intimacy could get me in trouble," she said.

Erin couldn't help but sigh before she continued. "After a while, I decided it wasn't worth the risk. I suppose I don't like being touched now because I've had so little physical contact. Most would probably crave it more but I guess I trained my brain to work in the opposite way. A defense mechanism of sorts."

A small silence passed as he considered her words. As always, she could hear most of his thoughts. How sad he was that she'd grown uncomfortable with physical touch. How she had sacrificed sex. More than that, how proud he was of her that she put other people's safety before her own needs. And for a man like Rònan, sex was right there at the top of what was most needed in life.

Then there was another thought he tried to repress. How she would never have to worry about something like that if she stayed with him. And he was more than willing to make up for all the lost intimacy she had suffered.

"This is why you're not on birth control," he murmured.

Erin nodded, not all that surprised he knew what that was considering Nicole's untimely pregnancy. "I got off it when I decided to give up sex altogether." She cast him a sidelong glance. "While you were down and out at the Viking fortress, Megan filled me in on how dragons can control getting pregnant so I figured sex was safe enough with you."

"Aye," he murmured, but she sensed an odd shift to his tone before he changed the subject altogether.

"You are verra proud of your time in the military," he said, voice gentle as his eyes stayed trained on the moon. "What of your promise to your Da? What of you pursuing singing?"

Her breath caught and she shook her head.

Rònan's hand slipped into hers but he kept his eyes averted. "You dinnae need to answer, lass. I was just curious."

And she wasn't going to...at first. It was none of his business. But flashes of his dragon spreading his wings and daring her to fly arose. He was determined that she fly and let go.

In more ways than one.

Though she meant to keep her mouth shut, it didn't work. "I did sing," she said. "Before I entered the military."

"And what happened?" he whispered into her mind.

"I failed," she whispered back. When a strange sort of fear filled her, Erin realized she was worried by how he might respond.

"How so?" He kept speaking within her mind, a place he knew she had become more and more comfortable with...maybe preferred?

"My voice started to crack."

Though he nearly said her voice would sound angelic even with cracks, he knew she would not want to hear that. "So you gave up singing."

"Yes," she whispered aloud, eyes moist. "But I had a few good years in the clubs first. Never made it big but got real close." Erin ran a finger down her throat. "The doctors never knew what it was exactly, just that shit was going downhill and losing my voice altogether was inevitable. They suggested I consider making a career change."

"And your change was the military," he murmured.

"Heck yeah," she said. "I needed a place that..."

When she trailed off, emotional, he said, "A place to find renewed strength. A new start."

"Yes," she said into his mind and looked at him. *"A new start."*

His thoughts swirled with hers. He understood that because he had felt it for the first time when she came into his life. The need for a new start. Except in his case, it didn't mean giving up a dream. No, for him it meant growing up.

Rònan sighed and again stared at the sky, voice whisper soft. "You might be half my size in dragon form but you are easily twice my size where it matters most, lass."

Touched, she squeezed his hand. "You might be bigger than you think, Rònan. Much bigger."

"Mayhap I'm heading in that direction." He propped up on his elbow and his eyes met hers. "But 'tis solely because I met you."

"I think we've been good for each other," she acknowledged.

Her heart began to thud a little heavier as she became overly aware of both the smoldering look in his eyes and their nudity. Yet there was something else now. Something new. When she embraced her dragon, she took on a deeper understanding not only of herself but him. How well-matched they really were. Not because they were half dragon but because of the way their souls somehow fit together...complimented one another.

When had she ever thought about souls?

"When you traveled through time with Cullen, it had an effect on you," Rònan murmured. "You experienced something divine, something that made you see far clearer. Who you really are beneath your physical form."

A shiver rippled through her followed by a flash of heat when his hand brushed her cheek, brogue thicker than ever. "And though I didnae experience the divine as well, ye should know that I feel the same way, lass." He trailed his finger down the side of her neck. "I've never met another who better suits me than ye. 'Tis not just the lust but something far deeper...better." There was a whole new look in his eyes when he whispered, "Something I dinnae want to lose."

She was so used to keeping men at arm's length that it was on the tip of her tongue to say what she always said. What she had been convinced of up until a few days ago. No, I can't. I won't. Now she wondered...could she? Would she? Being with a man like him was risky. "You're not the settling type, Rònan. I know you think you are right now but our situation has been extreme since we met. Ever hear the saying, relationships that start under duress never last?"

His finger stilled on the outer edge of her collarbone and his eyes searched hers. "Then explain how every Broun, MacLomain connection up until now has lasted. Every one of them began under duress."

"But I doubt most of the men were as promiscuous as you."

Rònan snorted. "'Tis well known that Bradon MacLomain had a way with lasses and enjoyed them fully before he met Leslie."

"But then Bradon ended up in the twenty-first century with far less temptation around him on a daily basis," she pointed out.

Rònan frowned. "Are you implying that my uncle would have been unfaithful had he and Leslie stayed here?"

Erin flinched. It had sort of sounded that way. But then she had a history she supposed she ought to share. "All right, I wasn't entirely truthful." She sighed and fiddled with a blade of grass. "Though I was super nervous about it, I tried at a relationship once in my late teens. He was in my band and persistent...and I thought maybe, just maybe..."

"What happened?" Rònan said. "Did you set him on fire?"

"No, thankfully, though at the time I thought he deserved..." She shook her head. "Never mind. He might've said he wanted to get serious but it turned out all he wanted to do was get in my pants. Shortly after he accomplished that, he cheated on me. After that, I figured I better stick to plan A and keep things brief with guys. No heart involved and hopefully no threat of flames."

Rònan eyed her with a new level of understanding before he spoke.

"I know 'tis hard for you to believe given your past but I wouldnae hurt you like that, Erin. Every lass I've been with were well aware I didnae want more than sex. I never once deceived any of them and gave hope where there was none." Rònan tilted her chin until her eyes were with his. "This that I feel for you is different. 'Tis unlike anything I've felt before. 'Tis frightening but addictive. You're all I can think about. Not only the man within wants you to stay with me always but the dragon." He stroked the pad of his thumb over her cheek. "I love you, lass."

Erin tried to speak but couldn't. He meant every word.

But love didn't prevent cheating...did it?

Following her every thought, he said, "Though I swear I would never be unfaithful, there is a way for you to be sure. Something I want so much 'tis making my bloody heart ache."

Erin frowned, confused and caught by the intensity in his eyes and voice. Her heart started to pound and her throat grew dry. Still, she managed to whisper, "And what's that?"

"Marriage can bind us and what I want but 'tis not nearly as strong a connection as my other desire." He kept stroking her cheek. "I want you as my dragon mate, lass. 'Tis as eternal as the ring you wear but more so. Neither of us would ever desire another. Dragons mate for life and 'tis a verra strong bond."

Oh, shit. Yet...

"That sounds intense," she said softly. "Maybe too much so."

"'Tis intense." He shifted closer. "You should not agree unless you're sure you want the same."

Erin inhaled deeply. "I'd be lying if I said I haven't grown to like you a lot but love..." She shook her head. "Love scares me."

"Because you loved your Da and he died," he murmured. "Did you love this man who cheated on you?"

"Honestly? I have no idea. I felt strongly but I was young," she said. "Looking back, I'm pretty sure what I felt was anything but love. Maybe just a need to have someone close to me again. I was pretty lonely."

"You wouldnae be lonely here," he murmured, his body against hers now. "You would have my family and me. Your friends." He cupped the side of her neck. "You can come to my castle or Castles Hamilton or MacLomain and start a new life. I dinnae want you to be with me unless you feel as I do." His lips were close now. "Though 'twould be hard to see you with another, I care for you so deeply that I only want the best for you. Whatever makes you happiest."

"Hell," she whispered, touched by his words. Again, he meant every last one. "You've gotta understand that I'm just not there yet. I haven't known you that long." She swallowed. "But out of curiosity, how exactly do dragons become mates?" Her brows shot up as something occurred to her. "Do they have to have sex in dragon form?"

"Nay." A small, interested smile came to his lips. "Though I can only imagine what that might be like." His hand drifted down to her waist and wrapped around half of it. "It can be done when in human form. From what I've heard, it takes place during sex and is nothing more than one dragon claiming their partner as their mate and the other agreeing."

"Claiming?" She quirked the corner of her lips. "That sounds pretty primitive. So what, do you say 'I claim you' or something?"

When Rònan ran his weapon-roughened fingers along her hipbone, thinking became more and more difficult. The conversation might be heavy, but they were both aroused as hell. "I dinnae think words are involved. All I know is that the feeling must be mutual. It must be as true as the heart and as powerful as the soul for the dragon bond to form."

"Damn," she murmured. "So we would know for sure that things are for real between us if it happened."

"Aye." He dropped a feather-light kiss on her lips. "Some say dragon mates find each other again lifetime after lifetime. That it cannae be any other way 'tis so strong a connection."

"But I was born over eight hundred years after you," she managed as he peppered kisses along her jaw. "So it seems like pretty much an impossible idea for us."

His whisper came close to her ear as his hand found its way between her legs. "Who's to say we're both not simply living the first life since last we met. 'Tis hard to know, aye?" She bit her lower lip hard and groaned as he worked at her swollen flesh. "Mayhap we were together hundreds of years before now. Mayhap my soul waited for yours to be reborn eight hundred years after mine."

Though she tried to respond it was impossible as his lips made their way down her body. His tongue twirled around her nipple before he latched on and sucked hard. Erin cried out, pleased when his touch grew more aggressive. He seemed to know precisely what worked for her. But again, that was the added bonus of being inside each other's mind. They felt not only their own bodies but each other's.

It was wild and she wanted more.

The ache between her thighs built like a volcano and she whimpered with relief when his mouth finally made it down there. Red flared in her vision as climax instantly found her. She half roared, half cried out and gripped at the grass to try to ground

238

herself. Within seconds, he managed to tear another orgasm from her with an especially creative way of using his fingers, tongue and maybe even his teeth.

Erin knew he was going to pull far more from her soon and she might be rendered useless. So she sat up and pushed him onto his back. Two could play this game. Another faint orgasm rolled through her as she traced her tongue along his tats then down his chest and abs, thrilled with the feel of all the hard muscles at her disposal.

"Bloody *hell*," he groaned as she made her way to his groin then took him into her mouth.

As a singer, she had been trained how to use her vocal chords to full advantage. Rònan never stood a chance because she was damn good with her mouth and tongue. More than that, her throat. She could hold her breath longer than most and while his size was substantial, she did things to him that she knew had never been done before. Things that had him digging his hands into her hair with a vice grip. Things that had him thanking not only her but his gods over and over between long groans and, at last, a mighty roar as he found release.

Erin licked her lips then kissed her way back up his body. He might have seemed done for and liquefied but when her mouth came close to his, the look in his eyes was ferocious. Grabbing the back of her neck, he pulled her lips to his. Their mouths were ravenous when they came together. No, *crashed* together the passion was so escalated. Teeth, lips, tongues, their kisses were far hungrier than ever before.

Their need so great that tears came to her eyes.

He sat and pulled her up until she straddled him. Their lips never separated. How could they? She'd never tasted anything so good, had never needed anything so much. Their bodies pressed together as he gripped her ass and slowly, carefully pulled her onto him. He might have just gotten off but it didn't seem to slow him down any.

They both growled as he filled her. Heat steamed off of their skin. Shaking, overwhelmed by what was happening, they pulled back and stared into each other's eyes. Like hers, his were of the dragon. Brilliant and emerald green. She wasn't frightened by the light sheen of glow that covered his skin any more than she was by her own dragon sheen.

Then it happened.

Trails of tingling sensation spread over her arms and shoulders moments before delicate swirls of ink appeared in their wake. Not too many. Just enough. A flourishing collage of designs she would always take pride in.

Her very own dragon markings.

"Ye couldnae begin to know how bloody beautiful ye look right now," he whispered into her mind with not only lust but immense pride in his eyes.

Forget heat, downright fire sizzled around them as she brought his lips back to hers. Legs wrapped around him, it almost felt like she separated from her body as they began to move. She had never wanted to become a part of someone until now. Though merging their bodies was astounding enough, she'd never craved such a heightened level of intimacy.

Kissing, stroking, they worked the fever between them to a higher pitch. Fire flared at the corners of her vision and she swore she smelled smoke but was so far gone it might have been her imagination.

Then they started rolling.

Him on top thrusting.

Her on top thrusting.

Then more rolling.

At some point, he ended up behind her as she lay halfway on her side. Her chest was pressed against the ground with his over her. Because it had been heated and torn up so much, the scent of not only their arousal but fresh cut grass permeated the air. His teeth were clamped on the side of her neck as she gripped at the ground.

Erin whimpered with pleasure as his thrusts only increased. They couldn't say each other's names enough as they struggled toward something far more profound than an orgasm. In and out, faster and faster, they moved their hips well, anticipating each other's every move.

He pressed her to the ground, dominating, before she grunted and he rolled so that she could once again straddle him and regain control. Yet as she gripped his shoulders and continued moving, something again shifted between them and it wasn't just their bodies.

No, it was far, far deeper inside.

Soul deep.

Hers.

His.

Theirs.

"Rònan," she mouthed and shook her head as she moved faster.

Whatever was happening between them had his breath increasing along with hers. Sharp bursts of air that met their pace. Fire might still flare but it was nothing compared to the red that swamped her vision. Not total dragon but close.

Tempting.

She leaned down and kept her lips close to his as they continued to move. He would not take back control. He was giving this to her.

Power.

Him.

Everything he was.

Their lips hovered against one another's as her pace increased, as not only her body but mind took him for all he was worth. Somehow through all the bliss and desire and lust, she understood her own self-worth.

How much strength she had.

Would always have.

It wasn't something she would ever lose. Nor was it something he would ever want to take from her. He saw her as an equal. He saw her as everything he wanted to be, no...*was*. The inner light within himself he never knew existed until she ignited it.

Just like she ignited in a whole new way.

Clear as day, she saw exactly who she was and had always been.

A good soul.

Never dark or bad in the least. Never a freak. Never a murderer. What she found in that singular moment was the stark truth about them both.

Though different they were very much the same.

One.

How could she have ever thought otherwise?

She wanted this man in every way possible.

Mind, heart and soul.

Hands pressed to the ground, she rocked forward one last time, released a strangled cry, and...took him. A throb of release didn't just blow through her but pounded over her wave upon wave. Red blinded her as his mind wrapped around hers and the Earth trembled. Whatever happened now felt far better than sex.

Far better than embracing her dragon.

Whatever happened forced him to release and he wrapped his arms around her as his roar met hers with equal force. Sobs broke from her as she locked up against him and gave up on drawing breath. Everything seemed to shake and she had no idea if it was them or the ground itself.

Sweet pain mixed with sharp pleasure ripped and shredded her to pieces as red continued to fill her vision. Everything she felt, everything she was…was Rònan…and her. A mutual, shattering release and acceptance that had her aflame in surrender.

Whatever happened after that was wet, hot and never-ending. Their minds, bodies, all that they were, seized around one another in a tight coil. It was everything she saw in her far future but still somehow right here and right now.

Still within her control.

Or was it?

Lost, gone, wrapped around him, she didn't much care. Nothing mattered but the bliss and freedom she'd found. The light at the end of a tunnel she had built long ago. An endless tight place that was long and thorough and without forgiveness.

A forgiveness she finally allowed herself.

The feelings fluctuating within not only mentally but physically were so strong she gave up…or gave in…she had no idea. All she knew was that she wanted to hold on to this man for as long as possible.

Rònan MacLeod.

Not just her friend.

Not just a dragon.

No, far more…far better.

"We need to go," he said from what sounded like far away.

"No we don't," she whispered. "Trust me, I'm already gone."

Those were the last words she uttered before one reality got ripped away to be replaced by another. Erin had a split second to realize Cullen Stewart, Darach, and her Viking posse had joined them. Then she had less than a second to see how searing and bright Cullen's eyes were before he roared, "We need to go now!"

A loud sound burst over them that she could only compare to a sonic boom that broke the sound barrier. It was as if an F/A-18E/F Super Hornet jet fighter had just passed over.

Then silence.

Rònan had leapt to his feet but kept her close. Somehow they were both dressed. She in her dress and him in nothing but his plaid and boots.

"Bloody hell," Cullen muttered from a distance before their surroundings swirled away and she was standing alone in an unfamiliar armory.

Darach appeared at the door, desperate eyes scanning the weapons.

Erin frowned, totally confused. "Where are we, Darach?"

He gave no response but stalked around the room, muttering, "I never should have kissed her. Now he knows how much she means to me."

"Kissed who?" she said.

He didn't respond but kept scanning the walls and talking to himself. "I need that sword. 'Tis the only thing that can keep her safe."

"Darach?" She waved a hand in front of his face. "Hello?"

Then she realized...like it had been at the Viking fortress with Rònan, Darach couldn't see her. Super. Back to being a ghost. But why?

"Too much bloody passion betwixt us," he said under his breath. "Rònan was right. I should have stayed away."

What the *hell* was he talking about?

She was about to try to get through to him again but was swept away in a maelstrom of magic. The next thing she knew she was in the Celtic Otherworld. Baffled, she looked around before something caught her attention.

A black, oily whip.

Someone was being beaten. Her heart slammed into her throat when she realized who it was.

Rònan.

The three dark shadows and the demi-god were attacking him ruthlessly. They had even managed to singe his hair. Long hair. Though confused, she raced toward him. Who cared if she didn't have a weapon. She would fight to the death if she had to. Anything to save him.

But it turned out it went far easier than expected.

Shock froze her in her tracks when her ring ignited a bright, glowing green. The demi-god roared in rage and his three minions squealed in distress before all of them vanished. Rònan remained face down and unmoving.

"Oh God," she cried and started toward him. "Don't you dare be dead."

"Nay, lass," came a deep voice before an old man with snowy white hair and a cane materialized in front of her. "You saved him well enough. He will survive. But 'tis not the right time for him to meet you."

"To meet me? What are you talking about?" She frowned, aware that a beautiful blond was walking their way. Eyes on the man, she said, "Who *are* you?"

A twinkle lit his eyes. "I am Adlin MacLomain." Then he gestured at the woman. "And this is Chiomara the Druidess. My mother."

Chapter Eighteen

Scotland
MacLomain Castle
1281

"WHERE IS SHE?" Rònan roared the second he realized Erin had not returned with them. The only people who stood alongside him were Cullen, Tait, and Bjorn.

"Erin's in here," Darach called from another room in the armory.

It might have been a few moments since they left Stewart land and traveled back to their own era, but not seeing her here immediately had his nerves raw. So he pulled her into his arms with relief when he laid eyes on her.

"I'm okay," she murmured, a stunned look on her face as her eyes drifted around the room. "Where am I now?"

"MacLomain Castle's armory," Rònan replied.

"I was just here...I think." She pulled away and her eyes locked on Darach. "Are you real this time?"

Darach frowned, as confused as the rest of them. "I dinnae ken, lass."

"And I wouldn't expect you too. After all, I didn't even know till now." She looked at Cullen. "Do you know what just happened to me? Everything I just learned here and then in the Otherworld?"

What was she talking about? Rònan was shocked to discover her mind completely closed off to him. How was that possible? Her eyes went to his. "I'll fill you in later." Then she headed for the door. "The shit's gonna hit the fan any time now. We need to find Niall, Jackie, and little Robert right away."

"They're here," Grant said, arriving at the door at the same time as Erin. Rònan was pleased to see his mother as well.

"Good to have you both back," Torra said. "As Erin said, trouble comes verra soon. Gather as many weapons as you can."

Erin nodded, relieved when Niall, Nicole, and Jackie joined them.

Nicole gave her a quick hug. "One sec you're at MacLeod Castle then poof, gone, before you show up here. Where've you been? I was getting worried."

"No time for that." Erin's eyes shot to Niall. "You need to give that sword to Rònan." Then her eyes flew to Darach. "And you need to work through your crap and protect Jackie."

"Aye," Grant agreed.

Darach frowned and avoided Jackie's eyes. "Of course, I'll protect her."

Erin shook her head and looked at Grant. Whatever passed between them made a flicker of surprise then determination pass over his face before he looked at Niall then gestured at Rònan. "I'd say the time is right, lad."

Niall nodded, clearly having full faith in the advice because he handed the blade to Rònan. The instant he made contact with the sword, magic rippled over him. Not only the sword glowed briefly but something else.

That's when he saw it.

Erin's ring. More so, the stone at its center.

A blazing emerald to match his eyes.

When his dragon roared up, Erin put a finger to her lips and shook her head. But their eyes remained locked as happiness surged through him. Not only had the ring bonded them but something far better.

Her dragon had claimed *him*.

And his dragon had eagerly accepted.

They were mates.

"'Tis good to see your ring's stone ignited, Erin," Grant said, not missing a thing. "Despite the fact you stole it."

Erin's brows shot up as her eyes locked with Grant's.

"Aye, Torra and I always knew you came by that ring in an unorthodox fashion." A tempered smile came to his lips. "As I learned from the Viking King, 'twas the Broun in you that was drawn to it but 'twas your dragon magic that allowed you to take it off on occasion." Then he winked. "As to you stealing it to begin with, it seems you're just the sort of lass who will protect herself at all costs. Mayhap by taking another's blade or even a ring. Though you didnae know it at the time, both your inner witch and dragon recognizes a weapon above all others when she sees it."

Ah, well that made sense.

"Interesting," she murmured, making no apologies for her sense of self-preservation even if it *did* involve a little bit of thievery. Sometimes you had to do what you had to do to survive...or to protect others.

"Now 'tis as Iosbail MacLomain said it must be." Torra's eyes met Rònan's. "Niall gave you the sword when the time was right. Now you must trust your lass and do the same for Darach when the time is right."

Rònan would always trust Erin. *His* lass. *His* dragon. As he was just as much hers. Based on how little she wanted him to say aloud not to mention her closed off mind, it was clear she was purposefully keeping their recent bond from the enemy.

Rònan eyed Darach, a challenge in his eyes when he said, "I will give the blade to you when Erin says to. As it is, this is one thing you cannae avoid, aye, Cousin?"

When Darach's eyes narrowed, Erin frowned and headed for one of the adjoining rooms. "Sorry everyone but I need a moment alone with these two."

"Aye," Grant and Torra said at the same time.

"Ye bloody well do," Grant added.

It seemed Uncle Grant might be as fed up with his son's evasiveness as Rònan was.

"We'll grab our weapons and wait outside," Torra said.

Darach and Rònan followed Erin. They had no sooner entered the bow and arrow chamber when she spun, planted her hands on her hips and narrowed her eyes at them. "Whatever this is between you two needs to stop right now."

Her eyes locked on Rònan's. "I know you look down at Darach because you don't respect him avoiding his responsibilities and becoming Laird." Her brows slammed together. "But it seems to me you weren't all that much better until recently. From what I've heard, you were a pretty immature leader. So cut him some slack."

Before either could respond, her eyes shot to Darach. "And you need to get over Rònan stealing a girl from you way back when. It obviously wasn't meant to be. Besides, women are all over you and I'm sure they have been for a long time."

"Aye, just not any of the Broun lasses," Rònan remarked, still irritated over his cousin spending so much time in the future.

"You need to get over that attitude because it makes you seem insecure." Erin frowned at Rònan. "And I know you're not. I think deep down you feel guilty for not getting to the future sooner. That it might've been a smart move to get to know us Brouns before we ended up here. That it might've been the responsible thing for a laird to do considering not only the future King of Scotland's life was at stake but the safety of your own clan."

Rònan was about to bite back but the words died on his tongue when he realized she was absolutely right. Neither Darach nor Niall were lairds yet they made a point of going to the future. In Niall's case, it was to better understand Nicole's disability. In Darach's case, mayhap it did have something to do with putting the lasses' minds at ease.

And though Rònan could say the responsibility of being laird kept him too busy, he knew two things. One, Logan had found the time to go to the future often. Secondly? Rònan wasn't busy leading his clan. No, his time had been spent being markedly frivolous and self-centered.

Disgruntled, Rònan and Darach eyed one another before Erin kept talking. "Now I've said what I needed to, I want to know exactly what's going on inside your head, Darach, because Jackie's depending on you."

"I dinnae ken," Darach said. "I will do my best to protect her. 'Tis simple as that."

"Don't lie to me." She crossed her arms over her chest. "Because I recently learned that my witchy trick involves hearing people and not being able to speak back. I sort of become a ghost."

Both men looked at her with confusion.

"At some point, you were in this armory seeing if Niall had left the blade here." Her eyes stayed trained on Darach. "You were muttering about how you never should have kissed her. That because you had 'he' would know. I got the sense you put 'her' life in great danger with that kiss." Her eyes narrowed. "It was Jackie."

"How could you possibly know..." he started and frowned. "You're guessing."

"About the Jackie part? You bet." She sighed. "But now I have my answer. At least some of it. What I don't understand is why kissing her puts her life in danger."

Darach ran a hand through his hair in frustration. "It doesnae matter."

"I'd say it does, Cousin," Rònan said, baffled by Darach's behavior.

"Och," Darach muttered and his voice grew softer, pain in his eyes. "I have avoided becoming Laird with good reason. And I should've never kissed Jackie because I know something nobody else does, not even my Da."

He was about to speak when a loud roar ripped across the sky.

The enemy was coming.

"Shit," Erin muttered and eyed Darach. "We'll continue this later."

He offered no response as they sprang into action and started loading up on weapons. The men strapped on arm guards before Darach raced out. Rònan stopped Erin before she could get far. Cupping the sides of her neck, he made sure she understood how serious he was. "I will fight alongside you every step of the way. I dinnae have a shred of doubt about your skills as a warrior but promise me you willnae shift unless you have absolute confidence in your abilities. You are new in your dragon skin and the enemy will likely try to exploit such."

"I know." Her gaze stayed strong. "Don't worry about me. I got this."

His eyes searched hers. "Aye, you do, lass."

Before she could dart away, he cupped her cheeks and kissed her hard and with enough passion that she'd never forget how strongly he felt about her. When he pulled back, her eyes had changed. They were glazed with lust and shimmered purple. Yet the battle lust was there as well. "Let us go fight then, my wee dragon."

By the time they made it outside, enemy soldiers had flooded the field. Hundreds of MacLomain clansmen were already engaging them. Instead of closing the portcullises, Torra shifted to a dragon and guarded the drawbridge.

"The clan has already lost too many good warriors to this threat," Rònan said. "I'm going to fight on the ground first."

"I'm coming," Erin said and strode after him.

Though a small part of him would rather keep her safe behind the castle walls, he knew better than to say it. Erin was as good a warrior if not better than most so he set aside his fear and nodded. "Fight well then, lass."

"Back atcha," she said, a dagger in each hand. She had little experience with a sword, so he thought her decision to fight with smaller blades wise. With any other he would say don't bring a knife to a swordfight but she had a particular talent with them. For starters, he knew many would underestimate her and she would use that to full advantage.

Nicole and Niall met them before they made it to the first drawbridge.

"I will fight alongside ye and yer lass, Brother," Niall said.

Nicole held up the shield Rònan had made for her and the Celtic dagger Niall made and winked at Erin. "I'm gonna head back into the castle and stick close to Robert. You sure you don't wanna join me?"

"No, I'm gonna follow the guys." Erin gripped Nicole's shoulders, eyes serious. "Let Robert know that I'll be there to protect him if things go wrong. I'll be right there alongside you, okay?"

"You got it," Nicole said. "Watch your back, Sweetie. I'll hold down the fort...or castle."

Erin nodded and wasted no more time talking but headed over the drawbridge with Rònan and Niall. As always, her Viking posse was close behind. Logan and Darach were already fighting on the field. Cullen remained on the battlement, eyes trained on his surroundings as he likely waited for his sister and her dark laird.

They went into this battle with more magic than ever before. While he knew most of the women of the Next Generation were inside protecting the king, the men were out here.

So they had five elder wizards, four younger, five dragons, and one angel.

Not too bad.

Rònan wasn't surprised when Tosha's words entered his mind. She had somehow ended up here along with the rest of them. *If Erin needs me, I will be there.*

"Thank ye, my friend," he said.

After that, it all became the thrill of battle. Rònan loved shifting but there was something equally satisfying about fighting in human form. The way his muscles heated and rage mixed with war lust. Adjusting easily to the weight of the blade Niall had given him, he cut down three before their swords swept through the air once.

Meanwhile, Erin was as impressive as always as she took down one man before he saw her coming. In a way, her fighting style was similar to Darach's. Both moved fast and with a certain finesse that most warriors didn't possess. Even as Rònan crossed blades with two more clansmen, he couldn't help but grin when Erin chuckled.

She had managed to bring a man to his knees and sliced his throat while side-kicking another. The chuckle was her berserker side. Something he didn't realize she had until now. When his cousin, Machara whooped with laughter and fell in beside Erin, he realized that the two were of similar spirits on the battlefield.

Half crazed, half wild and damn talented.

Yet they all had one thing in common and that was an absolute love for battle.

Rònan lost count of how many men Erin took down as the fighting continued. Any fear he had for her vanished entirely when he realized how confident she was. Sure, he had sensed it all along but to actually see her in action gave absolute truth to it.

Like his uncles and cousins, he occasionally used magic but for the most part, everyone kept it physical. Until the threat worsened, it made no sense to drain themselves. Almost as if his thoughts fed his surroundings, another loud roar echoed across the sky moments before the demi-god's large dark shadow filled the horizon.

Shortly after that, the dark shadow's minions, the *Genii Cucullati,* swooped down.

Seconds later, Brae Stewart appeared. Shock flashed in her eyes when they locked with Cullen's. Very non-angelic fury ravaged his face as her brother shimmered, spread his wings and swooped toward her.

When the Vikings saw the dark demi-god, they shifted and headed for it. Like Rònan, Erin fought viciously while her eyes remained trained on the sky. Whether or not she liked it, he moved even closer. Their eyes met for a split second but it was long enough for them to whip a dagger over each other's shoulder to take down men sneaking up on them. They grinned at how well they worked together before the action above stole their attention.

Whatever the evil laird was doing it kept Tait and Bjorn from being able to get close. Even Torra was unable to stop him when he flew toward the battlements.

"Damn it, I had hoped he wouldn't know that was why I steered clear of them. He knows my ring ignited so he's going after Robert and Jackie!" Furious, Erin muttered, "I think the hell not," and did what Rònan had hoped she wouldn't.

She shifted.

Though she wobbled some, he was impressed by how well she lifted off. Rònan ignored how terrified he was for her and shifted then swiftly followed. Sword locked in his talons, he sailed after her as she headed right for the demi-god. What was she doing? Somehow he knew that though Torra, Tait and Bjorn could not get close, the god would allow Erin to.

"Erin!" he roared into her mind. "Stop!"

But she didn't. She was too determined to get to Jackie and Robert to see good reason. Meantime, Cullen and Brae had ended up in the courtyard and were having a fight for the ages. Twisting, turning, black magic crashed against white as they fought. A storm consisting of thunder, lightning, and even rain thrashed around them making the wind shear more unstable than ever.

Though everything inside him wanted to protect her, Rònan had made Erin a promise. He would support her. So when her little body started to lose control, he came up under her so that she could stand on him and regain her balance.

Once she did, he whispered into her mind, *"Go do what you need to, my wee dragon,"* and arched his back so that she could take flight again. As soon as she did, he shifted back to his human form, grabbed his sword and dropped to the battlements. He figured the demi-god could take him easily enough in dragon form so he might as well do his best with a blade in hand.

What he did not expect to find when he landed was a man forming within the black mass. This was who Erin must have seen in the Otherworld. Swarthy, with black hair and dark lightning crackling around his aura, he dripped evil.

His eyes went to Rònan's blade and his words were gravelly and deep. "Ye'll need a wee bit more than that to defeat *me*, lad."

An Irish accent?

252

"I'll take my chances," Ronan growled and swiped. Naturally, the demi-god evaded. No matter how much he tried to attack, he never got the sword close enough.

"Bloody hell," Grant said from the courtyard as he stared up. "It cannae be."

A grin slithered across the demi-god's face. "Does my appearance look so familiar then, Grant MacLomain..." He cocked his head. Sort of a jerky motion. "Or is it Grant *Hamilton* now?" He pointed at the castle and roared, "Before all of this is said and done, ye *will* release my son from that tapestry!"

His *son*? The man his Ma and the Next Generation had fought twenty-seven winters prior was trapped in that tapestry. *Keir Hamilton.* Ronan suddenly understood why the demi-god had tracked Erin. More than that, their dragon blood. He had somehow made a connection with Keir. And that tapestry literally trapped Kier between here and his Viking kin.

Gods above, this was worse than anyone could have anticipated.

Grant immediately threw magic at the demi-god but it barely affected him.

Then things happened very quickly.

Erin landed in the courtyard and took up a defensive stance directly in front of Jackie.

Of all people, Heidrek appeared.

Ronan frowned when the Viking pulled Jackie into his arms.

Though they couldn't get close, Tait and Bjorn landed on either side of Ronan and the demi-god, their eyes zeroing in on both Erin and Heidrek. It was clear that though he was no dragon, they had a great deal of respect for the Viking King's successor.

Yet something beyond the obvious was happening.

Ronan could feel it bone deep.

When Little Robert came running out of the castle and flew down the stairs, the demi-god immediately went for him. Luckily, between Grant, Torra and everyone else throwing magic at him, he was slowed down.

Ronan leapt from the battlement and fell to one knee in front of Erin. She lowered her head and her dragon eyes locked with his.

"It's time to hand over the sword," she whispered into his mind. *"Trust me and do it now."*

If it was time for his cousin to have the blade, so be it.

"*Nay!*" Darach roared into his mind as he skidded to a halt next to Erin. Pain flickered in his eyes when they went to Jackie and Heidrek. "*Throw the blade to Heidrek. He can protect her best now, Rònan!*"

This made no sense. He was supposed to give it to Darach next so that *he* could protect Jackie. Long seconds passed as the orange sun sat low in the sky, steeping the distant mountains in purple as he held out the blade, tip to the ground and struggled with the decision. This sword was ultimately supposed to help defeat the enemy when in a MacLomain wizard's hands. Yet now he was to hand it off to a Viking ancestor?

"*Now!*" Darach roared again.

"*Please. For me,*" Erin whispered into his mind. "*It's the only way.*"

His eyes again met hers and his dragon responded to the soul-deep calling she sent to him. Without another moment of hesitation, he stood and tossed the sword to Heidrek. The Viking caught it, nodded to Darach, pulled Jackie close and they both vanished into thin air.

Something about the sword being gone gave the demi-god just enough power to push past everyone's magic and rush toward little Robert.

But Erin was faster.

She wrapped her wings around the wee king until he was completely covered. While Robert might be temporarily safe, she by no means was. Like her Viking posse, when Rònan shifted to a dragon and rushed to protect her, he was flung back as not only the demi-god but his shadow minions swooped in.

Horror filled him as Erin cried out in pain, her body trembling as she suffered under the onslaught of far too much power for her little dragon to handle.

"*Get to her!*" he roared within Tait and Bjorn's minds as he struggled through the thick waves of dark power fluctuating around her. Their minds met his with equal fury. They were as desperate as he was and struggling just as hard.

Though she was being brutalized, Erin never once moved but kept her head beneath her wings, a safe haven over Robert. Rònan flailed and roared as her scales began to sear off.

"Save her!" he roared at anyone willing to listen.

Grant, his mother, father, his cousins, uncles, *anyone*.

Then a distant sound filled his ears. It sounded so far away, he barely heard it...

Singing.

Beautiful, incomparable singing.

Erin.

Though her voice was growing weaker and weaker along with her body and life force, she was singing to the Bruce to comfort him. It was that, her unbelievably gentle and untouchable voice, that renewed his strength. Rònan focused on the sound and leapt once, twice, then covered her with his wings. Digging his talons into the earth, he locked up his muscles, pressed his cheek against hers and prayed to his gods to give him every ounce of strength they could spare.

But it seemed he would not need it.

The moment their bodies touched, the demi-god screamed in pain and backed off. When Rònan glanced over his shoulder, it was to see the cloud wisp away followed by the dark shadows. Despite his anger, he shuddered with relief not because he was safe but because Erin was.

"All is well, lass," he whispered into her mind. *"You did it. You protected the wee Bruce."*

Only when Rònan spread his wings and stepped back did he realize she had sunk down onto her haunches with her chin resting on the ground. She had Robert tucked safely between two talons as she...slept?

Because she slept right? The battle had worn her out.

Grant crouched nearby and held out his arms to Robert, voice soft. "Come here, lad."

Rònan cocked his head and lowered his wings. *"Erin?"*

He was vaguely aware of her friends, Nicole, and Cassie nearby. Vaguely aware of Tait and Bjorn with their dragon heads lowered as they emitted a low keen of sorrowful mourning that only their breed could hear. Then he was only remotely aware of Tosha trotting out and all of his Ma's kin, the Next Generation, surrounding them.

"Rònan," his Da whispered from somewhere around his left flank. "I'm so sorry, Son."

Why was his Da sorry? Nothing was getting through to him as he crouched down beside Erin and lifted her muzzle with his. *"Wake up, lass. You've done well."*

Somewhere far in the back of his mind, he knew her heart had slowed to a crawl...that her body was too badly damaged. *"Erin? My lass?"* he said over and over as he kept nudging her. *"Regenerate. Heal."* He tried to keep panic from his voice. *"'Tis something you can do if you just put your mind to it."*

But even he knew it took time to heal and that dragons could not do it with a simple thought. They might be able to heal faster than humans, but it still took time.

And time was something she clearly did not have.

When her heart thumped even slower, he swung his head around and searched for Cullen. *"Where did the angel go? He can help her!"*

His mother, once more in human form, touched him, her eyes sad. *"He and Brae vanished in the midst of battling, son. Cullen is no longer here."*

"Nay," Rònan whispered.

Then it happened.

Erin's heart crawled to a stop.

Simply stopped beating.

Rònan roared in grief, sunk to his haunches, pulled her close and wrapped his wings around her the best he could. This couldn't be happening. This couldn't be their end when they had only just found each other again.

Because they *had* just found each other again.

It could be no other way with his dragon mate.

But he knew as the luster of her shiny scales dulled and her body remained limp, she was gone. His best friend, his true mate...was gone.

Erin was dead.

Chapter Nineteen

"WHY CANNAE I hear you anymore?" came a soft voice.

Erin blinked and tried to sit up, tried to see, but her body remained unresponsive and her eyesight equally so.

"Robert, is that you?" she said, worried but keeping it out of her voice. "Are you all right?"

"Aye, but I'm scared," he whispered. "You stopped singing."

She had, hadn't she? But when had she stopped? For the life of her, she couldn't make sense of anything save her concern for the little boy.

"I'm sorry," she whispered. "I don't know why I stopped singing just that I'm...tired."

"I dinnae want ye to be tired," he whimpered.

"Me neither," she said. "Because that means I can't protect you like I should." Erin felt exhaustion swamp her but didn't want the wee King to be scared after she fell asleep so she tried to explain things to him the best she could. "You know how I'm losing my voice?"

"Aye," he murmured. "'Tis sad that."

"Maybe," she agreed. "But there's something to be learned from it."

"What?"

"That sometimes there's more to be learned by listening and paying attention to your surroundings." She struggled to stay with him. "There's a certain wisdom to be gained by speaking at only the most important times. That way, your words carry more weight and are respected in a way they might not have been otherwise."

Erin heard the tears in his voice and wished she could make things better.

"Then I will say the most important words now," he whispered. "Thank ye for protecting me, my friend."

"Anytime, little King," she managed to whisper before darkness closed around her more tightly.

After that, everything went very, very silent until she heard a heartbeat.

Thump. Thump. Thump.

Robert?

No, while she loved the little wannabe king this was by no means his heartbeat but a much stronger one. A calling that came from far, far away but ever so slowly pulled her closer. The closer it pulled her, the more the sounds around her increased. Wind. The waves lapping in the distance. Crying.

Yet always there was a heartbeat.

One she already knew better than her own.

His.

Green eyes. Unending devotion. True love.

Her dragon…her mate.

Rònan.

Erin tried to cry out to him but instead inhaled sharply and sucked in air that burned her lungs. Then she gasped as her lungs seized. Strong arms wrapped around her as she struggled for air.

"I've got you, Erin," Rònan rumbled against her ear, his voice thick with emotion. "I'll always have you, lass. Relax and breathe. You're not alone. Never alone."

His words said aloud and within her mind calmed her as her lungs worked to take in oxygen. After several blinks, blurriness slowly gave way to clarity.

The first thing she saw was Rònan's handsome face.

"Thank the bloody gods." His hand trembled slightly as he cupped her cheek. His bloodshot eyes were locked on her face. There could be no doubt he'd shed tears for her. "Welcome back, lass."

"What happened?" she said but nothing came out. Even so, he apparently heard her within the mind.

"You saved not only Jackie but the wee Bruce," he said into her mind. *"Yet again, you are a hero, my lass."*

Only then did she realize that he held her on his lap on the castle stairs and not only her friends but Viking posse and even Robert stood nearby.

258

She teared up when she saw the little king and held out her arms. "I'm so glad you're okay. Come here, Sweetheart."

Even though the words didn't actually come out of her mouth, Robert crawled onto her lap and wrapped his arms around her. Erin knew he tried his best to hide his tears as he whispered in her ear, "Thank ye for saving me and trusting me to hold yer ring for ye. 'Tis so verra good that it brought ye back to us."

Erin kissed the top of his head as her eyes met Rònan's.

She knew at that moment that everything had gone exactly how Adlin MacLomain said it might.

"So when you touched me without the sword in dragon form, our magic drove the bad guy away yet again, right?" she said into Rònan's mind. *"And as I asked him to when I first gave it to him, little Robert made sure the ring was returned to me. That was the key to bringing me back from the brink of death, right?"* Her lips curled with satisfaction. *"Better yet the power of the love that we share?"*

"Aye," he murmured. *"How did you know all that would happen?"*

Though saddened, Erin was well aware that her voice was permanently lost and sent out a general message she hoped all could hear while looking at Rònan. *"I think Robert could use some rest. If we could all go somewhere private, that'd be good."* She glanced at her Viking posse and managed a small smile. *"You're more than welcome too, my friends."*

Evidently everyone heard because they nodded and Grant crouched beside them, eyes on Robert. "'Twas no easy task keeping yer Ma in the castle all this time. Might ye go rest with her now that ye know Erin is safe?"

The Bruce pulled back and his little bloodshot eyes met hers. "I think mayhap 'twould be ill of me to leave a true Lady alone at this time."

Erin wished she could speak into his mind but knew she couldn't so she pointed at her throat, tried to talk then shook her head while offering a warm smile. She put a closed fist to her chest and mouthed, "I am strong. Thank you." After that, she put a hand against his heart then one against hers before she pointed between them and mouthed slowly, "I love you."

Robert paid attention to every little detail before he finally nodded and whispered, "'Twas a wise mistress who once told me fewer words mean I'm paying attention and will have more impact so I will only give you five more." He wrapped his arms around her and whispered, "I love you too, Erin."

Erin smiled, kissed the top of his head and held tight before Grant took his hand and led him away. When Rònan seemed unwilling to let her go, she eyed her limbs then her ring before she cocked a brow at him and spoke the only way she could now. Within the mind. *"I think despite what happened, I'm doing okay. That means I can walk."*

When he frowned, she winked. *"But I wouldn't mind you staying close."*

Rònan eyed her for a long moment before he nodded. *"Aye, always."*

Despite her strong words, Erin was never more thankful when her legs worked and she was able to walk without issue. Her friends pulled her into a group hug before she got too far. Though Cassie could no longer see, Nicole could barely hear and Erin was officially mute, they had found a place that their disabilities didn't hinder them nearly as much as they thought they would.

Or maybe it was merely their friendship that kept them so strong.

But even Erin knew it had as much to do with the men they found…the MacLomains who were theirs.

All that aside, they weren't whole and they all felt it. Jackie was gone and it slowed their steps. It kept worried looks on their faces alongside the relief they felt that Erin was alive. It was an odd mix of emotions and it affected each and every one of them.

But right now she had to stay focused on a friend who needed her more.

So she fell into step beside Darach. Though she knew he was glad to see her alive, she had never seen anyone try to disguise a heavy heart as he did now. She wrapped elbows with him and whispered into his mind, *"It'll be okay. Though I don't understand your reasoning yet, I know you did the right thing. The best thing possible for Jackie."*

Darach offered no response, his frown deepening.

Grant led them to a wall walk a few floors up and off the backside of the castle. A few torches burned and several mugs of whisky were served before she sat down beside Rònan and eyed the others. She spoke within their minds.

"Before I came here I made a brief visit to the Celtic Otherworld." Her eyes went to Rònan. *"As I soon found out, I had traveled there when you were first taken by the dark demi-god. I arrived when they were torturing you."* When surprise flickered in his eyes, she slid her hand into his. *"When I went to stop them they fled. As it turned out, the last time we were intimate, we ignited the power of the ring and became dragon mates."*

"But…" Rònan started yet she shook her head.

"The demi-god knew that we would likely ignite the ring, that we were meant for each other. That's why he went after me when I was a teenager. Why he made me hate dragons. Anything to keep us from finding love. It's also why he kept pursuing me during all those strange moments after I traveled back in time. Like when I thought Jackie called to me from the fire in the cave. How Robert somehow talked to me that night you were sleeping at the Viking fortress. And then when I thought I saw my father at your castle that night Cullen took me. The only thing I remain unclear about is seeing Brae's ghost." She sighed. *"But I'm sure we'll figure that out soon enough."*

"I dinnae ken why you were there when I was tortured, though," Rònan said.

"I learned about all that from Adlin MacLomain and…" Her eyes went to Grant and Torra. *"Chiomara the Druidess."*

Shock registered on their faces before she turned her eyes back to Rònan. *"Ever wonder why you took such a severe beating yet you were still alive when Nicole joined you in the Celtic Otherworld? Why you two weren't destroyed in an instant?"*

"Aye," he murmured.

"It was because I showed up before Nicole ever arrived," she said. *"I'm not sure how but I got there just in time. When I did the power of the ring stopped him from hurting you. Yet until we'd lived the moments leading up to the ring igniting, the Otherworld could still pull you in and through our connection, me as well. Apparently, we were there in some sort of dream state that made hurting us far more difficult. Not to say we didn't have added protection from not only Chiomara and Adlin but even Jackie when she watched over me. I'd still love to know how she managed that."*

She shook her head. *"Anyway, I found out from Adlin that the demi-god had no idea we eventually mated as dragons."* Erin quirked her lip. *"Neither did I for that matter but I'm glad we did. It became our ultimate, but unexpected weapon. Though he knows about it now, it's a weapon that'll come in handy when we fight him again. One he never expected."*

"So the demi-god meant to...kill my son had you not arrived?" Torra asked softly.

"Yes, but don't give me any credit. It was Adlin and Chiomara that were at the center of this plot," Erin said just as softly. *"They're the true heroes because bringing me there stopped the demi-god from killing Rònan."*

"Why did they want to kill Rònan to begin with?" Niall kicked in, upset.

"To prove a point." Erin kept her eyes steady and answered matter-of-factly. *"Rònan's not only a wizard but he's got the blood of a dragon. It made sense to kill him and weaken all of you in spirit at the very least."*

"So he never meant to use Rònan to fight his battles?" Grant asked.

"No. He was a pawn used to weaken you." Erin met Rònan's eyes. *"Besides, my man couldn't be taken and used by dark magic no matter how hard they tried."*

Rònan tried hard not to, but she knew he preened at her compliment.

"Though I'm grateful beyond words, 'tis a bit strange that Chiomara the Druidess was part of all this, aye?" Torra remarked to Grant.

"Now that's where it gets really interesting." Erin kept her eyes on Rònan's. *"It seems she's been acting like someone else to get you to the twenty-first century so we would meet and put this all in motion."*

Rònan eyed her and shook his head as he figured it out. *"All along I thought she was Jackie."*

"Yup." Erin shrugged. *"She and Adlin are great masterminds even from the afterlife."*

"Bloody hell," Grant and Torra whispered at the same time.

Erin nodded. *"They were very informative. I know Chiomara is your ancient Irish relative, the woman who pretty much started this clan.*" Her eyes went to the ghostly stranger standing in the corner. *"But who is she?"*

Torra's eyes followed hers and froze.

"Ma?" she whispered.

"Aye, lass," the woman murmured as a man appeared beside her. "'Twas I assisting my grandbabe."

"Who are they?" Erin whispered to Rònan when he stood.

"My grandparents," he whispered aloud. "Iain and Arianna MacLomain."

Arianna's eyes went to Erin. "'Twas a pleasure meeting you, lass. You are and will always be the love of my grandson's life."

Erin instantly recognized her voice. *"You were in Tosha."*

"Aye." Arianna nodded. "A name that meant satisfaction and has that not been proven time and time again with everything you and Rònan did together...what you found. Not just love but perfect unity. An unbreakable force for dragons...mates."

Erin tended to think of things far more sensual when it came to satisfaction with Rònan but wasn't above nodding her head. *"For sure...it's definitely been satisfying."*

Arianna and Iain chuckled, obviously understanding the humor in her response. When a neigh resounded from below, Erin strode to the railing and looked over. Tosha pranced around, clearly happy to be left alone on the shore of the loch.

"She's yours, lass." Arianna nodded down at Tosha. "I simply merged with Salve. 'Tis why Tosha came out of your horse trailer in New Hampshire. She's still your horse but now you better ken her soul and as time passes she will look more like the horse you remember. Care well for her." Her eyes went to Rònan. "And though I know it doesnae need saying, care well for my kin."

Holy shit. Well, now it all made sense. Erin grinned down at Tosha, also known as Salve.

She hadn't lost her horse after all.

"Wait," Torra said but Arianna and Iain embraced, Iain's words catching on the wind. "Your son is safe, daughter. We love ye both and will see ye soon enough."

Rònan frowned as they vanished.

Erin chuckled inwardly and glanced at Rònan. *"They were pretty lusty in life, eh?"*

"Nay," Torra said, a frown on her face as well. "Though affectionate, my parents were always…more refined."

Grant smirked then winked at Torra. "I guess that's changed some in the afterlife, Cousin."

Torra narrowed her eyes but a small smile played on her lips. "Apparently so if my Ma merged herself with a horse named 'Satisfaction.'"

"Not so different than me naming my horse Salve," Erin piped up. *"Short for Salvation. Hers not mine in that I saved her."*

They gave her an odd look but seemed to understand the comparison.

Grant, however, was the first to get back to business. "I feel time is limited." He eyed Darach and Erin. "I need to better ken why you two decided to give the sword meant to save Jackie to Heidrek." His eyes landed squarely on Darach. "More than that, I need to know why you sent your lass away with the Viking."

When Erin saw pain flash in Darach's eyes and sensed how he struggled with his words she shook her head.

"No." She crossed her arms over her chest and faced Grant. *"With all due respect, this is where I need to ask you and Torra to leave so that I can speak to Darach and his cousins alone."*

Grant's eyebrows lowered sharply and he was about to respond before Darach cut him off. "Please, Da." When Grant's eyes flew to him, he clenched his jaw. "I need to speak with Erin and my cousins alone. 'Tis important."

Rònan had never seen Darach stand up to his father. Not that Grant intended it in the least, but he suddenly realized that it took a lot for Darach to step out from under his father's ever powerful shadow.

"Nay, we must know everything," Torra started but Rònan cut her off. "Erin and Darach have done much for our clans. Might we not respect their wishes?"

Surprise then something close to pride flickered over Grant's face as he looked between Rònan and Darach. "Aye," he said softly. "We will honor their wishes indeed."

Rònan's mother gave Erin a smile and nod of approval before she wrapped elbows with Grant and left. Meanwhile, Darach downed half a mug of whisky.

"What were you trying to tell us in the armory earlier, Cousin?" Rònan said. "What secrets do you keep?"

Darach's eyes went from Erin to Rònan and he shook his head, clearly debating if he should share.

Erin felt Darach's internal distress as much as they all did. *"What is it Darach? Does all of this have to do with guilt over being with another woman in Scandinavia? Because even despite the kiss, I don't think Jackie would hold that against you. She's pretty understanding."*

Darach's eyes perked in surprise because she knew about the Viking girl. He ran his hand over his face in frustration and shook his head. "'Twas not what everyone thinks. 'Tis important that Jackie steers clear of me. Nothing good can come from us being together."

"But why when 'tis obvious there is affection betwixt you?" Rònan frowned with concern. "Does this have something to do with why you've avoided becoming laird?"

"Aye," Darach murmured, more troubled by the moment. "I cannae become laird or 'twill be the end of us all."

"Bloody hell," Rònan said. "Why not tell me sooner? Any of us? 'Tis ill of me to have thought so poorly of you."

"Nay." Darach shook his head. "You were right to feel as you did. I would've felt the same had our positions been reversed."

Rònan eyed him for a long moment, clearly trying to understand what was going on. In the end, he gave all he was capable of considering the circumstances. All he could think of to make things right.

"Well then let me at least say sorry for the lass I stole so long ago. I didnae know you felt so strongly." Rònan sighed. "Even if you hadn't, I never should've gone near her."

Darach eyed him for a long moment before he nodded. "Aye, lad. Like Erin said, 'twas a long time ago and 'tis well past time that I let it go. Besides..." His eyes went to Erin then back to Rònan. "You ended up with a far better one."

"Thanks, Sweetie," Erin said. *"And while I'm glad you boys have made up, I still want to know what's going on. I get that you're trying to push Jackie away to keep her safe but she's wearing a ring. That means she can only end up with a MacLomain wizard, right? Last time I checked, you're the only one left."*

"I think there's a way around that," Darach said softly. "Something that has to do with shifting the passion betwixt us to another." He pointed to the corner of his eye. "Because of her birthmark."

The crown shaped birthmark! She had forgotten about that.

"Passion shifted because of a birthmark?" Logan frowned. "I dinnae ken."

"Is this why Adlin told me in the Otherworld that you would soon hand off the sword to another...that you must... but he never said why?"

"Aye," Darach whispered. There was no mistaking the fresh round of pain that entered his eyes. "Now that I know Adlin supported my decision with the blade I cannae share more. Not yet. Mayhap never." He shook his head. "Jackie is safe where she is." He met his cousins' eyes before meeting Erin's. "All is well enough for now. I'm bloody proud of you, lass. Verra much so."

"Back at ya." She narrowed her eyes. *"You know I love you no matter what you're going through, right? That I'm here for you?"* Her eyes flickered from his cousins then back to him. *"All of us are."*

"Aye. I know." He hugged her before he squeezed Rònan's shoulder then strode off the wall walk.

Erin knew he needed space but she wasn't above saying to Niall and Logan, *"You two should go after him. He's fighting some demons and needs support."*

"Aye," they agreed before turning to Cassie and Nicole.

"Go on," Nicole said to Niall. "Erin's right. Darach could likely use some guy time. We'll catch up with you later."

"Aye then, lass," Niall said.

The men kissed their women then left.

Her friends had been amazingly quiet up to this point but it was clear both sensed she was ready for some time alone with Rònan.

"Why don't we go find something to eat, Nicole?" Cassie suggested.

"You read my mind." Nicole gave a little wave to everyone before she wrapped elbows with Cassie and winked at Erin. "Enjoy your man. We'll see you guys in a bit."

Erin nodded. "You bet."

After they left, she eyed her Viking posse who stood on either side of the wall walk doing their best to give the family privacy. First she went to Tait and cupped his cheeks. *"So what do you think? Can I handle myself alone now?"* She nodded over her shoulder at Ronan. *"He's pretty devoted considering we're mated and all."*

"So it seems." Tait narrowed his eyes at Ronan nonetheless. *"I could love you far better, woman."* The corner of his lip shot up. *"And please you much better."*

Erin ignored Ronan's growl and shook her head before hugging Tait and whispering, *"You wish, Gorgeous."*

That, it seemed, was exactly what Tait needed to hear because he puffed up and shot Ronan a triumphant look.

Erin met Tait's eyes. *"Thank you for all you did for me, my friend."*

Before he could respond, she went to Bjorn.

Unlike Tait, he had trouble meeting her eyes.

"Hey?" Erin gripped his forearms and angled her head until their eyes met. When they did, she was surprised by his emotions. She might've thought Tait was the dragon for her in a pinch but little did she know that there was one who cared for her every bit as much as Ronan.

A dragon who thought himself in love.

"Bjorn," she whispered and cupped his cheeks. *"You had to know I was never the girl for you."* She stood on her tip-toes and brought his ear down close to her mouth. Who cared if they spoke within the mind, it felt more natural. *"Just wait until you see who you end up with. She's gonna be something else."*

When she sank back down and their eyes met, she winked.

The corner of Bjorn's lip twitched, the first inkling of a smile she had seen since meeting him. His eyes stayed with hers before they met Ronan's, sizing him up yet again before his gaze returned to Erin. Their gaze held for several moments before he nodded.

True to form, he made a firm declaration. *"I feel you are safe."* He looked at Tait. *"We must go."*

Bjorn embraced Ronan swiftly and ordered Tait to do the same before both men bowed to Erin, leapt into the air and shifted. She went to the railing and waved as they flew into the moonlight and vanished.

Erin couldn't help it.

267

She cried.

Not loud and obnoxious, just a few tears. Tears that meant everything. Those dragons had protected her every inch of the way without expecting a thing in return. Yet what she thought was only going to be a few tears turned out to be more as Rònan held her from behind.

"I had my girls in the twenty-first century, women who had my back," she whispered. *"But those Vikings gave me as much loyalty if not more without even knowing me."*

"'Tis what we dragons do," he murmured. *"We protect our own."*

"I know," she whispered, eying the horizon for another long moment before she turned in his arms. Her eyes rose to his. *"Thank you, Rònan. Not only for protecting me as well as they did but... for loving me so perfectly."*

"Perfectly?"

"Yeah." She put her hands on his chest and kept her eyes with his. *"You did this thing between us right every step of the way."*

His brows lowered. *"I wasnae trying to do anything right or wrong, lass."*

"And that's what made it so perfect." She cupped the sides of his neck. *"You followed your heart and I love you for it."*

He lifted her onto the edge. Instead of pressing his obvious arousal against her, he cupped her cheeks and held her eyes, concerned. *"You knew that protecting Robert would mean losing your voice, didn't you?"*

"Yeah." She nodded, thinking nothing of it. *"I would've given my life for that kid."*

"I know you would have. You verra nearly did." His eyes searched hers, still worried. *"Are you truly all right, lass?"*

She answered without hesitation and with all her heart. *"Rònan, I'm better than I've ever been and though it's disconcerting as hell not being able to talk...I still am, aren't I?"*

"Aye." His lips brushed hers. *"You are."* A small smile came to his lips. *"And you're still able to sing. We all heard it when your dragon was protecting the Bruce. And 'tis even more beautiful within the mind."*

Erin swallowed a rush of emotion. Outside of mating with Rònan, it had been the most intense experience of her life. But right now it wasn't about her.

"I never would've tried singing if you hadn't given me the idea at the Viking fortress," she reminded.

"I just wanted you to know that all wasn't lost if—"

She put a finger to his lips and shook her head. *"Like my Dad, you encouraged me to never give up on my dream no matter what life threw at me,"* she murmured. *"Thank you for that."*

"You dinnae need to thank me, lass," he said softly. "Like your Da, I understood 'twas not a dream to let go of."

"Apparently not." She pulled him in for several soft kisses before she pulled back, concerned. *"Do you think Darach is going to be okay? And what's with Jackie and the Viking?"*

Rònan cupped her cheeks, eyes never more serious. *"We will protect those we love. So whatever is happening with Darach and Jackie, we'll be there every step of the way. Your family is mine as mine is yours."*

"You promise?"

"I promise, my wee dragon," he whispered before he closed his lips over hers.

Erin might have murmured a thousand times how much she loved him. That she had fallen in love with him. But dragons were dragons.

They took what they wanted.

She wrapped her legs around him. He slammed her back against the wall.

He growled.

She growled.

The perfect thing about being dragon mates? Words were no longer necessary. The love they rediscovered was thorough, timeless, endlessly lustful and theirs for all eternity.

Untouchable.

So though the enemy had not been defeated, it now had a face.

A face that would be remembered by the dragons it had tried to destroy.

In the end, the oath of a Scottish warrior had nothing to do with what he set out for but everything he ultimately needed.

True love, a mate, and someone to share a future with.

The End

Determined to keep Jackie protected from the dark demi-god, Darach flees MacLomain Castle without telling anyone his destination. As foretold by Celtic Goddess Brigit, that *should* have made the enemy pursue him. But nothing is as it seems. When he learns the demi-god isn't after him but chased Jackie to ninth-century Scandinavia, he races to get there only to find something unexpected. Things have changed. There might be hope for them. Maybe he can finally be with her. After all, he's been dreaming about her for years. The only problem? There's another man involved. One that Darach insisted she be with. Viking Heidrek.

Find out how everything unfolds in *Passion of a Scottish Warrior*, the final installment in the MacLomain Series: Later Years.

Previous Releases

~The MacLomain Series- Early Years~

Highland Defiance- Book One
Highland Persuasion- Book Two
Highland Mystic- Book Three

~The MacLomain Series~

The King's Druidess- Prelude
Fate's Monolith- Book One
Destiny's Denial- Book Two
Sylvan Mist- Book Three

~The MacLomain Series- Next Generation~

Mark of the Highlander- Book One
Vow of the Highlander- Book Two
Wrath of the Highlander- Book Three
Faith of the Highlander- Book Four
Plight of the Highlander- Book Five

~The MacLomain Series- Later Years~

Quest of a Scottish Warrior- Book One
Honor of a Scottish Warrior- Book Two
Oath of a Scottish Warrior- Book Three
Passion of a Scottish Warrior- Book Four

~The MacLomain Series- Viking Ancestors~

Viking King- Book One
Viking Claim- Book Two
Viking Heart- Book Three

~The MacLomain Series- Viking Ancestors' Kin~

Rise of a Viking- Book One
Vengeance of a Viking- Book Two
Soul of a Viking- Book Three
Fury of a Viking- Book Four

~Calum's Curse Series~

The Victorian Lure- Book One
The Georgian Embrace- Book Two
The Tudor Revival- Book Three

~Forsaken Brethren Series~

Darkest Memory- Book One
Heart of Vesuvius- Book Two

~Holiday Tales~

Yule's Fallen Angel
+ Bonus Novelette, Christmas Miracle

~Song of the Muses Series~

Highland Muse

About the Author

Sky Purington is the best-selling author of over twenty novels and several novellas. A New Englander born and bred, Sky was raised hearing stories of folklore, myth and legend. When combined with a love for nature, romance and time-travel, elements from the stories of her youth found release in her books.

Purington loves to hear from readers and can be contacted at Sky@SkyPurington.com. Interested in keeping up with Sky's latest news and releases? Visit Sky's website, www.SkyPurington.com to download her free App on iTunes and Android or sign up for her quarterly newsletter. Love social networking? Find Sky on Facebook and Twitter.

Made in the USA
Middletown, DE
02 April 2018